MURDER IN
THE GREEN

MURDER IN THE GREEN

LESLEY COOKMAN

Published by Accent Press Ltd – 2010

ISBN 9781907016080

Printed and bound in the UK

Cover Design by Nathan Mackintosh,
Zipline Creative

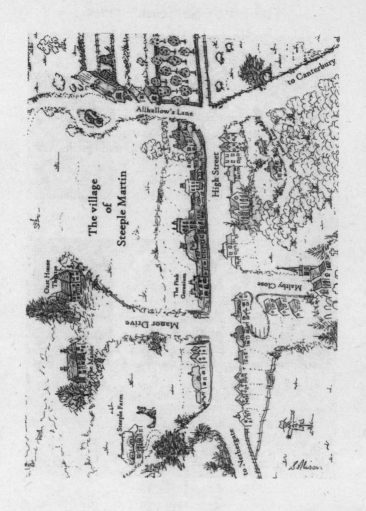

The village
of
Steeple Martin

Allhallow's Lane

High Street

Oast House Theatre

The Pink Geranium

Manor Drive

The Manor

Steeple Farm

Malby Close

to Canterbury

to Nethergate

S.Allison

The Libby Sarjeant Series
by Lesley Cookman

9781905170159

9781905170845

9781906125028

9781906373306

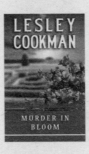

9781906373771

9781907016080

9781907016462

For my granddaughter, Kitty

Acknowledgements

First, I'd like to rectify a mistake I made in Libby and Fran's last adventure by acknowledging Miles Cookman and Chris Coates as the inspiration behind *Murder In Bloom*. Thanks, lads.

There are a number of people and organisations to whom thanks are due for background information to *Murder In The Green*, chiefly the original Mepal Molly Men and Bogshole Mummers; Dixie Lee and the organisers of Whitstable's May Day celebrations; and special thanks to my daughter Louise who had the idea in the first place.

And to fellow members of the Romantic Novelists' Association, Happy 50th Birthday to us!

Chapter One

OUT OF THE DARKNESS they came, bells silenced, boots muffled on dead leaves. The whites of their eyes caught the torchlight and reflected an ancient excitement. Above them, budding branches whispered, ahead of them the need-fire was already burning.

The path wound down the shallow hillside among the trees. Two figures broke away, feathers nodding above black faces. Neither of them returned.

'Please, Libby. Just come and talk to them.'

Libby Sarjeant frowned at the phone. 'Gemma, I can't.'

'Why not? You've been involved in murders before.'

Libby squirmed. 'Not intentionally.'

'But you have. You're like – like – oh, I don't know, bloody Miss Marple or something.'

Libby closed her eyes and squirmed some more. 'No, I'm not, Gemma. Let me tell you, the police always get there either ahead or at the same time as the amateur in these cases. Let well alone. They'll find out what happened.'

'It's nearly two months now. How can they find out now?'

'Just think of all the cold case reviews they do these days,' said Libby. 'They solve those, don't they?'

'They do on telly,' grumbled Gemma.

'Anyway,' said Libby, hastily returning to the point. 'I can't see your lot welcoming a batty old woman asking a lot of impertinent questions, can you? Be sensible.'

There was silence at the other end of line. Eventually Libby said, 'Are you still there, Gemma?'

'Yes. I was thinking,' said Gemma. 'Couldn't you at least come along? See the celebrations?'

'On the longest day?'

'Yes. We start at sunrise.'

'What? You must be joking!'

'It's traditional.' Gemma sounded defensive. 'Even the Mayor comes out to watch.'

'Good for him,' muttered Libby.

'Well, if you can't come then, you could come to one of the public displays during the day. Or even,' Gemma was disparaging, 'to the Saturday parade.'

'What's wrong with that?' asked Libby. 'I seem to remember that being good fun. I used to go with the kids.'

'Oh, yes, how are they?'

'Adam's working with a garden designer locally, and Belinda and Dominic are both working in London. How are yours?'

'Still at home,' said Gemma gloomily. 'Anyway, will you come?'

Libby sighed. 'Possibly to the Saturday parade,' she said. 'Where does it finish up?'

'Same as we always do – on the mount.'

'What time?'

'Two-ish. But you won't get a chance to talk to

anybody then.'

'I didn't say I'd talk to anyone,' said Libby.

'But I want you to talk to them,' wailed Gemma. 'You don't understand!'

'Oh, yes, I do, Gemma. Believe me.'

Libby put the phone down and frowned at her sitting room. Sidney the silver tabby twitched an ear in her direction and buried his nose more firmly under his tail. Libby sighed again, picked up the phone and sat down on the cane sofa.

'Fran? It's me.'

'Hi. What's up?'

'I'm fed up.'

'You sound it. Been missing me?'

'As it happens, I did, but I've seen you twice since you've been back, so I think I've recovered.'

'From the shock of my marriage, or my enforced absence on honeymoon?'

Libby laughed. 'Both. No, I'm fed up about lots of things.'

'Lots of things? Good lord!'

'Two anyway,' said Libby. 'One is Steeple Farm, which is turning into a monster, and the second is – well, someone's asked me to Look Into Something.'

Fran sighed. 'I don't believe it. A murder?'

'Yes. Have you ever met my old friend Gemma Baverstock?'

'No. Should I have?'

'No, I just wondered. She's a member of the Cranston Morris, if you've heard of them.'

'No, I haven't, but don't forget I've only been in Kent for a few years. And aren't Morris sides supposed to be men only?'

3

'Used to be, yes, and purists still argue about it, but there are loads of female sides now. Cranston have a male side, a female side and a mixed side, but still uphold the old traditions.'

'Well, I don't know anything about that,' said Fran, 'except that they dance at May Day.'

'Hmmm,' said Libby. 'Well, on May Day their Green Man was killed.'

'Sorry, you'll have to explain,' said Fran. 'I thought that was a sort of gargoyle.'

'Can be,' said Libby. 'Often carved up high in churches and cathedrals. But in this case it's a bloke inside a sort of conical wire frame covered with vegetation.'

'And this bloke was killed?'

'Stabbed inside the cage. No one knew until he didn't start to move when everyone else did.'

'People would have seen blood, surely.'

'I didn't think of that. Anyway, it's got nothing to do with me. I don't ever want to get mixed up with murder again. It's quite ridiculous.'

'Oh, I agree,' said Fran with a laugh in her voice. 'I bet Ben does, too.'

'Mmm.'

'Come on, Lib. There's something else, isn't there? You said Steeple Farm. And Ben?'

'Yes. I know I'm being silly, but –'

'Do you want to talk about it? Guy's at the shop and won't be home until at least half five.'

'Do you mind? I'll bring lunch with me.'

'Don't be daft,' said Fran. 'You can bring a bottle of wine, if you like. You'll be allowed one glass, won't you?'

'OK.' Libby brightened. 'I'll leave as soon as I can.'

Leaving a note in case anyone appeared and wondered where she was, she collected a bottle of wine from the kitchen, gave Sidney a perfunctory stroke, and left the cottage. The sky was grey, but as there was very little wind the air felt muggy, and much warmer than it had indoors. Romeo the Renault, now freed from servitude with Libby's son Adam, sat under the trees on the other side of the little green and started at the first turn of the key.

'I suppose I shall have to upgrade you sooner or later,' Libby told the car, as she turned round to drive out of Allhallow's Lane, 'but while you behave yourself, I shall keep you.'

The drive from Steeple Martin, the village where Libby lived, to Nethergate, the seaside town where Fran's cottage looked out over the sea, was quiet and pleasant, through undulating Kentish countryside and the occasional remaining hop gardens, but today Libby was too immersed in her thoughts to admire her surroundings.

Reaching the sign which announced itself as "Nethergate, Seaside Heritage town, twinned with Bayeau St Pierre", she drove past the entrance to the new estate and dropped down the hill to the high street, past Luigi's, the Italian restaurant favoured by Fran and her husband, Guy, and finally along Harbour Street, past Lizzie's ice cream shop and Guy's gallery until she reached Coastguard Cottage.

The heavy oak door stood open, and Libby found Fran leaning on the deep windowsill gazing out at the small harbour, the yellow printed curtains billowing round her. She turned and smiled.

'I still can't believe how lucky I am,' she said.

Libby gave her a hug. 'All this and a husband too, eh?'

Fran blushed. 'I can't get used to it,' she said. 'I'm Fran Wolfe now. How strange is that? I've been Castle for the last thirty years.'

'I bet people will still call you Castle,' said Libby, hauling the wine bottle out of her basket.

'I expect so,' said Fran, 'and I don't really mind, as long as it isn't the children.'

'No change there, then?' Libby followed Fran into the kitchen.

'No. I sent them all postcards from the honeymoon and while Jeremy was staying here until we got back he says Chrissie and Lucy never stopped badgering him. He was very rude to them eventually, and I haven't heard a word from them since he went.'

'He phoned me at one point,' said Libby. 'He was so sick of them, and they were being so selfish. Not that I could do anything, but by that time his lovely girlfriend had gone back to the States and I think he wanted to let off steam.'

'He said you had him over to dinner twice. He thought you were lovely.'

'Good.' Libby grinned. 'Adam was there too, so he had someone of his own age.'

'I thought Adam wasn't living with you now?' Fran handed over a glass of wine.

'He isn't. You know where he is, don't you?'

Fran shook her head. 'I've only been back a week, I haven't caught up.'

'In your old flat!' Libby announced triumphantly.

'Over the Pink Geranium?'

'And giving Harry a hand in the restaurant in the evenings if necessary. It seems to be working really well.'

'And Lewis?'

'Oh, Adam and Mog are still working on his gardens. They're going to be beautiful. And Lewis has got a new firm in to re-do the interiors. I don't think he wants to live there any more –'

'Not surprised,' said Fran, remembering the unpleasant events that had taken place at Lewis's house, Creekmarsh Place, only a few weeks before her wedding.

'– but he still wants to run it as a venue. He's going to get someone in as an events manager.'

Supplied with glasses of wine, they went back into the sitting room and sat either side of the empty fireplace.

'Still liking married life?' asked Libby.

'Yes.' Fran leant back and sipped her wine. 'It feels so good after all these years.' She fixed her eyes on Libby. 'And in that direction things are still not going well with you?'

Libby shook her head. 'Oh, we came to a sort of accommodation before your wedding, you know we did. But even though he's stopped pushing to get married, he's still banging on about Steeple Farm.'

Fran eyed her friend thoughtfully. 'Last I heard,' she said, 'he was going to do it up while you stayed at number 17 and then think again.'

'I know,' Libby nodded. 'But he's so

enthusiastic about it. He keeps dragging me off to have a look at what's being done – which isn't much yet, to be frank.'

'And don't you like it?'

'It's still Aunt Millie's house to me, even if I've stopped thinking of those dormer windows as eyes.'

'But you said –'

'I know what I said.' Libby was exasperated. '*You* said you wanted to live here on your own, and look where you are now? Married to Guy, with all that means.'

Fran pursed her lips. 'At least I was honest enough to admit I'd changed my mind. Love does that, doesn't it?'

'Yes, but I've admitted I love Ben. Ever since we came together over that girl's murder three years ago. We've got a lot in common – we're both divorced, we both love the theatre and we have the same social circle. His cousin Peter is one of my best friends.'

Fran looked doubtful. 'That's not love.'

Libby looked up quickly. 'I didn't say it was. I still fancy him.'

'You were the one who lectured me when I was dithering about Guy. I thought you had it sorted.'

'I did.' Libby sighed. 'Sort of.'

'And Steeple Farm's complicated matters?'

'Definitely. You remember why Ben's taken it on?'

'Of course. It belongs to Peter's mum Millie and while she's in care he won't sell it.'

'That's right. As all this happened just before your wedding, I wasn't sure how much you'd taken in. So Ben's going to do it up and live in it, and if Millie dies he'll buy it as a sitting tenant.'

'And the original idea was that you'd both live in it, wasn't it?'

'Yes.' Libby bit her lip. 'It is a lovely house – or it will be, but I love my cottage.'

'There would be much more room at Steeple Farm.'

'I know, I know.' Libby sighed. 'And Adam loves it. Lewis has promised to keep a watching brief over the renovations, and we've got that builder who's a qualified lime plasterer doing the work.'

'And?' prompted Fran after a minute.

'It still gives me a funny feeling when I go in.'

Fran gave a sharp little nod. 'In that case, don't go and live there,' she said. 'You know as well as I do, the atmosphere is paramount, and I know what I'm talking about.'

'I know.' Libby nodded. Fran had been a consultant to the Mayfair estate agents, Goodall and Smythe, who sent her into properties to divine whether there was anything in the atmosphere which would preclude clients from having a positive living experience, as they put it. Put another way, to find out if anything nasty had happened in the woodshed, the cellars or the attic which might make very rich clients very uncomfortable.

'You said you couldn't see me living there,' said Libby slowly. 'Remember?'

'Yes. I also said I could have been wrong. You know how often I'm wrong.'

'I think you were right.' Libby twirled her wine

glass. 'I won't live there.'

'What about Ben?'

'He was very understanding last time we spoke about it.' Libby stood up. 'Can I go outside for a fag?'

'You can have one in here, if you like,' said Fran.

'No.' Libby shook her head. 'It's bad enough me still smoking without contaminating everywhere else. I'll go into the yard. Perhaps Balzac will keep me company.'

'He'll be sleeping in the big flowerpot,' said Fran, also getting to her feet. 'Come on, I'll come with you. I want to know what you're going to do about Ben.'

Libby went through the kitchen and out into Fran's little courtyard. 'So do I,' she muttered.

Chapter Two

'SO HOW MUCH DO you know about this murder?' asked Fran later as she cleared plates into the kitchen sink.

'Only what I told you and what I remember from the local tv news. I noticed because it was Cranston Morris and I've known Gemma and her husband for ever. And a couple of the other members.'

'So just that the Green Man was killed?'

'And another member of the side has gone missing, yes.'

Fran raised her eyebrows. 'Isn't that significant?'

'The police looked into it at first, but he hasn't turned up and they seem to think it was a planned disappearance.'

'When he did he go?'

Libby frowned. 'That's the funny thing. They were all there for the May Day parade, apparently. It was after they'd discovered that Bill had been stabbed that the other bloke must have disappeared, because he wasn't there when they rounded them all up.'

'Very significant, then.'

'You'd have thought so,' said Libby, 'but he hadn't had time to get far, and there was no trace of him. Even his car had gone.' She shook her head. 'It's a real puzzle.'

Fran cocked her head to one side. 'And you don't want to look into it?'

Libby felt the colour creeping up her neck.

'Well ...'

'When does this Gemma want you to talk to them?'

'At the Summer Solstice. Apparently they get up really early and dance, then they go to various sites and dance some more. Then, of course, there's the Saturday Parade – either the Saturday before or after, whichever's closer.'

'Where's that? And which Saturday will it be?'

Libby wrinkled her brow. 'The day before at Steeple Mount. Longest day is June 21st.'

'Why don't we go to the parade together?' suggested Fran.

'You don't want to get involved, surely?'

'I wouldn't mind knowing more about it,' said Fran. 'What have I got to do these days? I wasn't cut out to be a stay-at-home housewife.'

'Guy won't mind?'

'Of course he won't. As long as I'm sensible and we don't get into trouble like we did before.'

'Ben'll mind.'

'Don't look so mournful. It's your life.'

Libby laughed. 'You've changed!'

'Yes,' said Fran thoughtfully, 'I have. Strangely, I've become more assertive. Guy's been good for me in so many ways.'

'Mmm,' said Libby.

'You find out the times and so on and we'll make arrangements,' said Fran. 'Hope the weather changes.'

No need to tell Ben, thought Libby, as she drove home through windscreen-wiper-defying drizzle. I'll just say Fran and I are going to have a day out together. But he knows Gemma and Cranston Morris, said an insidious little voice. He'll know why you're going to the parade. I'll have to think of an excuse, Libby told herself, and tried to think of something else.

Ben was in a particularly good mood when he returned from the Manor Farm estate office, where he worked looking after his parents rather diminished estate. Once the Manor had been the local centre of hop growing, but the gardens had all been sold off, the hopping huts knocked down, all but one small row which Ben wanted to turn into a museum, and the rest of the estate turned over to tenant farmers.

'They've actually finished ripping out the kitchen and repairing the walls at Steeple Farm,' he said, pouring himself a whisky. 'Want one?' He held up his glass. Libby shook her head.

'That seems quite fast,' she said, wiping her hands on a tea towel as she joined him in the sitting room.

'It is.' He grinned at her. 'Exciting, isn't it?'

'Yes.' She smiled and tried to feel keen. 'What's next?'

'They'll carry on stripping the whole house and repairing or restoring as they go. Lewis popped by today and was very enthusiastic.'

'Has he been at Creekmarsh?'

'He stayed down last night apparently.'

Lewis Osbourne-Walker owned Creekmarsh Place, where Adam and his boss Mog were restoring the gardens. Lewis was a carpenter whose appearances on a television homes show had given him a whole new career; a new series was being constructed round the renovation of the house and gardens. Adam was cock-a-hoop about appearing on television.

Libby nodded and threw the tea towel over her shoulder. 'Dinner in about an hour,' she said.

'How about a quick one at the pub, then?' said Ben. 'We haven't been down there for ages.'

Reprieve, thought Libby. He won't talk about Steeple Farm if we're in the pub. 'OK,' she said. 'Give me five minutes.'

The sun had made a belated appearance and threw their long shadows before them as they walked down Allhallow's Lane.

'So, what did you do today?' Ben slipped an arm around Libby's waist.

'Oh, I popped over to see Fran for lunch. She's–' Libby stopped and bit her lip. So happy, she had been going to say.

'She's what?' Ben cocked his head to look at her.

'Oh, I don't know,' Libby temporised, 'different, I suppose.'

'Happy?'

'Well, yes. But I didn't mean that.' Libby looked him in the eye. 'Assertive. She said so herself.'

'Oh.' Ben was taken aback, as she had intended.

'Anyway,' Libby went on, without giving him time to pursue the subject, 'she's suggested we have a day out, just the two of us, next Saturday.'

'Good. You've missed her, haven't you?' said Ben.

'Yes.' Libby smiled at him. 'I seem to be surrounded by males, don't I? And Fran is the first close female friend I've had in years.'

'I know.' Ben gave her a squeeze and opened the door of the pub. Libby immediately felt guilty because he was being understanding.

'Is that where you're going?' Returning from the bar with the drinks, Ben nodded at a poster stuck up beneath the clock.

"Midsummer Madness with Cranston Morris" it read. "Saturday Parade with fancy dress competition and Greet the Dawn at 5am on The Mount on Sunday 21st June."

Libby's heart sank. 'Yes,' she said. 'I used to enjoy taking the kids when they were younger. Fran suggested it –' true, she thought '– and I thought you wouldn't mind. Not the greeting the dawn thing, though.'

'I should think not.' Ben settled down beside her. 'We used to go, too. I expect we bumped into one another.'

'No.' Libby shook her head. 'You would have remembered me. If you recognised me when we met again a few years ago, you would have done then, too.'

'True.' Ben nodded, and paused for a sip of beer. 'I always fancied dancing morris.'

'Did you?' Libby was surprised. 'I wouldn't ever have guessed.'

'Apart from the stereotypical images – you know, Arran sweaters, beards and long hair – I thought it looked fun. I was put off by the women, though.'

'Really?' Libby twisted sideways in her chair to look at him properly. 'How come?'

15

'They always seemed to be homing in on a male preserve, and over-enthusiastic. I even researched it once.'

'Did you? What did you find out?'

'That there's evidence of women dancing way back in the sixteen hundreds, but the Morris Ring won't allow women's or mixed sides.'

'What's the Morris Ring?'

Ben wrinkled his brow. 'As far as I can remember, a sort of association of sides. Over two hundred, I think, but there are other organisations which allow the women.'

'Fascinating, and one up for the girls.' Libby lifted her glass.

'Yes, but there's no real evidence for women dancing in proper Morris sides, and it really was a men-only thing for years. The people who revived Molly dancing in the Fens in the seventies wouldn't have them, although even some of them do now.'

'Molly dancing?'

'Black-faced. They dance on Plough Monday –'

'You've lost me now,' said Libby shaking her head. 'Although Cranston Morris are black-faced. Would they have a connection?'

'No idea. As I say, I only did a bit of research a few years ago. And I used to have a friend who lived in the Cambridgeshire Fens and danced with a local Molly side.' Ben smiled reminiscently. 'Quite rough and earthy. They used to do a Mummer's play, too.'

'We have those here, too.' Libby was defensive.

'I know, I know.' Ben smiled again and patted her knee. 'Cranston Morris do a Mummer's play

16

themselves at the Saturday parade.'

'Of course,' said Libby, 'I should have remembered. St George and the doctor and all that.'

'We ought to do one for the theatre,' said Ben. 'We could do a pre-Christmas thing. That's when mummers used to go round, isn't it?'

'Wassailing?' Libby frowned. 'Something like that. I'll look it up. Perhaps we could do something round the pubs to promote the panto?'

To Libby's relief, Ben took hold of the change of subject and began to discuss next season's pantomime. The oast house owned by the Manor Farm had been turned into a small theatre, which was run by a consortium of Ben's cousin Peter, Ben himself, who was the architect behind the project, and Libby. The opening production had been marred by the murder of a member of the cast, but, since then, the theatre had gone from strength to strength and gained a formidable reputation in the area.

Peter and his partner, Harry, who owned between them the Pink Geranium, a vegetarian restaurant a few doors down from the pub, joined them at Number 17 after dinner.

Harry complained that the credit crunch was going to halve the takings if something didn't happen soon.

'As long as you break even it doesn't matter,' said Peter.

'Hardly doing that at the moment,' said Harry gloomily. 'That's why we've come here to ponce a drink off you rather than going to the pub.'

'And here was I thinking you were desperate for my company,' said Libby, handing over two large glasses of red wine.

Peter kissed her cheek. 'What, you, you old trout?'

Libby grinned.

'So what's been going on chez the Sarjeant Wilde household?' asked Harry, flinging himself on to the cane sofa and upsetting Sidney.

'Not a lot,' said Ben. 'Still working on Steeple Farm.'

Harry shot a look at Libby. 'Right,' he said.

'How's it going?' asked Peter. 'James was asking the other day.' James was Peter's younger brother.

'Has he decided he wants to move in?' asked Libby, a little too quickly.

'Good lord, no,' said Peter with a frown. 'He's far too ensconced in his nice flat in Canterbury with his new girlfriend.'

'New girlfriend?' said Ben and Libby together, and the conversation was once more turned away from Steeple Farm, to Libby's relief.

'Come on, then,' said Harry, a bit later, when Libby went to fetch another bottle from the kitchen. 'What's going on?'

'I don't know what you mean.' Libby gave him a wide-eyed look.

'You don't want to move into Steeple Farm, do you?'

'I didn't say that.' Libby wrestled with the foil covering on the bottle. Harry took it out of her hands.

'Just tell Ben. He won't mind.'

'But he will.' Libby looked up at Harry and

sighed. 'He really wants it. And he wants us to live there together.' She sighed again. 'Oh, he's said he'll live here until I'm ready, but that's not what he wants.'

Harry looked at her thoughtfully while pulling the cork from the bottle. 'And it's not what you want, cither, is it?'

Libby felt the colour creeping up her neck. 'Well, it's not ideal …' she began.

'No.' Harry handed her the bottle. 'If you want to talk about it, come down to the caff tomorrow. I think you're in serious need of therapy.'

'What were you and Harry talking about in the kitchen?' asked Ben later, as they got ready for bed.

'Steeple Farm,' said Libby, without stopping to think.

'Oh?' Ben stopped taking his shirt off and turned to face her. 'What about it?'

Closing her eyes and cursing herself, Libby sat on the edge of the bed.

'Come on, Lib, out with it.' Ben sat down on the other side.

'Harry wanted to know how I felt about it now.'

'Now?'

'Now the renovations have started.'

'They started weeks ago.'

'I know. He just wondered if I was happier about it.'

'Oh, so everyone knows you're not happy, do they?' said Ben grimly.

Oh, dear, thought Libby, here we go. 'No,' she said aloud, 'everyone – whoever everyone is – does not know I'm unhappy because I'm not.'

'Go on.' Ben settled back against the pillows, arms folded across his chest.

'It's just what I said before.' Libby stood up and belted her dressing gown round her waist. 'I love this cottage, and I made it what it is now. It's all me. It's very hard to think of leaving it.'

'And you've discussed this with Harry?'

'No!' The colour flooded back into Libby's cheeks. 'He was there when it was first discussed, wasn't he? And he knows me very well. He just sort of – picked up the – er – vibes, so to speak.'

Ben sighed and stood up to continue undressing. 'More than I can, then,' he said.

Libby escaped to the bathroom and heaved a guilty sigh of relief. It wasn't going to turn into an argument, then. Not tonight, anyway.

Chapter Three

LIBBY PUSHED OPEN THE door of the Pink Geranium despite the closed sign. Donna, Harry's waitress and second-in-command, still there after numerous offers from bigger and not necessarily better establishments, greeted her with a nod.

'Harry!' she called. 'Libby's here.'

Harry, already in his chef's checked trousers and white jacket, appeared from the kitchen wiping his hands on a tea towel.

'Hello, petal. Wine or coffee?'

Libby looked at her watch. 'It had better be coffee, hadn't it?'

'Go on, then. Take a pew. Be with you in a minute.'

Libby sat on the sofa in one of the windows, to the side of the front door. If she sat sideways she could see the village high street, Ahmed and Ali's eight-til-late, Bob's butcher's shop and the new farm shop, squashed into a gap between the Methodist Chapel and Ivy Cottage on the other side of the road.

'Have you met the people in the farm shop?' she asked, as Harry sat down beside her and put a tray on the coffee table.

'Course I have. So have you.'

'Have I?'

'They're the people who run Cattlegreen Nurseries on the Canterbury road. Nella and Joe. Nella says they weren't getting enough custom because people weren't stopping.'

'And is it better here?'

'She says so. People in the village are trying to shop in the village and not use their cars, so fresh veg is a good move. And did you know Ahmed's got a proper baker to deliver bread in the mornings, now?'

'Really?' Libby was impressed. 'Where from?'

'Steeple Mount, apparently. The bakery there does very well.'

'Oh, I know it. Run by Diggory something. He's a Cranston Morris man.'

'Richard Diggory. He sometimes supplies me with stuff. I didn't know he was a Morris man.' Harry pulled down the corners of his mouth. 'Might have to stop buying from him.'

Libby laughed. 'Go on, you don't subscribe to the old stereotype beard and Arran sweater image!'

'Well, no.' Harry leant forward to pour coffee. 'Rich is quite a suave individual, as it happens. Very surprising this is.'

'He's known as Diggory in Cranston Morris,' said Libby. 'I suppose that fits the image better than "Rich", doesn't it? I was introduced to him at a party, ages ago. I'll probably see him again on Saturday.'

'You're not going to that shenanigans?' Harry looked appalled.

'The parade? Yes. Fran and I are going.' Libby took a sip from her thick, white mug. 'Ben and I used to take the children years ago.'

'Together?' Harry raised his eyebrows.

'No, Ben and his wife and me and Derek. Ben

22

says we probably met, but I don't remember.'

'Which brings us neatly back to why you're here.' Harry leant back in the corner of the sofa. 'Shoot.'

Libby unnecessarily stirred her coffee.

'It's daft, really,' she said.

'So are you,' said Harry.

'Yeah, well.' She sat up and looked at him. Faint lines were beginning to show at the corners of his blue eyes and the handsome face was just that little bit fuller than it had been a year ago. 'You're looking very content,' she said.

'We're not talking about me,' said Harry. 'However, I am very content. I'm glad Pete and I got civilled, I have a failing restaurant and a lovely home. What more could a bloke want? Your turn.'

'You know I fancied Ben when I met him over that *Hop Pickers* murder?'

'I thought you already fancied him.'

'Well, I did, sort of, but I didn't know him very well.' Libby looked down at her mug. 'And I didn't think I stood a chance, to be honest.'

Harry's mouth twitched. 'Course you didn't.'

'Oh, come on, Harry!' Libby looked up and grinned. 'Short, plump and over fifty. Nobody's best catch.'

'Were you over fifty then? I thought you were younger.'

'Flatterer.' Libby put her mug on the table. 'Anyway. So we got it together, briefly, like a couple of teenagers. I reckoned it was that life-affirming thing you're supposed to do after death, you know?'

'I'll take your word for it,' said Harry.

'Then we drifted apart –'

'Your fault, I gather.'

'All right, it probably was, but then we got back together. And it was great. Well, you know, you've seen us through all of it.'

'But now –' said Harry.

'I think it started when he moved in.' Libby wriggled in her seat. 'I've come to realise that I like my own space.'

'So did Fran,' said Harry. 'I seem to remember she didn't want Guy moving in when she went to Coastguard Cottage. She wanted to savour the moment.'

'I reminded her of that,' said Libby, 'but she's changed. She loves Guy so much.'

'Which argues, petal, that you don't love our Ben that much.'

'I suppose it does,' said Libby gloomily. 'And now I don't know what to do.'

Harry cocked his head on one side. 'I know I'm not the expert on male-female relationships, but don't you think it's a bit unfair that you haven't told Ben all this?'

Libby nodded. 'But I don't want to lose him,' she said.

'Now that really is dog-in-the-manger,' said Harry. 'I want him, but only on my terms. Compromise, gal, is the name of the game.'

Libby sighed. 'You're not telling me anything I don't know. Ben and I went through all this only a few weeks ago, just before Fran's wedding. He's compromised, he's come to live in my cottage, when he had far more room at the Manor.'

'And you feel you can't chuck him out?'

'Of course I can't. But I feel crowded and pressurised.'

'Stating the bleedin' obvious, Steeple Farm would take care of all that, wouldn't it? Much more space. And Ben would let you do more or less what you liked with the inside, I betcha.' Harry sniffed. 'You could probably even take that creaky straw sofa. And the walking stomach.'

'Well, of course, I'd take Sidney,' said Libby with a grin. 'And my cane sofa is a statement, I'll have you know.'

'It makes enough noise,' said Harry, getting up. 'More coffee?'

'No thanks. I've promised Guy another pretty peep for his shop and I want to borrow Jane's sitting room to do a preliminary sketch, so I've got to go to Nethergate.'

'I thought you said Jane and Terry were turning that house back into one, now? Won't that be their bedroom?'

'Don't know,' said Libby, standing up. 'She said I could use it, that's all I know. And she's working from home today, so I'm going over.'

'They're getting married soon, aren't they?' asked Harry innocently, as he opened the door for her.

'Yes. Don't start.' Libby gave him a kiss on the cheek. 'And don't work too hard.'

Jane Maurice, local newspaper reporter, and her fiancé and ex-tenant, Terry Baker, lived in the beautiful, tall, terraced Peel House on Cliff Terrace,

Nethergate. It looked out over Nethergate bay and gave Libby a completely different perspective for her tourist paintings which Guy claimed to sell like hot cakes.

Jane opened the door, looking far less mouse-like than she had the previous summer when they had all been involved in some fairly hair-raising adventures. She kissed Libby's cheek and held the door wide.

'Terry at work?' asked Libby, toiling up the stairs behind her.

'Yes,' said Jane. 'Only five days a week now. He was doing six, but I said he didn't need to.' She opened the door to the room at the top of the house.

'I bet he didn't like that,' said Libby, when she'd got her breath back.

Jane looked sheepish. 'No, he didn't. But there's no mortgage on this place and I'm earning a reasonable salary, so why should he work all that overtime? I'd rather he was here with me.'

'What about when the children come along, though?' said Libby slyly.

Jane cleared her throat and went pink. 'We'll have to have a rethink then,' she said. Libby looked at her sharply, but she'd turned away.

'So how's the granny annexe going?'

Jane sighed. 'Mother's being difficult.'

'No surprise there, then,' said Libby, taking out her sketch pad and pencils. Mrs Maurice was a true daughter of the nineteen fifties and bigoted into the bargain.

'The flat was all right for old Mrs Finch, and we've already put in a new bathroom and kitchen,

26

but she's still saying she won't come.'

'Perhaps she just doesn't want to leave her own home and her friends,' said Libby, searching for the right viewpoint from the large window. 'It's a big step to take. I know,' she added darkly.

'*You* moved from somewhere the other side of Canterbury, didn't you?' asked Jane.

'Yes, but I didn't mean that. My old home was associated with my prat of a husband, so I didn't mind at all moving away, even though the kids were a bit uncomfortable with it.' Libby turned an armchair to face the window. 'I meant if I had to move from Number 17.'

'But I thought you were moving?' Jane looked surprised and Libby sighed. Everyone, as Ben had said, was indeed talking about it.

'Maybe,' said Libby. 'Any chance of a cuppa? I'm parched.'

'So what else have you done in the house?' she asked when Jane came back with tea.

'Turned the ground floor into a big kitchen and dining room, with a cloakroom, Terry's old flat into the sitting room and main bedroom, also with a cloakroom and an en-suite for us, and this floor's bedrooms and bathrooms. I'm using this one for an office at the moment.'

'Sorry,' said Libby, through a mouthful of BB pencil.

'That's OK.' Jane perched on the arm of another chair. 'I wasn't doing much. Not much to do.'

'Are you covering the Cranston Morris parade on Saturday?' Libby put down her pad and took the cup of tea.

'The – oh! You mean the Steeple Mount Solstice Parade? No, one of the juniors and a photographer will do that.' Jane frowned. 'Cranston Morris. Wasn't it one of their people who was stabbed at the May Day celebrations?'

Libby nodded. 'That's right.' She looked quickly at Jane. 'Matter of fact, a friend of mine wants me to look into it.'

'Oh, Libby, no!' Jane laid a hand on her chest, looking horrified. 'Remember what happened here?'

'Yes, yes, I know,' said Libby, testily. 'But Fran and I are quite interested.'

'Fran too? I thought she had more sense,' said Jane.

'Look, I'm only going to look into it as an intellectual puzzle,' said Libby. 'We're not police, or private detectives or anything. It's just people have got to know about our involvement with all these – um –'

'Murders?' suggested Jane.

'Well, yes.' Libby was uncomfortable. 'But, don't forget, Fran was actually asked to look into that business of the body on the island by the police.'

'By Ian Connell, anyway,' said Jane shrewdly. 'And he wasn't over-pleased, as I remember, when you turned up at Creekmarsh Place a couple of months ago.'

'But I was asked by the owner to look into that,' said Libby smugly.

'And then asked not to.'

'Oh, OK.' Libby sighed. 'Anyway, I've actually said I won't look into the Green Man murder, so you needn't worry.'

'But you said Fran was interested?'

'Yes.' Libby frowned. 'To be perfectly honest, I think she's a bit bored.'

'Well, don't let her drag you into anything,' said Jane. 'It was all a bit unpleasant, that murder.'

'Did you cover it?' said Libby, interested.

Jane nodded. 'I saw it – the Green Man, I mean.' She shuddered. 'Horrible.'

'And hadn't another member of the troupe, side or whatever it is, hadn't he disappeared?'

'It looked like it,' said Jane, 'because his car wasn't there and wasn't at his house, either.'

'Have they found him?'

Jane shook her head. 'Completely disappeared, apparently. Just another missing person.'

Libby looked out of the window over the grey-blue sea. Just another missing person, she thought. And perhaps not.

Chapter Four

THE PROBLEM, LIBBY TOLD herself as she drove home, was that she had no one to talk to. Except Fran, Harry and Ben, who, for different reasons, didn't appreciate what her problem was. She suddenly felt very alone and had to swallow hard against a painful lump in her throat.

'Pitiful,' she muttered to herself. But the feeling of ill-usage persisted. Ben (despite agreeing to stay at Number 17 for the time being) was really expecting her to live her life as he wanted it, Adam, although now living in the flat above the Pink Geranium, still tended to treat Number 17 as a hotel (and occasional laundry service) and her other children, Dominic and Belinda didn't get in touch anywhere near as much as she would have liked. And even Fran was now cocooned in a golden halo of marriage, more suited, in Libby's opinion, to a misty-eyed twenty-something. Although perhaps twenty-somethings were no longer misty-eyed but cynical and jaded these days.

Sniffing and swallowing, Libby drove past the turn for Steeple Mount, deliberately not looking towards Tyne Chapel, which at one time had been the scene of not only an illegal Black Mass but a murder. Vaguely, she wondered if Black Masses and covens had anything to do with the mythology surrounding the celebrations Morris sides took so seriously. Beltane and Samhain were certainly connected with witches, weren't they? She resolved to ask Gemma when she saw her on Saturday.

Obeying goodness knows what perverse prompting from her subconscious, Libby turned left instead of going straight on when she reached Steeple Martin and drove slowly up the sunken lane to Steeple Farm. Two small vans and a pile of timber were all that indicated the presence of workmen, so Libby parked the car and went round to the back of the house.

The kitchen door was open and through it Libby could hear Radio 2 quietly chuntering away.

'Lib!'

Libby swung round to face Ben, who had come up silently behind her.

'Hi,' she said weakly.

'This is a nice surprise.' He beamed at her and tucked a hand under her arm. 'Come and see what they've been doing.'

A tour of the house revealed much bare plaster work and open studwork and Libby felt her enthusiasm being very slightly rekindled.

'Coming on, isn't it?' said Ben, as they finished up in the empty kitchen. 'Look, they've just put a marble shelf in the larder.' He pulled open the planked door.

'Wow.' Libby put her head inside. 'I –' she stopped herself saying "I've always wanted one of those." '– I think it's fantastic,' she finished.

'I remember you saying you always wanted a larder,' said Ben. 'How do you feel about it now?'

'The house?'

'Of course the house.'

'It's going to be beautiful,' said Libby honestly.

'It really is. What a pity Millie changed it so much.'

Ben looked at her for a long moment. 'But you're still not convinced.'

Libby felt the colour creeping up again. 'I – er – I just need some time.'

'Mm.' Ben went to the back door. 'OK. Do you want to see any more, or shall I see you later?'

'I'll see you later,' said Libby, feeling absurdly guilty.

She took a last look at the paddock, imagining it with a couple of ponies resting under the trees at the end, frowned and went back to the car.

The answerphone light was winking when she got home.

'Lib, it's Fran. Can you give me a ring back?'

'Libby it's Jane. I found something out about that Green Man murder. Thought you'd like to know.'

Libby stared at the phone. Life wasn't giving her much of a chance to think about her personal problems.

'I just thought I'd look up everything we had on the Green Man murder,' said Jane, when Libby rang her. 'Apparently they looked into that bloke's disappearance more thoroughly than I thought.'

'And?'

'The police talked to his ex-wife and all his close friends, but no one could say whether anything was missing from his house. His wallet and keys were gone, but not his passport, and nothing's been heard from him since.'

'Dead?' asked Libby. 'Is that what they think?'

'According to my sources,' said Jane, with a

faint air of triumph, 'they think he's the murderer.'

'Well, obviously,' said Libby. 'Sorry, Jane, but if they've gone to a lot of trouble and the conclusions are what you've just told me, it stands to reason.'

'But that has never been released. He's still listed as missing.'

'And everyone concerned will have thought the same as the police, I bet,' said Libby. 'I wonder why Gemma didn't say anything.'

'Perhaps the people involved don't think it's connected?' suggested Jane.

'Or don't want to,' Libby mused. 'Perhaps that's it. Perhaps Gemma wants me to come up with an alternative theory. Well, thanks Jane. I'll keep you posted.'

'You are coming to my hen night, aren't you?' said Jane hurriedly as Libby was about to ring off.

Libby's heart sank. 'Yes, of course,' she said brightly. 'Next Saturday, isn't it?'

'The Saturday after,' said Jane, 'the 27th.'

'Right. It's on the calendar,' lied Libby. 'If I don't see you before, I'll see you then.'

She punched in Fran's number.

'Do we have to go to Jane's hen night?' she asked when Fran answered.

Fran laughed. 'Of course we do. We were instrumental in getting those two together. Or you were, anyway.'

'It's not going to be one of those awful learner plate and white veil dos, is it? We haven't got to get into a stretch limo and wave cheap champagne out of the roof?'

Fran snorted. 'Can you honestly see Jane doing

that? No, it's a very sedate evening at Anderson Place. Not many of us. A couple of Jane's old college friends, a few from work and us.'

'No Mum?'

'I hardly think so,' said Fran. 'But I wasn't ringing you about that.'

'No, sorry, Jane rang and reminded me, that's all. Why did you ring me?'

'I was thinking about that Green Man murder.'

Libby groaned. 'Jane was, too.'

'What did she say?'

Libby told her.

'Why didn't Gemma tell you anything about this other man?'

Libby explained her theory.

'That makes sense,' said Fran. 'If he was popular, they wouldn't want to think of him as a murderer. And you wondered if he was dead?'

'Yes. Well, if he hasn't been seen or heard of, presumably that means his credit cards haven't been used, that's the first thing that springs to mind, isn't it?'

'Ye-es,' said Fran slowly. 'I was just wondering what motive he had.'

'Oh!' Libby was surprised. 'I hadn't thought of that.'

'You hadn't thought of motive?'

'Yes. I mean, no. I hadn't. For either of them. I wonder if Jane knows anything.'

'Don't you go ringing her back,' said Fran. 'You said you didn't want to get involved – as usual.'

'Yes, well.' Libby cleared her throat. 'It's an intellectual puzzle.'

'Hmm. Not for the Green Man's widow, I suspect. What was his name, do you know?'

'Bill something. I've met them all in the past. Gemma belonged to my old amateur group, and we went to parties together.'

'And who is the Disappearing Man?'

'No idea. I expect we'll find out on Saturday.'

'It will have been in the papers.'

'It was, that's how I knew about it,' said Libby, 'I just don't remember the name. I could –'

'I said, don't phone Jane. What have you got a computer for?'

'Oh, yes!' Libby smiled. 'I'll look it up. Er – why do we want to know?'

'I'll look it up, too. We want to know before we see Gemma on Saturday so that you can confound her by telling her all the facts in the case and saying there's nothing you can do that the police can't.'

'I've already told her that,' said Libby, 'and in that case, why are we bothering to go?'

'Because we're bound to find something else out,' said Fran.

'You *have* changed,' said Libby.

The computer search yielded a plethora of news sites with everything from straight reportage to speculative ramblings about Celtic and Druidic rites and mystical vengeance. There was very little that Libby didn't already know, except the name of the Disappearing Man, who turned out to be John Lethbridge, a divorced financial advisor, who lived in a village a little way from Steeple Mount.

'Absconding with funds?' murmured Libby.

Monica, widow of murdered Bill Frensham, was

reported to be devastated, and her two student children had returned home to be with her.

'I hope neither of them was due to take finals,' thought Libby.

There were several theories about the celebration of Beltane, a festival that seemed to be based largely on sex, as far as Libby could see. At midnight on May 1st something called "need-fire" was lit to be carried back to the houses of the faithful (make that members of Cranston Morris, thought Libby) to light the fire to keep the house warm for the rest of the year and purify the cattle. Seeds were planted and courting rituals took place, all to ensure fertility for the coming season. There were earnest articles on the blood-letting which could be said to be the ultimate fertility rite and some which denounced the whole incident as a put-up job to call the whole of Druidism, Paganism and Celticism into disrepute.

It was all hugely interesting, thought Libby, but what Gemma thought she could do she had no idea. In this case, more so than in any other she had been involved with, she had no legitimate interest, and neither did Fran. And Fran hadn't even felt the slightest flutter of her psychic wings which had been so necessary in other cases, and the reason that the police, in the shape of Detective Inspector Ian Connell, as Jane had reminded her, had asked for her help.

Nevertheless, she and Fran would go to the Solstice Parade and talk to Gemma. It would be a day away from Steeple Martin at worst, and might turn up something interesting at best. Although being away from Steeple Martin might turn out to be the best of it after all, Libby thought, and went to put the kettle on.

'It was nice to see you this afternoon,' said Ben, later. He was pouring himself a drink before going up to shower and change.

'Yes,' said Libby, hesitating inside the kitchen doorway.

'Any more thoughts?' He cocked his head on one side, like an eager dog, thought Libby.

'A few,' she said slowly. 'I really like what's being done, and I can imagine how it will look when it's finished.' She sat down and smiled. 'And I even began imagining ponies in the paddock.'

Ben sat down opposite and patted her knee. 'That sounds hopeful.'

'Yes.' She sighed. 'I'm just being silly, I'm sure, but I do feel kind of pressured, and as I keep saying, I bought this cottage and did everything in it myself, so it feels like part of me.'

Ben looked at her for a long moment, then nodded. 'I do understand. And with me living here it doesn't feel like your house any more, does it?'

Libby was horrified. 'That wasn't what I meant!'

'I know it wasn't.' Ben gave her a crooked smile and stood up. 'I know we've been all through this before, and came to a compromise –'

'You did, you mean,' Libby interrupted.

'All right, I did,' agreed Ben. 'But it was that or lose you. And I don't want to lose you.' He dropped a kiss on her head and made for the stairs. Libby remained staring after him feeling guiltier than ever.

Now what, she asked herself. Before Fran and Guy's wedding Ben had indeed come to a compromise, putting his own desire to get married on hold and agreeing to live in Number 17 until Libby felt ready to live at Steeple Farm instead of moving into it straight away.

What she needed to do, she answered herself, getting up and going back into the kitchen, was to sort out what exactly she felt for Ben. Was the threat of leaving her cottage and moving in to a property owned by a member of his family affecting her feeling for him? She pulled a face at her reflection in the kitchen window. It made her sound like the heroine of a historical romance being imprisoned by the Duke's family.

Perhaps, she thought, absently stirring the pot on the Rayburn, she needed to get right away. Right away from Ben, the cottage, the farm and from Steeple Martin itself. Her world had been so bound up in its narrow confines for the last few years, even if there were excursions to Nethergate, she had hardly considered the outside world.

'That's it,' she said, raising her head. 'I shall have to run away.'

Chapter Five

THERE WAS NO OPPORTUNITY to run anywhere
before the Solstice Parade at Steeple Mount. Fran
and Libby met in the car park at the bottom of
Steeple Mount high street, which was almost at
bursting point. Libby drove round and round,
cursing each time she missed a space and getting
hotter and hotter and more and more frustrated.
Finally grabbing a tight space under the nose of
another irate motorist, she clambered damply out
and went to find the ticket machine, where she
discovered Fran looking enviably cool and
unflustered.

'I don't know how you do it,' she grumbled,
punching her registration number into the machine.
'You look as though you've just stepped out of an
air-conditioned Rolls.'

'Better than that,' grinned Fran. 'Out of Guy's
car. He dropped me off.'

Libby snorted.

Steeple Mount high street was *en fête*. Straighter
and narrower than that of Steeple Martin, bunting
was looped along both sides, and the few shops all
had relevant window displays, especially, Libby
noticed, Diggory's bakery, overflowing with bread
sculptures in the shapes of Stonehenge, the Oak
King and the sun.

'The Oak King?' asked Fran. 'Who's he?'

'Didn't you look it all up yesterday, as you
suggested?' said Libby with a lift of her eyebrows.

'No,' sighed Fran. 'So go on, tell me.'

'At the Winter Solstice, or Yule, the Oak King kills the Holly King, and then reigns until Midsummer, or Litha. Once the Summer Solstice arrives, the Holly King returns to do battle with the Oak King, and defeats him. The Holly King then rules until Yule. More or less. There are different versions according to whether you're reading Wiccan, Pagan, Celtic or Druid. I expect the Morris sides take a bit from each.'

'Litha's midsummer, then, is it?'

'And a great time for love and sex, apparently. Lots of tumbling in the bushes during the night.' Libby made a face. 'How uncomfortable.'

'But more cheerful than the black mass,' said Fran, remembering her experience a couple of years ago at Tyne Chapel just outside Steeple Mount.

'Well, I don't know about that,' said Libby. 'The Holly King kills the Oak King after sunrise – or is it sunset? – tomorrow. Not very cheerful.'

'Do Cranston Morris have an Oak King?'

'I don't know. I've never looked into it before. I just remember the parade and a lot of dancing up on the Mount.' Libby nodded towards the end of the high street. 'The parade's nearly there, look. If we want to see anything we'd better get a move on.'

Following the crowd, Libby and Fran reached the foot of the Mount and began to climb the path. It was some years since Libby had done this and now it was making her puff. Fran, as usual, looked unworried.

At the top of the Mount, in front of the large standing stone known as Grey Betty, Cranston

Morris were gathered round an odd figure wearing a mask and antlers. Other visiting sides grouped round them and all of them were singing.

'Oh, I remember this,' said Libby. 'It's about sunrise and the flame of love. They used to give out leaflets so everyone could join in. They've got a song for May Day, as well. The dances start after this.'

Sure enough, at the end of the song, which was greeted with cheers and applause by all the Morris sides and the onlookers, Cranston Morris formed up in front of the odd figure and began to dance.

'Do you suppose that's the Oak King?' asked Fran.

'Yes, could be,' said Libby. 'He's got an oak leaf crown, hasn't he? I don't remember him being around when we used to come with the kids, but I expect they just wanted to get to the fun fair.'

'Fair?' Fran looked around. 'Where?'

'They don't have it any more. Economic downturn, I suppose. There are a few roundabouts on the other side of the hill, look.' Libby led the way. 'And – oh! Gallopers!'

Sure enough, at the bottom of the Mount on the edge of the water meadows that ran down to the River Wytch, beautifully painted horses sailed up and down on a magnificent carousel.

'Can we have a go?' Libby turned excitedly to Fran.

'At our age?' Fran laughed. 'Come on, Lib!'

'What's wrong with it?' asked Libby, starting down the hill. 'There's a couple of pensioners on there already.'

'We're not quite pensioners yet,' said Fran, 'but I suppose there's no harm in it.'

After the carousel ride, Libby treated Fran to candy floss from the Nethergate Lions Club stall and Fran bought them each a turn on the coconut shy. By this time, Libby had noticed members of Cranston Morris, their duty now done, strolling among the crowds. On the edge of the Mount, outside the beer tent, sat Gemma Baverstock with the now mask-less Oak King.

'Hello, Gemma,' said Libby. 'This is my friend Fran.'

'Libby!' Gemma jumped up from her white plastic chair. 'Pull up a seat. Hello Fran. Oh, I'm so glad you came.' She sat down again and indicated the figure at her side. 'Do you remember Richard Diggory?'

'Yes, of course,' beamed Libby. 'Now I know why you had an Oak King in your window. Very impressive.'

'The bread or me?' Richard Diggory smiled back and shook her hand.

'Oh, both, of course,' said Libby. 'How long have you been Oak King?'

Gemma and Richard looked at each other. 'Only this year, actually,' said Richard. 'It was always Bill.'

'Oh?' Libby looked at Gemma. 'I didn't realise it was the same person. Was he always Green Man, too?'

'Yes.' Gemma nodded. 'So he could have been killed by anyone, you see. Everyone knew he was Green Man, the same as everyone knew he was Oak

King.'

'Only people who were interested in Morris and the celebrations. Outsiders wouldn't.' Richard picked up his empty glass. 'Can I get anyone a drink?'

Libby opened her mouth.

'No thanks,' said Fran, 'Libby's driving.' Libby glared at her.

'I don't remember an Oak King when I used to come with the children,' said Libby to Gemma when Richard had gone to the beer tent.

'No, he's fairly recent,' said Gemma. 'When Bill took over as Squire –'

'Squire?' Fran wrinkled her brow.

'Sort of captain,' said Gemma. 'Well, when he took over, and my Dan was made bagman – treasurer and secretary,' she explained, catching Libby's and Fran's expressions, 'they went into the whole history of Morris and incorporated the whole Oak and Holly King tradition into the solstice celebration. The Squire had always been the Green Man, so he became Oak King, too.'

'Who's the Holly King who has to kill him off?' asked Libby.

'Dan. And there he is,' said Gemma, standing up and waving.

Libby turned and saw a burly figure in a red and green cloak and tunic coming towards them.

'Hello, Lib,' he said, kissing her soundly on the cheek. 'Lovely to see you. Who's this?'

Libby introduced Fran, then touched the mask, similar to the one Richard had been wearing, which hung from Dan's belt.

'This is the Holly King mask, is it?'

He unhooked it for her inspection. 'Specially made for us by a bloke who does film and theatre make-up. We found a website with some on, and had them copied. I've got holly leaves and berries, Richard's got oak leaves and acorns.'

'And why the antlers?' asked Fran.

'It's all linked up with Herne the Hunter,' said Dan. 'If you go into the history –'

'Not now, Dan,' interrupted Gemma, laughing and patting him on the arm.

'No, but it's interesting, Gem,' said Libby. 'And you did want me to come and talk to you.'

'Yes,' said Gemma, her already rosy cheeks becoming rosier as she glanced at her husband, whose set mouth indicated his lack of sympathy with her views.

'You don't agree with Gemma,' said Fran.

'Bill's murder was bloody awful,' said Dan, ignoring the rather dreadful pun, 'and very upsetting for Monica. The police are still working on it and I don't see how involving amateurs –'

'Dan!' expostulated Gemma.

'He's right, Gem,' said Libby. 'I told you the police always get there in the end.'

'Not always,' mumbled Gemma.

'If they don't, then neither would anyone else,' said Libby. 'Sometimes Fran and I have been lucky enough to stumble on things, usually because one of us is in the wrong place at the wrong time, and it can be dangerous.'

'But you might be able to explain things to us,' said Gemma, her eyes imploring.

'How? I don't know anything about the murders.'

'Why do you say murders plural?' said Dan sharply.

Libby looked surprised. 'Sorry, I was just assuming that the other chap was being treated as a murder, too.'

'John Lethbridge?' Gemma looked shocked. 'He's just disappeared. He had money problems.'

'And trouble with his ex-wife,' said Dan.

'Ex-wife? That'd be old Willy.' Richard Diggory reappeared behind Gemma's shoulder and gave her a nudge. She winced and glanced up at Dan, who rolled his eyes.

Fran stared at him. 'Willy? Who's Willy?'

Richard gave a slight laugh. 'Wilhelmina. Wilhelmina Lethbridge. That's who you were talking about, wasn't it?'

'Was it?' said Libby.

Richards eyes moved swiftly to each of the group. 'I heard you say ex-wife. I only know one.'

'Could have been anybody,' said Libby, with a shrug. 'Come on, Fran, I ought to get back. My parking ticket will run out.' She stood up.

'You're going?' Gemma looked startled.

'I've seen the dancing and the Oak King and had a ride on the carousel,' said Libby, with a grin. 'Now I need to go home and have a grown-up drink.' She gave Gemma a quick kiss on the cheek and waved at Richard and Dan. 'Hope tomorrow goes well,' she said. 'Come on, Fran.'

'What was all that about?' asked Fran, as they climbed back up the Mount to where a troupe of small children were performing a largely uncoordinated fairy dance.

'There's something wrong with that Diggory person,' said Libby, pausing and panting by Grey Betty. 'You mark my words.'

'If there is,' said Fran, amused, 'I'm surprised you didn't start questioning him.'

'That's exactly why I left,' said Libby, starting down the other side of the Mount towards the high street. 'It would have warned him off and made the atmosphere even more uncomfortable than it was.'

Fran looked thoughtful. 'Yes, there was a certain amount of discomfort there, wasn't there?'

'Gemma's really uncomfortable.' Libby frowned. 'I don't know what it is, or why she's asked me to talk to people. She can't really mean that, can she?'

'She wants us to look into the murders,' said Fran calmly.

'Now *you've* said murders plural,' said Libby accusingly.

Fran nodded. 'And one of the reasons Gemma's uncomfortable is Richard Diggory.' Fran stopped outside the bakery. 'Notice anything about this window?'

'Apart from the Oak King and the sun?'

'And the Holly King on the floor.' Fran pointed to another bread sculpture of a Father Christmas head at the Oak King's feet.

'But that's just symbolic of the battle between them,' said Libby.

'But you said today the Holly King kills the Oak King, so this should be the other way round.'

'Oh.' Libby made a face. 'So Diggory's jealous of Dan? Why?'

'Oh, honestly, Libby!' Fran laughed. 'He's after Gemma.'

'Gemma?' Libby squeaked. 'But she's …well, she's …'

'Not very glamorous?' suggested Fran. 'No, maybe not, although I haven't seen her in mufti. But she's certainly got that sort of earthy sensuality that appeals to men.'

'Has she?' Libby's brows flew up into her hairline. 'Good lord! How do you know?'

Fran shrugged. 'I just do.'

'You've been having one of your moments, haven't you?'

'I suppose so.' Fran turned and began to walk towards the car park. 'I'm completely sure that whatshisname Letchworth –'

'John Lethbridge.'

'– was murdered, and that Richard Diggory has evil designs on your friend Gemma.'

'But the two aren't connected.' Libby hurried to keep up.

'Not on the face of it.'

'Oh, Fran, how could they be? Bill Frensham had nothing to do with Gemma; neither, as far as I know, had John Lethbridge, so Diggory wouldn't be knocking them off as rivals, would he?'

'As I said, on the face of it,' said Fran. 'I don't know. I'll have to go home and think about it. And talking of home,' she turned to Libby, 'will you give me a lift? Guy wasn't coming to get me until after closing time.'

47

'Of course,' said Libby.

They drove out of Steeple Mount and Libby glanced over to where the woods concealed Tyne Chapel.

'Reminds me a bit of all that Satanism at the chapel,' she said with a shudder.

'The Morris?' Fran nodded. 'It's all based in the old beliefs, and there's a connection with horned gods. The Morris is good, though, surely?'

'Oh, yes. Cranston Morris do loads of fund raisers and dance at church festivals.'

'I meant basically. The origins of Morris.'

'Oh. Right. Well, yes, as far as I could tell. Have a look online, but I warn you, there's absolutely loads of stuff on there, and you have to stop yourself going down all the unnecessary byways.'

'That's the same with all research,' said Fran.

Libby looked at her sideways. 'So we're looking into it, then?'

Fran, smiled through the windscreen as a view of her adopted town appeared over the horizon.

'Just for interest's sake,' she said.

Chapter Six

LIBBY COULDN'T SLEEP THAT night. Every time she began to drift off, she caught herself involuntarily and woke up. Eventually, thoroughly frustrated, she slid out of bed carefully, leaving Ben emitting whiffling little snores as he turned on to his back, and crept downstairs.

Sidney appeared in the kitchen in happy surprise and immediately started asking for breakfast. 'Ssssh!' she told him. 'It's not morning yet.' She felt the top of the Rayburn, which was barely warm, sighed, and dug out the electric kettle. Waiting for it to boil, she wandered out in the dark garden and noticed the slight lightening in the east.

'Nearly solstice time, then,' she said to Sidney. 'I suppose I could go and watch with the mayor.' She went back inside and peered at the clock. What time had Gemma said? Sunrise? 5 o'clock? Just time if she drank her tea while getting dressed.

Fifteen minutes later, in jeans, scarves and a denim jacket, Libby drove down Allhallow's Lane, hoping that the solstice celebrations were on the Mount. She hadn't thought to ask Gemma, having had no intention of coming. And now she wondered why she was. Had her sleepless night been somehow self-induced? Had she subconsciously intended to come all along?

She was surprised to find the Steeple Mount car park almost as full as it had been 12 hours earlier. A few stragglers were hurrying along the high street towards the Mount, where Libby could see a large group of people already surrounding Grey Betty. To her left, she noticed another group emerging from the direction of the woods.

'Don't be silly,' she told herself, 'they've come from the back lane. Plenty of houses down there.' But she found herself veering to her right and climbing the Mount as far away from the woods as she could.

The sight at the top was impressive. To one side stood the dancers and musicians, the accordionist and fiddler, to the other, several figures in long white robes, (Druids? wondered Libby) and in the centre, the fully clad Kings, Oak and Holly. And between them, to Libby's surprise, a female figure festooned in summer vegetation. The Goddess, the Earth Mother, obviously.

Libby stopped on the outskirts of the crowd and looked round. She saw the Mayor, looking uncomfortable with his chain of office sitting on top of a lightweight linen jacket, a gaggle of local press photographers, two of whom she recognised, and other members of Cranston Morris, the women in their traditional peasant girl costumes.

The sky began to get lighter and the Oak King began to speak. In spite of a certain amount of scepticism, or possibly cynicism, Libby found it impressive. As the light increased, so the two kings took up their positions, and as the sun weakly penetrated the cloud, they began to fight. It was a purely symbolic fight with staves, but to Libby it was chilling. As the Oak King fell, the Holly King took the Goddess by the arm and they ceremonially began a descent of the Mount. Behind them the dancers fell into formation, the musicians struck up, and the whole procession moved off, amid flashing cameras. The solstice song was sung again, and this time, Libby found herself remembering the words.

'Enjoy that?' Richard Diggory, mask hooked on to his belt, came up behind her, wiping his brow.

'Impressive,' said Libby. 'Do you ever hurt yourselves? Those staves must weigh a ton.'

'We're used to it. Dan isn't as – shall we say, committed? – as Bill was.'

'Doesn't hit so hard, you mean?'

Richard looked at her through narrowed eyes. 'You could say that.'

'Libby,' said another voice at her shoulder. She swung round.

'Ian! What on earth are you doing here?'

Detective Inspector Ian Connell's black eyebrows were, as usual, drawn down over his equally dark eyes. 'The same as you, probably,' he said.

Libby started. Aware of Richard Diggory on her other side, she shook her head. 'I – er – doubt it,' she said.

'I was watching the sunrise celebrations,' said Ian. 'Weren't you?'

Confounded, Libby gave a shaky laugh. 'Oh, of course.' She darted a look at Richard Diggory who had dropped behind and was watching thoughtfully. 'Do you know Ian Connell, Richard?'

'Detective Inspector.' Richard inclined his head. 'We've met.'

'Oh.' Feeling foolish, Libby realised that a) Ian

was probably here to keep a watching brief over Cranston Morris and b) that if so, Diggory would have been questioned by him after Bill's death.

'Mr Diggory.' Ian's own head bent slightly in acknowledgement. 'Are you going home now, Libby? Have you got your car?'

'Of course,' said Libby. 'I didn't walk from Steeple Martin.'

'I didn't suggest you did,' said Ian equably. 'I thought someone else might have given you a lift.'

'Fran's not here,' said Libby, and could have bitten her tongue out.

'No.' Libby could have sworn Ian's mouth quirked in a smile. 'I was merely going to offer you a lift if you needed one.'

'Oh. Thanks, Ian. No, I'm fine. The car's in the car park.'

'You're not still driving that rattletrap Renault, are you?'

'Romeo's very reliable,' defended Libby, crossing her fingers.

'If you say so,' said Ian, with a proper smile this time. 'I'll say goodbye then.'

Libby watched him stride off down the hill and wondered what he had really been doing here.

'So you know the saturnine Inspector?' Richard Diggory said.

'Yes,' said Libby.

'Well?'

'Good heavens.' Libby turned wide eyes on Diggory. 'What business is it of yours?'

He shrugged. 'Just wondered. Given your reputation and his.'

'Reputation?'

'Both investigators – of a sort.' Diggory gave a sly smile and veered off to his right. 'Got to go and join the others. See you around.'

Libby scowled and stomped off down the hill.

'Libby!'

'Good God,' muttered Libby and turned round to see Gemma hurrying down the hill after her, clad, surprisingly, in the draperies and vegetation of the Goddess.

'I didn't realise it was you under all that stuff,' said Libby, waiting for Gemma to catch up with her. 'I thought it was all very impressive.'

'Thanks,' said Gemma breathlessly. 'I didn't think you were coming.'

'I wasn't, but I couldn't sleep. Seemed like a good opportunity.'

'You haven't talked to anybody, though?'

'Gem, I didn't say I would. Richard Diggory talked to me, though.' Libby pulled a face.

'You don't like him?'

'Do you?' Libby raised her eyebrows. Gemma blushed. 'Oh, dear. Well, far be it from me –'

'But stay away,' finished Gemma on a sigh. 'I know. It's so flattering, though.'

'How long has he been – what? Flirting with you? Or is it more than that?'

'Oh, only while we've been preparing for this weekend, really. Because we did the King and the Goddess together.' Gemma looked away. 'It doesn't mean anything.'

It does to you, thought Libby. Oh, dear.

'How long have you been the Goddess?' she said

aloud.

'Only this year. Willy Lethbridge used to do it.'

'Willy? Wilhelmina?'

'Yes. Even after they split up, they were both still members of the group. Willy only really did the Goddess, though. She always used to do the May Day parade, too, although she didn't this year.'

'So did you do it because you're Dan's wife?'

'They all thought it made sense. Bill's wife Monica never used to do it, though. She's never been a member of the group.'

'What's she like?' asked Libby, as they resumed a path down the hill.

'Monica?' Gemma frowned. 'I don't really know her. Quiet. Didn't like being on show. She never even came to May Day or the Solstice.'

'So she never joined in socially?'

'Oh, yes, parties and things, and she even came to the pub after practice nights sometimes. A bit clingy, I always thought.'

'She must be devastated, then,' said Libby.

'Oh, she is,' nodded Gemma. 'She wouldn't see anyone after the murder, and she very nearly collapsed at the funeral. The children looked after her, but she didn't appear at the wake.'

'Where was that?'

'Oh, at their house. But the daughter – Julie, is it? – came down and said we were to carry on, it was what Dad would have wanted.'

'Poor kid. So did you?'

'We tried, but it was all too sad. Some of the other girls and I cleared it all up and we sort of crept away.'

'Have you seen her since?'

'No. No reason to, really. I suppose if they ever find out who – um – did it, we might see her.'

'Where though?' asked Libby. 'Still no reason to see her, I would have thought.'

'That's true.' Gemma nodded again. 'Oh – and by the way, did you see the police were here today?'

'I saw Ian Connell,' said Libby.

'Who?'

'Detective Inspector Connell. Was he in charge of the investigation into Bill's death?'

'Is he the very dark, sort of Celtic-looking bloke?'

'That's him.' Libby smiled. 'Fancied my friend Fran for a time.'

'I wouldn't have said no,' said Gemma, with a grin.

'She was in two minds at first,' said Libby, with an answering grin, 'but true love weighed, as they say, and now she's married to lovely Guy.'

'That's not Guy Wolfe? The artist?'

'The smallness of this part of the world never ceases to amaze me,' said Libby. 'How do you know Guy?'

'Well, he's sort of famous, isn't he? And he painted the dancers once, a few years ago. It was in the Royal Academy.'

'No! Really? Wow!' Libby was impressed.

'It was in the papers and everything,' said Gemma seriously. 'But I think it was before you moved to Steeple Martin, so you might not have seen it.'

'I'm surprised I didn't hear about it,' said Libby.

'I knew Guy long before I moved here. He's been selling my pretty peeps for some time.'

'Your -? Oh, yes, you paint, too, don't you?'

'Not as much as I used too, but yes. I do.'

'And do you still act? I haven't done anything with the old Players for ages.'

'Occasionally,' said Libby. 'I'm involved with our theatre in Steeple Martin now.'

'Oh, yes, of course. You had that murder, didn't you? That was the first one you investigated.'

'Look, Gem,' said Libby, standing still and turning to face her, 'I don't investigate murders. I'm not a private detective, or, God help me, a Miss Marple. That first time we were all suspects and it involved a lot of my close friends. My friend Fran came to help because she's –'

'Psychic, yes, I know,' said Gemma.

'And then her own aunt was murdered. After that, because she has this strange sort of – well, power, I suppose – the police asked her to help. And I helped her. That's all.'

'But there was that business over at Creekmarsh a few weeks ago, wasn't there?'

'My son Adam was working there.' Libby began walking again. 'Still is, as a matter of fact.'

'Really?' Gemma looked interested. 'So what's Lewis Osbourne-Walker like? He's gay, isn't he?'

Libby sighed gustily. 'Yes, he is, and he's a lovely bloke. Quite gorgeous to look at, of course.'

'Right,' said Gemma doubtfully.

'Oh, come on, Gemma! Surely you aren't homophobic?'

Libby watched unlovely colour flood Gemma's

face. 'Of course I'm not,' she said. 'I just –'

'What?' said Libby, now determined to make Gemma squirm. 'Just what? Don't know any?'

'I –' Gemma seemed to dry up.

'I expect you do,' said Libby. 'You just don't know you do. They are perfectly ordinary people, like you or me. They don't have a badge, or the mark of Cain. They just happen to have a different sexual orientation, and when I think how long and how effective their fight for non-discrimination has been, it makes me absolutely –'

'All right, all right!' broke in Gemma, as Libby's voice got louder and louder. 'Sorry. I guess I still haven't broken away from my parents' 1950s mentality.'

'A lot of people haven't,' grumbled Libby, quietening down. 'And I really, really object to making a fuss about it when no fuss should be needed.'

'I know.' Gemma placed a hand on Libby's arm. 'I'm sorry.'

They walked to the bottom of the hill in silence.

'Right, I'm off home for breakfast,' said Libby. 'I hope the rest of the day goes well.'

'And are you going to …' Gemma trailed off.

'Look into Bill's death after all?' Libby sighed. 'If Fran gets any sort of feeling about it, maybe. But that's all, Gemma.'

Shaking her head, Libby stomped off down the high street towards the car park, trying to subdue the investigating imp that was bouncing up and down beside her. Fumbling in her pocket for her keys and realising she was now too warm, she arrived at her car. Unwinding the scarves with relief, she got in and started the engine.

'Well?' said a dark brown voice at the window. Libby screamed.

Chapter Seven

'IAN!' HEART THUMPING, LIBBY wound down the window. 'You scared me to death.'

Ian looked sceptical. 'Am I going to get in, or are you getting out?'

Libby sighed, leant across and unlocked the passenger door. Ian folded himself inside and turned to face her. 'Well?' he said again.

'Well what?' Libby swallowed.

'I assume you *were* there for the same reason I was?'

'Watching the sunrise,' said Libby, avoiding his eyes.

'Bollocks. You're interfering again.'

'Ian!' Libby's voice trembled on the verge of a laugh. 'Are you swearing on duty?'

'I'd like to do a lot more than that on duty,' said Ian glowering at her.

'La, sir!' said Libby, and fluttered her eyelashes.

'Shut up, Libby.' Ian took a deep breath. 'Are you interfering in Bill Frensham's murder?'

Libby turned to face him. 'No, Ian. Gemma Baverstock asked me to, but I said no. I am not an investigator.'

'No, you're not,' said Ian, 'but that hasn't stopped you before. What about Fran?'

Libby wriggled in her seat. 'She came with me to the parade yesterday.'

Ian's brows drew down even more than before. 'Don't tell me,' he said.

'No – she hasn't had any moments,' said Libby hastily, 'she's just a bit bored.'

Ian's brows flew up. 'Bored? She's only just back from honeymoon!'

'Ah – um – that's the trouble,' floundered Libby. 'Guy's had to go back to work, Sophie's gone off to Europe and she's got nothing to do. Before the wedding there was all the preparation and – well –'

'Your little investigation at Creekmarsh,' Ian finished for her. 'Yes.' He settled himself more firmly in his seat. 'Now listen. We have been investigating Bill Frensham's murder for nearly two months –'

'And John Lethbridge's?'

Ian let out a breath. 'There, you see? You already know about that.'

'I didn't know he was dead,' said Libby innocently.

'I didn't mean that,' said Ian testily, 'I meant you know about Lethbridge's disappearance, presumably.'

'Oh, yes.'

'And is there anything else you know?'

'No more than you,' said Libby, looking out of the windscreen.

'Libby.' Ian took hold of her chin and turned her to face him. She blinked. 'Now listen. Don't go barging in to this investigation. It's complicated and fairly wide-ranging and nothing to do with you.'

Libby opened her mouth.

'No,' said Ian. 'Don't speak. I'm not saying that if Fran has some sort of vision about it I wouldn't be willing to listen, but that's it. Understand me?' He shook her chin a little for emphasis. She nodded, or tried to.

'Good girl,' he said patronisingly, and patted her cheek, opening the door with his other hand. 'Now off you go back to your Ben.'

Libby stared after him open-mouthed, forgetting to be annoyed about his uncharacteristic chauvinism. No wonder Fran had nearly been seduced by him.

'I'm going on a diet,' said Libby to Fran over the phone later in the morning. 'I'm far too fat.'

'You've been saying that for ages,' said Fran. 'What's changed suddenly?'

'I got very out of breath climbing the Mount.'

'I noticed.'

'No, this morning,' said Libby.

'You went to the sunrise?' Fran's voice rose. 'Why didn't you tell me?'

Libby explained about waking early. 'I couldn't ring you at that time in the morning, could I?'

'No,' said Fran grudgingly. 'So what happened?'

Libby told her.

'And Ian's warned us off in no uncertain terms,' she finished. 'Unless you have a spectacular moment about it all.'

'So what's new?' said Fran. 'We've been warned off every time.'

'Except when he's asked for your help.'

'Yes, but he only ever wants limited help,' said Fran. 'And we have got into trouble in the past.'

'I have, anyway,' said Libby, settling on the bottom stair more comfortably. 'You're more sensible.'

'Mmm.' Fran didn't sound convinced.

'Come on, Fran! Are you still bored?'

'I suppose I am a bit,' said Fran with a sigh. 'Although today we're going to Chrissie and Brucie baby's for lunch. That won't be boring.'

'Blimey! That's brave of Guy!'

'She is my daughter, when all's said and done,' said Fran, 'and I mean to start building bridges.'

'Even after they were so awful while you were away?'

'I'm going to tackle that over lunch,' said Fran. 'Then after I've talked to her, I shall go up to London and see Lucy.'

'Well, if you have any flashes of intuition don't forget to let me know.'

'I'll phone Ian direct,' said Fran, 'then you needn't get involved.'

'Oh,' said Libby, feeling a nasty little worm of disappointment. 'OK.'

'What was all that about?' asked Ben, rustling the Sunday papers at her from the sofa.

Libby sighed and told him.

'You want to investigate, don't you?' Ben put the paper down.

'Not really,' lied Libby. 'Fran said she did, the other day. She'll talk to Ian if she thinks of anything.'

'And today they're going to lunch with her daughter?'

'Yes. Don't know how Guy can bear it.'

'Well, I put up with your lot,' grinned Ben.

'Very true.' Libby nodded seriously. 'And I put

up with your dreadful family.'

Ben laughed. 'How about us having lunch with them, then?' he said. 'Shall I phone Mum?'

'If you like,' said Libby, brightening at the thought of not having to cook Sunday lunch. 'Will she mind?'

'Of course she won't. You know she'd feed us every day if we'd let her.'

Two hours later, when Ben and Libby arrived at the Manor, Libby wasn't surprised to find her son Adam already there, together with Peter, Harry and Peter's younger brother James.

'Turned it into a party, then, Mum?' said Ben, kissing Hetty's cheek.

'Caff closed today?' said Libby, as Harry gave her a hug.

'No bookings. So when Het called we decided to make a break for it.'

'Run away,' murmured Libby.

Harry lifted an eyebrow. 'And?'

'Nothing.' Libby smiled brightly at him.

Harry frowned. 'I'll be watching you, young Lib,' he said quietly.

Libby felt a rush of adrenalin as though she'd been caught out in some awful misdeed. She turned her back on Harry and went to give Ben's mother Hetty a hug.

'Hi, Ma.' Adam gave her a kiss on the cheek.

'You OK?' Libby returned the kiss. 'Haven't seen you for a few days.'

'Before I lived down here you didn't see me for months on end.' Adam was amused.

'Ah, but I've got used to you being around now.

And your washing,' said Libby, giving him a poke in the ribs.

'He's got his own washing machine, the rat,' said Harry. 'He uses the caff's whenever he wants.'

'Mum can peg it out, though,' said Adam, faintly colouring.

'If you did yours overnight you could peg yours out in the yard before you went to work,' said Harry.

'It'd be in your way,' said Adam, the colour getting deeper.

'Don't tease him, Harry,' said Libby, laughing. 'I don't mind.'

Adam and Harry grinned at one another and Harry turned back to Peter, who was having a low-voiced conversation with his brother.

'So how's the garden?' asked Libby. 'And Lewis?'

'Garden's coming on. Lewis was only saying yesterday you must come over when he's next down.'

'When will that be?'

'Next weekend possibly. He's got a job on for tv somewhere this week, then the whole crew will be down for some more filming. His mum's coming to look after him.'

'How is Edie?' Libby had only met Lewis Osbourne-Walker's mother a couple of times, but liked her.

'She's fine. I think having more to do has helped her. She seems much brighter and livelier. She's a fab cook, too.'

'Glad to hear you're not starving,' said Libby. 'I

suppose Harry feeds you, too?'

'I get the scraps,' said Adam, trying to look soulful.

Hetty called them in to the kitchen, where they sat round the huge table. Libby noticed Greg wasn't there, and leant over to whisper to Ben.

'Not very well today,' he whispered back. 'I'll go in and see him after lunch.'

Ben's father, wounded and imprisoned during the last war, had become increasingly frail over the last few years. He was an old-school gentleman who had deeply regretted having to hand over the management of his farm and hop gardens to his young wife after the war, although he was still able to run the estate office. Now, however, Ben, retired from his architect's practise, did it for him, though the hop gardens and most of the land had long gone.

How Hetty had managed it with such short notice, Libby didn't know. The enormous piece of beef must have been in the freezer, she supposed, but how had she thawed it out in time? Even in the microwave – if it had fitted – it would have taken ages. Still, thought Libby, tucking in to perfect roast potatoes, there it was, and hers not to reason why.

Lunch finished and cleared away, with Hetty insisting on doing her own "pots" as she always did, Ben went off to visit his father and the rest of them lay in various somnolent attitudes around Hetty's sitting room.

'Ben tells me the house is goin' well, Libby.' Hetty peered over the top of her spectacles.

'Very well, thanks, Het,' said Libby. 'How's Millie?'

'Much the same,' said Peter. He glanced at his brother. 'James and I went in to see her yesterday. I'm not sure she knew who we were.'

Hetty snorted. 'Her own sons? Course she knew.'

'No, Aunt Het,' said James. 'She really doesn't. Or what day of the week it is or anything. She talks about you, though, and your mother – Lillian? – and Flo and Lenny.'

'Oh?'

'But as though she was still a child,' said Peter. 'That bloody play.'

'You can't blame the play, Pete. She was already a bit ...' Libby trailed off and looked round helplessly.

'Barmy?' said Harry helpfully. 'Course she was, Pete.'

'But *The Hop Pickers* revived the whole story of you coming here, Het, didn't it? And that's what set her off.' Peter stood up and walked to the window. 'I'll never forgive myself.'

The rest of the little gathering fell silent and awkward. Eventually, James stood up. 'I'd better get back to Canterbury, Aunt Het,' he said. 'Tanya and I are going out tonight.'

'That's good, boy,' she said tapping his hand with her gnarled one. 'Time you settled down.'

Harry snorted and Adam gave him a nudge. Libby was amused to see how well the two of them got on. Fran would be worried that Harry, and/or Lewis Osbourne-Walker, would be turning Adam's head, but as far as she could see, her youngest son stayed resolutely heterosexual. Not that she was particularly worried about it either way.

As James left, Ben came back in to the room frowning.

'I think we should call the doctor, Mum,' he said. 'I don't like the look of him.'

Hetty gave him a sharp look. 'He's been as bad as this before.'

'Maybe, but we've always called the doctor.'

'He said not to,' said Hetty, setting her mouth in a firm line.

'Not even to make him more comfortable?'

Hetty's eyes lost focus. 'He's never comfortable,' she said, and Libby was appalled to hear a tremble in her voice.

Ben hunkered down beside his mother. 'I know, Mum. But I really do think we need to call the doctor.'

'Who is it?' said Libby, standing up. 'I'll do it.'

'The new one.' Hetty looked down at her hands clasped in her lap. 'The old surgery.'

The others in the room all looked at one another, reminded again of the tragedies of a few short years ago.

'All coming back to that fucking play again,' said Peter, and strode out of the room. Harry made an apologetic face and hurried after him.

Libby went outside to make the call. It was, of course, put through to an emergency service, but the operator told her she would try and get hold of Dr Harrison himself. When she rang off, she found Adam standing by her elbow.

'Mum,' he said quietly, 'I'm not sure I understand all this.' He jerked his head in the direction of the sitting room. Libby sighed. 'I'll just go and tell them I've made the call,' she said.

'You remember the play, don't you?' she said, coming back to Adam.

'Yes. We came down to see it.'

'And there was a lot of trouble about it? Remember that?'

'Could hardly forget it, could I?'

'Well, Pete blames himself for writing the play and insisting on putting it on. He doesn't think any of the problems would have happened if we'd never even thought about the theatre.'

Adam frowned. 'But you've put on lots of things since then, and he's been involved.'

'But now his mother and his uncle are both getting worse, and he sees it as a direct result of *The Hop Pickers*. It isn't of course, but you can understand it.'

Adam shook his head. 'I can't,' he said. 'It's like Lewis thinks he's entirely responsible for all the trouble at Creekmarsh. I tell him he's daft, but I don't think it makes any difference.'

Everyone stayed for a while, waiting for a call from the doctor. It came while Libby was making tea in the kitchen.

'He's coming over,' said Ben, coming to find her. 'He sounded –' he broke off.

'Concerned?' Libby put the big brown teapot on to the tray with mugs, a milk jug and sugar bowl.

'Yes.' Ben looked down at the tray and covered Libby's hand with his own. 'Lib, I'm sorry, but I think I ought to stay here tonight.'

Libby was conscious of almost equal parts of

worry and relief, and hated herself.

'Shall I stay with you?' she asked heroically.

Ben shook his head and picked up the tray. 'Better not,' he said. 'I don't think anything – well, that is, I don't think he'll –'

'Die tonight?' said Libby.

'Yes.' Ben looked at her. 'But it might be difficult.' He heaved a sigh, standing in the kitchen, the heavy tray in his hands, looking as though the whole world had descended onto his shoulders. 'He's been a creaking gate for so long that we've all got used to it.'

Libby nodded and leant across the tray to give him a kiss. 'I know,' she said. 'And what with Peter blaming himself it just makes things even more awful, doesn't it?'

Ben sighed and nodded, and they left the kitchen to take the tea into the sitting room. They were still there when the doctor arrived. Ben and Hetty took him straight up to Greg.

'Come on,' said Harry. 'Let's wash these mugs up and get out of the way. They won't want us hanging around.'

Peter, still looking like an aristo on his way to the tumbrel nodded vaguely and came away from the window. Adam began loading mugs on to the tray and Libby led the way to the kitchen, where she filled the sink with water.

'You three go,' she said plunging her arms in. 'I'll be quicker on my own. Then I'll just see if they need anything and get off home myself.'

Adam and Harry came up behind her and each gave her a kiss on the cheek.

'Come to us this evening,' said Harry. 'I've got some bookings at the caff, so if you feel like eating again later on I'll give you a share of Ad's scraps.'

Libby looked round at him and grinned. 'I'll do that,' she said. 'Be like old times.' She looked across at Peter, standing disconsolate by the door. 'Cheer up, Pete. It really isn't your fault.'

But, later, as she walked slowly down the Manor drive past the Oast House Theatre, she wondered if perhaps they didn't all share the blame.

Chapter Eight

IT WAS STILL BROAD daylight at a quarter to nine when Libby walked to the Pink Geranium. Ben had called at around six, to say that Doctor Harrison had arrived and organised some specialist equipment to be delivered, including oxygen, given his father an injection and said he would see them in the morning before surgery, but if they were at all worried they were to call him on his private number at any time.

'Seems a nice chap,' said Ben hesitantly. 'Don't know where he's living.'

'Over the surgery, perhaps?' suggested Libby. 'There is a flat there, isn't there? He must have bought the whole building when he bought the practice.'

'Maybe,' said Ben. 'Most practices have several doctors these days. The old village doctor has all but died out.'

'Not ours, obviously,' said Libby. 'And if he's nice, as you think, then thank God for it, I say.'

She glanced now across the road to where the doctor's surgery stood on the corner of Maltby Close. A light on the first floor confirmed her supposition that the new doctor had taken up residence in the flat. Bit small for a family, thought Libby, but at least there's a garden.

Donna installed her on the sofa in the window of the Pink Geranium and Adam brought over a bottle of red wine.

'Harry said you like this,' he said, wiping his

hands on his long French-waiter apron.

'I do.' Libby smiled up at him. 'Where's Pete?'

'He wouldn't come.' Adam pulled down the corners of his mouth. 'Said he'd got work to do at home.'

'Am I waiting until you two are free to eat with me?'

'Don't know.' Adam shrugged. 'I'm supposed to be plating up, so I'd better get back. See you in a bit.'

Libby sat gazing out onto the high street watching the sky get slowly darker. Eventually, she stood up, and carrying her wine glass, made her way to the back of the restaurant.

'Can I go through to the yard?' she asked Donna.

The yard, from where steps led up to the flat Adam was now occupying, had now become a designated smoking area. Libby sat at one of the little white-painted iron tables, and noted that the other two were full. She smiled evilly to her self and lit a cigarette. 'So much for the ban,' she muttered.

'What?' Harry slid a chair noisily away from the table and sat down. 'Gi's a fag, gal.'

Libby handed over her packet. 'Have you finished in there?'

'Yup. Be able to come out and play soon. Do you mind what you get to eat?'

'No, I'm looking forward to it.'

'So what's the news on Uncle Greg?'

Libby told him all she knew.

'Doesn't look too good, does it?' said Harry, stubbing out his cigarette half smoked and standing up. 'I'll just finish up in there and be out shortly.'

Libby finished her own cigarette slowly, then went back to the sofa to wait for Adam and Harry. Donna came over to join her and slipped off her shoes.

'Are you eating with us?' asked Libby.

'No.' Donna pushed her hair away from her face. 'Got a date.' She grinned at Libby. 'Finally, someone who isn't put off by unsocial hours.'

'Oh?'

'No one you know. He's a doctor.' Libby was surprised to see Donna blush.

'Not the new doctor over the road?'

'Oh, no. I'm one of his patients, couldn't do that.' Donna giggled. 'No, he's a houseman at the hospital.'

'Oh, right. Well. Congratulations. His hours will be even worse than yours.'

'I know.' Donna sighed. 'Can't get it right, can I?'

Harry appeared carrying two plates, Adam following with a third.

'Sure you won't join us?' said Harry. 'Or are you desperate for the doctor?'

Donna poked her tongue out and stood up. 'Will you sort out the last customers?' she said, indicating the two remaining tables of diners.

'Have they paid?'

'Of course.' Donna gave Adam a playful pat on the cheek and disappeared towards the kitchen. Harry nodded towards the empty table in the other window.

'She's a good girl,' he said. 'I hope she doesn't decide to start having babies and leave us.'

'She's got ambition,' said Libby, taking her seat at the table. 'You told me. That's why she came here from Anderson Place, isn't it?'

'But luurve might intervene,' said Harry. 'If this doctor sweeps her off her size tens.'

'Blimey!' said Adam, his mouth full of refried beans. 'I never noticed she had big feet.'

'Bye Donna,' said Libby loudly, and Adam choked. 'Have a good time.'

Donna encompassed them all in a smile and a wave.

'Anyway, babies aren't all they're cracked up to be,' said Libby with a darkling glance at her son.

'We were angels,' he grinned. 'It's Fran's lot who are so awful.'

'Not Jeremy, actually,' said Libby. 'You liked him, didn't you?'

'Yeah, but he's in America. Fat lot of use he is.'

'I met the other two at the wedding, didn't I?' said Harry, pouring more wine. 'The quite pretty one with the kids who couldn't decide whether or not to be a hippy, and the discontented one with the make-up and the husband.'

'Lucy with Rachel and Tom, who aren't too bad, I suppose, and dreadful Chrissie and Brucie baby, who have a cat, Cassandra. Fran and Guy have gone there today, as a matter of fact.' Libby sipped at her wine. 'Families, eh?'

'Yours is all right,' said Harry, with an odd look. 'The Parkers and the Wildes are a bit more of a problem.'

'Mmm.' Libby didn't want to think about it. 'I think there are quite a lot of family problems in

74

Cranston Morris, too,' she said.

'Cranston Morris?' Harry frowned. 'What have they got to do with anything?'

'You knew I was going to their parade,' said Libby. 'Well, I met Richard Diggory again. I said I would. Then I went to the actual sunrise celebrations this morning.'

'What time did you get up?' asked Adam, horrified.

'Four thirty. I didn't mean to, I just didn't sleep well. Anyway, it turns out Diggory is the Oak King and quite important in the whole Celtic festival thing. Bit of a ladies man, though.'

'Don't tell me he tried it on with you?' Harry threw his head back and laughed.

'Why shouldn't he?' said Libby, a little huffily.

'Trying to mate with a hedgehog comes to mind.' Harry patted her hand.

'He made me uncomfortable, anyway,' said Libby.

'And what else happened?' Harry had sat back in his chair and was watching her carefully.

Libby opened her eyes wide. 'Nothing, why?'

'Just wondering why you went to the parade and the sunrise party. Not your sort of thing these days, is it? You told me you used to go when he was small.' Harry jerked his thumb towards Adam.

'Something to do,' said Libby, bending to her plate once more.

'That bloke who was murdered on May Day,' said Adam indistinctly. 'Betcha.'

Libby looked up at two sets of eyes bent accusingly on hers.

'Well,' she said, clearing her throat, 'my friend Gemma did ask me to look into it.'

'Oh, *Libby*!'

'Oh, *Mu-um*!'

'It's all right,' she said hastily. 'Fran's had no moments about it –'

'So Fran's involved too?' said Harry.

'And Ian's warned me off comprehensively.'

'When did you see Ian?' asked Harry.

'This morning. He was there, too.'

'That bloke that got murdered May Day. Told you.' Adam glared triumphantly at his mother.

'All right, all right,' said Libby. 'But I said no, and that's that.'

'Where have I heard that before?' said Harry, casting his eyes up to the ceiling.

'You know what,' said Adam suddenly. 'You want to get away. Have a holiday. You haven't been away from Steeple Martin since you moved here, have you?'

Libby and Harry both looked at him in astonishment.

'Where did that come from?' said Harry.

'I just think she should.' Adam was defensive. 'She's spent the last few years looking into things for other people, and looking after people –'

Harry snorted.

'Well, she has,' said Adam, glaring once again, but this time at Harry.

'It's a lovely idea,' said Libby, 'but how could I? Ben and his family might need me.'

'He's packed you off home, hasn't he? He can always ring you if the circumstances change.' Harry leant forward. 'Look, petal. For once the incubus is right. You need a holiday. Even Fran's been on honeymoon.'

'But where would I go?' Libby's baser self was saying go – run away, while her more cautious self was telling her she couldn't possibly.

'Somewhere not too far away? But diffcrcnt?' Adam was thinking.

'This country,' added Harry.

'I know – Lewis is going somewhere this week – I told you.' Adam let his chair, which had been teetering backwards, bang to the floor. 'Somewhere nice, it is, I'm sure. He could find you a place.'

'You can't ask Lewis to do that.' Libby pushed her plate away.

'He wouldn't mind. He thinks you're great.'

'What is this strange power you have over young men?' said Harry, grasping her hand and looking deep into her eyes.

'Gay men,' said Libby.

'A fag hag to her fingertips.' Harry gave her hand a pat and stood up to take the plates away. On his way to the kitchen he stopped to speak to the last diners, who were preparing to leave. Adam dutifully went over to lend a hand.

Libby watched them both with a feeling that she had suddenly got out of her depth. It was only the other day she had been wanting to run away, and now here were two of her nearest and dearest telling her to do it. Not that they knew she wanted to, but it provided some sort of validation for her feelings.

The last diners had gone, Harry turned his sign to "closed" and Adam taken his apron off. Harry provided an ashtray. 'Not a public place any more,' he said.

'That's another thing,' said Libby. 'You can't stay anywhere these days. No one allows smoking in hotels or self-catering.'

'There's a loophole for hotels,' said Harry. 'It was in the catering mag. They can have smoking rooms.'

'Really? And how do you find out which ones they are?' Libby shook a cigarette out of her packet as Adam looked disapproving.

Harry shrugged. 'Google?'

'Choose a hotel and then ask them, I suppose,' said Libby. 'And then go on to the next one.'

'Are you going to go, then, Ma?'

Libby looked across at her son. 'It's an appealing idea,' she said. 'Although I do feel I'd be ratting on Ben.'

'And your "investigation"?' Harry put it in inverted commas.

'There isn't one,' said Libby firmly. 'I've said.'

Harry and Adam sighed in unison.

'So you did,' said Harry.

Chapter Nine

'HOW'S GREG?' ASKED LIBBY.

'No worse.' Ben's voice sounded tired at the other end of the phone.

'Have you had any sleep?'

'Oh, yes. Not as much as I'd like, but Mum and I both had a reasonable night's sleep.'

'Shall I come up and see him?'

'If you like,' said Ben. 'He's quite relaxed and perfectly compos mentis.'

'Much like normal, then?' said Libby with a smile.

'Exactly. So what did you do last night?'

'Went to the caff for leftovers with Ad,' said Libby, feeling slightly guilty.

'I'm glad you weren't on your own,' said Ben, and she felt even guiltier.

'No.' Libby took a deep breath. 'Ben, while you're at the Manor, would you – I mean – would it – er, well, I wondered –'

'Spit it out, Lib.'

'I wondered if I might go off for a few days,' said Libby in a rush.

'Off?' said Ben, after a short silence. 'Off where?'

'It was Adam's suggestion.' Libby hurried on. 'He said I needed a holiday.'

'Oh? Why?'

'Because I hadn't had one for so long, I suppose.'

'We could go away, if you want to.'

'You can't leave your Mum and Dad right now,' said Libby, feeling dreadful.

'No, but I'll be able to soon. Or is this simply to get away from me?'

'Of course not,' said Libby, now completely suffused in hot guilty colour and glad no one could see her. 'And it was only a suggestion. I don't want to leave if you need me.'

There was another short silence. 'Of course I need you, but if you want to get away, don't let me stop you. Where will you go?'

'I won't,' said Libby. 'You've made up my mind for me. I told Adam I'd feel I was ratting on you, and now I do, so I won't go.'

'Oh, God,' groaned Ben. 'Now you're making *me* feel guilty.'

Libby, feeling calmer and cooler, laughed. 'Right pair, aren't we?'

Ben gave a reluctant snort of laughter. 'We are.'

'I'll come up at lunchtime, shall I? See Hetty – and Greg, if he's up to it.'

'All right,' said Ben. 'And – thanks, Lib.'

Libby erased the Google search for rental cottages on her computer and switched it off. So that was that. She didn't know how she'd thought she was going to get away with it, and despite what Adam said, she didn't really feel in *need* of a holiday. It wasn't as if she worked particularly hard, after all, she thought, sending a guilty glance towards the conservatory and the blank canvases within.

Deciding to go the whole hog and prepare a

luxurious picnic lunch to take to the Manor with her, she collected purse and basket and set off for Ahmed and Ali's eight-til-late and Nella and Joe's new Cattlegreen farm shop. It was while she was selecting some very ripe brie from Ali's new deli counter that her mobile rang.

'Lib? Hi, it's Lewis.'

'Hello, Lewis!' Libby struggled with basket, purse and phone. 'I'm shopping. Can I ring you back in a minute?'

Ahmed's son, Ali's nephew, handed over a beautifully wrapped piece of cheese and took her money, handing it over for his uncle to put in the till. She smiled at him, thanked the brothers and went outside.

'Hi, Lewis, sorry about that,' she said. 'I was buying cheeses for Ben's lunch.'

'Ad said you was looking for somewhere to get away,' said Lewis Osbourne-Walker without preamble. 'Well, I got a suggestion.'

'Actually, Lewis,' she began, but Lewis interrupted.

'Now don't say you've changed your mind,' he said, 'because this one's right up your street.'

'How do you mean?' asked Libby cautiously.

'Well, you know we do a mini feature each week on the show?'

'I know you will be, when it goes out.'

'Well, it was your Ad talking about this Green Man effort set me off.'

'Oh,' said Libby with a groan.

'And I looked up all these weird folk-type things until I come to something that's going on now.'

'Now?'

'Well, in a few days' time. Why don't you come with me?'

'Lewis, did Adam tell you Ben's father's ill?'

'I thought that was why you could get away?'

'Well, yes, but it turns out Ben needs me here, and I can't really leave him. It's a bad time.'

Lewis let out a gusty sigh. 'Pity,' he said. 'I reckon it'd be good fun. Some of this Cranston Morris lot go. Seeing as how I thought you'd be looking into the murder, I thought you'd be up for it.'

'Where is it?' asked Libby, her interest now definitely piqued.

'Some village on the coast. They have this wicker thing – like the Wicker Man, I suppose.'

'Glory.' Libby shuddered. 'Not quite like that, I hope.'

'Something to do with John the Baptist?'

'Blimey! What are we talking about here? Pagan or Christian?'

Lewis sighed. 'No idea. I thought you'd know. Anyway, it's Thursday, 25th June.'

'It's Monday now,' said Libby. 'When were you thinking of going? Will you have to get the crew together?'

'Only the cameraman and the sound guy. We travel light. So, do you want to come?'

'Not much of a holiday, is it?' said Libby.

'No, but you'd get away for a couple of days. That's what you want, isn't it?'

'Did you tell Adam about this?' asked Libby. 'Only I don't know why he would be happy about it.

82

He wants to get me away from investigations, not get me in deeper.'

'He doesn't know what it's about,' said Lewis cheerfully. 'Go on. Be a devil. All found, nice little pub in the village.'

'You didn't answer me. When are you going?'

'Wednesday. Time to research the area a bit.'

Libby pulled at her lip. 'I don't know,' she said. 'I'll have to ask Ben.'

'You do that,' said Lewis. 'Give me a ring later.' And he was gone.

Now, thought Libby, trudging up the Manor drive, it will look as though this lunch is bribery. Bugger.

Ben opened the door as she approached the house.

'I've just had your mate Lewis on the phone,' he said with a grin. Libby's mouth dropped open.

'Apparently he wants your input into some feature he's doing for his show.'

'He said.' Libby cleared her throat and went past him and down the corridor to the kitchen. 'I said I'd think about it.'

'He told me.' Ben followed her into the kitchen. 'And if you were trying to protect me, thank you. Is this what you meant about going away?'

Libby unloaded her basket on to the table. 'No, I hadn't heard about it. He's only just phoned me, while I was shopping. I think it's a bit much of him to phone you. I told him what the situation is with your father.'

'I think he thought you were using me as an excuse.'

Libby looked up, surprised. 'Really? How odd.'

'Were you?'

'No.' She bit her lip. 'Well –'

'Come on, Lib. Wouldn't you like to go? He says you know more about this sort of thing than he does. And some of Cranston Morris are going.'

'I know very little about it all. Only what I've found out recently.'

'Ah,' said Ben. 'An investigation.'

'No. Fran and I just had a look, that's all. All this Oak King and Holly King stuff. Cranston Morris seem to have gone a bit farther down the old Pagan or Celtic path than most Morris sides.'

Ben turned her to face him. 'Why don't you go? I know I was a bit taken aback when you asked earlier – although it does seem a bit odd, you asking, then Lewis coming up with this scheme.'

'Think about it.' Libby stroked his cheek. 'Whose suggestion did I say it was?'

'Adam's.'

'And who does Adam work for?'

'Ah!' Ben grinned. 'All becomes clear. Adam's devious machinations eh? But why does he think you ought to go away?'

'He thinks I'm going to get involved in the Cranston Morris murder. He thinks it will divert my mind.'

'Doesn't he know where Lewis wants to take you?' Ben looked astonished.

'No.' Libby giggled. 'That's what's so funny.'

'If you go,' said Ben slowly, 'will you …' He trailed off.

'Get involved? I'll try not to.' Libby sighed and

kissed him. 'But if Gemma's there, and she probably will be, she'll definitely think I'm there on her behalf, despite what I said to her on Sunday. But,' she said, leaning back and looking into his face, 'I won't go if you'd rather I didn't.'

He gave her a squeeze. 'We don't have that kind of relationship, do we? And I'd hardly be jealous of young Lewis, would I?'

'Perhaps I could turn him,' said Libby with a grin. 'And now, let's sort out this lunch. Then I can go and see your father if he's up to it.'

Lewis was delighted when Libby called him later.

'See? I knew I could handle old Ben,' he said.

'Well, now you've got to handle young Adam, because he wants me to go away so I don't get involved in another murder investigation. And if he hears Cranston Morris are going to be there – well!'

'All right, all right. I won't mention them. I'll pick you up Wednesday morning at about nine, OK?'

'That early? Hell.'

'Lazy cow,' said Lewis. 'See you then.'

Libby called Ben. 'Lewis is picking me up at nine in the morning on Wednesday. Would you be able to come for a sleepover tonight? Or tomorrow? Or both?'

She could hear the smile in his voice. 'I think I might manage it,' he said. 'I'll stay here with Mum for dinner if you don't mind – but you could join us?'

'OK,' said Libby, never averse to avoiding cooking. 'I suppose I'd better start packing. What on earth do I take?'

'Ask Fran,' said Ben, and, blowing a kiss, hung up.

Libby chewed her finger for a moment, staring at the phone. She supposed she should tell Fran, but something was making her hesitate. Unwillingly, she realised it was the fear that Fran would want to come with her, or interfere in some way. Sitting down on the sofa, which Sidney vacated in a huff, she reasoned that Fran would hardly take off into the wilds of the West Country without her husband only weeks after her marriage. And she, Libby, could hardly *not* tell her friend she was going away. Sighing, she picked up the phone again.

'But why?' Fran said, after Libby's rather garbled explanation.

'It was Adam's idea that I needed a holiday,' said Libby. 'Ben agreed.'

'*Ben* agreed?'

'Yes, I know, but he has. He's busy with his mum and dad, so I'll be better out of his hair. I'm going to dinner at the Manor tonight and he's staying over here. I go at 9 am on Wednesday.'

'Whereabouts in the West Country?'

'A little village where they have some kind of pagan ritual to do with John the Baptist, I think.'

'June 25th?'

'How did you know that?'

'No idea,' said Fran. 'Is it his feast day? Yes, of course it is. He was born six months before Christ, wasn't he?'

'Was he? Anyway, what's it got to do with Wicker Men?'

'Wicker Men?' Fran sounded bewildered. 'Do you mean like that awful film?'

'Well, yes, I think so.'

'What that's got to do with John the Baptist I've no idea,' said Fran, 'but it sounds suspiciously as though you're getting involved again.'

'No, I'm just going because Lewis suggested it, and I think he's managed to swing it on his telly expenses.'

'Just you watch it, then,' said Fran. 'No crawling inside Wicker Men in the dark.'

'No.' Libby shuddered. 'I'll stick close to Lewis and his team.'

I'll try, anyway, she thought, as she climbed the stairs to start packing. Nothing's likely to happen.

Chapter Ten

LEWIS'S SUV, FOLLOWED CLOSELY by that of the cameraman, swung down a precipitous little lane between high banks. They had passed Plymouth and turned sharp left, as far as Libby could make out.

'Forgotten corner of Cornwall,' said Lewis, with a sideways grin. 'Not so many tourists. They by-pass it.'

'But I've heard of Whitsand Bay and Kingsand and Cawsand,' said Libby.

'The main road cuts it off, though,' said Lewis. 'And our little village doesn't seem to get anybody.'

'What's it called?'

'Portherriot. We're staying at the Portherriot Arms.'

'And when do all these shenanigans break out?'

'They start on Thursday night, I think,' said Lewis. 'I've got all the notes on the laptop, and I spoke to one of your mates at Cranston Morris. She was delighted.'

Libby groaned. 'Not Gemma Baverstock?'

'That's her. She's sort of the secretary, isn't she?'

'Her old man's currently the head honcho,' said Libby. 'He played the Holly King on Sunday.'

'So tell me all about the solstice celebrations that they do,' said Lewis, swinging the car round a sharp bend. A view unravelled before them.

'Oh, look!' said Libby.

Obligingly, Lewis drew up. Behind them, the

cameraman's vehicle also slowed to a stop. They all got out.

Ahead of them, green fields starred with poppies sloped to granite cliff tops, below which they could see a small cove guarded by rocky outcrops like bared teeth rising from a fretting sea. On the other side of the cove they could see a few buildings, above which thickly wooded cliffs marched away into the distance. The whole was isolated, and very beautiful.

'I guess the rest of the village is below us,' said the cameraman from behind a viewfinder. 'Great place.'

'Windy,' said Lewis, and shivered.

Libby looked at him sharply. 'What's the matter?'

'Nothing.' He gave her a strained grin. 'I get the old heebies in the country these days.'

'Because of Creekmarsh?'

'Well, it's not nice to have murders on the premises,' he said, climbing back into the car. 'Come on.'

'If you feel like that, why did you come down here?' Libby climbed in after him and fastened her seat belt.

'Work, innit? Anyway, I thought I'd be safe if you was with me.' Lewis started the car and moved slowly away.

'So that's why you asked me? Nothing to do with Adam?'

'He was talking about you and I saw an opportunity, as they say.' He slid her another grin. 'You don't mind, do you?'

Libby grinned back. 'Nah. I'm going to enjoy it.'

'So, you were going to tell me all about this solstice business,' said Lewis. 'Carry on.'

Libby related all she had heard, read and found out about the folk traditions followed by Cranston Morris. 'I don't know what else there is,' she said. 'Cranston Morris seem to have their own version of most of the traditions, all mixed up together. I don't think they're purists. They seem to take the bits they want from each.'

'And that includes this Wicker Man effort,' said Lewis, rounding a bend which took them to the top of a village street.

'I suppose so. It's a rebirth thing, isn't it? I read something about Manannán mac Lir.'

'Do what?'

'Manannán mac Lir,' repeated Libby. 'He was a sea god. Particularly in the Isle of Man, but also Wales and Cornwall, which seem to be the most pagan parts of the British Isles. The most steeped in the traditions, anyway.'

'Blimey, you're better than my researcher,' said Lewis. 'This looks like it, doesn't it?'

They had driven down the little village street past stone cottages bright with window boxes and emerged at the bottom in a tiny square (which wasn't) that fronted the cove. Small boats were drawn up on the mixed shingle and sand beach, and the terrace of a cafe, which seemed to have grown out of the cliff-side, lay to the left, while to the right stood a solidly Victorian hotel, The Portherriot Arms.

'Lovely,' said Libby, with a sigh of pleasure.

'Yeah,' said Lewis. 'Where's the car park?'

'I don't suppose there is one,' said Libby. 'There isn't room.'

'Do you mean to say we've got to lug everything from some bloody place up there?' said Lewis in horror.

'Let's ask,' said Libby, opening her door. 'We're cluttering up the square.'

But as she clambered down from the vehicle a man came hurrying out of the front door of the Portherriot Arms.

'Ms Osbourne-Walker?' he said.

'Er – no,' said Libby, suppressing a giggle. 'That's Mr Osbourne-Walker.'

The man, short, tubby and wearing a wonderfully flamboyant waistcoat over a checked shirt, rushed round to Lewis's side. Libby turned to speak to cameraman Jerry and soundman Boysie.

'Why Boysie?' she'd asked earlier.

Lewis shrugged. 'No idea. Ask him.'

Now, Libby eyed Boysie, with his long hair and tattoos and decided to wait until she knew him better.

'Do you know what exactly you're going to be doing while we're here?'

Jerry shook his head. 'Only filming this celebration or festival, or whatever it is. Then whatever takes his lordship's fancy.'

'Has he got permission?'

Jerry raised his eyebrows. 'He'd better bloody have,' he said. Boysie, a man of few words, nodded.

'Car park's round the back,' yelled Lewis out of his window. 'Follow me.'

He started up without waiting for Libby to rejoin him, so she plodded along behind Jerry's car, down the right-hand side of the hotel, which appeared to be another steeply rising lane bordered with more stone cottages and one startling pink and turquoise gift shop. Buckets, spades, inflated seagulls and seals, hats and kites fluttered outside in garish dissonance.

The small car park adjoined an equally small garden at the back of the hotel. In Libby's opinion, it was more pub than hotel, even though the little man in the waistcoat surely suffered delusions of grandeur.

Lewis got out of the SUV, Jerry and Boysie got out of Jerry's rather more battered one and waistcoat-man and two youths in jeans arrived to help with the unloading. Libby sat on a bench and watched. She was joined surreptitiously by several silent drinkers, who gathered behind her like so many ghosts.

'S'that Lewis bloke orff the telly,' came a sibilant whisper.

'Ar. 'Er said 'e'd be comin.'

'Fer Mannan night?'

'Ar.'

Mannan night? thought Libby. That fits with Manannán mac Lir. She thought of turning round to ask if that was the case, then decided against it. Villagers, if these were they, might be resistant to nosy strangers. Although they hadn't seemed opposed to Lewis.

The equipment had been unloaded and transported inside by the two youths. Libby was joined by Lewis, Jerry, Boysie and waistcoat-man. The Greek chorus behind her melted away.

'Now, let me show you to your rooms, or would you like a drink first?' said waistcoat-man. 'Such a long journey from London.'

'Kent, actually,' said Libby sweetly. Waistcoat-man looked as if he might say "same thing", in which case she would have countered with "Nice place, Devon," but with a quick look at Lewis, he held his tongue.

'Drink?' Lewis looked at his little entourage, who nodded.

The bar, lounge bar, Libby supposed, was dark, woody and red plush. A vase of dusty paper flowers stood in the fireplace, but, apart from that, it was inviting. Through a doorway, they could see the other bar, where the villagers must gather, judging by the buzz of conversation and occasional bursts of laughter. Waistcoat-man disappeared and reappeared like a magic rabbit behind the bar.

'What's your pleasure, lady and gentlemen?' he beamed.

Five minutes later, settled on a surprisingly comfortable bench seat in the window with a half pint of lager, Libby smiled at her fellow travellers.

'Nice 'ere, innit?' she said.

Jerry nodded. Boysie looked morose and Lewis looked anxious.

'I hope they won't cause trouble,' he said.

'Trouble?' asked Libby.

Lewis nodded towards a poster on the wall, depicting a highly coloured and improbable wicker giant falling into a positively Turner-esque sea.

Mannan Night! it proclaimed.

'My researcher said they were a bit sort of protective like when she spoke to them.'

'Who did she speak to?'

'I dunno. I spoke to your mate, and she was all right. Told me all she knew, anyway.'

'Which wasn't much, by all accounts,' said Libby.

'Just as long as they don't turn on us,' said Jerry, swallowing half his pint in one go.

'Do they, sometimes?'

Jerry shrugged. 'Don't care for meself, but they can damage the equipment.'

'Did you get the impression they might be like that?' Libby said to Lewis.

'Our Shannon said they was all right about us coming, but didn't want to talk about it.'

'Shannon? She the researcher?'

'Yeah. Worked on *Housey Housey* with us before.'

'A lot of people came with you from *Housey Housey*, didn't they?'

'Guess I'm just lovable,' said Lewis with a grin and Jerry and Boysie snorted.

'Anyway, we'd better see if we can get anybody to talk to us before tomorrow night.' Lewis finished his tonic water. 'I'll go and ask Trubshawe over there.'

'Trubshawe? Is that his name?' said Libby, delighted.

'Nah – he just looks like one.' Lewis grinned and went to the bar.

Waistcoat-man, whose real name turned out

disappointingly to be Jones, suggested Lewis talked to a few of the patrons of the public bar during the evening. He himself only knew of Mannan Night as a source of revenue and occasional damage. The committee, unlike many village committees, didn't even meet here, he said, a trifle huffily.

'Are any visitors staying here?' asked Libby, joining Lewis at the bar.

'Apart from yourselves, madam? I believe participating visitors are lodged with committee members or stay at the camp site at the top of the village.' Mr Jones sounded even more put out, now. Camp sites were obviously, in his opinion, beyond the pale.

'In tents?' asked Boysie suddenly in a deep and unexpected voice.

'I believe so,' said Mr Jones. 'And –' he hesitated before continuing with emphasis '– caravans!'

'Even worse,' muttered Jerry with a concealed grin.

'Wouldn't have minded a tent,' said Boysie. Mr Jones looked scandalised.

After assuring Mr Jones that they would be eating in his restaurant that evening, the little party adjourned to their rooms.

'See you downstairs about half past seven,' suggested Lewis, 'that'll give us time to get sorted.'

Libby unpacked her small suitcase, had a quick shower in her beautifully appointed bathroom and changed into a long skirt and suitably ethnic-looking top. Just right for traditional folk-type festivities, she thought. Although she didn't match the luxurious boutique-hotel style room, she reflected. That needed Versace or Armani.

It was still only a quarter to seven, so she decided to explore.

The sky was overcast and the wind was turning the grey sea into dirty washing-up liquid. Bells and buckets tinkled and clanked together outside the gift shop, and on the terrace of the little cafe a harried-looking member of staff was taking down umbrellas.

'Not sure if that means it's going to get windier or not going to get wetter.'

Libby turned to see Dan Baverstock beaming at her.

'Dan! How lovely to see you,' she said.

'Lovely to see you, too, but what on earth are you doing here?' said Dan giving her a peck on the cheek.

'Oh, a friend of mine's down here and offered to bring me away for a few days. Lewis Osbourne-Walker. I think he talked to Gemma the other day?'

A spark of interest lit Dan's face. 'Oh, right! He's a friend of yours, eh? Gemma didn't say. He's here to do a documentary, isn't he?'

'Just to film a bit, really,' said Libby. 'I expect he'll do follow-up stuff and interviews after editing.'

'Ah,' said Dan, looking bemused. 'So he'll be filming tomorrow night, will he?'

'Is that when the ceremony takes place?'

'First part.' Dan nodded. 'Then the second part in the morning.'

'So what are the first and second parts, then?'

96

'Burning of the Man tomorrow night,' said Dan, 'and then retrieving him from the sea in the morning.'

'Is there anything left to retrieve if he's burnt?' said Libby with a shudder.

'Oh, yes. He's only set alight just before he goes in the sea – up there, look.' Dan pointed to where the wooded cliffs rose up on one side of the bay. Libby could see some kind of edifice above the trees.

'Then the bonfire carries on and there's dancing,' explained Dan. 'Quite good fun.' He looked uncomfortable.

'You don't look sure,' said Libby.

'Oh, well,' Dan shrugged, 'some of them get a bit carried away, you know.'

'Not Cranston Morris, surely,' grinned Libby. Dan looked at her quickly, then away again.

'Course not,' he said. 'Come and have a cuppa. Gemma's up there.' He pointed to the cafe terrace. Libby was sure he'd been about to say something else.

'So where are you staying?' asked Libby once she was seated in a windy corner of the terrace next to Gemma. 'Someone said something about tents.'

'We've got our camper van,' said Gemma, 'but lots of them have tents.' Now it was her turn to look uncomfortable.

'Camper van's much better, I would have thought,' said Libby. 'Are you all together on one site?'

'Yes, a camp site owned by one of the Mannan committee,' said Gemma. 'It's right near the bonfire site, so it's really handy.' She looked up and smiled as Dan came to the table with three white china mugs.

'I'll have to come up and see you,' said Libby, quite fancying the idea of a camper van.

'Do,' said Gemma. 'I'll show you round. Dan'll be busy with Diggory and some of the others tomorrow.' A shadow passed over both the Baverstocks' faces and Libby wondered why.

'So.' Gemma sat up straight and looked directly at Libby. 'Why are you here, Libby? Have you decided to look into our murder after all?'

Chapter Eleven

I KNEW IT, THOUGHT Libby. 'No,' she said aloud. 'I just told Dan, I'm down here with Lewis Osbourne-Walker.'

'Really?' Gemma's face, as Dan's had, lit up. 'Of course! You're a friend of his, aren't you? I wondered why he'd phoned me and how he got the number.'

'He didn't get it from me,' said Libby.

'What about – um – Ben?' asked Gemma.

'He's glad to get me out of his hair. His father's ill, and he's up at the Manor helping his mother.'

'Didn't he want you there, too?' Gemma frowned.

'Apparently not. I did ask.' Libby frowned back.

'Sorry.' Gemma's colour deepened. 'So he's all right about you coming away with Lewis?'

'Oh, yes.' Libby grinned. 'After all, he's got nothing to be jealous about, has he?'

Gemma's colour had now turned to beetroot. 'Er – no, I suppose not.'

'Are you part of his – er – team?' asked Dan, clearing his throat and sending a minatory look towards his wife.

'For the filming? Oh, no,' said Libby. 'I'm just along for the ride.'

'Oh, of course,' said Gemma. 'It was his house where you found –'

'No, *I* didn't,' said Libby firmly. 'But yes. There was a murder there.'

'So are you really here to – ?'

Libby sighed. 'Gemma, I'm not here to do anything but have a couple of days off, and Lewis offered me the opportunity. He thinks of me as a second mum.'

'Has he got one, then?' Gemma looked interested.

'He hardly stepped fully formed on to the set of *Housey Housey*, did he? Of course he's got a mother. Very nice woman name of Edie.'

'Sorry, I'm sure.' Gemma lifted her chin and stared out to sea.

'Well, I'd better get back to the hotel,' said Libby, after a short uncomfortable silence. 'We said we'd meet at 7.30.' She stood up. 'Thanks for the tea.'

'Will you be coming to watch tomorrow night?' asked Dan, also politely standing up.

'If the others are going to film it, I shall be there. Who did they ask for permission, by the way? I know Lewis spoke to you, didn't he Gemma?'

'Someone spoke to the committee down here,' said Gemma. 'Not Lewis, I don't think. He only called me to get the local idea of it. I couldn't really tell him much.' She looked quickly at her husband.

'Right.' Libby looked from Gemma to Dan and frowned. There was something odd going on here, she was sure, but she couldn't quite decide if it was to do with Mannan Night or Cranston Morris itself. Whatever it was, they were ashamed of it, that much was certain.

'I'm off, then,' she said. 'I'll pop up to your camper tomorrow, shall I, Gem? Have you got your mobile with you? I could give you a ring to find out when it's convenient.'

Gemma fished into her tapestry shoulder bag and pulled out a mobile phone. Libby punched the number into her own, and with a wave, left the Baverstocks to their contemplation of the unsettled sea. It was by now almost half past seven, but before she went back to the Portherriot Arms she decided to pay a visit to the little gift shop.

She nearly fell down the step into its dark interior and was greeted by an uninterested voice. 'Mind the step,' it said.

The interior of the shop was as cluttered as its exterior. Presents and postcards from Cornwall, from Portherriot, even from the Eden Project, abounded. China dogs, wishing wells, piskies, and pirates jostled each other on the shelves, and a giant freezer hummed and shook slightly in the corner, covering "genuine Cornish Ice Cream" with crystals like the Snow Queen's palace.

At the back of the shop, behind a counter piled high with magazines and comics, Libby eventually discerned a shape. At first it appeared to be entirely round and dark, but on going closer, middle-parted hair fell to navy-sweatered shoulders, surrounding a swarthy face adorned with an incipient moustache. Male or female, Libby wasn't sure. Two bright eyes followed her progress round the shop.

'Do you sell cigarettes?' Libby didn't need any, but she felt she was expected to buy something. The shape nodded, and Libby asked for her brand.

'Good night, is it?' she asked, noticing another poster for Mannan Night as she accepted her change.

The sharp eyes fell, and there was a barely perceptible shrug.

'Thanks,' said Libby, and tripped up the step. 'Mind the step' followed her out into the lane.

Lewis, Jerry and Boysie were waiting for her in the "lounge". Mr Jones bustled over and asked once again after her pleasure.

'I just met my friends the Baverstocks,' Libby said, when he had gone to fetch her glass of wine. 'I'm going up to the encampment tomorrow and Gemma's going to show me round.'

'Can we come?' asked Lewis.

'No, I don't think so. This is an old mates thing, and you'd inhibit her. I'm going to see her camper van.' Libby smiled up at Mr Jones as he set her glass down in front of her.

'We'll have to find some of the other – what was it he called them? Participants.' Lewis took a small sip of tonic water. 'I need to talk to the main man, don't I?' He appealed to his sound and camera men.

'You got Shannon's notes,' said Jerry. 'Who is it?'

'I'll ask old Trubshawe,' said Lewis.

'The organiser?' said Mr Jones, thus appealed to. 'Well, I suppose Florian Malahyde would be the one to ask. I'm not sure.'

'Where would Florian Malahyde be found?' asked Libby.

'Just up the way,' said Mr Jones, gesticulating. 'The shop.'

'The gift shop?' Libby's eyebrows rose.

'Just so,' said Mr Jones. 'Now, if you'll excuse

me, the restaurant ...'

'Is Florian a man's or a woman's name?' asked Libby, as Mr Jones hurried away.

'Man's,' said Jerry. 'If it's a woman it's Flora.'

'Oh.' Libby looked at the table, frowning. 'I've met him.'

'How?' said three voices.

'I went into the shop after I talked to Gemma and Dan Baverstock,' said Libby. 'It's a funny little seaside gift shop up the lane there. He didn't seem to want to talk about Mannan Night, though. I asked.'

'Why?' said Lewis.

'There was a poster on the wall.'

'And you didn't know if it was a man or a woman?' said Jerry.

'No. You'll see, if you go and talk to him tomorrow. Could have been either.'

Jerry raised his eyebrows and shook his head at Lewis. Libby scowled at him.

'He won't be open after dinner, will he?' said Lewis.

'I don't know,' said Libby. 'There wouldn't seem to be much call for it. We haven't seen many visitors, have we? Maybe it's just day trippers.'

'And participants,' said Boysie. They all looked at him and Mr Jones arrived to tell them their table was ready.

The restaurant, and the food, spoke once more of the Portherriot Arms' ambition to become a boutique hotel. The trouble, of course, was that the villagers wanted it not to get above itself and stay as their local. The only other diners were very obviously visitors, and not those for Mannan Night, either.

Lewis decided a chat with locals in the other bar would be a good idea, so after refusing dessert in favour of an Irish coffee, Libby carried her glass through and perched on a stool by the bar. Lewis ordered another tonic water for himself and beer for Jerry and Boysie.

'Are they coming through?' asked Libby. 'I though they'd want to go off on their own.'

'There isn't anywhere else,' said Lewis, pulling a face. 'Jerry asked.'

'Bet he was popular,' grinned Libby.

However, Jerry proved to be more than popular when he managed to get into conversation with a group of locals and inveigle himself and Boysie into a game of darts. Libby and Lewis drifted over to watch.

'So,' said Jerry, positioning himself at the oche, 'what's all this going on tomorrow night, then?'

'Tha's what yer down here for, ennit?' said a tall, thin man in corduroys.

'Only 'cos the telly sent us,' said Lewis. 'We don't know nothing.'

'S'only Mannan Night.' Another man shrugged. 'Do 'un every year.'

'Tourist board stuff, is it?' asked Jerry, throwing his last dart and raising a few eyebrows at his score.

The thin man shrugged. 'No. Old Florian –'e does it. Done it for years.'

'What does he do, exactly?' asked Libby, edging a little nearer.

The group of men all turned to look at her,

surprised, and she realised she was the only woman in the bar.

'Gets they dancers organised.' The thin man shrugged again.

'Local dancers?' asked Libby.

'Goat's Head they calls 'emselves,' said another man.

'Goat's Head Morris?'

'That'll be it. Black coats and faces. They does a play at Christmas in 'ere.'

'A Mummers Play?' Libby was delighted.

'Aye. With Father Christmas and a dragon.'

'Great!' Libby turned to Lewis. 'You need to talk to the head of the Goat's Head Morris, then. If you can't find him, I'll bet Gemma knows him.'

'Bernie Lee, that's who you want,' said the thin man, stepping up to the oche and throwing the remark over his shoulder. 'Always into that there pagan stuff.'

'Pagan!' whispered Libby. 'See, I said it'd be interesting.'

'Did you?' Lewis made a face at her. 'I reckon you're just thinking of your old murders.'

'Course I'm not.' Libby was indignant. 'The murders didn't happen here. Anyway, there was only one murder. The other person has simply disappeared.'

'That's not what you think,' said Lewis. 'Unless you think the other person murdered the first person.'

'Very convoluted,' said Libby, with a grin. 'No, I don't know, and I'm not going to think about it. I am, however, very interested in the Goat's Head

Morris. The Goat is the symbol of the devil.'

Lewis frowned. 'I don't like this much,' he said. 'It's all a bit weird.'

'It was your idea,' said Libby. 'The Green Man, remember?'

'Yeah.' Lewis sighed. 'I must have been off me rocker.'

'It'll make good telly,' said Libby, 'as long as they let you film the actual celebration, or whatever it is.'

Lewis sighed again. 'We'll go and talk to that Flora person in the morning. You go and have a word with your mate and see if you can find out where this Bernie Lee hangs out. We need to talk to him, too.'

'Can I borrow your laptop?' asked Libby a few moments later, after watching Boysie throw three darts straight into the bull, looking bored.

'Yeah. What do you want it for?'

'To look up the Goat's Head,' said Libby, lowering her voice. 'See what it's all about.'

'Don't go messing with it, Lib.' Lewis shook his head at her. 'We'll just talk to these people and film tomorrow night. Then we'll go home.'

'But there's the second part of the ceremony,' said Libby. 'Your Shannon must have told you that.'

'Huh?'

'They fish the wicker man out of sea in the morning.'

'Oh,' said Lewis, looking gloomy. 'Yeah.'

'Anyway, you promised me a holiday. Two nights isn't much.'

Lewis looked at her with dislike. 'I don't know

why I brought you.'

'Yes, you do. For protection.' Libby grinned. 'You told me that up on the cliffs this afternoon.'

'Fat lot of protection you are,' said Lewis, picking up their glasses. 'You ready for a proper drink now?'

'Are you?'

'I want a cuppa,' said Lewis. 'I bet I can persuade them to make me one.'

Libby looked over to one of the jean-clad youths from this afternoon who now lounged behind the bar.

'I bet you could persuade him into anything,' she said with a wink.

Chapter Twelve

AFTER BREAKFAST THE NEXT morning, Lewis, Jerry and Boysie set off to talk to Florian Malahyde, while Libby, after a quick call to Gemma, climbed the rest of the way up the lane and came out on to a windy plateau at the top. To her left, in front of the thick trees, a large field contained what seemed like hundreds of tents, some caravans, camper vans and a couple of static caravans. Immediately in front of the trees stood a low stone building, which Libby guessed contained showers, loos and possibly offices.

She began to work her way down the left-hand side of the field as Gemma had told her, keeping an eye out for her friend. Who, as it turned out, was all too visible.

In the centre of a circle of chanting people, Libby could see the Oak King and the Goddess engaged in a ritual dance. She stopped and watched as the Holly King emerged from a tent and in mime, challenged the Oak King. The performance followed exactly the ritual she had seen the previous Sunday morning, and ended with all three performers bowing to their little audience, after which Gemma disappeared into a camper van behind her, while Richard and Dan talked to the members of the audience. Libby followed Gemma into the van.

'So what was that in aid of?' she asked, after looking round the neat interior and approving it.

Gemma had taken off her robe and her crown,

which she laid across one of the benches in the living area. 'Just explaining what we do in our celebrations. Everyone does something different.'

'And what about the Goat's Head Morris down here?' asked Libby, and was startled by the look of fear that crossed Gemma's face.

'They're – well, they're different,' she said finally.

'Black faces and black coats,' said Libby. 'That doesn't sound very different.'

Gemma looked at her for a long moment, then got up with a sudden abrupt movement and filled a kettle. 'It's what they do,' she said at last.

'What they do? I heard they do a Mummers' Play, but so do you, don't you?'

'Yes. It's not that.'

'What then?'

Gemma looked frightened again. 'Sacrifice,' she whispered.

'Sacrifice?' Libby hooted. 'Don't be daft, Gem! How could they ever get away with that?'

Gemma looked stubborn. 'They do. It's well known.'

'Pagan ritual?'

'I don't know. They all dress up like those Goths, only lots of them are much older. Do you want coffee?'

'Yes, please, black, no sugar. So where do you get this idea about sacrifice from?'

'Everybody knows. They have these meetings in the woods over there.'

'When? While you're here? How many times have you come down for this Mannan Night thing?'

'This is the second.' Gemma pushed a mug towards Libby. 'Only since Willy stopped doing the Goddess.'

'And Dan?'

'Same. Bill always came down, with a few members of Cranston Morris, but it all seemed a bit odd to us. Then we came last year, because Bill wanted Dan to play the accordion.' She shrugged. 'Then of course, this year – well, with Willy gone and Bill dead – we had to come.'

'So you don't really know that much about it?' Libby sipped hot coffee. 'Ow.'

'You hear things.' Gemma's mouth was set in a stubborn line.

'About sacrifice?'

Gemma sighed. 'Look, Libby, if you've just come here to laugh at me, you can go away again.'

'But you asked me –' began Libby, but Gemma interrupted.

'I thought you could reassure some of our members about the murder because you had been involved in cases before. You said you couldn't, but you still turned up at the Solstice. Now you've turned up down here. Are you investigating or not? And if you are, do the police know? And even if you are, why have you come down here? What have you heard?'

Libby stared at her friend in surprise.

'Good lord, Gem. I don't know what to say.'

'How about answering my last question? What have you heard?'

'I haven't heard anything.' Libby frowned. 'I honestly came down with Lewis for a few days' break. The only thing I've heard is that Florian Malahyde organises the Mannan Night and Bernie Lee is head of Goat's Head Morris. And that came from people in the bar of the Portherriot Arms last night. What *could* I have heard?'

Gemma looked at her searchingly. 'Are you sure?'

'Of course, I'm sure,' said Libby, exasperated. 'Are you suggesting there's something funny going on down here? And that it's connected with your murder?'

'I'm not suggesting anything,' said Gemma, snapping her lips shut.

'Except sacrifice,' said Libby. 'Come on Gem. You've already said that. You can't backtrack now.'

'Goat's Head Morris do that, I've told you.' Gemma looked over her shoulder and out of the window. 'They go into the woods at night.'

'You've seen them?'

Gemma nodded. 'And seen the bonfires.'

'In the woods?'

'Yes.' She leant forward. 'I'm serious, Lib. I didn't connect Mannan Night with Bill's murder, but since we've come down here ...' she trailed off.

'Has something happened?' asked Libby, after a moment.

'Not exactly.' Gemma frowned. 'It's just – well – I can't really put my finger on it.'

'Is it the people, Gem? Some of your friends?'

'Well,' said Gemma again, 'well, yes. I don't know how to put this without seeming disloyal, but some of them seem to have come down here for another reason altogether.'

'Another reason?'

'Than just Mannan Night. That's supposed to be a rebirthing ritual, and it ties in with our Solstice celebrations. It's Celtic, you see.' Gemma was earnest. 'But some of them – I'm not sure. They seem to have been whispering together.' She made a tutting sound and sat back in her chair. 'How pathetic that sounds. They're not a bunch of schoolkids.'

'But you think something secretive's going on?'

'Dan and I noticed a group of them went off together the night before last, then the same thing happened last night.'

'Are they a group of particular friends at home? Might they not have gone off for a drink?'

Gemma shrugged. 'They might, but we'd all organised to stay here and have a camp fire. We'd brought beer and wine with us.'

'Was Richard with them?' asked Libby.

'Richard?' Gemma looked startled. 'Not the first night. He stayed here with us. I didn't notice him last night.'

She looked uncomfortable and Libby guessed she'd been looking for Diggory.

'Why do you ask, anyway?' Gemma looked suspicious.

'No reason. I just thought he seemed quite – er – fond – of you when I saw you last weekend. I thought he might be, well, flirting with you. I told you that last weekend.'

Colour rushed into Gemma's cheeks. 'Of course not,' she said. 'He knows I'm married. Anyway, he's not really one of us. Dan's and mine, I mean.'

'Your what?' Libby frowned.

'Well, we were part of the original Cranston Morris – you remember, years ago, when we first started up after the Bogshole Mummers folded.'

'I remember.'

'Well, then Bill joined and John Lethbridge –'

'He's the one who's vanished? Married to Wilhelmina?'

'That's him. Well, Bill knew all about all the old Celtic and Pagan rituals, and began to introduce them. Some of the members got very enthusiastic, and that's when we started doing the Oak and Holly King rituals, with the Goddess.'

'The Goddess is around at Beltane, as well, isn't she?' asked Libby.

'And Plough Monday,' nodded Gemma. 'She is supposed to give birth to the Beltane at the Winter Solstice, then on Plough Monday she's supposed to be laid in the first furrow in the form of a corn dolly, then she courts the God at the equinox – this is where the Oak King comes in –'

'So it's a bit mixed up? Some of it's Green Man and the Goddess and some of it's Oak and Holly King? And then down here it's Manannán mac Lir.'

Gemma frowned. 'Who?'

'An old sea dog – I mean, god – which is where Mannan Night comes from.' I think, thought Libby.

'Well, they all come from the same root, whatever their names,' said Gemma. 'And a lot of the group took it more seriously than others. We just liked our dances and celebrations and rehearsals, but they used to meet at other times, too.'

'To do what?'

113

'I don't know. Discuss it all, I suppose. But then …'

'Then? You're not thinking of Bill's murder, surely?'

'No-o-o.' Gemma looked up under her brows. 'It's just that, with John going, and Willy having gone, I wondered.'

'Wondered what?' asked Libby, getting exasperated.

'If there was something else going on.' Gemma sat up straight. 'Which is why I wanted you to come and talk to everyone.'

'I still don't see how I could have done that,' said Libby, 'unless you'd gathered them all together and I'd given them a lecture.'

'I thought if they knew how the police can be – you know, thorough – they would all be honest and we'd get it cleared up quickly. You don't know how horrible it's been since May Day.'

'Murder is horrible,' said Libby, 'and you've got a hope if you think anything I said would encourage people to be honest. I know for a fact that people always conceal things from the police in a murder case, and not usually because it's anything to do with the murder, either. It annoys me, and it annoys the police, I know. Ian Connell is a particular friend of ours and he gets mad – generally at me – because people interfere, tell silly lies and do stupid things.'

'Like what?'

'Stupid things like trying to investigate when it should be left to the police,' said Libby, feeling the colour mounting into her face. 'That's why he gets mad at me.'

'See, you do know a lot about it,' said Gemma. 'I just thought –'

'That I could talk someone into confessing? Or into not shielding someone else? No chance. They wouldn't listen to me. People always think they know best. They watch television programmes and see the heroine go into the dark cellar, and they say "Oh, don't be daft! She wouldn't do that!" then they go and do virtually the same thing themselves.'

Gemma's shoulders slumped. 'Oh, well,' she said, in a dispirited voice.

'Do you actually suspect any of these people in Bill's group of being his murderer?' asked Libby. 'Or do you think there's something going on with them down here? That they'd have thought of him as a sacrifice?'

Gemma looked scared. 'I know it sounds silly,' she said, 'but I knew about Goat's Head Morris, and then all the others were going after them into the woods ...'

'But Bill didn't die down here.'

'No, but the Green Man is symbolic and in some rituals is killed off.'

'Not in modern south-east England he isn't,' said Libby. 'Not in the middle of a parade. Now, if there were any *clandestine* rituals it would have happened then.' She paused suddenly.

'What is it?' said Gemma, after a moment.

'Do you know anything about Tyne Chapel?'

Gemma's brow wrinkled. 'Isn't it somewhere near Steeple Mount?'

'Just outside, part of an old estate,' said Libby. 'Why did you want to know?'

'No reason.' Libby looked at her quickly. 'I just wondered if Cranston Morris had ever used it, that's all.'

'What would we use it for? Isn't it derelict?'

'Not completely,' said Libby. 'I thought you might use it as a rehearsal space.'

'Good heavens, no!' Gemma laughed. 'That has to be in a pub, or the men would want to know the reason why. Beer's part of the tradition of Morris dancing.'

'Ah, yes,' said Libby, 'the archetypal Morris dancer: Arran sweater, beard and pewter tankard.'

'Accordion, fiddle and bodhrun as side options. And the trouble is – it's true! Dan and I even conform in that we're teachers.'

'Oh, well, you can't have everything,' said Libby obscurely. 'At least you look more cheerful now.'

'I suppose you've made me see I was being a bit silly,' said Gemma, although Libby still didn't think she looked entirely happy.

'Well, if they sneak off into the woods tonight, why don't you follow them,' said Libby. 'Then you'll be able to have a good old laugh at whatever it is they're doing.'

'Not if it's sacrifice.' Gemma shuddered. 'It might be a rabbit or – or – a goat.'

'I shouldn't think so,' said Libby. 'Anyway, tonight's Mannan Night, isn't it? They won't do anything awful tonight. They'll be too busy showing off.'

Chapter Thirteen

LEWIS, JERRY AND BOYSIE had had no luck in tracking down Bernie Lee, but had managed to record some colourful locals talking about their previous experiences of Mannan Night. Florian Malahyde, however, despite being on view at his shop, refused to talk about it, or about anything, in fact.

'All he'd do was nod,' said Lewis over lunch at the terrace cafe. 'I asked if he'd given permission for us to film and he nodded. Then I asked him if he could tell us something about the history of the festival and he shook his head. And so it went on.'

Lewis bit into a giant-sized pasty. 'And you're right – he is weird,' he said with his mouth full.

Boysie nodded in agreement, long hair flying. 'Weird.'

'Swings both ways, I reckon,' said Jerry.

'Hangs straight down, more like,' said Lewis.

'Asexual,' Libby added sagely. 'A sort of hermaphrodite.'

'So Bernie Lee's off somewhere preparing for tonight and Florian Malahyde won't talk to us. What did your mate have to say?' said Lewis.

'Not a lot that was relevant,' said Libby. 'All she would say is that Goat's Head Morris have a reputation for conducting sacrifices.'

'What?'

'Bloody Hell!'

'Phmph!'

'That's what I said.' Libby took a bite of her pasty. 'As far as I can see it's only a rumour, probably put about by Goat's Head themselves to create a bit of mystery and perhaps keep people away if they're doing something a bit iffy.'

'Like what?' said Lewis.

'Drugs, maybe? Gemma said they're all Goth types. Or just simple, straightforward orgies. You never know.'

'Are orgies simple and straightforward?' asked Jerry, looking interested.

'How do I know?' Libby made a face at him. 'But they're not illegal, are they? Just immoral.'

'How do we find out?' said Lewis, wiping crumbs from his mouth with a paper napkin.

'That's not part of your remit, is it? You're just looking at Mannan Night and the history of it.'

'Yeah, but it'd be good to get a bit of smut in as well,' said Lewis with a grin.

'Bet your producers wouldn't like it, and anyway, you'd have to get permission or be sued.'

Lewis sighed. 'There is that, of course. So, what next? Do we go up and have a look at this wicker man thing before tonight?'

'I've had a look,' said Boysie. 'Can't get near it.'

'Oh.' Lewis looked dispirited. 'What do we do, then?'

'See if there's a museum?' suggested Libby. 'They might have something about it.'

Mr Jones, when applied to for information once more, suggested they try the museum in Plymouth. 'Nothing here,' he said, shaking his head. 'Although the reception at the holiday park might have something.'

'Holiday park?' said Libby. 'Where's that?'

'Up on the cliffs to the west,' said Mr Jones, waving vaguely. 'Not a holiday *camp*, you understand, more upmarket.'

Following his instructions, all five of the party crammed themselves into Lewis's SUV and set off for the upmarket holiday park, which proved to be a group of "lodges" set round a large central pavilion which housed a swimming pool and fitness centre. The reception area and attendant receptionist were both sleek and prosperous-looking, and the receptionist was extremely well informed.

'There's no museum nearer than Plymouth,' she said. 'All the local attractions have leaflets and things, but nothing else.'

Asked about Mannan Night, she simply shook her head. 'I know it happens, but it's just like a firework night, isn't it? There's no carnival or anything.'

'There's a bit of a fair, I think,' said Lewis.

'Oh, well, if you find out anything tonight, would you let me know? It'd be useful to tell the punters – I mean, clients.' She blushed prettily.

'It'll be on the telly, anyway,' said Lewis. 'You'll get a plug from that, won't you?'

'Oh!' She put a hand to her mouth. 'I'm ever so sorry – I didn't recognise you.' Her colour deepened. 'Here –' she fished out a notebook from a large handbag '– can I have your autograph?' Jerry and Boysie looked bored and Libby looked on with interest. This was the first time she'd seen Lewis in his role as a television personality.

119

'Well, we didn't get very far there,' said Jerry as they went back to the car.

'Yes we did. We found out that there's not much point in looking for a museum,' said Libby. 'And I like the look of those lodges. I wouldn't mind staying in one of those.'

Lewis shuddered. 'Right out here on the cliffs? With all that sea around?'

'Lovely!' Libby grinned at him. 'Come on, let's get you back to civilization.'

'If you call Portherriot civilization,' muttered Lewis, swinging himself into the driver's seat.

They made a detour to the top of the cliffs above Portherriot bay, in case they could see the erection that contained the wicker man, but were deterred by temporary fencing cutting off the point. Lewis wanted to go and question Gemma again about Goat's Head Morris and their supposed sacrifices, but Libby was firm.

'It was bad enough with me this morning,' she said. 'You'd throw her into a complete spin if you started in on her. We'll just watch what happens tonight.'

'If we can see anything,' grumbled Lewis.

'It's up to Jerry and Boysie to "see" things. You've got to talk to people.'

'If they'll talk to me. Haven't had much luck so far.'

'You said you talked to people this morning.'

'Yes, but they didn't know much. I want the history.'

'The dirt, you mean,' said Libby, amused.

'Well, yeah. Was it fertility, sacrifice, or what?'

'And you think because Goat's Head Morris have this reputation for sacrifice, that's what the Mannan figure will be? A sacrifice?'

'Well, why not? Stands to reason, dunnit?'

'I suppose so. I mean, it's chucked in the sea for the sea god, so yes, it is a sacrifice. Except it's not a real person.'

'It would have been once, wouldn't it?' said Lewis.

'When I looked it up, as far as I can remember, it said that the Druids burned men inside wicker cages made in human form. But after that, it was just wicker giants paraded through the streets. Like tonight, I suppose.'

'Yeah, but they don't parade it, do they? They just set light to it and chuck it in the sea.'

'It's the same thing,' said Libby.

Mr Jones had opened the restaurant early to accommodate visitors who wished to attend the celebrations, so Libby, Lewis, Jerry and Boysie congregated in the bar at 5.30 for a pre-prandial drink. Although Libby was the only one with alcohol.

'Can't,' said Jerry. 'Drunk cameramen are as much use as a chocolate teapot.'

'Oh, yes.' Libby looked mournfully down at the tonic water and two lemonades. 'I feel guilty, now.'

'We'll make up for it after,' said Lewis. 'Or they will, anyway.'

After dinner, Jerry, Boysie and Lewis collected their various items of equipment and met Libby outside the Portherriot Arms.

'Here we go a-wassailing, then,' said Libby.

'Huh?' Jerry looked puzzled.

'Never mind,' said Libby. 'Looks exciting, doesn't it?'

And, indeed, it did look exciting. Although the sky was still blue, torches had sprung up all over the little square, on the beach and up the lane beside the hotel. Libby noticed that all the seaside paraphernalia hung outside Florian Malahyde's shop had gone, presumably as it would cause a fire hazard, although, she realised, Florian himself wouldn't be there anyhow. He would be somewhere on the cliffs, presumably in whatever outfit suited his role as Mannan Night organiser.

Another path, not discovered as yet by Lewis's party, was lit, leading from the little jetty opposite the terrace cafe. As it appeared that this was the favoured route, Lewis set off to follow the steady stream of spectators. Libby trailed behind, feeling excited. There was something about this event that took her straight back to childhood. Perhaps it was torchlight against the evening sky, perhaps it was because, for the second time in a week, she could see the bright and garish colours of an old-fashioned carousel, but she could almost be twelve years old again and going across the common to the travelling fair, accompanied by her schoolfriend Mary and Mary's older brother, Stuart, whose instructions from both sets of parents had been to "stick close to those girls and don't let them go on the waltzers!" Needless to say, Stuart had disappeared the minute they'd arrived at the fairground and been enveloped in the special candy-floss, engine oil and fried onion smell of the fair.

Nearing the top of the lane and the site of the festivities, no longer roped off, Libby felt the same excitement that she had then, all those years ago. She wondered how Mary was now, how Stuart was, if he'd married his girlfriend. She really must write to Mary.

'What are you dreaming about?' Lewis turned round and came to a stop in front of her. 'You goin' to help me with this interviewing?'

'Am I supposed to be?'

'Thought you might want to. Don't have to. You can go off and do your own thing.'

'I'd rather, if you don't mind,' said Libby. 'I want to see if I can find Gemma.' And find out what goes on in those woods, she added privately, even though she herself had said there would probably be no time for private ceremonies that night. You never knew what might happen after the main event.

As the sky darkened, the revellers revelled harder. All the old-fashioned fairground stalls were there; coconut shy, hoopla, roll-down game, duck-shooting gallery and a fat lady photo-booth. As well as the gallopers, there was a proper helter-skelter and a chairoplane. Candy floss and hot dogs were almost as popular as the beer from the beer tent, manned, Libby wasn't surprised to see, by two of Mr Jones's youths, perspiring heavily and looking harassed.

At last a voice bellowed out from a megaphone – no electronic nonsense here, thought Libby – and the audience was exhorted to come to the site on the edge of the cliff where the giant wicker man stood on his plinth. All the rides shut down and all the lights went out. Libby joined the press of people around the enclosure and could just make out Lewis, with Boysie's fluffy microphone waving above his head.

Around the wicker man, fashioned in the form of da Vinci's Vitruvian Man, even down to two sets of arms and legs inside a giant wheel, stood three Morris sides. Cranston Morris had fielded only their male dancers, although a few of the women, including Gemma in full Goddess regalia, stood beside them. Another traditional side stood to attention, holding rappers and wearing startling white shirts and green and white faces and finally, on the far side, sinister in black, feathers floating from their jackets and hats, which were surmounted by animal skulls, were Goat's Head Morris. The only noise now was the hissing of the torches and the occasional jingle of bells.

A figure stood below the wicker man on the plinth. It appeared to have long white hair and beard and be dressed in an old-fashioned magician's robe. As the crowd watched, it bent forward and lifted a large shallow bowl, in which fire suddenly sprang up. Then in a voice which seemed to be neither male nor female, but carried over the whole headland, it chanted:

'On the day of Midsummer, the people of this place give tribute and sacrifice in honour of him who keeps the Gates between the worlds, their first king, Manannán mac Lir, Lord of the Waves, Son of Nine Mothers. Bring forth your offerings to he who makes possible all your journeys between the worlds.'

A member from each of the Morris sides, and Gemma, as the Goddess, stepped forward and placed something in the bowl. 'Salt, sea, flower, stone,' chanted the figure as they did so. As they stepped back, an even more imposing figure in black, complete with cloak, stepped forward from among the Goat's Head Morris and joined the white-haired figure. Together they lifted unlit torches high in the air before plunging them into the still-burning bowl in front of them. Then together with what seemed to Libby to be an elemental cry, they threw the lit torches into the wicker man.

Almost as soon as the torches landed, the whole edifice began to move, rolling down a prepared ramp towards the edge of the cliff, gathering speed. It was a terrifying spectacle, the figure of the man inside the wheel almost seeming to move as the flames swept along the limbs towards the torso. As it hit the edge of the ramp, it seemed to rear up into the air before plunging, turning over and over, towards the rocks below.

A huge cheer went up from the spectators and at once the air was filled with noise. The lights came on, the rides started up and, by the plinth, the dancers began to dance. Libby made her way over to where she had last seen Gemma and, sure enough, found her watching the traditional Cotswold Morris that the three sides were now performing in perfect unison.

'That was impressive,' said Libby.

Gemma turned quickly. 'Oh, Lib, it's you!'

'Well, duh! Who else did you expect it to be?'

'Could have been anybody,' said Gemma, looking round furtively.

'You have got the wind up, haven't you?' said Libby, tucking her arm into Gemma's. 'Are you off duty, now? Shall we go and get a drink?'

'We'll never get served,' said Gemma. 'Too many people. I've got a bottle of wine in my basket over there, though, if I can creep round and get it.'

'Sounds good,' said Libby. 'Shall I wait here?'

Gemma nodded and began to edge round the perimeter of the enclosure. The crowds had drifted off now, only a few diehards remaining to watch the dancers. The plinth above them was now deserted, the black and white figures nowhere to be seen. Gemma arrived back with her basket.

'Here,' she said, 'screw-top bottle and two plastic glasses. I bought one for Dan, but I expect he'll have beer with the boys.'

Libby found a convenient tree and eased herself down onto the ground, using it as a back rest. 'So were you up as close as that last year?' she asked.

'No.' Gemma shook her head. 'Last year I stayed back. Some of the other women go forward, but unless I need to I'd rather not.'

'And that was Goat's Head Morris, I take it? And was the figure in black Bernie Lee?'

Gemma nodded.

'And the white-bearded one Florian Malahyde?' Gemma nodded again, concentrating on pouring wine into plastic cups.

'Well, I don't see what there is to be so scared of. This Manannán person would seem to be quite benign, and there isn't any human or animal sacrifice involved, or any dark invocations.'

'You think I'm just being silly, don't you?' sighed Gemma. 'Well, just you wait. They'll all disappear off into the woods in a minute, and our lot with them.'

Libby had by now got a shrewd suspicion as to what was going on in the woods, and it wasn't sacrifice.

'Does Dan go with them?' she asked.

'Oh, no, it's only a few of them. Diggory, of course. Bill used to, and John and Willy. Some of the others.'

Libby looked down into her wine and then up at her friend. 'Gemma,' she said, 'I don't want to speak out of turn, but don't you think there's a rather obvious explanation for all these furtive goings-on in the wood?'

Gemma plucked at the fabric of her heavy robe. 'I expect that's what it seems like,' she said in a muffled voice.

'So why are you so sure the Goat's Head lot are up to no good? If they want to go off and have orgies under the guise of fertility rites or whatever, it can't matter to you, surely? Especially if Dan doesn't go?'

'Oh, I know that,' said Gemma, 'and I'm sure that's what a lot of it is. But why have all these rumours been circulating? Either there's something in them, or someone is trying to conceal something else.'

'By spreading rumours about sacrifice to keep people away from whatever they're doing? So what is it? Drugs, do you reckon?'

'I told you, I don't know.' Gemma was impatient. 'I just know they scare me.' She looked across at where the dancing was coming to a stamping, shouting end. 'That Bernie Lee scares me.'

'He isn't there now, is he?'

'Yes, look.' Gemma pointed. 'Standing at the back. You can see that awful hat.'

The lowering figure almost disappeared into the dark of the trees behind him. Libby could make out nothing but the occasional glint of white from his eyes.

'I bet he's a pussycat really,' said Libby. 'I wonder if Lewis got to talk to him.'

'He's always in the background,' said Gemma, 'except for that bit where they set light to the Mannan.'

'He's not now,' said Libby, levering herself upright. 'I must see this. Look. Lewis caught him!'

Chapter Fourteen

THE BLACK FIGURE WAS hemmed in by Lewis, Jerry and Boysie. Seeing Libby approaching, Jerry waved her over impatiently.

'Here, hold this,' he said, flipping something open with a practised flick of the wrist. She found herself holding a portable reflector, which she nervously adjusted according to Jerry's barked instructions.

'... Bernie Lee,' Lewis was saying, 'who I hope will tell us a bit more about this ceremony. Mr Lee?'

'It's been revived to do honour to the sea god Manannán mac Lir. Used to be sacrifice inside that wheel.' The voice seemed to arrive in the air without conscious volition.

'And how long has it been going on?' asked Lewis.

'Like this, ten years or so.'

'Like this? What happened before then?'

'No one remembered it.'

'So who revived it?'

'We remembered it.' The voice deepened, grew more gravelly, and Boysie made a face, leaning forward.

'We? Would that be you and Mr Malahyde?'

'Malahyde built the first wheel,' said Bernie Lee.

Lewis was beginning to sweat. Bernie Lee was not exactly forthcoming. 'Well, thank you Mr Lee,' he said. 'Perhaps we could talk to Mr Malahyde now?'

But Bernie Lee was gone, already disappearing into the wood, only a slightly denser black than himself.

'Romanichal,' said Boysie, doing something complicated to his equipment.

'What?' said Lewis and Libby together.

'Gypsies. Romanies. That's what he meant.'

'What he meant what?' said Lewis.

'When he said "we".' Boysie stood up straight. 'Anyone for a beer?'

'He's Romany?' said Libby, handing over her reflector. 'Did you hear that, Gem?'

Gemma had followed Libby to the interview site and hovered in the background. She nodded.

'I didn't know Gypsies believed in Celtic or Pagan religions,' said Libby, frowning. 'I thought they were descended from far-eastern tribes.'

'I thought it was Romania,' said Gemma hesitantly.

'They got there a bit later, I fancy,' said Libby. 'Didn't they, Boysie?'

The others all looked at him. He grinned at Libby.

'Far as I know,' he said.

'You?' Lewis stared.

'Course. There's lots of us around,' said Boysie. 'Even Michael Caine.'

Lewis spluttered and Libby and Jerry laughed.

'True. His dad was a Romanichal. And Charlie Chaplin. And Elvis.'

'*Elvis*!' they chorused.

'His family were descended from English

Romanichals.' He looked round at the rapt faces. 'Come on. I want a beer.'

Lewis shook his head. 'I dunno,' he said. 'I don't believe it.'

'It looks like it's true,' said Libby. 'What's the matter?'

'I still can't catch up with that Malahyde bloke. I reckon he's the one I need to talk to.'

'I agree with you,' said Libby. 'I don't really buy the Gypsy's Warning back there. It was a bit too pat. Yes, I'm sure Bernie Lee's a Romany, but I don't believe it was tribe memory that reinvented the old Mannan man. I think it was Mr Malahyde, with a bit of help from his friend Bernie.'

'For profit? The old moolah?'

'Maybe he really does believe all the mumbo-jumbo.' Libby fell into step. 'Perhaps he was just looking for a hook to hang it on. Mannan man doesn't come from here, after all.'

'You know more about it than I do,' grumbled Lewis.

'Um,' said Gemma, bringing up the rear. Libby turned. 'What, Gem?'

'I don't think anyone knows why it was started here. It just sort of sprang up.'

'Who said that?' asked Lewis. 'Sorry, you're Gemma, aren't you? Nice to meet you.' He thrust a hand at Gemma who took it gingerly.

'Um,' she said again. 'Well, it was Bill Frensham, actually. He –'

'I know, he was the one who was murdered.' Lewis nodded.

'Well, he was the one who started coming down

here. I told Libby, I think. And he said it just grew up.'

'And you've been coming how long?'

'Only two years,' said Gemma. 'I don't know much about it.'

'You must know where to find this Malahyde, though?'

'Sorry.' Gemma shook her head. 'Only his shop. Although,' she said, glancing over her shoulder, 'I expect he's in the wood with the rest of them now.'

'This the sacrifice business?' said Lewis to Libby.

'That's what they put about,' said Libby. 'Have you heard anybody else talk about it?'

'No one does,' said Gemma, firmly for once. 'You won't get anyone to talk about it.'

Lewis regarded her thoughtfully. 'Hmmm,' he said.

'Oh, come on,' said Libby. 'Let's see if Boysie's managed to get to the bar. Are you coming with us, Gem, or are you going to find Dan?'

'I'll – er – I'd better go and find Dan,' said Gemma, searching the crowd with worried eyes. 'I hope he hasn't gone off with Richard.'

'Who is one of those who disappears into the wood for dubious pleasures,' said Libby, watching her friend weaving in and out of the throng in her Goddess dress.

'So what do *you* think's going on?' said Lewis, as they battled their way through the beer tent towards Boysie, whose dark head could be seen over nearly everyone else's.

'With this festival?' said Libby. 'I just think this

guy Florian Malahyde started it up having probably had an interest in esoteric stuff –'

'Esso what?'

'Esoteric – it means secret and meant only to be understood by a few. More or less.'

'So that's what all this Mannan stuff is?'

'All the Celtic, Pagan and Wiccan stuff, yes. I think he – or they – have mixed it all up to make a special legend for this village, and now they're capitalising on it. Whether there was ever an ulterior motive to it or not, I wouldn't know.' Libby accepted a slopping plastic glass of lager from Jerry. 'Mind you, I wouldn't *know* any of it, I'm only guessing.' She took a sip of slightly warm beer. 'But knowing that Cranston Morris have made up certain parts of their own rituals, I should think that's what most of them do.'

'What about them Goat's Head lot?' said Boysie. 'Reckon they're Romani?'

'Do you?' asked Libby.

'He is.' Boysie jerked his head in the general direction of the woods. 'The rest of them, don't know.'

'Well, whatever they are, I don't suppose you'll get anything more tonight. You've got enough to cut together haven't you?' said Jerry.

'Yeah, and we've got the second part in the morning,' said Lewis, sipping at a flat lemonade. 'Yuck. Can we go back and have a civilised drink at the pub?'

'Give us a chance,' said Jerry. 'I haven't even started my beer. You go, if you want to.'

'I'll come with you if you'll hang on a minute,'

said Libby, not wanting to upset Boysie by wasting her warm lager. 'That is, if you're sure you actually want a drink.'

'A cuppa would be nice,' sighed Lewis. 'Sad git, aren't I?'

Ten minutes later, burping slightly, Libby was following Lewis back down the path to the jetty.

'So, was it worth it?' she asked, panting.

'Yeah.' Lewis stopped and waited for her. 'Not sure about this on location stuff though.'

'You've done it before,' said Libby. 'You do it at your own house.'

'S'different, innit? I've got a team of cameramen and directors and continuity people then. I've had to do all this on me own.'

'But it'll go to the editors and the director when we get back,' said Libby. 'They'll cut it about until it's right.'

'They'll probably cut it all,' said Lewis gloomily. 'I expect it's crap.'

'No, it isn't,' said Libby. 'It's only going to be a short piece within a programme anyway, isn't it?'

'Yeah.' Lewis shrugged. 'Oh, well, I gave it me best shot, didn't I?'

'Course you did.' Libby looked down at the little boats in the harbour. 'But you haven't enjoyed it.'

'No.' Lewis sighed. 'I'm a city boy, aren't I?'

'Yes. Except when you're at Creekmarsh.' Libby led the way across the square to the Portherriot Arms. 'And I still don't really know why you wanted to come down here.'

'Told you,' said Lewis, collapsing onto one of the comfortable window seats in the almost empty bar. 'After all that solstice stuff I wanted to find another folky type thing I could feature. It's colourful and interesting. So I found this one.'

'Are you sure it was nothing to do with Adam wanting me to go away?'

'Do I look like some kind of charity?' said Lewis indignantly

Libby smiled across at Mr Jones, who had appeared behind the bar looking harassed. 'Could we have a tonic water and a lager, please?' she called.

He turned without a word to collect glasses and Libby, with a grimace at Lewis, stood up and went over to the bar.

'Busy tonight?' she asked.

'Hardly anybody. All up at Mannan Night, aren't they?' Mr Jones turned round with the tonic water and a glass before pulling the pump back on the lager. 'Including my barmen.'

'Ah, yes,' said Libby. 'We saw them in the beer tent. They were run off their feet.'

'That's some consolation,' said Mr Jones. 'I haven't set it all up for nothing.'

'Do you always do the beer tent?' asked Libby, handing over the money.

Mr Jones shook his head. 'First time. Malahyde organised it before with someone he knew. Let him down this year, so I was told.'

'Did he actually come and ask you?' said Libby. 'He seems not to talk to anybody normally.'

'You're right,' said Mr Jones. 'He sent some secretary person down.'

'Not Bernie Lee?'

'Not Bernie Lee. He wouldn't come in here to ask me anything.'

'So who do you suppose the secretary person was?' Libby asked Lewis when she got back to their table. 'The one you spoke to?'

'Must have been. But, I said, it wasn't me, it was Shannon.'

'Oh, yes. Couldn't we find a name? You must have one.'

'I'll look on me laptop in the morning,' said Lewis. 'Tonight I'm too perishin' tired.'

'Right,' said Libby.

Over breakfast next morning, Lewis told them he'd found the contact Shannon had made before they came down.

'Did you phone her?' asked Libby.

'Course I did.' Lewis looked a bit shamefaced. 'She was a bit cross. She'd given me all the details before we left.'

'And you hadn't bothered to look?' said Libby. Jerry and Boysie looked at one another and rolled their eyes.

'Yeah, well, it was all a bit of a rush.'

'And you would have got a lot further if you'd got in touch with this person as soon as we arrived, wouldn't you?' said Libby. 'Have you called him yet?'

'Er – no. I thought it was a bit early.'

'Oh, Lewis!' Libby was exasperated. 'If this person – he or she? – she, then, is involved with the celebrations, she'll be long gone. What's her name?'

Lewis looked even more shamefaced. 'Amynta Malahyde.'

'His wife?' Libby, Jerry and Boysie said together.

Lewis shrugged. 'Dunno. Got a phone number though.'

'Well, ring it!' commanded Libby. 'Honestly, Lewis.'

'Yes, Mum.' Lewis grinned at her. He stood up and went to the other end of the restaurant to make the call. Libby, watching, with relief, saw him begin to speak. It wasn't too late, then.

'Ceremony starts at 10.' Lewis pulled a face. 'It's his sister. Said she wondered why I hadn't been in touch yesterday.'

'Didn't you tell her you'd spoken to her brother and Bernie Lee?'

'Oh yes. She didn't sound too pleased.' Lewis sighed and sat down again. 'I said I'd see her up there.'

'Wasn't she there last night?' persisted Libby. 'She must have been.'

'I don't know!' Lewis frowned at her. 'I didn't go into the whys and wherefores. You can come and ask her if you're so mad to know about it.'

'All right, all right,' said Libby. 'Only curious.' She darted a glance at Jerry and Boysie who were both continuing to eat imperturbably. 'Aren't you?' she said.

They looked up, surprised. 'No,' they said together.

However, when they arrived at the top of the cliff once more, all of the party were as keen to see Amynta Malahyde as Libby was.

She turned out to be a lady of indeterminate age,

hung about with many beads and velvet scarves. Her wispy fair hair wafted gently in the cliff-top breeze and her forehead was creased with worry.

'My brother doesn't speak to people,' she said on being greeted by Lewis. 'Your young woman should have told you that.'

'Only if you told her,' said Libby. Ms Malahyde looked astonished at being addressed and shook her head vaguely.

'I don't know,' she said. 'I only make the arrangements. I thought she knew all about the festival.' She drew herself up and waved a regal hand over the brightly coloured scene. 'Mannan is famous.'

'In this part of Cornwall, maybe,' said Libby, 'but not in London or Kent.'

Ms Malahyde looked even more shocked and Lewis jumped in before Libby could offend her any further.

'We need to know everything about it from you, Mrs – er – ma'am. Would you be prepared to speak on camera?'

Amynta Malahyde preened and gave Libby a triumphant look. Libby subsided and sat down on the grass to listen.

It was as she had thought, reading between the lines. The Malahydes had both been members of some kind of pseudo-religious organisation and had incorporated some of its more esoteric (as Libby had said) ideas into the cult of Mannan, which they had lifted wholesale from the sea god of the Isle of Man. Amynta clammed up when asked about their other rituals, and when Lewis, greatly daring, happened to mention the sacrifices connected with the worship of the sea god, she became positively sibylline. Eventually, Lewis asked about the morning's activities, and they were pointed over to where a gathering was forming on the cliff edge.

'Looks a bit dangerous,' said Jerry.

'There are railings,' said Amynta, in a voice which suggested a soul above railings.

After she left, presumably to go and attend her brother, the little group made their way to the cliff edge, where, as Amynta had promised, there were railings. A moveable section which had obviously been moved last night to allow the passage of the wheel was now firmly in place, and at intervals along the barrier stood burly-looking stewards in yellow jackets.

'I didn't see any of them last night,' whispered Libby to Boysie as they established themselves in a good position.

'Yeah, they were there,' said Boysie. 'Kept outa sight, though. Spoil the moment, wouldn't they? Doesn't matter so much this morning, in the bright light o'day.'

'No,' said Libby, much struck. 'Of course.'

A slight diminution in the hubbub around them signalled the arrival of Florian Malahyde, once again in his arch-wizard costume, followed this time by Amynta, her hand on the arm of Bernie Lee whose black costume looked strangely bland in the sunlight. Boysie tried to edge nearer to catch Malahyde's words, which were flung away on the wind. Jerry was moving slowly with his heavy camera and Lewis was practically jumping up and down with frustration.

Eventually, a group of men, presumably last night's Morris Men in mufti, went forward and began to wind what looked like a sort of winch. The crowd watched in silence as slowly, bit by bit, the charred remains of the wheel rose into view. A cheer rose up, Malahyde spoke a few more words, and somewhere in the background a band, apparently made up of accordions and fiddles, struck up.

'That appears to be that,' said Libby.

Lewis growled. 'I'll have to get a few comments,' he said. 'Can't leave it like that. Did you get it, Jer?'

Jerry nodded. 'Don't know what Boysie'll have got, though. Bloody wind.'

Boysie agreed morosely.

'Well, I'm going to find Gemma to say goodbye and then I suppose we begin to make tracks for home?' said Libby.

'Yeah. I'll have another go at the black goat and old Merlin, and see you back at the pub in a bit.' Lewis made a face and set off through the crowd, followed by Jerry and Boysie.

Gemma was in her camper van.

'Hiya,' said Libby, following her knock inside. 'I just popped by to say goodbye.'

Gemma nodded, but said nothing.

'What's up, Gem?' Libby sat down on the bench beside her. 'You don't look happy.'

Gemma's eyes seemed to refocus on her friend. 'I told you what would happen,' she said, in a voice that sounded as though it was rusty from disuse.

'What do you mean? What happened?'

'This morning. On my step.'

'What?' Libby wanted to shake her.

'A rabbit and a chicken.' Gemma gulped. 'With no heads.'

Chapter Fifteen

'AH.' LIBBY REPRESSED A shudder of revulsion. 'So, sacrifice, you think?'

'I told you.' Gemma was angry now. 'You didn't believe me. And someone thinks I've been talking to you and this was a warning.'

'Why on earth should it be? Why couldn't it be something to do with Dan?'

'He hasn't talked to anybody.'

'And had he gone off with Diggory and the others into the wood last night?'

'No! He was in the beer tent over the other side from where you were. Only Diggory and a couple of others had gone off with those awful goat people.' Gemma put her head in her hands. 'He's gone to show them all the – the –'

'Bodies?' suggested Libby helpfully. Gemma gave her a look of dislike.

'Well, I'm really sorry, Gemma, but perhaps you shouldn't have wanted to talk to me in the first place. You've certainly done a complete about-face.' Libby stood up. 'Say goodbye to Dan for me.'

And that's that, thought Libby, as she went back down the path to the jetty. All very interesting and a bit silly. It looked very much as though, in previous years, a few members of Cranston Morris, Bill Frensham, John Lethbridge and Richard Diggory among them, had hooked up with Goat's Head Morris and probably Florian Malahyde while attending the Mannan Night festivities and disappeared to join in with whatever unsavoury high jinks went on under the unlikely patronage of the sea god. She thought fleetingly of the black mass held at Tyne Chapel a couple of years ago and wondered if it was the same misguided people involved. Anything as an excuse for some seriously skewed sexual shenanigans.

In which case, she said to herself, leaning on the little harbour wall, had it spilled over into real life when they got home, causing Bill Frensham's murder by John Lethbridge?

'No,' she said aloud. It surely wouldn't have taken from last Mannan Night to May Day this year for that sort of ill-feeling to bubble up.

Unless, she thought, resuming her walk towards the Portherriot Arms, something had happened, like a relationship started on Mannan Night which had then continued in secret when they went back to Kent. And then been found out. But that could only mean Bill Frensham's relationship with someone that affected John Lethbridge.

What was it Gemma had said about Lethbridge's wife? Wilhelmina, or Willy, who had been the previous goddess. And who had left John. A lightbulb went on in Libby's head. Willy and Bill Frensham! And John had found out and killed Bill before disappearing himself.

But, she said to herself as she climbed the stairs to her room to fetch her suitcase, Ian would have thought of all this. And he didn't seem to be pursuing that line of enquiry as far as she could see. Sighing, she checked drawers and wardrobe and went downstairs.

Lewis, Jerry and Boysie joined her in the bar after a few minutes.

'Got a few words with that Malahyde person at last,' said Lewis. 'Not that it helped much.'

Libby told them about the headless rabbit and chicken.

'Someone trying to tell her something,' said Lewis. 'Couldn't we talk to her about that?'

'No, we couldn't,' said Libby decisively.

'Put her off the scent,' said Boysie.

'Chicken and rabbit,' said Jerry with a grin, flapping his arms. 'Cluck-cluck.'

'Oh, I didn't think of that,' said Libby. 'You mean "you're a scaredy cat" sort of message instead of a "put you off the scent" message.'

Jerry shrugged. 'Whatever. Doesn't matter, does it?'

'No,' Libby said thoughtfully.

Eventually, half an hour later, the bill settled and the two vehicles loaded up, they began the long journey back to Kent, or, in Jerry's and Boysie's case, back to London. They stopped on the cliff top where they had stopped on the way in and got out for one last look at Portherriot. On the other headland they could see the bright colours and hear the faint music of the fairground, and just make out the blackened wheel re-mounted on its dais. Jerry got out the camera and took a last panning shot, then nodded with satisfaction and climbed back into the driving seat.

'See you,' he said. Boysie raised a hand and they drove off.

'I don't reckon I did a very good job,' said

Lewis.

'Why? You got as much as you could out of people, and Jerry got a lot on camera. As I said, it'll be edited down anyway.'

Lewis shrugged. 'Yeah.' He turned and gave her a grin. 'Did me best, didn't I? come on then, Mum. Time to go home.'

The journey home seemed endless. They stopped at the first service station they came to after joining the M4 and bought an indifferent meat pie, which Lewis insisted on eating in the car as he'd been recognised. Libby wandered round looking at the books, bought a magazine and a bar of chocolate, then they were on their way again.

'So,' said Lewis once they were on the M26, 'did you find anything out about your murder?'

'Eh?' Libby turned to look at him in surprise. 'I thought I was being taken away to stop me looking into it.'

'I told you, that had nothing to do with it. But I thought you'd have a poke about as your mates were down there.'

'Well, apart from Gemma being spooked by all the sacrifice stories and then her headless bodies there wasn't anything to poke into.'

'Bet you thought about it, though. Whatever goes on in those woods. Must have given you ideas.'

'Sort of.' Libby could feel herself blushing. 'I did wonder if the murder was anything to do with Mannan Night.'

'Go on, then, why?'

Libby explained her earlier theories. 'It doesn't quite ring true, though,' she said. 'And anyway, the police will have looked into that aspect of it by now.'

'You reckon this Lethbridge person killed the other one? The Green Man?'

'Well, he did disappear immediately after the murder and no one's seen him since,' said Libby.

'Figures.' Lewis concentrated on filtering onto the M20. 'Did you tell Ben when you were coming back?'

'I haven't spoken to him today,' said Libby guiltily, aware that she had only called Ben once, yesterday, since she'd left. 'But I said it would be today.'

'How's his dad?'

'Much the same,' said Libby. 'I'll give him a ring now.'

Ben was delighted to hear from her, which made her feel even guiltier.

'Would you like to come to the Manor for dinner?' he asked. 'Mum always makes too much.'

'Oh, thanks,' laughed Libby. 'But are you sure she won't mind? I mean, it's a difficult time.'

'It's no different from how it was a week ago, to be honest. I might just as well move back out again, except that she seems to like my company.'

'Is Greg confined to bed?'

'That was my doing, I'm afraid,' said Ben. 'After I insisted she call the doctor the other day. He'd be perfectly all right downstairs in his own chair, I'm sure. It's just the getting up and down stairs that's the problem.'

'At least you've got a downstairs loo if he does come down,' said Libby. 'If you're sure, then, I'll

146

come up after I've had a freshen up.'

'He was pleased, then?' said Lewis, after she'd switched off.

'Seemed to be. His dad's no worse.'

'So he could come back to you?'

'Yes,' said Libby, turning to look out of the side window.

'You don't sound very pleased.'

'Of course I am,' said Libby. She turned back to Lewis. 'Actually, it means I've got to make up my mind about Steeple Farm,' she said, in a burst of honesty, 'and I'm not sure about it.'

'Yeah, I know.' Lewis slipped her a sideways grin. 'Ad does, too. Doesn't matter that we both like it and think you'd love it there, does it? It's what you think matters.'

'Yes, but it seems so churlish not to want to live there. It's the opportunity of a lifetime.'

'Does churlish mean rotten? In that case, yeah, it does, but it's how you feel. You have to have a feel for a house.'

'I know. And when I first went there, when Peter's mother was still living there, I hated it. And even though it's different now, I can't shake off that feeling.' She bit her lip. 'And Fran said she couldn't see me living there, although she's reneged a bit on that since.'

'Stop using long words,' said Lewis. 'You mean she's had second thoughts?'

'Not exactly,' said Libby. 'She just said that she could be wrong, she often is.' She sighed. 'The trouble is, she's nearly always right.'

'So tell Ben you don't want to move there. You

can't live there if you're not going to be happy. Like me with Creekmarsh. I'd never be happy living there permanent, like. So I just pop in and out. Me mum wants to go and spend some time there, though. I'll look for a manager and some staff soon, then we can start turning it into a proper venue.'

Happy to change the subject, Libby said, 'So are you still going to do weddings and conferences?'

'Maybe,' said Lewis, 'but I'd like to do a festival, too. You know, have a proper music festival.'

'You'd have to have camping facilities for that,' said Libby.

'There's plenty of room if you go up the other way from the river. Make an ideal site, it would.'

'I don't think the locals would like it.'

'Oh, come on. It'd only be for a few days and hardly any people around there, anyway.'

'Suppose so. Adam would love it.'

He grinned. 'So would I.'

By the time Libby had showered and changed, it was nearly eight o'clock before she set out for the Manor. Sidney, who had been fed alternately by Adam and Ben, chose to ignore her completely, and scratched the sides of the cane sofa viciously just to let her know who was boss.

Ben met her at the bottom of the drive and enfolded her in a bear hug.

'I've missed you,' he said.

'Missed you too,' said Libby, feeling guiltier than ever.

He tucked his arm through hers and led her slowly towards the house. 'So tell me how it all

148

went.'

She gave him a brief outline of their adventures in Portherriot, and then, as they came level with the theatre, converted from the Manor's oast house, she stopped and turned to face him.

'Look Ben, I've got something to say,' she said, trying to keep the shake out of her voice.

He looked at her with a wry expression on his face. 'Why am I not surprised?' he said.

'No, listen.' She took a deep breath. 'I just can't fancy the idea of living at Steeple Farm. I'm sorry, and I know you've already put a lot into it, but it just doesn't feel right to me.'

He looked at her for a long moment. 'You don't want to live there, or you don't want to live with me?' he said eventually.

'Oh, no! Only the house,' she said, and, with a rush of relief, realised it was true. 'Oh, Ben, I've missed you.' She wound her arms round his neck and pressed her cheek to his. She felt him chuckle.

'You've only been gone a couple of days,' he said into her ear. 'I'll send you away more often if this is the reaction I get.'

'It puts things into perspective,' she said, pulling away and looking into his face. 'I got very muddled about Steeple Farm.'

'I know you did, and that's why I said we would carry on as we are.' He pulled her arm through his and they resumed their stroll towards the house. 'What worried me was that you didn't seem sure about me either.'

'I thought you still wanted us to get married,' said Libby. 'I was terribly worried.'

'Don't be,' said Ben. 'We'll just let Steeple Farm take care of itself. At the end of the renovations, either I or Pete will pay the bill, and if I don't want it, Pete will sell it on the open market. Unless he decides to have it himself.'

'And for now?'

'For now, I'm hoping to be able to move back home.' The blue eyes twinkled at her.

'To me?'

'Yes, to you. Hetty will be quite happy. After all, I'm not far away, am I? And she still says I was over-reacting to call the doctor last Sunday. We've got Dad downstairs for dinner this evening.'

'Wow! You said you thought he could manage it earlier.'

'Yes, so I went straight up and told him. He was delighted. Hetty grumbled a bit.' They'd reached the house and Ben pushed open the door. 'Come on, he'll be pleased to see you.'

Greg looked better than when she had last seen him, thought Libby, but the portable oxygen cylinder beside him looked frighteningly alien.

'Don't mind that,' he said as she bent to kiss him. 'Precautionary measure only. Tell us all about Cornwall.'

Chapter Sixteen

'WHAT DOES ONE WEAR to a hen night?' Libby, clad only in underwear, appeared in the sitting room. Ben grinned.

'From what I've seen on the streets of Canterbury on a Saturday night, not much more than that,' he said.

'Not at Anderson Place,' said Libby. 'Sir Jonathan would have a heart attack.'

'Is that nice girl Melanie still there?' asked Ben.

'Mel? No idea. I liked her.'

'Is that where Jane and Terry are getting married?'

Libby nodded.

'Long way from Nethergate,' said Ben.

'She couldn't find anywhere nearer that would hold enough people or have room to stay overnight,' said Libby. 'Oh, well, if you can't help me with clothes I'll go and continue rummaging.'

'I'll help you out of them, if you like,' said Ben, coming towards her purposefully.

When eventually Libby was successfully clad in black trousers and a floaty black top, Ben was lying back sultan-like on the bed.

'You've certainly been re-invigorated by your trip to Cornwall,' he said. 'As I said, I think you'll have to go away more often.'

'I'll start thinking you want to get rid of me,' grinned Libby, patting his naked stomach. 'Come on, make yourself respectable. Fran and Guy will be here soon.'

'At least this is one outing with Fran that I don't have to worry about,' he said, heaving himself to his feet.

'What do you mean?'

'This time you're not going off ferreting for information.' Ben disappeared into the bathroom and Libby laughed.

Guy deposited Fran and Libby at the foot of the steps up to the front doors of Anderson Place.

'Hasn't changed,' said Libby, looking round at the foyer. 'Where are we meeting Jane?'

'In the bar,' said Fran, pointing. 'Look, there she is.'

Jane was at a table in a corner with three other young women; she introduced them to Libby and Fran, who felt like geriatrics.

'Ben thought there'd be mini-skirts,' Libby said in a whisper.

'Dirty old man,' said Fran. 'Why?'

'He said that's what they wear on hen nights in Canterbury. Not much more than underwear, he said.'

'That's true. You've seen them yourself.'

'Not in the flesh,' said Libby, and giggled.

Jane had bought champagne, and, by the time the final guests had arrived, happily nearer to Libby and Fran in age, everyone was relaxed and beginning to have a good time.

'So, what do you do?' one bright young thing asked Libby.

'Do?' Libby was confused.

'For a living.'

'Oh!' Libby laughed. 'I paint pictures.'

'Cool. Really? Do you sell them?'

'My husband does,' said Fran with a smile. 'In our gallery.'

"Our" gallery, Libby noted.

'And that's what you do?' the girl asked Fran with interest. 'The gallery? Wow. So much more interesting than my job.'

'Do you work with Jane at the paper?' asked Fran.

'I used to, but I was made redundant.' The girl shrugged. 'I work for Frensham Holdings now.'

Libby's champagne went up her nose.

'What do you do?' asked Fran smoothly, ignoring her.

'I work for one of the directors. He's all right, it's just so boring.'

'What does Frensham Holdings do?' asked Libby, recovered.

'Owns lots of smaller companies.' The girl held out her hand to Fran. 'Sorry, I don't think I got your names when I came in. I'm Trisha.'

Fran and Libby introduced themselves.

'What sort of companies does Frensham Holdings own, then?' said Libby.

Trisha looked surprised. 'Well, they're more divisions, I suppose. There's Frensham Marketing, Frensham Supplies and Frensham Media. That's how I got in, because I'd been working for the paper. Mr Phillips is the director in charge of the media division.'

'Ah,' said Libby, nodding.

Jane chose that moment to call her party to order and marshal them into the restaurant, where Libby was unsurprised, but pleased, to be greeted by Melanie, the events manager, who had organised Peter and Harry's civil partnership, and was now, obviously, organising Jane's wedding.

'Did you recommend us?' she asked Libby quietly.

'I think I mentioned you,' said Libby with a grin.

'Well, thanks. Word of mouth is the best recommendation.'

'How's Sir Jonathan?' Fran leant across Libby.

'Very well. Still pottering about upstairs. You can pop up and see him if you like.'

'Maybe after dinner,' said Libby. 'I think we're at Jane's beck and call just now.'

'I'll tell him you're here, anyway,' said Melanie.

'Of course, you'd know Melanie, wouldn't you?' said Jane. 'It was that other murder, wasn't it?'

A sudden silence fell around the table.

'Murder?' squeaked Trisha. 'Oooh!' She leant forward. 'Someone from our firm got murdered, you know.'

'Oh,' said Libby weakly, while various other questions erupted from other guests.

'Sorry,' said Jane, and clapped her hands. 'I shouldn't have said that. And there wasn't a murder here, so don't worry about it.'

Not here *exactly*, thought Libby, and sighed. The guests subsided, trying not to look too obviously at Libby and Fran. Trisha, however, was not to be subdued.

'Did you know about our murder?' she asked,

still leaning forward. 'It was Mr Frensham himself.'

'Yes, I heard,' said Libby.

'Awful, it was,' said Trisha with a certain ghoulish relish. 'He was in some silly costume with the Morris dancers.'

'I know,' said Libby.

'Miss Martin was gutted.' Trisha said with satisfaction and sat back in her seat.

'Miss Martin?' asked Fran.

'Elizabeth Martin. She's the exec director of Frensham Holdings. My Mr Phillips fancies her rotten.'

'Office politics and romances, eh?' said Libby with a laugh, trying to hold these new names in her head for later.

Jane leant across and tapped Trisha's arm. 'Not murder on my hen night, Trish,' she said.

Trisha coloured. 'Sorry,' she said, including them all in a shamefaced smile. 'I'll shut up.'

'What do you think of that?' said Libby sotto voce, as a waitress placed a bowl of soup in front of her.

'Interesting, but I thought we weren't investigating?' said Fran, with a sly grin.

'Again!' said Libby, with an answering grin.

The meal was as excellent as Libby had expected, and after it they retired to the bar, where Jane was presented with various slightly risqué presents, which amused Libby and vaguely shocked Fran.

Melanie appeared and leant over Libby's shoulder. 'If you can be spared, Sir Jonathan would be pleased to see you,' she said.

Libby looked across at Jane. 'How long are you gong to be here?' she asked. 'Only we'd like to pop up and see the owner, if that's OK?'

Jane shrugged and smiled. 'I'm staying overnight,' she said, 'so it's fine by me.'

Libby and Fran followed Melanie up to the room they had been to before, where, beyond the double doors, Sir Jonathan himself stood before the great marble fireplace. Tall and well-built, his hair was completely white, but still plentiful, as were his large moustache and eyebrows.

'Libby and Fran!' he said coming forward and shaking them both by the hand. 'Come and sit down. Would you like coffee?'

They sat together on the same small sofa Libby remembered from their previous visits.

'No thank you, Sir Jonathan,' said Fran. 'We've just had some downstairs.'

'Of course, of course.' He beamed on them and sat down. 'So tell me. What adventures have you been having since we last met?'

Libby laughed. 'Oh, lots!' she said. 'Somebody must have been talking.'

'You can't keep anything quiet in a place like this,' said Sir Jonathan. 'As you know, I like to pop round and have a look at each of the departments and chat to people. And Melanie always tells me if you've made the papers.'

Libby and Fran exchanged glances. 'We've only been mentioned briefly,' said Libby.

'Oh, I know, but there was that business with the body on the island, wasn't there? Didn't that concern the young lady downstairs, your hostess?'

'Yes,' said Fran. 'That's how we met her.'

'And this year, the young man at Creekmarsh Place?' They nodded. 'Well, tell me all about it, then!'

Briefly, they filled Sir Jonathan in on their "adventures" since they had last seen him eighteen months before.

'And nothing going on now?' he said when they'd finished. 'What about old Bill Frensham? You ought to have a look into his death, you know.'

Libby's mouth dropped open.

'Did you know him?' asked Fran.

'Of course! Frensham Holdings have used Anderson Place for meetings and conferences for years.' He narrowed his eyes at them. 'You *are* looking into it, aren't you?'

'Not exactly,' said Libby hastily. 'A friend of mine from the Morris side he belonged to asked me to – well – to speak to the other members, although why, I can't think. We're not investigators.'

'No, but you've been involved, unwillingly, I admit, but definitely involved in several murder investigations. And with Mrs Castle's rather – ah – unusual talents,' he winked at her, 'it's not surprising if people think you *are* investigators.'

'Hmm,' said Libby.

'It's an interesting case,' said Fran, 'but Inspector Connell – do you remember him? – has more or less told us to keep off.'

'Ah, well.' Sir Jonathan shrugged. 'I suppose he would have to say that. But if you came up with anything useful, he'd be pleased, wouldn't he?'

'What do you mean, Sir Jonathan?' Libby

frowned suspiciously.

'I know you haven't got time now, but if you fancied popping along for a coffee one morning, There are one or two things I might be able to tell you.' He grinned like a naughty schoolboy and stood up. 'Now you must get back to your party. You will come and see me, won't you?'

'The old rascal,' said Fran as they made their way back to the bar. 'If he's got anything to say, he should have told the police.'

'If he has, it's probably something the police would dismiss,' said Libby. 'Ian would, anyway.'

Fran looked at her. 'He's not that bad,' she said.

'He scared me to death the other morning at the Mount,' said Libby. 'But I can see that you would find him – um – appealing.'

'Well, don't you go finding him appealing,' warned Fran. 'You're having enough trouble with the relationship you've already got.'

The taxi booked to take them home arrived after another half an hour, and they said goodbye to Jane after settling their part of the bill. As they went out of the bar, Trisha scooted up behind them.

'I say,' she said in a breathless whisper, 'somebody was just saying that you are actually detectives.'

'No,' said Libby and Fran together, 'we're not.'

'But you've done murders? I mean you've sort of – been involved?'

'Yes,' said Libby reluctantly.

'Only I think there's something funny going on at work. I don't know whether it's to do with Mr Frensham, or what. I don't know what to do.'

'If you think there's anything going on that could possibly be to do with Mr Frensham's death you should go to the police,' said Fran.

'Yes, but it doesn't seem like much,' said Trisha, looking uncertain. 'Couldn't I tell you?'

Libby sighed. 'OK. But not now.' She took out her mobile and pressed a few keys. 'There – put your number and name in. I'll ring you.'

'So much for not ferreting things out,' said Libby in the taxi. 'Who would have thought it?'

'Two people offering us information on a crime we're not involved with,' said Fran, amused. 'And somewhere we wouldn't even have dreamed could have any connection.'

'Mad.' Libby shook her head. 'I suppose we'll have to talk to them, now.'

'Don't sound so smug,' said Fran. 'You know you wanted to, all along.'

Libby sighed. 'Like a bloody drug, isn't it? I know I shouldn't, yet I want to. It's like Steeple Farm in reverse.'

'Eh?'

'Well, I know I ought to love Steeple Farm, but I can't.' She turned to her friend and grinned. 'So, which one do we start with, then?'

Chapter Seventeen

AS IT WAS SUNDAY the following day, Libby decided it would not be politic to start making enquiries. Hetty had once more invited everybody to lunch, after which Ben played chess with his father, who was looking considerably better, and Libby and Harry went out into the garden for a cigarette.

'Well, petal?' Harry sat down on a bench. 'How are things now?'

'Much better.' Libby perched on the stone wall that ran round the terrace. 'I've told Ben I don't want to move to Steeple Farm.'

'And?'

'He was fine with it. I wasn't being fair to him, was I?'

'No. And how was Cornwall? It was Cornwall, wasn't it?'

Libby told him all about Cornwall.

'Did you find anything out about your murder?'

'It isn't my murder. Although –' she paused.

'Don't tell me. Fran has had one of her moments and you're hot on the trail.' Harry shook his head at her. 'It'll all end in tears.'

'No, it won't.' Libby hesitated. 'What's happened, you see, is that we've been presented with a couple of leads. No –' she held up a hand as Harry opened his mouth 'We didn't look for them. It happened last night.'

'And they were?'

Libby told him.

'So Cornwall was no use, then.'

'It made my mind up about Ben and Steeple Farm. And although there was all the spooky goings-on in the woods I couldn't see that any of that had anything to do with Bill Frensham's murder.'

'Unless they're part of a cult that gets together down there,' suggested Harry. 'They do that sort of thing in Cornwall, don't they?'

'Well, in a way that's what Mannan Night is all about,' said Libby, 'although it appears to be a once a year sort of cult.'

'How do you know?' asked Harry.

'Cranston Morris only go down there once a year, so they couldn't be part of it.'

'It doesn't have to be your Mannan stuff,' said Harry. 'It could be a cult that has branches everywhere.'

'Like the WI?' Libby laughed. 'I suppose so. I did wonder if there was any connection to the group that used the old chapel for black masses.'

'Why not? Satanists or something. That's what the lot at Tyne Chapel were, wasn't it?'

'I'm not sure we ever found out. I thought they were just in it for the sex.'

'I reckon most of these odd groups are in it for the sex,' said Harry. 'The witchcraft, or devil worship or whatever just adds spice.'

'I don't think they'd agree with you.' Libby stubbed out her cigarette and poked it into a flowerpot. 'I do wonder what the point of frightening poor Gemma with all the sacrifice business was, though.'

'Do you think it was simply to frighten her?'

'Well, she said everyone knew about it, but I wonder who told her that?'

'Her husband? Whats'isname?'

'Dan. He seemed as bewildered as she did. I think there's a sort of splinter group of Cranston Morris, and I think Bill Frensham was in it, and so was – or is – Richard Diggory. He went off into the woods with the Goats Head lot.' She thought a bit. 'And I bet John Lethbridge was in it, too.'

'Who?' said Harry.

'The bloke who disappeared. Who might have murdered Bill.'

'Blimey, it's complicated,' said Harry, shaking his head. 'Come on, let's go back inside. I must sweep my young man off home soon.'

'Will he want to be swept?'

'Yes,' said Harry firmly. 'He needs to unwind in the comfort of his own bathrobe. He went to see Mad Millie this morning and it always upsets him.'

'It's such a shame that seeing your own mother should upset you,' mused Libby. 'I hope I don't do that to my kids.'

'Oh, you already upset them,' said Harry, ducking. 'I practically live with your son, don't forget.'

It wasn't until the following morning that Libby phoned Fran.

'I wondered if I ought to phone Trisha and you ought to go and see Sir Jonathan,' she suggested. 'I think he likes you better than me.'

'Don't be daft,' said Fran. 'You phone Trisha, yes, we can hardly both do it, but we go and see Sir

162

Jonathan together. He said coffee, didn't he? We could go now.'

'Now?'

'I'll come and pick you up on the way. You can phone Trisha while you're waiting.'

'She might not be able to talk at work,' Libby demurred.

'Well, make arrangements for a more convenient time, then. Come on, Lib, you're usually the one who rushes ahead –'

'Like a bull in a china shop,' Libby finished for her. 'Yes, I know.'

Sure enough, not only was Trisha unable to talk while at work, she showed distinct signs of having changed her mind about talking at all.

'It was the champagne, I expect,' she said giggling nervously. 'It's nothing really.'

Frustrated, Libby puffed out a sigh. 'If you change your mind, give me a ring,' she said, and gave Trisha the number.

'Right,' said Trisha. 'Er – I'll maybe, um – ring you some time. Like –' she stopped suddenly. 'Later,' she almost whispered after a moment.

'It was so strange,' Libby said later to Fran, as they bowled along the road to Anderson Place once more. 'First of all she didn't want to talk to me, then she said she'd ring me.'

'Perhaps there was someone in the office,' said Fran.

'Yes, but all she had to do then was say she'd call me back. She was – odd.'

Fran pulled in to the car park. 'Do you think we should have called ahead?' she said. 'He might not

163

be here.'

But as they walked into the impressive foyer of the Place, Sir Jonathan was coming towards them, obviously on his rounds, and professed himself delighted to see them.

'Come up to the flat,' he said. 'More comfortable up there.' He led the way to the gilt lift cage and they ascended slowly to the second floor.

When they were provided with coffee, Libby sat back in her chair and put her head on one side. 'So, Sir Jonathan. What was it you wanted to talk to us about?'

'First of all, are you going to look into his death?'

'You know we can't actually do that. We said so on Saturday night.'

'And you remember what I replied. I only ask because I knew the man and I know his wife. I don't think the police are looking in the right direction.'

'I don't know where the police are looking,' said Libby. 'Frankly, I doubt if they'd tell me, either.'

'Of course they wouldn't,' said Sir Jonathan, 'but I gather the investigation has centred on the Morris connection.'

'Because of where and when he was murdered,' said Fran. 'I still find it amazing that someone could be killed like that in full view of everyone in broad daylight.'

'But the other dancers were milling around all the time. Any one of them could have got close enough to do it,' said Libby. 'That's why the police are concentrating on that side of his life.'

'And the fact that John Lethbridge has

disappeared.'

'And why haven't they found him?' asked Sir Jonathan.

Libby and Fran looked at him. 'Why?'

'Yes. If he killed poor Bill, he's gone into hiding. That's what they think, don't they? But *why* did he kill Bill?'

Libby looked bewildered. 'Why?' she said again.

'Think about it,' said Sir Jonathan, his eyes sparkling under the bushy white eyebrows. 'If John Lethbridge killed Bill, there must have been a reason. If it was to keep himself safe from some threat he wouldn't go into hiding. He might go into hiding to avoid the threat, but he wouldn't kill – do you see?'

Libby was still looking bewildered, but Fran nodded slowly. 'I see. If Bill was killed to keep a secret safe, that must mean that the killer wanted to carry on living as he'd always done.'

Libby's face cleared. 'Oh, I see! That's clever, Sir Jonathan. Why didn't I think of that?'

'Oh, please, drop the Sir.' The old man chuckled. 'I must say, awful though this is, I'm quite enjoying working things out.'

'I can see that,' said Fran, amused. 'What made you want to, though?'

'I told you. I knew Bill, and his wife. Funny little thing, she is. Very quiet.'

'And you'd been doing business with Bill and his company for some time?'

'Oh, yes. Since we first opened. Frensham Marketing did all our publicity, set up the website, everything. Even found us Mel.'

'Really?' said Fran. 'They interviewed her?'

'Not exactly. She was working for another of their clients. I'm afraid we poached her.' He chuckled again. 'Stripy hair and all.'

'Yes, she's changed since I first saw her,' said Libby.

'Did you know John Lethbridge?' asked Fran.

'No. I'd met him when he came here to one of Bill's functions, but that was all. But you see, if he's disappeared and they suspect him, they must have linked him to Bill, and it surely wouldn't just be because of any connection to the Morris men.'

'Something outside, then. Perhaps he was having an affair and Bill found out?' said Libby.

'No, he was divorced, remember? Your friend told us,' said Fran.

'Oh, yes. Willy.'

'But, as Jonathan says, if he killed Bill to stop him telling all, he would have meant to stay around.'

'Oh, yes.' Libby frowned. 'Complicated isn't it? So do we believe Lethbridge's disappearance has nothing to do with Bill's death?'

'That's what I think,' said Sir Jonathan. 'I think someone from outside mingled with the Morris dancers.'

'Outside the Morris side, you mean?' said Libby. 'So it could be anyone? A business associate?'

'It seems logical to me,' said Sir Jonathan.

Fran and Libby looked at one another. 'In a convoluted way, it does to me, too,' said Fran.

'And Trisha!' said Libby excitedly. She turned to Sir Jonathan. 'Trisha works at Bill's company for a man called – what was his name, Fran?'

'Phillips, was it?'

'Yes, Phillips. And she wanted to talk to us because she said she thought there was something funny going on.'

'Really?' Sir Jonathan's eyebrows almost met his hairline. 'I'd never have thought it. Bill was always the most honest and straightforward businessman I knew.'

'Maybe,' said Libby slowly, 'she didn't mean business-wise. Maybe she meant personnel-wise.'

'Ah.' Sir Jonathan nodded. 'That could be it, of course. I think there was a bit of friction with a woman there at one time.'

'Trisha said someone was gutted about Bill's death,' said Libby, 'but I'm not sure in what way.'

'Well, you'll find out if Trisha phones you, won't you?' said Fran, and stood up. 'Thank you for the coffee, Jonathan, and for the ideas. If we find anything else out we'll let you know.'

'Please do,' said Sir Jonathan, looking wistful.

Libby impulsively kissed him on the cheek. 'And if we go off looking for something, you can come too.'

Sir Jonathan brightened immediately. 'Good stuff!' he said. 'I'll see you out.'

Back in the car, Fran turned to Libby with a frown. 'Why did you say that?'

'What, that he could come too? Well, why not. If we go and see someone to ask questions he could be useful.'

'Has it occurred to you that we have no right to ask anybody any questions? We're only looking into this as an intellectual exercise, remember?'

Libby turned to look out of the window. 'Sure,' she said.

'That's all very well,' she told Sidney later, 'but Fran was the one who was interested in the first place. She's just dying to find out more about this, I know she is.' Sidney put his ears back, but didn't move. 'What she needs is a good "moment" that will send her off on the right track, then she can make the excuse that she's actually helping the police. And,' she added gloomily, 'she probably will be.'

A trip to the Cattlegreen Nurseries Farm shop seemed indicated in order to buy vegetables for a stir fry, so Libby collected her basket and set off down the lane. Just as she reached the bottom a car turned in rather fast and shot past her, only to pull up abruptly almost in front of number 17. Libby stood and watched, frowning, as the car door opened and a blonde head poked out.

'Trisha!' Libby started back up the lane again.

Trisha got out of the car and stood looking uncomfortable, her hand on the door handle.

'Hello,' she said. 'Sorry, I didn't see you.'

'No,' said Libby in an admonitory tone. 'I could tell. Did you want me?'

Stupid question, she thought, seeing as she's standing in front of my house.

'Yes. Am I holding you up? Were you going out?'

'Yes, but it's not important.' Libby fished in the basket for her keys and unlocked the door. 'Watch the step – oh, and the cat.'

Sidney, affronted, darted between their legs and off up the lane.

'So, is this your lunch hour?' asked Libby. 'Can I get you anything?'

'No, no that's all right, said Trisha, perching uncomfortably on the edge of the armchair. 'I don't want to disturb you.'

'Tea, then? Or coffee? I'd offer you a glass of wine, but you're driving.'

'Coffee, then, that would be lovely.'

'Right.' Libby went into the kitchen and tested the kettle on the Rayburn. She moved it onto the hotplate and left it to boil.

'Come on then, you've obviously got something to tell me that you didn't want to over the phone.' Libby sat on the sofa. 'How did you know where I lived?'

'Jane told me.' Trisha looked down at her hands twisting together in her lap. 'I thought I ought not to tell you, it seemed disloyal, somehow, but I talked to Jane about it, and she said you were very discreet' (really? thought Libby) 'and you were very good at making sense of things.' Trisha looked up. 'You and Fran, of course.'

'Of course,' said Libby. 'So what it is it?'

'Well – ever since Mr Frensham died Miss Martin and Mr Phillips have been arguing. It's always behind closed doors, and they never do it in front of anybody, but it's been really horrible.' She paused. 'And then, last week ...' her voice tailed off.

'Last week?' prompted Libby.

'I had to go back into the office to collect

something. Everyone had gone home and I got my files and then,' she swallowed, 'I heard someone moving about in Mr Frensham's office.'

'Go on,' said Libby.

'I knew nobody should be in there, because the police had cleared it of everything they thought they might need and sealed it. So I – I went and knocked.'

'And who was it?'

'That's just it! I don't know. First of all there was no more movement, then there was a sort of noise, then nothing. So I opened the door.' Trisha was looking frightened now, and Libby guessed it had taken a good deal of courage to attempt to face up to an intruder.

'And when I opened the door,' she continued, 'the room was empty. And the only other way out was the door into Miss Martin's office. And there was no one in there either.'

'Did you tell anyone?"

Trisha nodded. 'I told Mr Phillips. I called him right then, on his mobile.'

'And what did he say?'

'Nothing. He laughed and said it didn't matter, just lock up and he'd see me on site in the morning. That's why I'd needed the files you see. We had a site meeting.'

'And you're not happy about this?'

'Well, no. If someone's snooping round Mr Frensham's office, when there's nothing much left in there, what do they want, and why is it such a secret? And why are Miss Martin and Mr Phillips fighting?'

Libby shook her head. 'I've no idea, Trisha, but it can't have anything to do with Mr Frensham's death, can it?'

'But the next day when we got back to the office, Mr Phillips went in to see Miss Martin and they had another row. And the door was a little bit open.' Trisha coloured. 'I couldn't help hearing, you see. Miss Martin was speaking. Sort of almost hissing at him.'

'And what was she saying?'

Trisha swallowed again. 'I'll kill you. That's what she said. I'll kill you.'

Chapter Eighteen

'SO WHAT WE HAVE to do,' said Fran later on the phone, 'is talk to this Miss Martin.'

'Elizabeth Martin,' said Libby. 'but how do we do that? We can't just barge into Frensham Holdings and demand to see her.'

'We'll have to find out a way to talk to her outside of work. Find out where she goes, what she does.'

'Oh, come on, Fran, be sensible,' said Libby. 'How on earth do we do that? We know nothing about her, we have no connection to Frensham Holdings and the only person we know willing – just – to talk about her is Trisha.'

'Barry Phillips, then,' suggested Fran. 'How about him?'

'Same applies. Let's face it, we're out on a limb here, despite you wanting to find out all about it. No way in anywhere. At least we've had *some* kind of connection in the past, but this time we've nothing.'

'What about your friend Gemma? She was the one who asked you in the first place.'

'We – ell,' said Libby.

'Look, she's been marginally involved all the way through so far,' said Fran, sounding, to Libby's ears, far too excited. 'She'll be only too willing to help.'

'But she was scared in Cornwall,' said Libby. 'I'm sure she's still of the same mind.'

'Give her a chance,' said Fran. 'Ask her if we

can both come and talk to her.'

Libby sighed. 'All right,' she said, 'but don't blame me if she says no.'

She told Ben about it over stir-fried vegetables, which she had eventually managed to go and buy after Trisha, a twittering mass of qualms and misgivings, had departed.

'It's not like Fran to be keener than you about an investigation,' he said, forking rice into his mouth.

'I told you,' said Libby, 'she's changed since she got married. Much more assertive and – well, aggressive, even.'

'Fran? Aggressive? Never.' He laughed. 'Boredom, is it?'

Libby considered. 'I think it is,' she said. 'Her life's sorted, after years of living on the breadline in a horrible London flat, at odds with her children, suddenly she's got a lovely home and a lovely husband. There's nothing to aim for any more.'

'Except harmony with her children,' said Ben.

'Ooh, yes,' said Libby, 'I forgot to ask how her visit to Chrissie was. She wanted to start building bridges.'

'In order to throw Chrissie off?' asked Ben.

'That's an idea,' said Libby, 'but no. Jeremy's OK, but he's in America. Lucy is a whining pain with her kids, always wanting handouts, and Chrissie at least has a good standard of living and doesn't keep demanding things of Fran.'

'But she moans about Fran's inheritance,' said Ben. 'And they both disapprove of Fran's marriage.'

'I know,' said Libby. 'That's why she was taking Guy over there to try and get them to know him.'

'As far as I could see, Brucie baby only respects money men,' said Ben. 'He almost unbent to me when he found out I was an architect, which in his book is respectable. But artists and actors, no way. I'm surprised he married Chrissie knowing her mum was an actor.'

'She probably didn't tell him,' said Libby, standing up and collecting plates. 'And anyway, that's got nothing to do with Fran being enthusiastic about this Green Man murder. And she wants to go rushing in talking to people who we have no connection with, which of course we can't do.'

'Who does she want to talk to?' asked Ben, following her into the kitchen with the serving bowls.

'Oh, the other directors of Frensham Holdings,' said Libby, dumping plates into the sink. 'You know it was Bill Frensham who got murdered?'

Ben frowned. 'That would be – let me see – Elizabeth Martin and Barry Phillips?'

Libby turned round. 'Do you know them?'

'I've met them.' Ben put the bowls down on the draining board. 'We designed a building for Frensham Holdings a few years ago. It's a pseudo-barn where they mount exhibitions and hold functions.'

'Oh, wait a minute,' said Libby slowly. 'Over towards the Elham valley somewhere? Backs on to woodland?'

'That's it,' said Ben. 'Have you been there?'

'Yes, a couple of times.' Libby picked up a wine bottle. 'Come on, let's leave this for a bit.'

'So what did you go to Frensham Barn for?'

asked Ben pouring wine into their glasses back in the sitting room.

'First time was some kind of business function with Derek, just before we split up,' said Libby, sipping appreciatively. 'Second time – was – what was it? Oh, I remember. A charity do for someone's birthday. I don't know whose. I went with Peter and Harry. Before I moved here.'

'Was the business function to do with them, too?'

'Oh, I expect it was. As far as I remember, we were the guests of a colleague of Derek's and his wife. I don't remember meeting any Frensham Holdings people, though.'

'I don't suppose you would have done,' said Ben. 'But didn't you meet Bill Frensham when you knew Gemma and her husband years ago?'

'Oh, yes, but he was new to Cranston Morris and no one really knew him. It was later that he sort of took over, as far as I can make out from Gemma.'

'So why does Fran want to speak to Martin and Phillips?'

'Because Trisha heard them arguing.'

'Trisha?'

Libby told him about Trisha and her dramatic pronouncement.

'I told her it was just something people said, not to be taken seriously, but she seems to be worried about the atmosphere at the place, and the fact that someone has been searching the office.'

'Well, I expect I could engineer a meeting somehow with Martin and Phillips,' said Ben. Libby choked on her wine.

'You what?'

'Just to satisfy Fran.' He grinned at her. 'And stop you going off the deep end and getting into mischief.'

'How, though?' she asked, after she'd kissed him.

'Let me think about it,' he said. 'Although I'm officially retired, I still own most of the shares in the practice. I'll think of something.'

'I couldn't believe it,' Libby told Fran the next morning on the phone. 'I don't know why he's doing it. He hasn't taken an active interest in a murder investigation since *The Hop Pickers*.'

'It's a ploy,' said Fran, a smile in her voice. 'To get you on side.'

'Oh,' said Libby. 'You could be right. But I'm on side already. He knows that. I came home from Cornwall a reformed character.'

'Ah, but what about Steeple Farm?'

'He's OK with that now. Meanwhile, let's hope he comes up with a foolproof method for meeting Elizabeth Martin and Barry Phillips.'

And, in fact, he did.

'I'm in the office,' he said, calling in the early afternoon.

'The estate office?' Libby frowned.

'No. Wilde and Partners. I had a look and discovered that the directors of Frensham Holdings are still on our Christmas card list, as it were. They have all been guests, in the past, at our infrequent drinks parties.'

'And?' prompted Libby.

'I thought we should maybe have another one.'

'What?' squeaked Libby.

'Well, I never had an official retirement do for the clients, did I? I just sort of slid out unnoticed. I thought perhaps we should rectify that.' He paused. 'And due to our connection with it, I thought we could ask if we could hire Frensham Barn.'

Libby became aware that her mouth was hanging open.

'Blimey,' she said eventually. 'When you go for it, you certainly go for it. How will you ask them?'

'With care,' said Ben, and hung up.

Libby phoned Fran.

'Hmm,' said Fran.

'What do you mean, hmm?'

'It's an awfully big coincidence.'

'What him knowing Martin and Phillips? You didn't say that earlier.'

'I've thought about it since then.' Fran paused. 'And he's known about your interest in this –'

'And yours.'

'All right, and mine, but anyway, he's known about it since we went to the Mount at least. He knew who'd been murdered, didn't he?'

'Ye-es.'

'Why didn't he tell you about this connection straight away?'

Libby's heart felt as though it missed a beat. 'What are you suggesting?'

'I'm not suggesting anything,' said Fran. 'I'm asking a question. He must have known he knew the man. Why didn't he tell you?'

'Because he thought it would fan my interest? He didn't want to get involved?'

'He didn't want *you* to get involved. If he'd told you then you would have wanted to follow it up.'

'So why is he getting involved now?'

'To get you on side, as I said before, but there must be another reason.'

'Well, it can't be anything sinister,' said Libby. 'Ben's just not like that.'

'You suspected him in that first murder, though, didn't you?'

'I didn't know him well then. And let's face it, he's hardly likely to be a suspect in this one, is he?'

'No. But he's got an ulterior motive, I'm sure,' said Fran.

Libby was ready for him when Ben arrived home, looking dapper and sexy (she thought) in an unfamiliar dark suit. She handed him a whisky almost as soon as he set foot through the door.

'What's all this?' he asked with a grin. 'That grateful, are you?'

'Yes,' she said, sitting opposite him on the sofa. 'But far more interested in why you're doing this. It isn't just for me and Fran, is it?'

He looked her steadily in the eye. 'No. I told you, I never had a farewell do for clients.'

'Nah,' she said, sitting back against the cushions and disturbing Sidney. 'That's not it.'

He raised his eyebrows. 'Oh? Who says?'

'Fran.'

'Ah.' He put his whisky down and shrugged off his jacket. 'A famous moment.'

'No. She just thinks about things.'

'And comes up with wrong answers.' Ben picked up his drink and crossed his legs.

Libby was watching him closely. 'No, she hasn't. There is another reason, isn't there?' She waited, but there was no answer. 'How well did you know Bill Frensham?'

Ben sighed and sat back. 'A business acquaintance.'

'And?'

He looked at her for a long moment. 'Look, Lib. I'm going to tell you this because you'll probably find out anyway, but I didn't trust Bill Frensham any further than I could throw him. He did everything he could to wriggle out of payment for the Barn, while keeping a huge friendly smile on his face.'

'So why on earth invite his co-directors to a do?'

'Because there was something funny going on in that business and I'd quite like to find out what.'

Libby gaped. 'But why haven't you told me this before?'

'Because you'd be on the phone to Fran, or trying to tell your bloody Inspector Connell as soon as I did.'

'I thought you liked Ian?' said Libby artlessly.

Ben let out a gusty and somewhat irritated sigh. 'Don't change the subject.' He shifted position and leant forward. 'Look. I knew, whether you admitted it or not, as soon as Gemma Thing got in touch with you you'd be like a dog after a rabbit. Eventually, you'd want to get in touch with Elizabeth Martin and Barry Phillips. And I could just see you breaking into their offices or something and getting into real trouble. Look what happened to you over that business in Nethergate.'

'I wouldn't break into anywhere!' said Libby, shocked. 'I haven't yet, have I?'

'No, but you've been in a couple of tight places, and you know exactly what your nearest and dearest think of that. I'm surprised Guy's so laid back about it.'

'Actually, so am I,' said Libby. 'Especially as Fran's been more interested in this one than the others. Except her old aunt's death, of course.'

'Perhaps he doesn't know,' said Ben.

Libby shook her head. 'No, she tells him everything. Anyway,' she stood up and held her hand out for his glass. 'That's beside the point. What decided you to help?'

'Because I could at least save you from getting into worse trouble.' He handed over his glass. 'Elizabeth Martin is a seriously scary lady, and I don't want you falling foul of her.'

'You don't think..?' Libby stopped in the act of pouring whisky.

'That she killed Bill? No, of course not. That really is far-fetched – although some of the other murders you've been involved in have stretched credulity a bit. No, but I do think the company has been guilty of some – er – creative thinking, and –'

'Oh, I get it!' Libby turned excitedly. 'That's what Trisha heard them quarrelling about. They think because of Bill's death the company will be investigated and it will all come out!'

'Well,' Ben looked startled, 'I hadn't quite got that far, but I did think Martin and Phillips would be extremely unhappy if you started poking your nose in.'

'So why introduce me?'

'Because I might find out what has been going on, and, incidentally, get back the last of the money they screwed me out of, and so that any interest you have in them will be legit.'

Libby screwed up her face. 'Just because I've been introduced formally, I can hardly go up to them and say "Right, now we know each other, did you murder Bill Frensham to keep your dodgy dealings under wraps?'

Ben let out an irritated sigh. 'No, but at least you can talk to them, or engineer a meeting. If you'd never met them, how could you?'

'No, I see that.' She paused. 'I don't suppose you could say I was looking for a job? Give me a glowing reference as a – a – oh, I don't know, a perfect PA?'

Ben spluttered into his whisky.

Chapter Nineteen

'WHAT DO WE KNOW about John Lethbridge, apart from the fact that he was married to Wilhelmina?' asked Fran on the phone the following day.

'He was a financial adviser,' said Libby. 'At least, I think so.' She stopped to think. 'I'm still puzzled about the police not looking for him.'

'I expect they are,' said Fran, with a strange note in her voice that Libby recognised.

'Oh? Come on Fran, out with it. What do you know?'

'I don't *know* anything,' said Fran slowly, 'but I'm pretty sure he's dead.'

Libby let out her breath in a whoosh. 'Just as we thought. They were both murdered.'

'Ye-es, but someone must have set it up to look as if Lethbridge murdered Frensham.'

'Why?'

'Well, he hasn't been seen since Frensham's murder and his car wasn't where it should have been.'

'That's right.' Libby frowned. 'So what are you saying?'

'Lethbridge was killed before Frensham.'

'Are you certain?'

'I keep seeing trees in the dark. And fire. And you know that suffocating feeling I get?'

'I know, but I don't know why you're getting it now. You've no connection to Lethbridge and you haven't touched anything of his, have you?'

'No.' Fran sounded uncertain. 'But I think perhaps it's because I've been concentrating on it so much. Mind you, it could be my mind playing tricks. We don't know for certain.'

'Could we follow it up somehow? Could we ask Ian?'

'Of course not,' snapped Fran. 'Be sensible.'

'Trees at night and fire,' mused Libby. 'How about if I ask Gemma if there's anything in that she recognises?'

'I don't think that's a good idea. Given her reactions when you were down in Cornwall she'll get scared again, and I bet she regrets asking you in in the first place.'

'She does,' said Libby. 'All that sacrifice stuff and the Goat's Head Morris really turned her up.' She stared out of the window to where Sidney was stalking a piece of paper on the tiny green outside the house. 'What about the Tyne Chapel mob? Do you think they know anything about – well, whatever goes on behind the scenes at Cranston Morris?'

'It's a Goddess Cult,' said Fran.

'Eh?'

'Goddess Cult. John Lethbridge's wife was the Goddess before Gemma. It was Frensham and Lethbridge who introduced the more esoteric elements into what had been an ordinary Morris side, wasn't it?'

'And Diggory had something to do with it,' said Libby. 'How do you know, anyway?'

'I don't know,' said Fran, in some surprise. 'But that's it. And you've just given yourself the clue.

183

Diggory. You can ask him.'

'He's creepy.' Libby shuddered.

'No more than the Tyne Chapel mob, who are supposed not to exist now.'

'What about if they all defected to Cranston Morris?'

'That's stretching it a bit,' said Fran. 'You think about it. See if any of what I've seen makes any sense.'

The more Libby thought about it, the less keen she was to make any sort of approach to either Gemma Baverstock or Richard Diggory. In fact, if she were honest, she was beginning to regret getting even marginally involved with the whole Green Man murder. What with Ben organising a party just to introduce her to two of the suspects, who had nothing to do with the Green Man aspect anyway, and now Fran being sure Lethbridge was murdered and wanting her to find out about Goddess Cults – well.

She turned away from the window and went out into the conservatory, where she wasted a considerable amount of time staring alternately at blank and half-finished paintings. This was what she should be doing, painting, to bolster her barely adequate income. Oh, Ben always said he had enough money for both of them, and had been contributing to household expenses since he moved in, but Libby was determined to keep her financial end up, and, besides, she wouldn't ask him for anything personal, like clothes, presents (especially for him!) and cigarettes.

With an effort, she set about her preparations to

work on the half-finished picture she'd started in Jane Maurice's house. Eventually, it took hold of her, and when Sidney butted his head against her leg, she was surprised to find she'd been working for well over two hours. Which made it lunchtime. She stood up and stretched.

There was nothing in the cupboards or the fridge that she fancied, which meant a trip into the high street to buy something. She went upstairs to make herself presentable, collected her basket and set off down Allhallow's Lane.

It was while she was in the new farm shop that she saw Harry gesticulating madly outside the Pink Geranium. She paid for her salad ingredients and crossed the road.

'Wassup?' she said. 'Going in for semaphore?'

'Got someone here who wants to buy you a coffee,' said Harry holding the door open for her.

'Someone who doesn't know me very well, then,' said Libby.

'Libby!' said Richard Diggory, standing up from the table in the window and holding out his hand. Libby's heart sank.

'Hello, Richard,' she said. 'How are you? Recovered from Cornwall?'

Looking disconcerted, Diggory sat down again.

'We were just sorting out orders when we saw you trotting about like the good little housewife you are and decided to bring a little light into your life,' said Harry. 'Coffee? Or a glass of wine?'

'It's lunchtime, isn't it?' Libby looked round at the few other patrons. 'Wine, I think.' She gave Diggory a cool little smile and sat down on the opposite side of the table, pushing order pads and Harry's laptop out of the way.

'We were only talking about you this morning,' she said, bending the truth a little.

'Oh? Who's we?' Diggory was looking now as though he regretted inviting Libby in the first place. If he had, of course. It was probably Harry.

'My friend Fran and I. Remember her? You met her at the Mount.'

'Oh, yes. At the Solstice Parade.'

'That's it. She was wondering, actually,' said Libby, making it up as she went along, 'about some of the other Morris traditions. Or Celtic, or whatever they are. I mean, the whole Mannan Night thing – that isn't traditional, is it? It's been made up.'

Diggory looked horrified. 'Made up? What on earth do you mean? Of course it isn't.'

'Oh, come on, Richard,' said Libby. 'It's a complete fabrication made up by that creepy Malahyde bloke and his sister.'

'Based on true folk history.'

'But incorporating all sorts of other stuff that doesn't belong. I mean,' went on Libby, getting into her stride and completely forgetting that she was fed up with the whole thing, 'all that sacrifice stuff and going off into the woods. What was *that* all about?'

Diggory's face was now a fetching pink. 'It's part of the ceremony that's private,' he said at last.

'I bet.' Libby sat back and stared at him. He fidgeted. 'Connected to the Goddess Cult.'

His colour fled from his face, and almost as quickly returned. 'Wha -?' he said.

Harry returned at this moment with a glass of red

wine and a fresh cafetière. Diggory looked as though he would like to get up and leave, but served with fresh coffee and with uncompleted orders from a good customer all over the table, he was stuck.

Libby turned to Harry and compounded Diggory's discomfort.

'I was just asking Richard about the Goddess Cult,' she said. Diggory's hand shook as he tried to pour coffee and covered his paperwork in brown splashes.

'Goddess Cult?' Harry narrowed his eyes at her.

'It's a fertility thing,' said Libby blithely. 'Celtic in origin, isn't it, Richard?'

'Um, yes.' Diggory cleared his throat.

'Not part of the ordinary Morris dance tradition, is it?'

'Er – no.'

'So what is it?'

'The earth mother,' said Diggory, 'you know, that sort of thing.'

'You use some of the traditions of the solstices, don't you? Corn dollies, and the Oak and Holly Kings. The Goddess comes into those.'

Diggory relaxed a little. 'Oh, yes. Morris celebrates all the old seasons and rites, you see.'

'Like May Day?'

'Yes. Beltane, and the need-fire.'

'Need-fire?' Libby sat up straight. 'Gemma told me about that.'

'We light it the night before May Day.' Diggory cleared his throat again. 'It's – er – a cleansing ritual.'

'Oh?' Libby looked interested. 'Where do you do

that? On the Mount again?'

'Near the Mount, yes.'

'Do you dance? Are you dressed up?'

'Well, yes, but it's a private ceremony.' Diggory frowned. 'Sorry, why exactly are you interested?'

'Well, I told you. All that business down in Cornwall, going off into the woods – was that the same as the need-fire business?'

Diggory's colour was fluctuating again. 'Similar,' he said.

'But the Goddess Cult is a part of it? But not one that all the members of Cranston Morris are aware of?'

'What are you implying?' Diggory finally summoned up righteous indignation. 'That there's something underhand about our rituals?'

'No, of course not,' said Libby, smiling at him. 'Not underhand.'

Harry poked her in the ribs. 'Cut it out, Lib,' he said. 'You're making my supplier uncomfortable.'

'Sorry.' Libby was penitent. 'But he did ask me to have coffee with him.'

To Diggory's obvious confusion, she then proceeded to be charming to him, while Harry looked suspiciously on.

'I must be getting on,' she said at last, finishing her glass of wine. 'I only popped out for some stuff for lunch.'

Harry stood up to make way for her to ease round the table. She leant forward to Diggory.

'Very interested in the Goddess Cult,' she murmured. 'I'll ask Gemma.'

Diggory looked alarmed. 'Don't do that,' he said.

'I'd be pleased to – er – tell you all about it.'

'Good.' Libby beamed and straightened up. 'I'll look forward to it.' She edged past Harry, bestowing on him the ghost of a wink. He followed her outside.

'OK, what was that all about?' he said, hands on hips. 'Your idea of interrogation and harassment?'

'Sort of.' Libby grinned. 'His own fault. He shouldn't have asked me to join you.'

'So it's Sarjeant and Castle – sorry, Wolfe – on the case again, is it?'

'Could be,' said Libby. 'Even Ben's got involved in this one.'

'Omigod,' groaned Harry. 'Where will it all end?'

'In tears, I expect, as you said,' said Libby cheerfully. 'Thanks for the wine.'

'It'll go on Diggory's bill, believe me,' said Harry darkly.

Libby made her salad when she got home, sat with it at the table in the sitting room window and phoned Fran.

'Fire,' she said. 'Need-fire. The night before May Day.'

'Eh?' said Fran. 'Oh, I see, Fire, trees. Where did you get this from?'

Libby told her in between mouthfuls. 'And I asked about the Goddess cult,' she said. 'He was gobsmacked.'

'So it is that.' Fran paused. 'I'll look it all up.'

'So will I,' said Libby, 'and Diggory is going to tell me all about the Goddess Cult. Once he'd got over his shock, I indicated that I'd be quite interested. He didn't want me to talk to Gemma, though.'

'Libby! Don't go there!'

'Oh, I shan't meet him, or anything like that,' said Libby. 'I didn't even give him my number, but it's an avenue to explore, isn't it?'

'All I hope is that he won't go and tell any of the rest of the clan and you don't come to a sticky end.'

'Oh, I shouldn't think so,' said Libby. 'After all, we think Frensham and Lethbridge were the prime movers in the underground Cranston Morris, don't we?'

'Do we? Well, in that case it's even worse. They're both dead.'

Chapter Twenty

LATER IN THE AFTERNOON Fran's car drew up behind Libby's Romeo the Renault outside number 17 Allhallow's Lane.

'I've got the kettle on,' said Libby, opening the door, 'and I've made a few notes on the Goddess.'

'Me, too,' said Fran, 'but it's all a bit confused, isn't it?'

Libby pulled out chairs on either side of the table in the window, where the computer sat winking its little eye at them. She tapped the keyboard and the screen sprang into life.

'There,' she said. 'That's the most inclusive explanation, but you can go off into all sorts of highways and byways.'

'I know.' Fran nodded and sat down. 'Gaia seems to be the oldest figure, but the Goddess movement itself is modern.'

'There's very little to indicate naughty goings-on,' said Libby. 'I'll go and make the tea.'

Fran had opened her notebook and found a site on the internet which mentioned the Portherriot Mannan Night when Libby brought in two mugs of tea.

'Did you bother to look any of this up when you got back?'

'No.' Libby looked surprised. 'I should have done, shouldn't I?'

'I thought you wanted to look up those Goat people,' said Fran.

'I did. What does it say there?'

'Very little. Just a description of what goes on, its roots with the ancient sea-god Manannán mac Lir and that's about it. There's an email address and a phone number, but that's about all.'

'Well, they didn't seem over-keen on media interest,' said Libby. 'The Malahyde person and his sister seemed positively discouraging. I don't know how Lewis's researcher managed to get permission to film.'

'Well, there's no mention of the Goddess cult there, and as far as I can see it isn't really known as the Goddess cult.'

'No, but there are mentions of her and a horned god, representing the two sort of high gods. And that she is connected with the old Earth mother.' Libby peered at Fran's notes.

'And the Maiden, Mother, Crone image which came from Robert Graves, so is very modern.' Fran sat back frowning. 'But there are indications of her being the symbol of rebirth and fertility, so if there are little pockets of Goddess worship, they could well have worked it into a nice little rite of fertility.'

'Like bonking each other in the name of the Goddess.'

'Something like that,' said Fran, amused. 'After all, that's what that mob at Tyne Chapel were doing, weren't they, all in the name of the devil.'

'It seems to me that most weird cults are set up specifically to indulge in orgies,' said Libby. 'And it looks like this is what's happening here, or are we getting ahead of ourselves?'

'You said on the phone that Richard Diggory

was a bit –'

'Discombobulated,' said Libby. 'That's what makes it suspicious.'

'But he said he'd tell you all about it.'

'Yes, but only because I made it sound as though I might be up for whatever it was.'

'You be careful,' warned Fran. 'This is exactly what Ben doesn't want you to do. That's why he's gone to all the trouble of setting up this party for you to meet the Frensham Holdings people.'

'All right, all right. If he rings me, and I doubt if he will, I'll prevaricate. But I want to know if that's what all the goings-on are about which Bill Frensham introduced to Cranston Morris. This sub-culture, which was what was going on in the woods in Cornwall, I'm sure of it. And they put about the sacrifice rumour to stop people interfering.'

'But surely that would make people interfere? If they thought sacrifice was going on, wouldn't they report it to the police?'

'Not if they were threatened,' said Libby. 'Gemma was terrified.'

'She could have reported the animals on her doorstep before she left for home. The Goat people wouldn't have come after her.'

'She didn't know that.' Libby shook her head. 'I tell you, she'd been threatened – or warned – before they even went to Cornwall. Which is daft. Why did the underground Cranston Morris bother to take Dan and Gemma and the other normal ones with them? Why not just go off on a jiggy-jiggy jolly without them?'

'To keep the authenticity of the side going?'

suggested Fran.

'Anyway, what we really want to know is whether it has anything to do with the Green Man murder.' Libby pulled the keyboard towards her. 'Beltane night and need-fire, that's what we need.'

'I've done that,' said Fran. 'It's an old cleansing ritual. They used to drive their cattle through it, and all lights in the village or settlement had to be extinguished or it wouldn't work. Then the villagers took home little bits of the fire to rekindle their own. And it was led by two chaste young men.'

'Have trouble finding any of them these days,' said Libby, 'but yes, Gemma told me all about it.'

'It's a practice that has survived with some of the other old Celtic traditions, just for effect,' said Fran. 'I think they all jump through it, or something. Anyway, it was that night that John Lethbridge was killed.'

Silence fell. Libby stared at her friend, her mug half-way to her mouth.

'OK,' she said after a minute. 'When did you come up with that?'

Fran looked surprised. 'I told you. Fire and trees – he was killed in trees in the dark. It was Beltane night.'

'But how do you know it was Beltane night? You didn't at first.'

'Well, I do now,' said Fran. 'And I'm going to tell Ian.'

'I think you should,' said Libby, 'and right now, or he'll think you've been holding out on him.'

Fran sighed, nodded and swallowed the last of her tea. 'Can I use your landline?'

'Be my guest.' Libby waved a hand. 'Give him my love.' Fran scowled.

As it happened, Ian Connell wasn't at his desk and whoever was on the other end of the phone wasn't keen on giving him any messages unless he, the desk sergeant, was put in full possession of the details. Fran declined, and finally got a grudging agreement that her name would be mentioned if Inspector Connell happened to be passing.

'Try his mobile,' said Libby. 'We've both still got the number.'

'But only for an emergency,' said Fran. 'I don't like to.'

'This *is* an emergency,' said Libby. 'I'll do it.'

Fran sighed. 'No. If he sees your number come up he'll get annoyed and probably won't answer.'

'Hmmph,' said Libby.

However, Ian's mobile went straight to voicemail, and, unwilling to say too much, Fran asked him to ring her.

'He will,' said Libby, 'because he'll guess the only reason you'd call would be with information, concrete or not.'

'I expect so,' said Fran, turning her attention to the computer again. 'Let's look up Goat people now.'

But the only page on Goat's Head Morris contained just a list of where they were performing and a contact telephone number.

'Secretive, these Cornish, aren't they' said Libby. 'I did wonder if they really are Morris men, or if they themselves are another sort of cult.'

'Oh, let's not get into that,' said Fran. 'Whoever

killed Frensham was nothing to do with them. He might have linked up with them to perform weird and wonderful rites in Portherriot, but I think that's where their involvement ends.'

'I think I ought to go and see Gemma again,' said Libby 'despite what I said. I want to know who threatened her and when.'

'I doubt if it's got anything to do with the case, I've just said. Leave it.'

'I want to know why she's still worried,' persisted Libby. 'If she is.'

'Why don't you leave it until we hear back from Ian,' said Fran.

'What do you expect him to do?'

Fran's brow wrinkled. 'I'm not sure. Search the area where they held their Beltane night celebrations?'

'If it was near to the Mount, wouldn't they have searched already? Once they realised he'd disappeared?'

'No idea,' said Fran. 'I wish I knew more about police investigations.'

Libby went to make more tea while Fran amused herself searching for unlikely combinations of cults on the computer until her phone rang.

'Ian, hello,' she said.

Libby brought the two mugs back in and sat down at the table, watching her friend's face.

'No,' said Fran, 'it was just that I had a – well, I thought John Lethbridge might have been killed the night before the murder.'

Libby saw her face change.

'What?' she said, almost in a whisper. 'How?

196

What happened?'

She listened for a long time, while Libby fidgeted on her chair and tried to contain her impatience. Eventually, she said goodbye and switched off the phone.

'Well?' said Libby.

'They've found John Lethbridge's body,' said Fran.

'Bloody hell,' said Libby.

'In the woods near the Mount. There's a path that leads through them on the edge of a sort of escarpment. Very thick woods. He was found at the bottom of this sort of cliff.'

'How did he die?'

'Ian wouldn't say. He just wanted to know why I'd thought it had happened on Beltane night. He wants to talk to me.'

'But you don't know anything else.'

'I know. I think he wants to try and drum something else up, like he has before.'

'Guy won't like that.'

'I can make sure he's there with me.'

'What about me?' said Libby indignantly. 'Why can't I be there, too?'

'After Ian's warning to you? I don't think he'd like that.'

'Well, as long as you tell me everything afterwards.' Libby was grumpy.

'When don't I?' said Fran. She stood up. 'I'd better get home. I think he wants to speak to me tonight.'

'I've just made more tea,' protested Libby.

Fran sat down again. 'Sorry. But I'd better be

quick.'

'So, now we know Lethbridge was murdered,' said Libby. 'Does it change things? We've suspected it all along.'

'So have the police I think,' said Fran, sipping tea.

'How did they find the body? Without hearing from you first?'

'Just a plain old search, I think. They'd tried to find him alive, you know, credit card transactions, sightings, all ports and airports covered, but no trace, so they had to search for a body. Someone had seen him earlier that day – the day before May Day – and he was all right but a bit jumpy.'

'Did Ian tell you that?' Libby said in surprise.

'Yes.' Fran looked equally surprised. 'Oh, I suppose I'm going to be cast as an expert witness again. He shouldn't really tell me anything.'

'No.' Libby looked thoughtful. 'I tell you what, that body had been there for nearly two months. I bet it was in a state.'

'Oh, yuck, Lib. Don't even think about it.'

'Good job you didn't see that in your mind's eye, wasn't it?' Libby grinned wickedly. 'Put you off your cornflakes, that would.'

Fran put down her mug. 'Right,' she said, 'that's it. I'm going. I'll let you know what Ian says.'

'Oh, by the way,' said Libby as she stood on the doorstep. 'Is this common knowledge yet? Have they released it to the press?'

'Why?'

'Can I tell Ben?'

'He's told me, so it can't be classified. I expect they'll release it on the news this evening.' Fran got into her car. 'Talk to you later.'

Libby went back inside, brow furrowed in concentration. Now the situation was a lot clearer and seemed to remove several suspects. She sat down at the table and drank the remainder of her cooling tea. She remembered her feelings of this morning, when she had almost decided to give up amateur detection.

'What,' she said out loud to Sidney, who had appeared and was winding himself round her legs, 'do I actually have to do with this case? Only Gemma wanting me talk to her silly Morris side. Because I've been foolish enough to get myself involved in murders before. But why did she want me to *talk* to them? She's never really explained that.' She stood up. 'I'm just a sucker for a mystery, I suppose, and because of that, other people get me involved.' She took the mugs to the kitchen and stood looking through the conservatory to the garden.

'I can't help it,' she sighed, as Sidney jumped up to the work surface and began nosing at the bread bin. 'Satiable curiosity, like the elephant's child. An intellectual exercise.' She frowned as she decanted cat food onto Sidney's chipped Victorian saucer. 'Except that it's real people, not characters in a television drama.'

She put the saucer on the floor and reflected on the real people. The proposed meeting with Martin and Phillips now didn't seem relevant, if, as seemed certain, Lethbridge's and Frensham's murders were linked. But now there was a new suspect. The Goddess herself. Wilhelmina Lethbridge.

Chapter Twenty-one

TRUE TO HIS WORD, Ben had begun preparations for his "leaving" party. His gift to Libby was to send her as a special envoy to Frensham Barn.

'What do I have to do?' she asked, when he told her that evening.

'See which rooms are available, facilities like cloakrooms, and what catering arrangements they have.'

'Couldn't Harry do the catering?'

'Not everyone's a vegetarian, Lib. Unless Harry soils his fingers with a bit of meat I think that's out of the question.'

'Yes.' Libby sighed. 'Pity. And who do I meet?'

'Barry Phillips. He's in charge of marketing, which is where Frensham Barn fits into the organisation.' Ben frowned. 'I've always quite liked Barry. I don't like to think of him mixed up in any of Bill Frensham's dirty work.'

'Are you sure there was dirty work?'

'Pretty sure. Apart from trying to chisel money out of us, dodgy deals with the suppliers and a lot of cash deals which I'll guarantee didn't go through the books.'

'Doesn't sound too awful,' said Libby.

'I suppose not, but definitely illegal.' He smiled. 'And immoral.'

'But old Sir Jonathan said Bill Frensham was one of the most upright and straight businessmen he'd ever met. And they used to hold functions at

Anderson Place. Why do that when they had the barn?'

'More prestigious,' said Ben, 'and let's face it, Frensham wouldn't let Sir Jonathan get wind of anything underhand, would he?'

'Another thing,' said Libby, chewing her lip, 'won't they think it's odd you booking the place when you'd had a run-in with them?'

'The girl I spoke to didn't comment,' said Ben.

'I wonder if that was Trisha.'

'Barry Phillips PA, she said she was.'

'That's Trisha,' said Libby. 'I hope she isn't there when I go. She'd never be able to pretend she'd never met me.'

'Why should she?'

'Well, she spilt a certain amount of beans, didn't she?'

'Nothing much, from what you've told me. Now, stop worrying. The appointment's set for tomorrow morning at eleven, so let's get an early night so you can catch up on your beauty sleep.' He leered at her.

'Satyr,' she said, making for the stairs.

Libby was nervous as she drove across country towards Frensham Barn. She didn't know quite what Ben expected her to get from this meeting, and as John Lethbridge's body had now been found, she couldn't see any link between Frensham Holdings and Bill Frensham's murder. She wondered privately if Ben was doing this in some way to get back at the company, but in that case, why hire them?

'Or,' she said to herself, as she turned into a tarmac drive signposted "Frensham Barn", 'perhaps he doesn't actually intend to hold the party after all. Perhaps he'll leave them in the lurch.' She scowled at the building in front of her. Surely Ben wouldn't be that devious.

The barn looked like every other converted barn Libby had ever seen. Most of its front was glass, and as far as she could see there was nothing special about it. She wondered if that was one of Ben's problems. Perhaps they had watered down his design and then tried not to pay for it?

There were three cars parked in marked parking bays to one side of the forecourt. Libby parked next to a large silver Mercedes and got out. There was silence except for distant summery country sounds. She walked slowly towards the open door, taking a deep breath and summoning her courage.

'Mrs Sarjeant?' A shortish, well-built man appeared in the doorway.

'Yes,' said Libby.

He held out a well-manicured hand. 'I'm Barry Phillips, very nice to meet you.'

'Er – yes,' said Libby shaking the hand.

'So Ben Wilde has forgiven us, has he?' Barry Phillips made this sound jocular, but there was a sharp look in his small blue eyes.

'I'm not sure I know what you mean,' said Libby.

'You know he designed this building?'

'Hurrum – yes,' said Libby.

'I believe there was some trouble over the bill. We had to modify the design.' Barry Phillips was watching her carefully.

Just as I thought, Libby told herself. Out loud,

she said, 'I rather gathered that when I saw the building.' Coolly.

'Ah.' Phillips round face broke into a grin. 'Well, it was nothing to do with me,' he said, 'even though I am a director and the barn comes under my control. I preferred Ben's original design. Still,' he took her elbow and led her through the lobby and into a large conference room, 'I'm glad that he's decided we're on speaking terms again. I liked Ben.'

And I like you, thought Libby, smiling back at him. I'm glad you're not a suspect.

'I think Ben's argument was with Bill Frensham personally, rather than with Frensham Holdings,' she said artlessly, 'and of course, now he's dead ...'

'Ah, yes.' Phillips looked solemn, but Libby thought she detected a certain relief in his expression. You didn't like Frensham either, she thought.

'Terrible business, that,' he said. 'They haven't caught the man who did it yet?'

'Not as far as I know,' said Libby, slightly surprised. 'No leads at all.'

'But the man who disappeared ... they haven't found him yet.' He shook his head. 'Shocking. It's been two months now.'

'Oh,' said Libby, 'they've found *him*.'

'They have?' Phillips turned, his eyes widening in shock. 'My God! Why has no one told us? Have they told Monica?'

'Monica?' Libby frowned.

'Monica – Bill's wife. They must have told her. How do *you* know?'

Sidestepping this question, Libby said with a

certain amount of internal glee, 'But why should they tell her?'

'What?' Phillips looked at her as though she was mad. 'Surely they tell the murder victim's wife when the murderer's caught?'

'Oh, I *see*!' Libby feigned sudden understanding. 'Oh, no, they haven't caught the murderer. They just found John Lethbridge's body. He was the man that disappeared. And it turns out he'd been dead longer than Mr Frensham.'

Luckily, Barry Phillips didn't ask her again how she knew, but simply looked as though his world had fallen apart. That's interesting, thought Libby. That's made him think the murderer must be someone else. And he's worried about *who*.

'Anyway,' said Libby brightly, 'I'm not here to talk about Mr Frensham. I mustn't waste your time. You know the reason for Ben holding this reception?'

Barry Phillips pulled himself together with an effort. 'Ah, yes.' He cleared his throat. 'According to my secretary,' Trisha wouldn't like that, thought Libby, 'he's holding a sort of retirement party. Is that right?'

'Yes. He didn't hold one when he retired from active service, as it were, so he thought he ought to make it official.'

'He hasn't actually left the company, has he? Sold his interest?'

'Oh, no.' Libby shook her head. 'But he no longer practises. He manages his father's estate.'

'Oh?' Libby could see Phillips's ears prick up. 'Where's that?'

Time to depress pretension. 'Steeple Martin,' she said. 'So, can you tell me what facilities you have and what catering arrangements you usually make? Parking and so on?'

Barry Phillips switched on his professional manner and led her through the barn's multiple, if bland, facilities. Libby decided she would much prefer Anderson Place, but smiled and nodded throughout.

'Now, would you like a cup of coffee?' he asked at the end of the tour. 'Real stuff in the office.' He smiled at her and she reminded herself that she liked him.

'Thank you, that would be nice,' she said and followed him into a spacious office to the left of the main lobby.

'Who lives in here normally?' she asked as she seated herself by the desk.

'Whoever's here from head office. It's not in constant use, so there's no reason to have someone here all the time.'

'Oh. Whose are the cars outside then? There were three there when I parked.'

'Gardeners.' Phillips placed a cafetière between them on the desk. 'They come in twice a week or more if we have a function. They have their own building hidden away in the grounds.' He frowned suddenly.

'Where they keep their tools I suppose?' said Libby. 'That would have to be alarmed as well as this place, wouldn't it? Expensive equipment, I would have thought.'

'Yes.' Phillips lifted his gaze from the cafetière.

'Funny, you know, I wondered if it was something to do with that when Bill was murdered.'

'Really?' Libby's heart thumped. 'Why?'

'We had a break-in down there a while ago. Bill looked into it, but wouldn't call the police.' He sighed. 'I couldn't understand why.'

'Was much taken?'

'No, that was the point. Bill made a report for the estates department, and then – well, it was brushed under the carpet. Or that's what it seemed like to me.' He was frowning again.

'Should you be telling me this?' asked Libby.

'Oh, sorry.' He looked up and smiled again. 'I suppose I shouldn't. I expect it was because you told me about that other bloke being found that Bill's murder was in my mind.'

Libby fought a battle with her sensible side and won. 'Actually, I knew Bill myself, slightly,' she said, crossing her fingers. 'I'm still friendly with some of the members of Cranston Morris.'

'Really.' He looked wary. 'Strange bunch, I always thought.'

'Oh, I agree. In fact I was down in Cornwall last week filming them, and some of the things they get up to are really weird.'

'Filming?'

'Oh, a friend of mine was doing a small feature about them on a television programme.'

Barry Phillips looked as though he'd like to have asked, but didn't.

'Lewis Osbourne-Walker,' said Libby, putting him out of his misery. 'He does a programme –'

'Yes, I know what he does. And he owns

Creekmarsh.' He put his head on one side. 'And I know who you are, now, too.'

Libby's heart sank.

'You're the one who found that body –'

'No, I *didn't*,' Libby interrupted. 'Why does everyone think I did?'

'But aren't you the one who's been mixed up with all those murders? Is that why you're interested in Bill?'

'Well,' Libby hesitated, 'it's actually because my friend is a psychic. She's helped the police on a couple of occasions, and I've helped her.'

'So *is* it why you're interested?'

'Why do you think I am?'

'Because you brought his name up very early on, and you seem to know something that the general public don't know. Even members of his own company, who would be expected to be told.' Phillips sat back in his chair. 'And now I've given you fuel for your fire by telling you about the gardeners' shed.'

'Have you?' Libby tried to look innocent. He laughed.

'Oh, it's all right, Mrs Sarjeant,' he said. 'I don't mind at all. I wish the police would get to the bottom of Bill's murder so we could all stop tip-toeing round one another with suspicious faces.'

'Is that what you're doing? Who's all?'

He shrugged. 'Elizabeth Martin and me, for a start. And Monica, of course.'

'His wife? Why? Is she a director of the business?'

'She has an interest financially – or rather she

had a small one which is now a much bigger one. She doesn't take much of an *actual* interest in the business, never has, as far as I can see.' He sat back and looked up at the ceiling. 'But there's been no motive discovered, you see.' He looked back at Libby. 'And everyone suspects each other.'

'How do you know Monica does?'

'Oh, she was here after he died, hysterical. Accusing Elizabeth and I of killing him to gain control of the business.' He shook his head. 'We got her calmed down, and her children took her home, but she's popped up two or three times since then, snooping around.' He sighed again. 'And we can hardly stop her, can we?'

'I suppose not,' said Libby. 'But surely you and Miss Martin don't suspect each other?'

'It's Mrs Martin, actually, and no, of course I don't suspect her.' Libby's was interested to note a slight heightening of Barry Phillips's colour as he said this. Does he fancy her? she wondered.

'Well,' she said, 'it's all very interesting, and thank you for telling me all about it, but –'

'You didn't tell me if you *are* looking into Bill's death,' he said.

'Not really, although my friend has been helping the police a bit.' Libby crossed her fingers again. 'But I was going to say, I shouldn't worry too much. Now John Lethbridge's body has been found, it looks as thought the murder was more connected to his private life than his business life.'

The door of the office crashed open. A tall, striking redhead stood there and Libby thought she could almost see flames coming from her nostrils.

'And exactly what is going on here?' she said.
Elizabeth Martin had arrived.

Chapter Twenty-two

'LIZ!' BARRY PHILLIPS STOOD up in a rush. Elizabeth Martin's eyes swivelled to him under lowered brows.

'Elizabeth,' he corrected himself. 'This is Mrs Sarjeant –'

'I know.' The fierce eyes turned back to Libby, who was sitting fascinated and rooted to her chair. 'I want to know what she's doing here.'

Libby opened her mouth but Barry Phillips beat her to it.

'To check out the facilities for Ben Wilde's retirement party,' he said, going round the desk and attempting to take Elizabeth Martin's arm. She shook him off.

'So I'm told,' she said. 'And I want to know why. Bill would never have allowed it.'

'Of course he would.' Barry Phillips was flustered. 'Whatever had happened –'

'No. Ben Wilde tried to get money from us after giving us a sub-standard design. He was – is, I should say – a chiselling fraud.'

Libby opened her mouth again, but once more Phillips beat her to it.

'Elizabeth!' His voice had taken a completely different tone, and Elizabeth Martin turned to him in surprise. 'That was totally uncalled for and extremely rude. Apart from the fact that Ben Wilde's design was far superior to that which we've got now, he is anything but a fraud. And I would remind you that Frensham Barn is under my jurisdiction, not yours, and if I wish to let it to anyone, I will.' He sat down again, looking thunderous.

Elizabeth Martin stood rigid except for her eyes which flicked between Libby and Phillips.

'How dare you!' she whispered finally. 'This is to get back at me, isn't it?' She leant across the desk, her face inches from Phillips's. 'Because he's dead and you still can't have me.' She straightened, cast a scathing glance at Libby and stalked out of the room, slamming the door behind her.

Libby didn't know where to look. She could hear Phillips breathing heavily and kept her eyes fixed on her coffee cup, wondering how soon she could decently get up and make her escape.

'Sorry about that,' said Phillips eventually. She looked up at him and shook her head with a slight smile.

'She – er – she was very – um – *fond* of Bill. She's not exactly – well, she's not –'

'Got over him?' suggested Libby.

He nodded.

'Were they having an affair?' Libby winced at her own bluntness.

'Yes.' He sighed. 'Sorry, this is a most unprofessional meeting.'

'On both sides,' said Libby. 'Don't worry. But her attitude was fairly self-explanatory. I don't think anyone's ever called Ben a chiselling fraud before.'

'No, and of course he couldn't ever be.' Phillips sighed again. 'She's just overwrought and –' he stopped, colouring faintly again.

Libby was dying to ask him if he was in love with Elizabeth Martin, but even she wasn't tactless enough to do so. He stood up and turned away from her, jingling something in his pocket.

'Well, I'd better go.' She stood up, too, and put her coffee cup down. 'I'll get back to you if I think of anything else.'

Phillips turned back to her, frowning. 'Yes, of course,' he said. 'And if you hear anything else about Bill's murder – do you think you could possibly let me know?'

Libby's eyebrows shot up. 'Well, of course, as long as I'm allowed to.'

'Allowed to?'

'By the police,' said Libby, colouring in her turn. 'We – that is, my friend and I – are supposed to keep everything in confidence. In fact, perhaps I shouldn't have told you about John Lethbridge's body.'

Phillips's expression lightened. 'But you did – and just before Elizabeth came in you said it looked as though the murder wasn't connected to his business life.'

'But to his private life.' Libby looked him in the eye. 'And Mrs Martin certainly looks as though she was his private life.'

Phillips's shoulders slumped and he sat down again. 'But not any more,' he said.

'Well, obviously. He's dead.'

'No, no, that's not what I meant. He'd broken off the relationship months ago.'

'Oh, I see.' Libby sat down. 'And she was mad?'

'You saw her.'

'I certainly did. Powerful lady.'

Phillips smiled slightly. 'She's not always so – so –'

'Awful?' suggested Libby. 'No, I'm sure she isn't. But a tartar in business.' She leant her elbows on the desk. 'How does she get on with Monica?'

'Monica?' he looked up, startled.

'Hated her?'

Looking uncomfortable, Phillips nodded.

'Well, that's about all for now,' said Libby and stood up again. 'I'll be off.'

'You sound like Columbo.' Phillips attempted a smile and got to his feet. 'I wish I could say it had been a pleasure, Mrs Sarjeant.'

'Call me Libby. Everyone does,' said Libby blithely. 'And if I hear anything else about Bill I'll let you know. Unless it's prejudicial, of course,' she added solemnly.

Barry Phillips walked to her car with her and held the door open.

'Don't think too badly of Elizabeth,' he said.

'I'll reserve judgement,' said Libby with a smile, 'but tell me. Why does she want –' she stopped.

'Want what?' He frowned.

'Why does she seem to hate you too?' Libby hurriedly revised.

'I don't think she does really.' He held out his hand. 'Goodbye, Libby.'

Thank goodness I stopped myself in time, Libby said to herself as she drove down the drive. Fancy asking the poor man why his beloved wants to kill him!

She turned all she'd learnt over in her mind on

214

her way home, desperate to talk to Fran about it. In the end, she stopped in a lay-by and pulled out her mobile.

'Would you be free if I came over now?' she asked.

'Yes, I'm sure I could put aside my pressing engagements. What's up?'

'I've got so much to tell you. Could we go to Mavis for coffee?'

'It's lunchtime. We could go to the pub.'

'I don't feel like the pub. It's nice and sunny. We could sit under Mavis's gazebo.'

Twenty minutes later they were sitting under the gazebo outside Mavis's Blue Anchor cafe, looking out over Nethergate Bay, the two trippers' boats, the *Sparkler* and the *Dolphin* bobbing gently below the hard, while their owners, Bert and George sat at another table with their large mugs of strong brown tea. Libby summarised her meeting at Frensham Barn, including everything Ben had told her.

'So, what do you think?' she finished, nodding thanks to Mavis, who put down two mugs and an aluminium ashtray.

Fran didn't say anything for a minute, staring out at Dragon Island in the middle of the bay.

'Well,' she said at last, 'it looks as if Martin and Frensham were having an affair, Phillips is in love with Martin but she doesn't want him and Monica is snooping round the business.'

'Yes, I know all that,' said Libby. 'But what else? What about the gardeners' shed?'

'What about the gardeners' shed?' said Fran. 'I can't see that has anything to do with anything.'

'I thought perhaps Frensham was using it as a – a – oh, I don't know. A hidey-hole.'

Fran laughed. 'A hidey-hole? He was a grown man, Lib, not a seven-year-old.'

'Well, you know, perhaps for aspects of their Goddess Cult thing. Or papers he didn't want found relating to the business. Or even to meet Elizabeth Martin.'

'I doubt if he'd risk that with the gardeners in and out about their lawful business.'

'Perhaps we should tell Ian, anyway.'

'Oh, I intend to,' said Fran. 'He wants to see if I can come up with anything else about Lethbridge's murder, so I'll tell him everything we've learnt from Cornwall onwards.'

'Will you?' Libby was doubtful. 'Will he listen? And will he do anything about it? He'll probably laugh and tell you to tell me off again.'

'He wants to take me to the spot where they found Lethbridge's body. I think you could probably come too, as it'll be fairly informal.'

'Could I?' Libby brightened. 'Great!'

'Don't sound so ghoulish,' said Fran. 'I can tell you it's not much fun going to a murder scene.'

'No, of course not,' said Libby, 'but at least Ian's taking us – I mean you – seriously.'

'He always does as long as we're not interfering.'

'But we usually are interfering,' said Libby.

'Anyway, I'll ask him. He wants to take me this afternoon. Will you be free?'

'I'm free!' said Libby.

They sat in the sun outside the Blue Anchor for

another hour, eating Mavis's meat pies and drinking more tea. Libby phoned Ben to tell him she was spending the afternoon in Nethergate with Fran.

'And I met Barry Phillips *and* Elizabeth Martin at Frensham Barn,' she said.

'Martin as well? What did you think?'

'You were right. She is scary. Bad mouthed you, for a start.'

Ben chuckled. 'I thought she might. I didn't tell you she actually made a play for me when it looked as if I was going to take them to court over the contract.'

'No! What did you do?' Libby's stomach curled a little with jealousy.

'Oh, took her to bed and cast her aside like a broken toy,' said Ben. 'What did you think I did?'

'Um, nothing?'

'Almost. I let her know what I thought of a woman who, not only had an affair with her married colleague, but then tried it on with someone else.'

'Apparently Frensham cast her aside himself a few months ago,' said Libby. 'I wonder who for?'

'Maybe nobody, Lib. Don't go looking for things that aren't there. Enjoy your afternoon with Fran.'

'What you two up to these days, then?' Bert waggled his pipe at the two women as they got up to leave the café.

'Nothing much, Bert,' said Libby. 'How about you?'

'We ain't never doin' nothing,' said George, 'but you two – I reckon you'll be stirring up mud again, eh?'

'Who, us?' Libby widened her eyes at him.

'Never!'

'Holiday-makers already,' said Fran, looking over the sea wall on to the sands.

'Mainly families with pre-school children,' said Libby, watching a sandcastle being demolished by a determined toddler.

'And senior citizens.' Fran nodded towards a group of ladies in deckchairs, sensibly dressed in wide-strapped sandals and crimplene.

'I didn't know they still made crimplene,' said Libby. 'Perhaps it's the modern equivalent.'

'But the same old designs,' said Fran as she put the key in the lock of Coastguard Cottage. 'I wonder who sells them?'

'Back of the newspapers, I should think, along with the trusses and incontinence knickers.'

'Don't mock,' said Fran. 'You'll need them all eventually. And you'll be searching the small ads for Indian dresses because you can't get them any more and you're still stuck in the seventies.'

'I am not stuck in the seventies!' Libby was horrified. Fran grinned.

'What time did Ian say he would come for you?' Libby was leaning on the windowsill looking at her favourite view.

'He said he'd ring as soon as he could, so I'll ask him then if you can come too.'

'Hadn't you better check your messages then? Or would he have called your mobile?'

'He might have,' said Fran, 'if I'd taken it with me.' She picked it up from the table by the fireplace. 'I'm always doing that.' She pressed a button. 'Yes – there we are, one missed call.'

She crossed to the landline and sure enough, there was Ian's voice saying he would pick her up at two, and that he would call her mobile.

'Oh, well, that's that,' she said, looking at her watch. 'He'll be here in a minute. We'll have to hope that he's in a good mood.'

Chapter Twenty-three

LUCKILY, WHEN HE ARRIVED Ian was at least not in a bad mood. 'I suppose so,' he said resignedly, when Fran asked tentatively if Libby could come with them. 'This isn't a strictly official trip.'

Libby fed the parking meter she'd found for Romeo, and climbed into the back of Ian's car. 'Nice,' she said, patting the leather seats. 'Must be fun to be a detective inspector.'

'I could call it other things,' said Ian, swinging the car round in front of The Sloop, under the watchful eyes of George and Bert, still sitting outside the Blue Anchor.

They drove out of Nethergate towards Steeple Mount, but, to Libby's surprise, turned off the main road at the sign for Tyne Hall, now on a proper signpost. Last time she had seen it the name had been on a very dilapidated wooden one. Ian turned into the little lane Libby remembered, past cottages, a wide stream and a small stone footbridge. Libby looked in vain for the crested grebe she'd seen before.

'We're on foot from here,' said Ian, parking by the bridge.

'This is the valley where Tyne Chapel is,' said Libby, climbing out of the back seat.

Ian nodded, locking the car. 'But we don't have to go near it. Just through the woods on this side of the valley.'

They set off across the footbridge and along the

footpath Libby had taken before, emerging at the top of the valley. Opposite them stood Tyne Chapel, looking no different from the last time Libby had seen it. Fran, of course, had seen it in the dark when it had been the scene of a murder.

'That's where I first met you,' she said to Ian. He nodded and turned to his right. 'Along here,' he said and plunged into woodland.

At first, the trees were fairly sparsely planted, but further along the path they became more dense. On their left the ground dropped away sharply to the foot of the valley, still thickly wooded.

'They came this way on Beltane Night,' said Ian over his shoulder. 'It comes out near the foot of the Mount.'

'Oh, yes, I remember seeing them coming that way at the Solstice,' said Libby. 'I didn't realise this was the other end.'

'Why do they come this way?' asked Fran. 'Where do they come from?'

'They were fairly reticent on that subject.'

'This is a murder enquiry,' said Fran, shocked. 'They have to tell you.'

'I didn't say they didn't.' Ian looked over his shoulder, amused. 'Just that they were reticent. They used to start from the chapel.'

'Oh, no,' Libby panted, struggling with the slightly uneven ground and the pace of the other two. 'Not that bloody chapel again.'

'They can't get inside now, and there's a security fence round the perimeter now. Didn't you see it back there?'

'No. I didn't look very closely. It gives me the

creeps.'

Ian stopped, and they realised they were facing police tape.

'You didn't tape the path off from the beginning?' said Fran, looking round.

Ian shook his head and got down on his haunches. 'No one comes this way except the Morris men. Unfortunately, as Libby said, they came this way at the Solstice, so any remaining signs would have been messed up, if they hadn't already after nearly two months.'

'So would the body,' said Fran, and Libby felt sick.

'What about the cottages back over the bridge?' she asked, to take her mind off it. 'Did you ask them anything?'

'Of course.' Ian got to his feet, still amused. 'They used to be part of the Tyne Hall estate, but they're all privately owned now. No one saw anything except the Morris Men going over the bridge on Beltane Night. They're used to it.'

'Do they leave their cars there?' asked Fran. 'Do they come back this way to pick them up?'

'No they leave them in Steeple Mount and walk here.'

'What puzzles me,' said Fran, as she stared down the hillside to where they could just see a tent at the bottom, 'is why he wasn't missed.'

'It's dark, don't forget, and they're blacked up. I don't suppose they did a head count.'

'But the following morning. They all thought he was there.' She turned to Ian. 'They were all convinced he was there. Why was that?'

'We haven't got that far yet,' said Ian, looking faintly disconcerted.

'I know,' said Libby. The other two looked at her in surprise.

'It stands to reason, doesn't it? They dance in the May Day parade. There had to be the right number of dancers. They'd have noticed if they were one short. Which means that whoever killed John Lethbridge took his place that morning. And, presumably, the night before.'

Fran nodded slowly and Ian was scowling. 'Bloody hell,' he said.

'I can't believe you didn't think of that,' said Libby gleefully.

Ian shook his head at her. 'One day,' he said.

'You'll have to get me in the force? Isn't that what they always say?'

'Heaven forbid,' he said. 'What do you think, Fran? Is she right?'

'I should think so,' said Fran. 'I'm not getting anything up here, though. Could we go down?'

'Must we?' said Libby.

'You can stay here,' said Ian. 'Don't want you clumping over everything anyway.'

'Gee thanks,' said Libby indignantly. 'And after I've solved your case for you.'

He grinned at her. 'I expect us simple plods would have got round to it eventually,' he said. 'Come on Fran.'

Libby watched as he and Fran picked their way slowly through the undergrowth. She could see a flattened sort of path that she guessed, with a shudder, might have been the route John

Lethbridge's body had taken to the bottom. Fran stopped just short of the tent, frowning at the ground. Libby saw her look up at Ian after a moment and say something, but she couldn't hear what it was. Then Fran turned and began to make her way back up the bank.

'What happened?' said Libby. 'What did you say?'

'Not sure,' said Fran, slightly out of breath. 'It was odd. Just something about a woman. I couldn't tell anything else. Because of a woman? I think that must have been it.'

'Nothing about the murderer?' Ian came up beside them.

Fran shook her head. 'Just something about a woman.'

Fran and Libby looked at each other. 'Elizabeth Martin?' they said together.

Ian sighed. 'OK,' he said. 'What have you been up to now?'

After ascertaining that Fran could get nothing more from the scene, they started back the way they had come, while Libby told Ian all they knew, including her morning's visit to Frensham Barn.

'I assume you were going to tell me all this sometime?' said Ian.

'We were,' said Fran. 'In fact we were discussing it earlier. But you must know all about Frensham Holdings already.'

'We do. And even we could see that Martin and Frensham had been having an affair and that Phillips wanted to step into his shoes.'

'Oh.' Libby was downcast. 'And what about

Martin telling Phillips she could kill him?'

'Your Trisha could be exaggerating,' said Ian, as they came out on the hillside opposite the chapel. 'People do say that in the heat of the moment. Perhaps he'd been trying it on.'

'And what about someone snooping in the offices at night?'

'Monica Frensham. She's now the major shareholder in the business, but she's always been kept in the dark, and she wants to know.'

'Oh.' Libby almost bumped into Fran as they crossed the little stone bridge. 'Oi! What did you stop like that for?'

Fran lifted her head. 'There's something here,' she said. 'A disturbance. Suffocating.'

'Like the feeling when Aunt Eleanor was murdered?' Libby went round until she stood in front of her. 'Did someone die here?'

Fran shook her head. 'I don't know. It's just very unpleasant.'

Ian was examining the stone parapet and then getting down on his haunches to look at the ground.

'I know!' said Libby again.

'What?' Ian and Fran looked even more surprised.

'I bet this is where the impostor joined the group.' Libby almost bounced in excitement. 'See, if they all came over this bridge, they'd all be sort of squashed together, and it would be easy for someone to slip in at the back if they were waiting hidden at the side of the bridge. Just wait until Lethbridge came along and bingo.'

Ian nodded slowly. 'But not that easy. You could

be right, though.' He looked round. 'Where would he hide?'

'Over there.' Libby pointed. On the side of the bridge where it joined the little village street, trees came right up to the edge. 'If he walked here before the Morris side did, he could wait in there until they arrived and pick his moment.'

Ian crossed the bridge and began examining the ground the other side.

'There won't be anything there now,' murmured Fran.

'Are you getting anything else?' asked Libby quietly.

'No. Just nastiness. Let's go.'

They followed Ian across the bridge and went straight back to his car.

'Pity,' said Fran. 'It's such a pretty spot.'

'It is.' Libby turned to look at the row of cottages with their bright, traditional front gardens. Even the crested grebe had reappeared on the stream. 'I wonder if he's the one I saw two years ago,' she said, going over to the bank to watch.

'Its grandson, I should think,' said Fran.

Ian rejoined them and opened doors. 'Anything else, Fran?' he asked as he climbed into his own seat.

'Nothing. Just there's definitely something about a woman.'

'The motive, you think?'

'That would make sense,' said Libby, leaning forward from the back seat. 'If it was someone's wife Lethbridge was playing with – here! Could it have been Monica Frensham? Perhaps Bill killed him?'

'Then who killed Bill?'

'Ah.' Libby sat back.

'Someone who's wife both Bill and John had been playing around with?' said Fran.

'That could link it to the Goddess Cult,' said Libby, and realised she hadn't filled Ian in fully on her exploits in Cornwall. She gave him the potted version and finished up with Wilhelmina Lethbridge. 'So it could be her, except the same thing applies as it does to Monica Frensham.' She sighed gustily. 'I can see why Bill or John might kill each other, but not why someone would kill them both.'

'Excuse me for interrupting,' said Ian, swinging out on to the main road, 'but have you forgotten the obvious?'

'What?'

'That Frensham was killed because he saw who killed Lethbridge.'

Fran and Libby looked at each other.

'Aren't our policemen wonderful?' said Libby.

Chapter Twenty-four

NOT HAVING HAD TIME to shop or cook, Libby took Ben to the Pink Geranium that evening, and over lentil soup and mushroom lasagne told him about the day's events.

'So you're officially on the case now, are you?' he said, twirling his wine glass between his fingers.

'Not officially, no, but Fran's being asked to help again, and I did give Ian some ideas.' Libby smiled triumphantly. 'I am of some use sometimes.'

'I can see that.' Ben gave a wry grin. 'I suppose I shall have to put up with it.'

'Don't say that.' Libby put her hand over his. 'I won't have another thing to do with it if you don't want me to.'

'I was the one who made the excuse for you to investigate Frensham Holdings, remember?' He patted her hand. 'Don't worry about it. I shall rest easier now I know Ian's aware of your snooping.'

'I was wondering,' said Libby, forking up the last of her lasagne, 'if you really wanted to have this party after all. If it was just an excuse. Elizabeth Martin was so vicious I wouldn't put it past her to come and mess it up on purpose. I'm sure they both actually wondered why on earth you'd chosen the barn.'

'I suppose it was a bit childish, wasn't it?' Ben stared out at the darkening high street. 'Hoping I could scare them into admitting dodgy dealing.'

'Was that what you wanted to do?'

Ben refocused on her. 'In a way. I'd like to know what was going on in that company. I told you.'

'I know you did, but I couldn't see how holding a party there would help that.'

'I suppose I wanted to sneer at what they'd done to my lovely design.'

'In public? That's not like you.'

'No.' Ben sighed. 'Oh, well. They won't be surprised if I pull out after this morning, will they?'

'Not in the least,' said Libby. 'But I told you Barry Phillips wanted me to tell him if they found out anything more about Frensham's death. He was convinced Lethbridge had killed him and disappeared.'

'That was what everyone was supposed to think, wasn't it?'

'Yes, and he really did. When he realised it wasn't true he was scared shitless. I think he must have thought Elizabeth Martin had done it.'

'Well, I wouldn't put it past her,' said Ben. 'I told you she was scary.'

'But why would she? Phillips said they broke up months ago and Frensham wouldn't have her back. I can imagine her going for him when they broke up, or during a row, but not planning something like this. Anyway, why would she kill Lethbridge?'

'Is Ian sure they were killed by the same person?'

'Surely it's got to be,' said Libby, reasonably. 'Someone dressed up in Lethbridge's Morris clothes on May morning.'

'Are you sure they're Lethbridge's clothes?'

'No, they're not, actually, because he was still

wearing his when he was found, but the murderer was wearing Cranston Morris clothes – had to be, or he'd be noticed in the crowd on Beltane Night. Then he put the same ones on in the morning and danced all through the parade before killing Frensham and disappearing.'

'I still don't understand how he could just disappear like that.'

'Everyone would have been milling about, and they weren't the only black face Morris there. He just wandered off into the crowd.'

Ben nodded.

'And they reckon it's Monica Frensham who's been snooping around the offices?' he said, after a while.

'So Ian thinks. She's the major shareholder now and according to him she's always been kept in the dark so she wants to find out.'

'That surprises me,' said Ben. 'She's such a quiet mouse of a woman. I didn't think she took any interest in the business. She would be quite happy to let Martin and Phillips run everything, I would have thought.'

'But if she knew Martin and her husband had been having an affair? Perhaps she wants to find something against Martin to get rid of her.'

'You can't just get rid of a director,' said Ben, 'and she's a shareholder too, don't forget.'

'Perhaps Monica thinks there were fraudulent dealings, like you. Then she could get rid of her, couldn't she?'

'And land the business in trouble,' said Ben. 'And much as I would like to see them get their come-uppance, a lot of people are employed by Frensham Holdings, either directly or indirectly. It wouldn't be fair on them.'

'So you'd let them get away with it?'

'I don't think I ever thought I'd go to the authorities. Just make life a bit uncomfortable for them.'

'You said you like Phillips.'

'He was the best of them, and I don't think he was involved in whatever it was.'

Adam emerged from the kitchen, flushed of face and with his hair on end.

''Lo, Ma, Ben.' He bent to kiss his mother.

'Hello, darling.' Libby beamed at him. 'Working hard?'

'Harry's a slave-driver,' said Adam, pulling out a chair and sitting down. 'Much worse than Mog.'

'Mog is far too mild to be a slave-driver,' said Libby, referring to Adam's garden designer boss. 'And what about Lewis? Is he still around?'

'Down tomorrow. We're filming another segment for the programme.'

'So you've got to be bright-eyed and bushy-tailed for the cameras in the morning, then?'

Adam preened. 'I always am,' he said.

Harry joined them and swung a chair out, swinging a leg astride. 'Case conference?'

'How did you guess?' said Ben.

'Libby's got her Sherlock face on.' Harry helped himself to a glass of their wine. 'Want some, Ad?'

'Can I get myself a beer?'

'Yeah, go on, drink the profits.'

Adam grinned and went to the counter.

'Deadly Morris men then, is it?' said Harry. 'Arrested Diggory yet?'

'Not yet,' said Libby, 'but give me time.'

'He's a good baker. Don't know what else he deals in, but the bread's good.'

'What do you mean, deals in?' Ben asked, frowning.

Harry shrugged. 'Just an expression. He always seems to be on the verge of giving me a nudge and a wink and offering me dirty postcards.'

'He is a bit like that, isn't he?' said Libby. 'I think he's in with this business of the Goddess Cult. Well, I know he's in with it. An excuse for a bit of hanky-panky.'

'You don't think he's into anything else?' Ben was looking worried. 'Drugs, or something?'

'Or something? Can't think what else it would be, unless it was under-the-counter gingerbread men.'

'So you *do* think he's dealing?'

'Come on, Ben, how would I know?' Harry turned to where Adam was pouring a beer and chatting to Donna. ''Nother red for your mother, sunshine,' he called and turned back to Ben. 'No, I wouldn't know. There's definitely something a bit lairy about him, but apart from sounding me out about kinky goings-on when we first got the business he's always been straight with me.'

'Kinky goings-on?' Libby giggled. 'Sounds a bit dated, whatever it is.'

'Bona!' said Harry, and gave her a grin. 'One has to put on the polari occasionally, dear heart. Punters expect it sometimes. But no. He was just hinting at sordid little parties as far as I could make out. I made it very clear that I was a serious young man with a reputation to uphold and he left me alone after that.'

'So does he do all his baking himself?' asked Libby, making room for Adam as he returned to the table.

'Some of it. Does the decorative stuff, and to be fair he's a great confectioner and pâtissier, but he leaves his staff to do most of the everyday stuff. He comes and takes orders and keeps on the right side of the customers. Takes orders for Frensham Supplies, too.'

He looked round the table, surprised at the effect his words had produced. 'What?' he said. 'What did I say?'

'It was Bill Frensham who was murdered,' said Libby.

'Yeah, even I know that,' said Harry, uncorking the wine with an enormous corkscrew. 'What's that got to do with the price of fish?'

'It's a coincidence,' said Libby.

'And the great detective doesn't like coincidences,' said Ben.

'Do you get stuff from Frensham Supplies, too?' asked Libby.

'Not into office equipment, dearie.' Harry poured wine.

'Office equipment?'

'You could have worked that one out, Lib,' said Ben. 'Can't see Frensham Holdings going into catering, can you?'

'No, I suppose not. What are they? Marketing,

Supplies and – what was the other one?'

'Media. Small-scale promotional films and radio commercials.'

'Why doesn't that come under Marketing? Surely it's all the same thing?'

Ben shrugged 'Ask your friend Barry Phillips. He's Marketing, alarming Elizabeth is Media. Bill was Supplies.'

'Bill was MD, too, wasn't he?'

'Chief exec, dear, these days. Martin is executive director. Although what they are now is anyone's guess.'

'Excuse me, dears, but we're still here, you know,' said Harry.

'You brought the subject up,' said Libby. 'Asking about Diggory.'

'He can't be a crook with a name like that,' said Adam.

'Out of the mouths,' said Harry, giving him a pat. 'Bless.'

'What sort of office equipment?' asked Libby, going back to the conversation before last.

'No idea,' said Ben. 'The usual, I suppose. Printers, scanners, cartridges, stationery. We never used them, and they certainly didn't push themselves.'

'Sir Jonathan,' said Libby. 'I bet he did. I'll ring him tomorrow.'

'Why are you so interested all of a sudden?' said Ben.

'She's probably unearthed a drugs distribution ring,' said Harry. 'Leave her alone with her fantasies.'

'I'm just trying to find a motive for Bill Frensham's murder,' said Libby. 'We can't find one yet.'

'But I thought you'd got two murders now. There must be a joint murderer,' said Ben.

'Ian thinks Bill saw who killed Lethbridge so he had to be killed.'

'In that case,' said Harry, 'assuming Lethbridge is this person who vanished like the mist in May, it would be the motive for *his* murder that mattered, wouldn't it? So you're looking in the wrong direction.'

Adam, Ben and Libby stared at him.

'Bugger,' said Libby.

Chapter Twenty-five

'LISTEN,' SAID LIBBY ON the phone to Fran. 'It's John Lethbridge we should be looking at.'

'Yes,' said Fran. 'So?'

'Well, we've been looking at Bill Frensham.'

'You have. Ever since we came back yesterday I've been thinking about the motive for Lethbridge's murder, if what Ian said was right.'

'Oh,' Libby said, deflated. 'Harry pointed it out last night. I hadn't thought of it.'

'Wilhelmina would be a good place to start,' said Fran. 'How do we get to her?'

'She has kept cropping up, hasn't she? I could ask Gemma.'

'What about that Diggory person?'

'He cropped up again last night, too,' said Libby, and repeated the conversation.

'You could always get on to him about the Goddess business,' suggested Fran.

'Yeah, right,' said Libby.

But the next person she spoke to on the phone came as a total surprise.

'Is that Mrs Wilde?' The female voice was soft and hesitant, timorous almost, thought Libby.

'Not exactly,' she said. 'I'm Ben's partner, Libby Sarjeant. Can I help you?'

'I don't really know,' said the voice. 'Did you go and see Mr Phillips at Frensham Barn yesterday?'

'Ye-es,' said Libby.

'Oh, I'm sorry, I should have introduced myself.'

236

The voice gave a nervous laugh. 'I'm Monica Frensham.'

Libby's eyebrows flew up. 'Mrs Frensham?' she repeated.

'Er – yes.' Monica Frensham cleared her throat. 'I hope you don't mind my phoning you, only I understand you've been asking some questions.'

Libby's stomach rolled in acute embarrassment. 'I'm sorry –' she began.

'No, no, please,' interrupted Monica. 'I don't mind at all. In fact, I was wondering – could we meet?'

Meet? Libby's brain started flying in all directions. 'Of course, if you feel –'

'Yes, please. And your friend? Mrs – Wolfe, is it?'

'No,' said Libby. 'I mean, yes.' She stopped for a moment. 'May I ask how you know – um – about us?'

'Oh, yes, of course. Barry Phillips called me yesterday. And Gemma Baverstock has called once or twice to see how I am – was.'

'I see,' said Libby slowly. 'Well, of course we'd love to see you, if you think we can help in any way. Where and when do you suggest?'

'Oh, I don't mind. Shall I come to you? Or would you like to come to me? Or somewhere else?' Monica's voice sounded stronger now.

'Why don't Fran and I come to you?' suggested Libby, deciding it would be a good plan to have a look at Bill Frensham's home ground.

'Certainly. Whenever you want.'

'I'll get in touch with Fran – Mrs Wolfe – and

call you back. And thank you for calling.'

'Well!' said Libby to Sidney as she dialled 1471 to obtain the Frensham number. 'That takes the biscuit. Would you believe it?'

She punched the button for Fran's number and prowled round the sitting room waiting for it to be answered.

'Hello,' said Fran's surprised voice. 'Did you forget something?'

'Not exactly,' said Libby, and explained.

'Well I'll be –' said Fran.

'So was I,' said Libby. 'So we want to go, don't we?'

'I'll say we do,' said Fran. 'Any time she says.'

'Today?'

'Whenever she wants,' said Fran.

'This afternoon?' suggested Monica when Libby called back.

'Yes, if you're sure that would be convenient,' said Libby. 'About three?'

The Frensham house turned out to be in a hamlet deep into hop-farming country. Fran picked Libby up on the way, and after negotiating some very narrow lanes between very high hedges, they came out on a ridge looking down into a shallow valley, where a cluster of houses huddled round a church. Hop gardens lay to one side, while rolling green fields lay to the other, a wood topping the rise on the other side of the valley.

'I wonder if this valley continues to Steeple Mount,' said Libby, as Fran set the car to drive slowly down the steep lane to the hamlet.

'It's called Steeple Cross,' said Fran, 'so it's sure

to be connected. I bet we could have got here easier than coming via Steeple Martin.'

'All right, all right,' said Libby. 'Here, look. That's the house.'

The road flattened out just as two redbrick gateposts topped with white pineapples appeared on their right. A curving gravelled drive led to a pristine neo-Georgian house, flanked on all sides by manicured lawns, regimental cypresses and depressed shrubs. Libby and Fran looked at each other.

'I'm glad we didn't bring Romeo,' muttered Libby, as they got out of Fran's little Roller Skate. 'He's not half smart enough for this place.'

Monica Frensham opened the panelled front door before they could get near it.

'Hello,' she said breathlessly. 'I'm so glad you could come.' She stood back to allow them entry, then with a quick, bird-like nod, showed them into a huge room on their left.

Windows looked out over the drive, and at the other end, french doors led into what appeared to be an enormous conservatory. A faux fireplace sat against the side wall, with a spiky and formal arrangement of twigs and silk flowers on its hearth and a group of photographs on the mantel. Monica gestured to a corner sofa arrangement in pale green and took a large leather rocking chair herself, her thin body and mouse-brown hair overwhelmed by its opulence.

'I'm so pleased you're here,' she said again. 'I can't tell you how frustrated I've been.'

Libby swallowed and blinked.

'Oh – oh, I'm sorry.' Monica stood up. 'Tea? Would you like tea? I should have asked as soon as you got here. And cake. I won't be a moment.' And she hurried out the way they had come in.

'Frustrated, eh?' murmured Libby.

Fran nodded. 'By Frensham Holdings. But let her tell it.'

Libby nodded and went to the mantelpiece to look at the photographs. There were two family groups, one from several years ago when the two children were small and one comparatively recent. She was surprised at Bill Frensham's appearance, which she barely remembered. Tall and good-looking, with a sharp, pointed face which was reflected in the two children's features, he bent solicitously towards his wife, who was turned slightly away from him, her own sharp features softened as she looked at her children.

Monica must have had everything prepared, for she returned in a very short time pushing a tea trolley – a tea trolley! thought Libby – with cups, teapot, milk jug, sugar bowl and two-tier cake stand. She gave a nervous little laugh.

'I never get to have proper tea any more,' she said. 'You must excuse me for indulging myself.' She sat down and sighed. 'This is such a treat.'

When they were all served with tea and Libby had taken two small chocolate cakes, Monica put her cup on a side table and looked down at her hands.

'I know this must have seemed an odd request,' she began, 'but when I heard you'd been asking questions, I though you might help me. I've been

240

wanting to ask questions too, you see, and no one will answer them.'

'I'm not sure I quite understand how you knew we *were* asking questions,' said Fran.

'I told Mrs Wilde – I mean Sarjeant – Barry Phillips told me.'

'But I didn't actually ask him questions,' said Libby, feeling uncomfortable. 'I went there to hire the barn for my – for Ben. It was Eliz – Mrs Martin – who put the cat among the pigeons.'

Monica's eyes narrowed and her expression changed. She looks like an angry mouse, thought Libby. 'Elizabeth Martin. Yes.' She was silent for a moment and Fran and Libby exchanged stealthy glances. Eventually, she took a deep breath and looked up.

'Barry said he'd told you Martin and my husband had an affair?'

Omigod, thought Libby. 'Yes,' she said aloud.

'And that it was over but she wouldn't let go?'

Libby nodded.

'Well, that's only half the problem.' Monica picked up her cup and took a sip. 'She's actively preventing me from looking into the firm's business. I'm the major shareholder now, and although when he was alive Bill never wanted me to get involved in the business, unless I sell out to Martin and Phillips, or float my shares, I need to know what's going on.' She smiled. 'I'm shrewder than I look, and without Bill's knowledge I kept up with a lot of the firm's dealings. Not so much the supplies side – he'd have been down on me like a ton of bricks, but I could always poke around media and marketing.' She put her head on one side. 'I could never understand why those two divisions were separate.'

'Me neither,' said Libby. 'I said that yesterday.'

'Anyway,' said Monica, ignoring the interruption, 'what I wanted to know was have you found anything out, and why you were asking questions in the first place.'

Another silence fell. At last, Fran, with a quick glance at Libby, spoke. She explained about Gemma Baverstock's concerns, Trisha's vague worries and finally Ian Connell's request.

Monica kept her eyes fixed on Fran's face, and when she'd finished speaking, nodded slowly.

'So it's official,' she said.

'Official?' said Libby.

'Your enquiry.'

'Well – not exactly.'

'But the police know you're asking questions.'

'Yes.' Libby raised her chin a little. 'Mind you, we don't tell them everything.'

Fran shifted on her end of the sofa and Libby ignored her.

'So you can tell me what you've found out?' said Monica, leaning forward a little.

'Some of it's still confidential,' said Fran quickly, before Libby could speak. 'Inspector Connell trusts us to keep a lot of the information to ourselves.'

'Even stuff *you've* found out?' Monica sounded incredulous.

'It might be prejudicial.'

'What about –' she paused and swallowed 'John Lethbridge?'

Libby and Fran exchanged another quick glance.

'You know they found his body?' said Libby.

Monica nodded. 'I wouldn't have. Barry told me.'

'He was under the impression that Lethbridge had killed your husband.'

'Yes.' She nodded again. 'So was everybody.' She shook her head, looking down into her lap. 'So silly.'

'Silly?'

'John wouldn't hurt a fly.' Monica looked up and away towards the front windows. 'He was so gentle.'

'Oh.' Libby looked helplessly at Fran, who gave a slight shrug. 'So you never agreed with the official verdict?'

Monica looked back. 'The police never said they suspected John of Bill's murder. After the first few times they left me alone.' She bit her lip. 'I wasn't very well, you see.'

'The first few times?' said Fran.

'When they came to question me. Would you like more tea?' She stood up and Libby and Fran handed over their cups with murmured assent.

'Would you like to know what happened?' asked Monica, as she handed their refilled cups back.

'What happened?' said Libby cautiously.

'When they came to tell mc I was just about to leave.' She turned towards the french windows and began pacing.

'She wants to talk,' mouthed Fran. 'Let her.'

'Leave?' prompted Libby.

'For the parade. I always went to the finish,

243

where they danced and had the maypole. And I was just leaving.' Her voice quavered on the last word. Libby and Fran kept quiet.

'And they wanted to know when I'd last seen Bill – which was stupid, because I'd seen him when he left two hours before. And after that they came back a couple of times to ask about Bill and Cranston Morris, and John, and their relationship.' She took a deep breath. 'I told them, John couldn't have had anything to do with Bill's death. They were friends. *We* were friends.'

'Did you get on with John's wife?' asked Libby.

'Willy?' Monica gave a tremulous laugh. 'I was scared of her. She's terribly glamorous and a bit – er, well. Have you met her?'

'No,' said Fran, 'but we were hoping to speak to her. Could you introduce us?'

'Oh, no, she wouldn't like that,' said Monica firmly. 'She never liked me.'

'What about the night before Bill's death?' said Libby after a pause. 'Do you know anything about what happened then?'

'That was when they say John was killed, was it?'

'Yes. Beltane night,' said Fran.

Monica shook her head. 'Why would I know anything about that?' She made a face. 'Silly business. Jumping over fires. Ridiculous.'

'You didn't go, then?' said Libby.

'No, I didn't! I never did. I was never interested in any of the Morris stuff. Especially that Goddess business.'

'Goddess?' said Libby and Fran together.

Monica looked confused for a moment, and Libby wondered if she hadn't meant to mention the Goddess.

'Oh, you know, the Oak King and all the extra stuff.' She turned back to the french windows. 'All the brother and sister gods.'

'Is that what it is?' said Libby surprised. 'I thought the Goddess was the mother figure.'

Monica turned back towards them and shrugged. 'Oh, I don't know. It's all fairly disgusting, isn't it?'

'And Bill was into all that, was he?' said Libby. Fran frowned at her.

'Yes. He said it was all part of our cultural heritage.' She came and sat down again in the leather chair. 'Wilhelmina was always the Goddess.'

'But Gemma was the Goddess this year, and she doesn't seem to want to be part of – of – well, all of that.'

'No. Sensible of her.' Monica sat up straight and lifted her chin. 'Wilhelmina had left though. After she and John split up.'

No one seemed to know what to say after that, and eventually, Libby cleared her throat and edged to the front of the sofa.

'Well, if we've answered your questions, Mrs Frensham, I think we ought to go now,' she said.

'But you haven't answered my questions.' Monica's voice was tremulous again. 'You haven't really told me anything.'

'I told you everything that's happened since Gemma Baverstock got in touch with Libby,' said Fran gently. 'There isn't any more.'

Monica's face twisted. 'But what about John's

body? You must know more about that?'

'I'm afraid not,' said Fran.

'Except –' began Libby.

'Except what?' Monica turned to her eagerly.

Libby felt her cheeks growing hot and turned to Fran for help.

'Where it was found,' said Fran. 'In the woods near Steeple Mount.'

'Woods?'

'Where they walked to the Mount.'

'Oh.' Monica frowned. 'So that's when he was killed? When they were walking to the Beltane fire?'

Fran sent Libby a warning look. 'They think so,' she said. 'But you said you knew it was Beltane night just now.'

'But I don't see ...' Monica stopped. 'How did no one notice?'

'We don't know,' said Libby. 'The police only give us a small amount of information. We're not part of the inner circle.'

Monica gave a short laugh. 'Sounds like Cranston Morris,' she said.

'Oh?' said Libby innocently.

'You already know about the Goddess business, and the Oak and Holly kings. All that incestuous stuff.' She looked as though there was something rotten under her nose.

'You're saying not everyone was part of that? That it was a separate – um – organisation?'

Monica surveyed her shrewdly. 'I'm sure you know that already.'

Libby's cheeks began to burn again.

'I think we ought to be going, Libby,' said Fran, standing up hastily. 'Thank you for the tea, Mrs Frensham.'

Monica stood up, a slight figure in pale blue. 'You've spoken to Richard Diggory, haven't you?' she said.

'Yes.' Libby was on her feet, too. 'Why?'

'No reason.' Monica's voice was hard. 'He knows all about the Goddess. You know that.'

'Er – yes.' Libby cleared her throat.

Monica looked at her. 'Yes. He told me.'

'You've spoken to him as well as Barry Phillips?' said Fran.

'I've spoken to everybody,' said Monica, moving to the door. 'And no one will tell me anything.'

Chapter Twenty-six

'WELL!' SAID LIBBY, AS she climbed into the car beside Fran. 'That was a most uncomfortable session.'

'But telling,' said Fran, putting the car into reverse. 'Especially who she'd talked to.'

'We should have taken Sir Jonathan with us,' said Libby. 'He said he liked her, and we did promise him.'

'She would have gone all sugary if he'd been there,' said Fran. 'At least we saw her more-or-less normal.'

'That was normal?' said Libby, leaning back out of the way while Fran negotiated the turn into the road. 'She started out by putting on an act, didn't she?'

'Seemed like it,' said Fran. 'And she certainly isn't overcome with grief about her husband.'

'I couldn't quite work out what she *was* concerned about,' said Libby. 'John Lethbridge mainly, I thought.'

'Oh, yes. Even though she made sure we realised that, I think it's safe to say they were having an affair. Or *had* had an affair.'

'Really?' Libby turned to Fran in surprise. 'Her?'

'Not a likely candidate for an affair, you think?' said Fran with a grin.

'Well, no. Too thin, and not in the least glamorous.'

'I bet she's got hidden depths,' said Fran. 'And

I'm pretty sure there was something with Diggory, too.'

'What?' gasped Libby. 'Come on, Fran, you're guessing.'

'Yes, I am, but it came through very strongly. I think Barry Phillips phoned her, but she phoned Diggory.'

'So which one is she having an affair with now?' Libby made a face. 'Not that I don't believe you, of course.'

'I don't think there's anyone at the moment,' said Fran. 'That was one thing she said that was true.'

'Frustrated, you mean?' Libby laughed. 'I thought that was what she meant, but you said by the firm.'

'It was a subconscious revelation, I think,' said Fran. 'But she is being frustrated by Elizabeth Martin, isn't she?'

'Obviously. So she's got two reasons to hate her; one, Martin had an affair with her husband, and two, she's trying to prevent her, Monica, from taking over the company.'

'I doubt if Monica wants to take over the company, she just wants to know what's going on, which she's entitled to do as the major shareholder.'

'Which means she thinks there's something not quite right going on,' said Libby.

'I expect it just means she wants to make sure she's getting the right payout,' said Fran.

'Can they alter that?' said Libby. 'Don't the accountants make the payments?'

'Creative accounting,' said Fran. 'They've got an

accounts department, and I expect not everything goes through it.'

'You're making a lot of assumptions,' said Libby.

Fran sighed. 'I know. It all feels right, but you know what I'm like. This is probably my conscious mind telling me what I think should be going on.'

'It's logical, though,' mused Libby. 'What we really need is a mole in the accounts department.'

'Libby!' Fran almost stood on the brakes. 'Who do you think we are? Some television cop series?'

'No, sorry.' Libby was abashed. 'I get carried away sometimes.'

'You're telling me,' said Fran. 'Look, all that happened was that Monica Frensham asked to see us because she thought we might know more about her husband's murder than she'd been told.'

'She's right,' said Libby. 'We do.'

'What has *not* happened is us being asked to look into and find the murderers of John Lethbridge and Bill Frensham. That's the police's job, and Ian's on the case. Just because he's kind enough to let us in on part of it doesn't mean we have carte blanche to go galloping through the evidence, or question all the suspects.' Fran took a deep breath. 'There.'

Libby stared at her in admiration. 'Gosh,' she said. 'You do put things well.'

Fran shot her a narrow-eyed glance. 'Are you being sarcastic?'

'No. You're absolutely right. But we've done exactly the same as this every time we've got mixed up with a murder. And let's face it, you were keener than I was at the beginning.'

Fran sighed and slowed down to turn into the road leading to Steeple Martin. 'I know. It's addictive, that's the trouble. But in the first two cases we were actively involved. You were even a suspect.'

'I wasn't!'

'Well, you were questioned,' said Fran. 'And then it was my aunt who was murdered, so I had a valid reason for being involved.'

'And after that it was the police who asked you in. And Ian asked you in this time, too. Don't forget that.'

'Not until just now, though,' said Fran. 'And he warned you off at the beginning.'

Libby shrugged. 'Oh, well. We'll just have to carry on doing it as an intellectual exercise again.'

'And everybody'll believe that,' said Fran with a grin.

'Let's go over it all back at mine,' said Libby. 'Intellectual exercise or not, I'm intrigued. And don't try and tell me you're not.'

'Wouldn't dream of it,' said Fran.

A fine rain was falling as Fran pulled up behind the little Renault opposite Libby's cottage. Sidney appeared at the window as soon as they got out of the car.

'I swear he knows the sound of every car,' said Libby, opening the front door and falling down the step.

'More like November than July,' said Fran, going to stand by Sidney at the window.

'Warmer, though,' said Libby. 'Tea? Or are you still full of Monica's dainty cups?'

'I'd like a decent cup,' said Fran. 'Hers was a bit weak, wasn't it?'

'Like her,' said Libby, going into the kitchen.

'She's not weak,' said Fran, following.

'She's giving a very good impression, then,' said Libby.

'Exactly,' said Fran. 'I should think it suited her all this time to be thought of as the little woman at home. And she admitted to being shrewder than she looks, didn't she?'

'Not shrewd enough to know what was going on in the business, though.' Libby got two mugs from a cupboard.

'But shrewd enough to know there *is* something. You said that yourself.'

'You said she just wanted to know the money was right.' Libby swirled hot water round her teapot.

'It doesn't matter, does it. She's hiding something, and I'm certain it's to do with John Lethbridge.'

'They had an affair,' stated Libby.

'We think.'

'And the dreaded Wilhelmina? What about her?'

'I'd still like to talk to her,' said Fran. 'Find out why she left Cranston Morris.'

'Because she and John split up, I suppose,' said Libby, pouring boiling water into the pot. 'But we're not supposed to be talking to the suspects. You said.'

'I know, I know. But I'd still like to.'

'So what else did we find out today?' Libby got milk from the fridge. 'Monica and John had an affair, she didn't like Willy or Elizabeth Martin, both of whom may have had affairs with Bill. John was kind. According to her. Martin and/or Phillips are blocking her from finding anything out about Frensham Holdings.'

'Martin, not Phillips. He rang her.'

'I wonder if Lethbridge had any business dealings with Frensham Holdings.' Libby poured tea into the mugs. 'He was a financial adviser, wasn't he?'

'He could have handled their insurances,' said Fran. 'Or their portfolio.'

'He'd know all about their financial situation, anyway,' said Libby, her eyes brightening. 'Could that be why he was killed?'

'You're not suggesting Bill killed John and someone else killed Bill in revenge?'

'Could be the same person,' said Libby, warming to her theme. 'Suppose there is something dodgy going on at Frensham Holdings – presumably in the bit that Bill looked after.'

'Supplies,' said Fran.

'Yeah, supplies. Then John finds out – or is involved – and the person who's behind it all has to kill him. Then Bill finds out so she has to kill him too.'

'She?'

'Sorry, I was thinking of Elizabeth Martin.' Libby sighed and picked up her mug. 'Suppose that's too good to be true.'

'You really didn't like her, did you?' said Fran, amused.

'No, I bloody didn't,' said Libby. '*And* she made

a pass at my Ben.'

'If there was something going on at Frensham Supplies Bill would have been sure to know about it,' said Fran. 'It isn't a huge business.'

'Diggory would know.' Libby sat on the sofa and moved Sidney.

'You said you were going to ask him about the Goddess,' said Fran, 'but I don't think you should. He doesn't strike me as a very savoury character.'

'You said earlier I should.'

'I know, but I've thought about it and now I don't think so.'

'Perhaps it's him?' Libby suggested. 'Perhaps Bill was fiddling the company and –'

'Oh, come on, Libby! Why would Diggory kill John?'

'John found out when he was auditing the books?'

'Financial advisers don't audit books,' said Fran.

'Oh.' Libby chewed her thumb. 'Perhaps it isn't to do with the firm, then. Perhaps it really is to do with the Morris stuff. Or the Goddess cult, anyway.'

'Or something else entirely,' said Fran. 'I wonder which woman it was I could see when we were with Ian yesterday.'

'Monica? No, she wasn't there. She said she didn't go to any of the Morris events except the end of the May Day parade.'

'She *said* she didn't. She could be lying.'

'Hmm,' said Libby doubtfully. 'Then there's Martin and Wilhelmina. Could be either of them.'

'I don't see why Martin would kill John, although I suppose as Wilhelmina was his ex, she might have a motive.'

'It's motive all the time, isn't it?' said Libby.

'But the police don't go for motive first,' said Fran. 'They go for means and opportunity. So they'll have been all through this with everyone, and it looks as though everyone has alibis –'

'Hey, we don't know that,' said Libby. 'They've only just found John's body. They won't have checked everybody out yet.'

'That's true,' said Fran slowly. 'Of course they haven't. Monica said she wouldn't have known had Phillips not phoned her.'

'I wonder if Jane's heard?' said Libby. 'It would have missed this week's edition, but she could get it on to the Mercury's website.'

'We're not thinking about Jane,' said Fran, 'we're thinking about our suspects.'

'Would they have told Wilhelmina? After all she was his wife.'

'That's another point,' said Fran. 'We don't know if they were divorced or merely separated, do we?'

'Does it make a difference?'

'It will if he's got anything to leave,' said Fran. 'If she's his widow she'll be entitled to the estate unless there are children.'

'It all depends on whether she was still dependent on him,' said Libby. 'But otherwise it won't make any difference. She only left last year, didn't she?'

'Perhaps you ought to get in touch with Diggory after all,' said Fran. 'He'd probably have all the answers, especially if Wilhelmina was the Goddess.'

'Perhaps.' Libby looked thoughtful. 'I could ring while Ben's here. I'd feel safer.'

'He's not going to do anything to you over the phone,' said Fran. 'When I said don't get in touch with him, I meant in person.'

'I know, but I'd still feel safer. So what else do we know?'

'We know there's a subversive branch of Cranston Morris, which it would appear they are glossing over by inviting Gemma and Dan to take leading roles.'

'Not in the subversive branch.'

'No, but as Goddess and one of the Kings they're figure heads. Makes me wonder if they have a real Goddess and King hidden away for nefarious purposes.'

'Wouldn't they have taken them with them to Cornwall, though?' said Libby. 'They all went off into the woods, so they were indulging in their nefarious practices down there, but they had Dan and Gemma as Goddess and Holly King.'

'Told you, as cover. Don't forget Lewis was going to film them.'

'Oh, yes! I didn't think of that. But – hang on, Lewis didn't decide to film them until the last minute.' Libby finished her tea. 'I'll call Diggory tonight.'

'What will you say?'

'No idea. I shall wait for inspiration to strike.'

'You can't do that. You've got to have a cover story. What did you say to him at Harry's?'

'I just said I was interested in the Goddess Cult and I would ask Gemma. He said not to do that but to talk to him.' Libby shook her head. 'Which means that Gemma doesn't actually know anything about the Goddess Cult.'

'We'd already figured that out,' said Fran. 'So what will you say?'

'As I've already ridiculed the whole thing it's going to be difficult. I think I just go in for a bit of nudge, nudge, wink, wink.'

'Well, be careful.' Fran put down her mug and stood up. 'We haven't got much further have we?'

'Perhaps we won't,' said Libby. 'Perhaps that's the last we'll hear about any of it until the police announce they've caught the murderer.'

'Except for whatever Diggory tells you tonight,' said Fran, and opened the front door. 'Keep me posted.'

Chapter Twenty-seven

BUT DIGGORY WAS NOT destined to tell Libby anything that night. Libby tried his phone number, obtained from Gemma on the flimsiest pretext, several times during the evening with no result. Ben, getting tetchy around ten o'clock, suggested sarcastically that she went and staked out the bakery.

'Not a bad idea, actually,' she said. Ben snorted.

'No really. I'll pop over there tomorrow. It's Saturday, so there'll be lots of people around.'

'So no chance to chat him up about nasty goings-on,' said Ben.

'But it will make him see I'm serious,' said Libby. 'Make him think so, anyway.'

'Do you want me to come with you?'

'That would rather defeat the object, wouldn't it?'

'You wanted me here tonight.'

'I know,' said Libby uncomfortably, 'but in broad daylight on a Saturday morning I won't feel so bad.'

Ben sighed. 'All right. But I could always come and wait in the car, or in a pub.'

Libby brightened. 'Yes, you could! And I could just be shopping, and be meeting you for lunch.'

'Don't push the boat out too much,' said Ben. 'I didn't say lunch was on offer.'

'Don't be a skinflint. Anyway, I'll buy you lunch as a thankyou.'

The following morning the rain had disappeared leaving everything sparkling. Ben went to the Manor to fetch the four-wheel drive, whose existence he justified by driving it over the track and into the top – unmade – of Allhallow's Lane.

Steeple Mount high street was almost as busy as it had been on the Saturday of the Solstice Parade. Ben disappeared towards the strangely named Bell and Butcher and Libby wandered across the road and tacked slowly towards Diggory's shop. This time, there were no crowns or other cultish regalia in the window, simply some beautiful decorative loaves and an iced cake covered in bronze roses.

A woman wearing an alice band and pushing a pushchair manoeuvred her way out of the shop looking harassed. Libby hurried to hold the door for her.

'I suppose they didn't have pushchairs when this shop was built,' she said cheerfully. The woman gave her a look and scurried off without saying thank you. 'Charming,' muttered Libby, and went inside.

To her surprise, the shop was empty.

'Hello?' she called. She heard a chair scrape on the floor and a rustling as the curtain covering the doorway behind the counter was pushed aside.

Diggory, in full old-fashioned baker's costume, stood in the doorway, his mouth a big O of surprise.

'Richard!' beamed Libby. 'Ben had to come over this way today so I cadged a lift with him. Did you get my messages?'

'Er – yes.' Diggory turned his head slightly as if to look over his shoulder. 'I was going to ring you back.'

'That's all right.' Libby looked round. 'There's no one here. You can tell me what I want to know now, can't you?'

'Not really.' Diggory's colour was changing. Libby thought she'd never met a man whose face went red so frequently.

'Oh, why not? I only want to know what goes on at your underground meetings.' Libby gave him her best salacious smile. 'I found out about another group a couple of years ago, but they were broken up.' She nodded knowingly at him. 'I mentioned the Tyne Chapel mob to you before, didn't I?'

'So you're interested are you?' A woman's voice came from the back room, followed immediately by a woman. And what a woman, thought Libby.

Tall, with wavy blonde hair and raspberry glossed lips, her figure wouldn't have looked out of place on page 3 of one of the redtops. Libby gained an impression of a lot of leather and a good sprinkling of lace, before returning her gaze to the sculpted face.

'Are you Wilhelmina?' she asked.

Both the man and the woman stared at her.

'Yeah,' said the woman eventually. 'Who wants to know?' she clicked her fingers. 'Oh, of course! The person who's interested in the Goddess. Gemma's little friend.'

Libby swallowed an instant rush of anger. 'Hardly little, I feel,' she said, abandoning any attempt to fool Diggory. 'And you probably know why I'm here.'

'I know why you *said* you were here,' said

260

Wilhelmina.

'You have no idea?' Libby peered at her as closely as she dared. 'Have the police not been in touch with you?' She knew Fran would by now be warning her not to say anything else, but she was determined to establish some kind of ascendancy over this woman. Childish, but understandable, she thought.

'The police?' Wilhelmina and Diggory exchanged glances, Diggory's colour fading to white.

'Why would the police want to talk to me?' asked Wilhelmina, a catch now in her voice.

With a belated sense of propriety, Libby shook her head. 'I'd better not tell you until they do,' she said, aware of how annoying that would be. 'I don't suppose Monica's spoken to you?'

'Monica?' Diggory's voice sounded as thin as a reed. 'Why?'

'No, of course she hasn't.' Libby was now feeling out of her depth. She really had no excuse to be here asking questions, and now she didn't know how to extricate herself.

'Who are you, exactly?' Wilhelmina started forward and came up against the counter.

'Libby Sarjeant,' said Libby. 'I thought you said you knew who I was?'

Wilhelmina shrugged.

'Are you still the real Goddess?' Libby was all interest. 'I was going to ask Richard about that, wasn't I, Richard?' She turned to him with a smile. He smiled weakly back.

'Oh, come on, Diggory! You didn't fall for that?'

Wilhelmina swung round and glared at him. 'She's nosing around.'

'That's why you were in Cornwall, wasn't it?' he said. His voice hadn't recovered. 'You were trying to find out about us?'

'No – I told you. I was with my friend –'

'The telly-poof. I know.'

Libby knew what it meant to have your breath taken away. Stunned, she was silent for a moment.

'I'd been asked,' she began, and had to clear her throat, 'to look into Bill Frensham's murder.'

This time they both gasped together.

'But we didn't have anything to do with that!' Wilhelmina's voice was high and reedy now, too. 'It's nothing to do with – with –'

'You? Or the Goddess Cult?'

Wilhelmina looked round desperately at Diggory. He put his head in his hands. Libby frowned.

'Look,' she said, 'I don't actually think you did have anything to do with Bill Frensham's death, but it looks very much as if you're afraid of something. What is it?'

Wilhelmina pulled herself together. 'Don't be stupid,' she said. 'We haven't got anything to be afraid of.'

'You might not be afraid,' said Libby, pointing, 'but he is.'

Diggory lifted his head. 'I knew you were trouble that first day at the Solstice Parade,' he said. 'Poking around. Nosy bitch.'

Wilhelmina snorted. 'She's nothing but a nosy old cow. God, Diggory, how did you get taken in?'

Diggory shook his head. 'I saw her with that Inspector at the Solstice. And both of them were up at the valley with him the day before yesterday.'

'Both of who?' asked Wilhelmina.

'Her and her spooky friend,' sneered Diggory.

'How do you know that?' said Libby.

'One of our members lives in Tyne Cottages.'

'Oh, the pretty little cottages this side of the bridge?'

He gave a look of dislike. 'Yes. She called me. Wondered what you were doing.'

Libby's stomach clenched. 'But there must have been quite a lot of activity round there over the last – um – couple of months. That's the way you walk to your – er – your festivities, isn't it?'

'Yes.' Diggory's eyes narrowed. 'There's been a fair amount of police activity over the last few days, actually. So what's going on?'

Oh, bugger, thought Libby. Now I've lost the initiative. Aloud, she said 'Continuing their investigations into the – er – incidents, I suppose.'

'And you think our harmless little group have something to do with it.' Diggory stood up. 'Well, you're wrong.'

'I told you,' said Libby, 'I don't think you do, actually, but I'm not sure that the Goddess Cult, or whatever name it goes under now, is legal. You were part of that nasty little coven that used to meet at Tyne Chapel, weren't you?' She watched as their expressions changed yet again. 'And you know that the Black Mass is illegal?'

'Oh, shit,' said Wilhelmina.

'So what's with all this sacrifice business down

in Cornwall?' said Libby, relieved that she seemed to be in charge again. 'I assume it's not virgins?'

'I'm not saying another word,' said Diggory. 'You'll have to arrest me. But I swear on my life, I had nothing to do with Bill's death. None of us did.'

Libby, congratulating herself on a couple of good guesses, regarded them thoughtfully.

'So, tell me,' she said finally, 'when exactly did you set up the Goddess side of things? And why Goddess?'

They looked at each other.

'It was Bill's idea,' said Diggory. 'He worked out something with Florian Malahyde.'

'Who had already written his own script for Mannan Night,' said Libby. 'Go on.'

'It's all based on fact,' said Diggory. 'All the old religions. They're all related in some way.'

'Sex,' said Libby. Diggory went white and Wilhelmina went red. 'All right. So people were encouraged to join by invoking the "old religions". And presumably the lure of illicit sex. That's why they all belonged to that other coven, where Nurse – I mean Joan – Redding died.'

Neither of them said anything.

'And what about your husband, Mrs Lethbridge? Was he involved?'

'He went along with it at first,' said Wilhelmina, 'but he backed out after a bit. Didn't like it.'

'And that's when you left him?'

'Yes.' She cleared her throat. 'After a – after I – after –'

'After he discovered your involvement as the Goddess was slightly more than he'd anticipated?'

suggested Libby. Wilhelmina looked as though she'd quite like to kill her. 'I'm surprised you left him. I thought it would be the other way round.'

Diggory sent Wilhelmina a look of dislike. 'He threw her out.'

'Ah.' Libby realised she couldn't go any further with this without revealing the fact of John Lethbridge's death. She also wondered what Ian Connell was going to say when he found out about her inquisition.

'What about the old religion, though,' she said, determined to get to the bottom of at least one thing before she left. 'Is it based on Mother Earth, the season, or what?'

Wilhelmina sighed. 'It's all the same, really. Everywhere has a different version, but you have the mother who is also the sister and the daughter and the King who is father, brother and son. They all mate and kill each other and rise again. Even that phoney Malahyde's got some of it right.'

'And the Morris is part of it?'

'Developed out of it,' said Diggory. 'Bill went into it quite deeply. Fascinating, some of it.'

'And the Black Mass?'

Diggory's colour fluctuated again. 'All to do with fertility,' he said shortly.

'Right,' said Libby. 'Well, I'll be on my way. I think you might get a visit from the police fairly soon.' She looked away. 'I hope – I mean ...well. Just be aware of it.'

When she emerged on to the high street she discovered she was sweating. Just how much good or damage she'd done she had no idea, but at least she'd confirmed a few things she and Fran had suspected. And surprisingly, she felt sorry for Wilhelmina Lethbridge.

She found Ben in the pub behind a newspaper.

'At least you're not hunched over a mobile or an MP 3 player,' she said, peering over the top at him.

'Should I be?' He put the paper down.

'It's the way people get news these days,' she said.

'Young people get news, not old dodderers,' said Ben, standing up. 'What do you want to drink?'

When he returned with her half pint of lager, Libby told him most of what had happened inside Diggory's bakery.

Ben shook his head. 'You took a hell of a chance,' he said. 'Suppose one of them got nasty?'

'They were too scared to get nasty,' said Libby, not really believing it.

'That's just when people *do* get nasty,' said Ben. 'And half the stuff you were saying to them –'

'Was guesswork,' said Libby. 'I know.'

'How on earth did you link them to that Black Mass mob?'

'It was the chapel, I think,' said Libby. 'And it was suggested, can't remember whether by me or Fran, right at the beginning. It's the sex angle.'

'I know, but you had no proof, not even a grain of a suspicion. All you had was your visit to Cornwall and a fertile imagination.' Ben shook his head again. 'You'll be the death of me one of these days.'

'Or of me,' said Libby.

Ben covered her hand with his own. 'That's

exactly what I'm afraid of,' he said. 'Now come on, drink up. I don't want to stay here any longer. I don't feel Steeple Mount is a healthy place for you.'

'Fran's cousin Charles comes from here, doesn't he?' said Libby as they made their way back to the car park. 'I should have remembered that.'

'Why?' asked Ben.

'He was a bit of a loser, wasn't he? Seems to breed the wrong sort of people.'

'Based on Cousin Charles and Richard Diggory?'

'And the others.'

'They don't come from here,' said Ben. 'Or at least most of them don't.'

'Gemma and Dan do.'

'Well, they're not on the list of suspects, are they,' said Ben, beginning to sound exasperated. 'Come on, for goodness sake. Let's pop down to Nethergate and have lunch at The Sloop.'

Chapter Twenty-eight

FRAN EXPRESSED MUCH THE same sentiment as Ben when Libby related the events of the morning. After lunch at The Sloop, Libby dropped in to Coastguard Cottage while Ben went along to Guy's shop and gallery.

'We're no further, anyway,' said Libby. 'It doesn't look as though anyone had a motive to kill Lethbridge except Wilhelmina, and she seems to have fallen on her feet. There was no suggestion that she'd had nowhere to go. And why kill Bill?'

'Perhaps we're approaching it from the wrong angle,' said Fran.

'You said we had to find the motive for Lethbridge,' said Libby, 'that's what we're doing.'

'But there was something Lethbridge was doing – or had done – which we don't know about.'

'Exactly – that's the motive.'

'But what was he doing? Do you see what I mean? Did he have an affair?' Fran stopped. 'Well, we know he did, with Monica. Did he have one with anyone else? And isn't it odd that he should throw his wife out when he himself was playing away?'

'Perhaps that didn't start until after Wilhelmina had gone,' said Libby. 'And, we've already said, the affair with Monica might give Bill a reason to kill him, but who would then kill Bill?'

'I suppose Monica might,' mused Fran.

'Let's find out where she was, then,' said Libby, jumping excitedly out of her chair.

'And how do you propose we do that? She's already said she was just about to leave the house when the police came to tell her. I doubt if she'd just got in from stabbing her husband.'

'You never know,' said Libby. 'Were there any civilians around when he was killed? You know – ordinary members of the public?'

'I've no idea, but I'm pretty sure if Monica was there she'd have been recognised.'

'Oh, yes,' said Libby gloomily. 'Of course she would. So – she was in disguise.'

'As a black-faced Morris man?' Fran laughed. 'How would she have got the stuff off before the police came?'

'Oh, I don't know.' Libby scowled into the fireplace. 'She's the only one I can think of, that's all.'

'What about Elizabeth Martin and Barry Phillips?' said Fran.

'Oh, heavens.' Libby sighed. 'Do you think Ian's going to look into the business?'

'In case there is something wrong with Frensham Supplies? I don't know. Does he think there is?'

'We don't know, do we,' said Libby. 'That's the problem. And no way in the world that we'll ever find out.'

'We had the polis round here today,' said Harry on the phone when Ben and Libby got back to Allhallow's Lane.

'The police? Whatever for?'

'Drugs!' said Harry in an underworld voice.

'What?'

Harry laughed. 'Apparently, there's a distribution organisation somewhere in the area and a link in the chain's been broken.'

'And what do they think you are? The link or the baron?'

'Neither. They were asking if I'd ever been offered any by any of our suppliers. Subtly, but that's what they were asking.'

'And how do they know this link has been broken?'

'They've been watching someone, apparently, and he – or she, I don't know – hasn't followed normal procedure.'

'Why don't they ask them, then?' said Libby. 'Oh, I suppose they don't want to alert the big bosses.'

'That's about the size of it,' said Harry. 'I don't think they knew who the distributor was for this person they've been watching, and if they could track down any more of the customers they could put the finger on him – or her.'

'Why did they think you might know?' said Libby indignantly. 'How dare they?'

Harry laughed again. 'Because this other person is also in the catering trade. I don't know what branch, but that's what they did. Go round to everyone in the area who might have deliveries from a catering supplier of some sort.'

'Like Richard Diggory,' said Libby.

'Oh, come on, Lib! He's hardly a supplier. He only sells a few of his products to a very few restaurants and delis.'

'Bet it makes sense, though. Who was in charge

of the investigation?'

'I don't know, do I?' said Harry. 'Just two uniformed cops.'

'Oh – not even CID?' Libby was disappointed. 'Can't ask Ian, then.'

'Well, you could. I wouldn't mind being questioned by him.'

'Stop it, you flirt,' said Libby. 'I shall have to think about this. Thanks for telling me, Harry.'

'Oh, I knew you'd be interested,' said Harry. 'I said the other night you'd got a whole drugs ring set up, didn't I?'

Libby told Ben what Harry had said.

'It just seems such a coincidence after what Fran and I were saying earlier,' she said.

'But you were talking about Frensham Supplies,' said Ben, 'not catering supplies. You can't have it both ways.'

'Do you think we ought to talk to Ian about it?'

'No, I don't,' said Ben. 'If he thinks there's anything to connect either Richard Diggory or Frensham Supplies to a drugs ring or Bill's murder, he will look into it. Probably already has. You are not the police, my darling, nor are you, as you so frequently say, Miss Marple. I think you're busy making something out of nothing, and you ought to leave it alone.' He bent down and kissed the top of her head. 'Sun's over the yard arm. What do you want to drink?'

'Wine, please,' said Libby with a sigh. 'And I suppose you're right. I ought to stop thinking about it and concentrate on something else.'

'Exactly,' said Ben, fetching red wine from the

kitchen. 'It's Jane and Terry's wedding next Saturday, isn't it? Concentrate on that, instead.'

Libby brightened. 'Oh, yes. I've got to go shopping, haven't I?'

'Shopping?' repeated Ben warily. 'For a present, you mean?'

'No, of course not. No, well, of course I will have to buy a present, but I meant a new outfit. I can't wear the same one I wore for Fran and Guy's, can I?'

Fran and Libby hit Canterbury on Monday. A morning spent scouring the clothes shops and department stores left them hungry and thirsty and they repaired to the little side street pub where they had first been introduced. Their favourite barman was back, even more outrageously dressed than before, and again asked mournfully after Harry. Libby assured him that Harry and Peter were going from strength to strength and squeezed behind the table with Fran to await their shepherd's pie.

'We ought to ask him if he's on the drugs distribution route,' she whispered, as the barman disappeared to take their order to the kitchen.

'Sssh!' Fran looked round, alarmed. 'Honestly, Libby, you ought to be more careful.'

'Well, he could be,' said Libby. 'City centre pub, lots of students.'

'I'm sure the police would have done a thorough search,' said Fran. 'If they were asking Harry, you can bet they've asked every establishment in the area.'

Libby sighed. 'I know. And Ben thinks it's to do with Frensham Supplies, who do office equipment anyway.'

'Eh?' Fran frowned. 'Then why are they asking restaurants?'

'No – they aren't connected. It was me connecting things up,' said Libby. 'In my usual fashion, apparently.'

'Bricks and straw,' said Fran, nodding.

'You needn't agree,' said Libby huffily, and startled the barman by bestowing on him a brilliant smile.

It was no surprise when Ben received a letter later on in the week from Frensham Holdings, informing him that due to circumstances beyond their control, they were unable to accommodate him at Frensham Barn.

'After the reception I got I'm not surprised,' said Libby, 'and I did say you ought to cancel, didn't I?'

Ben raised an eyebrow. 'Yes, dear,' he said.

Neither Libby nor Fran heard anything from Ian Connell or anyone connected with the Green Man case all week. Libby spent a lot of time painting in the conservatory and the remainder sitting under the cherry tree in the garden, while Fran spent several days helping in the shop, and the rest exploring Nethergate on foot.

Saturday rolled round, and with it, Jane Maurice's wedding to Terry Baker. Fran and Guy drove over to Allhallow's Lane, where they were to stay overnight, and joined Libby and Ben in their taxi. Other members of the Steeple Martin community were invited to the evening reception, even Harry having agreed to take a Saturday evening off from the Pink Geranium.

The guests were directed up the steps at Anderson Place, and to the right of the reception hall, through double doors into what must have once been a formal drawing room, with a large marble fireplace on the left-hand wall and enormous french doors leading onto a balcony, which in turn led on to the imposing front steps. This was where Peter and Harry had celebrated their civil partnership, and, when the registrar came into the room, Libby was delighted to see he was the same small, round man with a jolly, smiling face, who looked as though he'd be more at home in a red suit with white whiskers.

Jane and Terry appeared in the doorway and everyone stood up. For the first time, Libby noticed Jane's mother, still apparently firmly stuck in the 1950s, by the look of her pale pink two-piece suit and matching hat. She nudged Fran.

'Mrs Maurice, look.'

'She doesn't exactly look thrilled, does she,' whispered Fran and earned a frown from Guy.

Jane, in a glorious 1920s style dress of oyster satin, paused as they came level with Libby. Moving in front of Terry, she reached across Ben, who sat by the aisle, and kissed Libby's cheek. 'Thank you,' she whispered, before turning a brilliant smile on her fiancé and continuing towards the celebrant.

Libby, bright red, with tears ruining her eye make-up, accepted a tissue from Fran and a hug from Ben and tried to concentrate on the short ceremony.

As wedding organiser Melanie had once told Harry and Libby, the happy couple were able to go straight out on to the balcony for photographs, followed by their guests, who drifted down the steps after the obligatory group pictures and across to the marquee where the reception was to be held.

'Bit bigger than ours,' said Fran.

'I liked yours better,' said Libby, 'but just look over there!'

'Where?'

'That waitress with the tray – the blonde one.'

Fran looked at her. 'There are at least three blonde ones.'

'The Marilyn Monroe look-alike,' whispered Libby. 'With the very short skirt.'

'Right.' Fran nodded. 'What about her?'

'I can't believe the coincidence,' said Libby, 'but that's Wilhelmina Lethbridge!'

Chapter Twenty-nine

'HOW EMBARRASSING,' SAID FRAN, turning away.

'Embarrassing? Why?'

'Well, you practically accused her of murder last week. Don't you think it's embarrassing?'

'Oh.' Libby stared across at Wilhelmina, who was by now smiling brightly at a succession of male guests who had lined up to relieve her of glasses. 'I think she's beyond embarrassing.'

'She might be, but you're not.'

'Oh,' said Libby again. 'Well, I'll just have to try and avoid her. I wonder why she's here?'

'Working, I should imagine,' said Fran dryly. 'The same as Diggory who's standing behind the buffet table.'

Libby caught her breath and choked. 'Oh, bugger,' she said.

Ben appeared at her side and gave her a considering look. 'Whatever you're plotting, my love, could I remind you that we're at a wedding, and our first duty is to the happy couple, who have just arrived to do the receiving line?'

'Oh, right.' Libby smiled brightly and straightened her jacket. 'Come on, then, Fran.'

'Why is Diggory here?' she whispered, as they approached the uneven receiving line, consisting of Jane, Terry, Mrs Maurice, hanging back and trying to remain inconspicuous, and Terry's mother, a small, jolly person wearing a bright pink and blue floating creation that made her look like a plump fairy godmother.

After being presented to both mothers as "the person who brought us together", and being acknowledged by Mrs Maurice with a baleful eye and a brief 'We've met', Libby escaped towards a table laden with full champagne glasses.

'Have one of these,' said a voice in her ear and she nearly jumped a foot in the air.

'Willy!' she gasped. 'I mean, Mrs Lethbridge.'

'Willy will do.' Wilhelmina looked round the marquee and turned her back on the guests, handing Libby a glass as she did so. 'I'm glad I've run into you.'

'You are?' Libby took a fortifying swig of the champagne and coughed.

'You knew about John when you saw us last week, didn't you?'

Libby risked a quick look at Wilhelmina's face, which was bent over her tray of glasses. 'Yes,' she said. 'I'm sorry I couldn't tell you.'

Wilhelmina shook her head. 'That's OK. I understand how suspicious you were.'

'You do?' Libby's eyebrows reached her hairline. 'I thought I was probably a bit rude. And I certainly jumped to a lot of conclusions.'

'Yes, you did. But they were mostly right.' Wilhelmina looked up, and Libby was surprised to see her long eyelashes were wet. 'And there's something I ought to tell you.'

'Should you not tell the police?'

'I'd rather tell you. After all, you're in with them, aren't you?'

'Er – well – yes.' Libby crossed her fingers over

277

her handbag. 'Should I fetch my colleague? She's just over there.'

'No.' Wilhelmina shot a look towards the buffet, where Diggory was in conversation with a tail-coated individual of imposing aspect.

'Yes, I was going to ask, what's he doing here?' said Libby, following her gaze. 'Come to think of it, what are you doing here?'

'He does outside catering. Didn't you know?' Wilhelmina looked at Libby. 'That's why I'm here. He takes pity on me every now and then and hires me as a waitress. I'm crap at it, but it helps with the rent.'

'Who hires him?' asked Libby. 'Anderson Place or the client?'

'No idea,' said Wilhelmina. 'Does it matter?'

'I suppose not,' muttered Libby.

'Anyway, I'd better get moving or he'll be down on me like a ton of bricks,' said Wilhelmina, turning to face the guests once more. 'He won't want me talking to you.'

'So why did you want to?'

'Not now. Can I ring you up? Or come and see you?'

'When people say that they often don't do it,' said Libby. 'I'll come to you if you'll tell me where. And don't tell anyone you're going to talk to me, either.'

Scenarios from various television police dramas played through her head showing her pictures of Wilhelmina's battered body, cut down before she could tell her tale.

'All right. I've got a flat in Nethergate. Just off

Marine Parade. "Marine View" it's called.'

'I know it,' nodded Libby.

'Do you?' Wilhelmina looked surprised.

'Yes. I used to know someone who lived in the same road,' said Libby, omitting any mention of the murderer who had also stayed there. 'When shall I come?'

'When you like. Here.' She fished in the pocket of the tiny apron she wore over her skirt. 'I scribbled this down when I saw you come in. Ring me.'

Libby looked down at the number scrawled on a scrap of paper. 'OK,' she said. 'Please take care of yourself.'

Wilhelmina's face twisted in a parody of a smile. 'Sure,' she said.

Libby took another glass of champagne and went in search of her party. She found them talking to Sir Jonathan, who had put in his usual appearance to check that his guests were happy.

'Do you hire the caterers, Jonathan?' she asked after being courteously greeted with a kiss on the cheek.

'Sometimes, I believe so,' he replied, his eyebrows raised. 'Why do you ask?'

'I was surprised to see Richard Diggory here,' she said.

'Ah!' Sir Jonathan twinkled beneath his white eyebrows. 'Diggory's bakery supplies us regularly. His catering service is small – he's only probably here for the cake.'

'Ah! That makes sense,' said Libby, turning to where she could see the impressive three-tier construction set on a side table. 'I didn't think he would bring waiting staff too, though.'

'I believe they often bring staff to swell the numbers,' said Sir Jonathan.

'Right.' Libby nodded.

'What was all that about?' hissed Fran when Sir Jonathan moved away to talk to the bride and groom.

Libby told her as much as she could of her conversation with Wilhelmina. 'I suppose it isn't a coincidence after all,' she finished. 'Diggory's a baker and confectioner – of course he's likely to have made the cake.'

'And you're going to see Wilhelmina?'

'I hope so. I just kept thinking of all those TV programmes where the witnesses say I'll tell you all tomorrow, and then are found dead before they can say anything.' She shivered. 'Scary.'

'Perhaps she'll go home with Diggory tonight and be safe,' said Fran. 'Where does she live?'

'You'll never guess,' said Libby. 'In the same road as Sue Warner. Remember the house called "Marine View" and we said the servants in the attics would have been the only ones who could have seen the sea? Well, that's it.'

'Good lord.' Fran shook her head. 'Shall I come?'

'I don't know,' said Libby. 'When I asked if I could bring you over just now she said no, but that was because she didn't want to draw attention to herself. She's given me her number, so I'll ring before I go and ask her.'

After the buffet, the speeches and the cutting of

the cake, Libby looked round for Wilhelmina, but she was nowhere to be seen. Diggory had taken the cake into the kitchens, presumably to divide it into guest-size pieces. Perhaps Wilhelmina would reappear handing it out.

But neither of them reappeared, and Libby was left wondering if she would, in fact, ever see Wilhelmina again.

After six o'clock, evening guests drifted in and the party took off. Terry's talented sister unsurprisingly had a cabaret spot during the evening, playing the piano and singing, and a local band supplied danceable music the rest of the time. Jane and Terry floated round the marquee on a cloud of champagne and happiness, and, all in all, Libby thought, it was the third lovely wedding she been to in the last couple of years. The thought did make her wonder if she should be planning her own, but the involuntary shudder it provoked made her reconsider immediately. Poor Ben, she thought, stealing a look at him as he danced gracefully with Jane's mother, who was visibly thawing.

On the way back to Allhallow's Lane, as they shared a people carrier taxi back to the village, Libby invited Harry and Peter to join them for a nightcap.

'She looked lovely, didn't she?' said Libby, when they arrived. 'Gorgeous dress.'

'All brides are lovely,' said Guy, sitting on the arm of Fran's chair. 'Especially mine.'

'Oh gawd,' said Harry. 'Young lurve.'

'Not so young, whippersnapper,' said Guy. 'You

were, though.'

'Old married couple now, aren't we, me old dutch?' He poked Peter with his foot from his place on the hearthrug.

'Don't you start taking me for granted,' said Peter. 'I'm still a desirable property.'

'Anyway, I agree with Lib,' said Fran. 'She did look lovely. And Terry looked so smart. His mum's nice, isn't she?'

'So's his sister,' said Ben, 'But Jane's mother. How difficult is she?'

'We told you that last year,' said Fran, 'when we went to see her in London.'

'And Jane wants her to live with them? She's mad.' Harry lifted his glass for a refill.

'She's not, you know,' said Libby getting to her feet and fetching the gin bottle. 'Her mother would always be on at her to go up to London to look after her as she gets older, and Jane's still upset that she wasn't nearer when her aunt died. If her mother's in the flat downstairs, she's independent but Jane and Terry are on hand. I think it's a great idea. I'm busy planting it in Ad's mind already.'

'Adam?' scoffed Harry. 'He couldn't look after himself, let alone anyone else.'

'Come off it, Harry,' said Peter. 'He's a sensible young man, is Adam. And he's holding down two jobs. Yours and the one at Creekmarsh. And even the flat over the caff's quite clean and tidy.'

'Really?' Libby was interested. 'Can I come and have a look?'

'No.' Harry glared at her. 'He'd never trust me again.'

'So,' said Ben, deeming it wise to change the subject, 'you found out what Diggory was doing there.'

'Well, yes,' said Libby. 'You were there. It was obvious really.'

'Diggory?' said Harry surprised.

'Who's Diggory?' asked Peter, whose life as a journalist in London precluded him from knowing a lot about Libby's various, and nefarious, doings.

'He's a baker,' said Libby, 'and he's involved in this funny cult with Cranston Morris, where Bill Frensham was killed. And he knew John Lethbridge who was also killed. And he's friends with Lethbridge's wife, who was there today as a waitress. He made the wedding cake, by the way.'

'Right,' said Peter, wrinkling a patrician brow and pushing back a lock of straight blond hair. 'I think I get all that. Does this mean you two are up to your old tricks again. Miss Marple and Miss Silver join forces?'

'No!' said Libby and Fran, while Harry was heard to mutter 'Miss Silver? Who's Miss Silver?'

'Yes, they are,' said Guy. 'Libby was asked by a member of this Morris side, then Fran was asked by her old flame.'

'Oh, yes! I didn't see him there tonight,' said Libby, hoping to change the subject again.

'No,' said Fran. 'Jane said he'd sent his apologies, but he was called out.'

'Well, I'm not terribly distressed about that,' said Guy, with a grin.

'Oh, you!' said Fran, giving him a nudge which nearly sent him off the arm of the chair.

The conversation turned in another direction and Libby relaxed. She didn't want anyone peering too closely at her proposed activities, which she had a strong suspicion might appear dangerous to those of her friends who had been involved involuntarily in her past escapades. She thought particularly of the adventure last year where she, Fran, Ben and Guy had all been in the way of a murderer, and not only interrupted a failed attempt at burglary, but she and Fran had been attacked personally.

Taking a healthy swallow of scotch, she put it all from her mind and set out to be entertaining.

Chapter Thirty

ON SUNDAY MORNING LIBBY braced herself to tell Ben she was going over to Nethergate. She could hardly say she was going to interview a suspect, and as she'd spent most of the previous day, and breakfast that morning, with Fran, she couldn't use visiting the Wolfes as an excuse.

However, Ben announced as soon as Fran and Guy had left that he was going up to Steeple Farm if Libby didn't mind, and he would see her at the Manor around one o'clock for lunch.

'Won't you come back here to change?' she asked, surprised.

'No, I don't need to. I've kept some overalls at the farm. What will you do?'

'Oh, I don't know. Washing? Change the spare bed?'

'They've only just got out of it,' grinned Ben. 'You're not usually that efficient.'

But he left it at that and disappeared as soon as he'd helped clear away the breakfast things. Libby watched him drive away and then scrabbled in her handbag for Wilhelmina's phone number.

It rang for a long time, and Libby's heart was beginning to beat uncomfortably fast when a sleepy voice answered.

'Wilhelmina?' said Libby. 'It's Libby Sarjeant. You said you'd like to meet. I'm free this morning.'

'Oh.' It sounded as though Wilhelmina was struggling to sit up. 'Sorry I was still asleep. What time is it?'

'After ten,' said Libby, trying to keep disapproval out of her voice. After all, she frequently stayed in bed until after ten on a Sunday herself.

'Do you want to come over, then?'

'If you still want to talk to me.'

'Yes,' said Wilhelmina, her voice stronger. 'I do. I need some advice.'

'OK,' said Libby. 'Can I bring my friend with me? She's the clever one in our investigations. I promise you, she's very discreet.'

'She the one who sees ghosts?'

'Ghosts? No. But you've obviously heard of her.'

'Yes.' There was silence for a moment. 'She can see things, can't she?'

'Some things, yes.'

'That sounds a bit – well, dangerous.'

'She's never actually had a vision of somebody killing someone else,' said Libby.

'Right.' More silence. 'OK, then. Give me an hour. You know where it is?'

'I know where it is,' said Libby, and rang off.

'Lib, I've only just got in,' complained Fran, when appealed to. 'I don't know what I'm going to say to Guy.'

'You said he didn't mind you taking an interest. Anyway, won't he be opening the shop? It's a summer Sunday – good for trade.'

'Oh, all right,' said Fran with a sigh. 'Where shall I meet you?'

'On the prom,' said Libby, 'And we can always

have an ice cream afterwards if we don't take long.'

Déjà vu, thought Libby an hour later as she waited for Fran on the promenade at Nethergate. In the second adventure she and Fran had together they had come to Nethergate (Fran didn't live there then) and watched elderly holiday-makers braving the summer weather. It was much the same today, sea whipped up into meringue points, threatening steely clouds in the sky and a nasty little wind blowing up swirls of dust and sweet wrappers. Thank goodness yesterday had been sunny. Libby turned and looked up at Cliff Terrace, where Jane and Terry lived in Peel House. Not that they were there now, of course.

'Ready then?'

Libby turned to face Fran and beamed. 'Come on then,' she said.

Marine View was a tall Victorian house in a terrace. Most of the others appeared to be guest houses, but this one was divided into flats. Libby found the bell marked Lethbridge and pushed.

'Nothing as fancy as an entryphone,' she said, as they waited for a response. Eventually the wide front door opened a crack and Wilhelmina's tousled head appeared.

'Come in,' she said, standing back.

Libby and Fran trooped in and waited for her to close the door and lead the way. Libby couldn't help comparing the way she looked now with the glossy image she'd presented yesterday and last Saturday. Her hair stood out round her head in a halo of spikes, her eye make-up had slipped under her eyes and her lipstick had spread up to her nose and down to her chin. Grey sweat pants and a grubby T-shirt completed the effect. Exchanging glances with Fran, she followed Wilhelmina up the stairs.

The flat was on the first floor. The front room had tall windows and a beautiful fireplace which had been boarded up. Wilhelmina sat down on a sagging sofa and indicated chairs on the other side of the room.

'This is Fran Castle,' said Libby.

'Wolfe,' said Fran.

'Oh, yes. I keep forgetting. Fran Wolfe. She's just got married.' Libby leant forward. 'So, what did you want to talk to us about? You said you wanted advice.'

'Yes.' Wilhelmina tucked her feet under her and examined her nails. 'You know my husband was killed.'

'Yes,' said Fran. 'On Beltane night. Before Bill Frensham was killed.'

'Yeah. So it couldn't have been him, could it? John, I mean. He couldn't have killed Bill?'

'Of course not,' said Libby.

Wilhelmina shifted uncomfortably. 'Only you see, I went to see him that day.'

'The day he died? Have you told the police?' said Fran in a surprised voice.

'No. That's why I wanted advice.'

'But why me?' said Libby. 'You were fairly angry with me last week.'

'But you were right.' Wilhelmina's colour was rising. 'We were all part of this Goddess thing, and Bill and Diggory had got it all tied up with some coven thing.'

'I knew it,' said Libby.

Wilhelmina looked up under her brows. 'Yeah. Some black magic thing that happened and they broke up.'

'And reformed as the Goddess cult as an offshoot of Cranston Morris,' said Libby.

'John joined in, but he didn't like it when I got too friendly with people, especially Bill.' She was looking down at her hands again.

'And Diggory?' said Fran.

'Only since John left,' said Wilhelmina. 'Bill and I had broken up by then.'

Libby raised her eyebrows. 'Really?'

'Really what?' Wilhelmina looked belligerent.

'You'd broken up?'

'He was off with that woman from his work, wasn't he.'

'Ah, yes. Anyway, you went to see John the morning he died, you were saying,' said Fran.

'Yes.'

'Why?'

'I needed money.' Wilhelmina lifted her chin.

'So what do you need advice about?' Libby was frowning. 'You can tell the police that, can't you?'

'Not that.' Wilhelmina stood up. 'I'm going to have a coffee. Want one?'

Libby and Fran both shook their heads and she wandered off, presumably into the kitchen, leaving them looking at each other in puzzlement.

'What's she on about?' said Libby quietly.

'Something he told her, I expect,' said Fran. 'She's working up to telling us.'

Wilhelmina returned carrying a large blue mug.

'You were saying?' prompted Libby.

'Well.' Wilhelmina sighed, took a sip of coffee and winced. 'See, it was John. He said he couldn't give me much at the moment but he would soon.'

'Meaning?' said Libby, after a pause.

'I don't know. He was angry.' Wilhelmina looked up. 'This is why I thought I'd talk to you.'

Libby regarded her silently for a moment, then heaved a deep sigh.

'Look, Willy,' she said, 'let's get this straight. You're not making much sense at the moment. Start from the beginning. You were married to John Lethbridge. He and Bill Frensham were friends, right?'

'Some kind of business connection,' said Wilhelmina. 'They knew one another before we got married.'

'Right. So did Bill suggest you both joined the coven?'

'I never belonged. I think John did, but there was this murder, you see –'

'We know about the murder,' said Fran.

'Oh, do you?' Wilhelmina looked surprised. 'Well, anyway, then John suggested this Goddess thing, and it sounded fun, you know, one up from wife swapping. Sort of gave it an extra – I don't know – thrill, somehow.'

'And you got too friendly with Bill Frensham?' said Libby.

'Yeah, well, he and me were the King and the Goddess and we had to do it.' She paused, gazing out of the window. 'In front of the others, too. They all pretended it was sort of religious, but it wasn't. They just used to get turned on and go off and shag each other.'

Libby glanced sideways at Fran's pained expression. 'So you and Bill carried on outside the group?' she said.

Wilhelmina nodded. 'And John found out and I left. The he took up with that Monica. To pay Bill out, I reckon.'

'And Diggory?'

'Oh, he'd always fancied me. We thought we might as well, but we had to keep it sort of secret because Richard was still in the group. But they couldn't get another Goddess like me, see?'

'Gemma certainly wouldn't be up for it,' said Libby.

'Well, no. But they had to keep the Goddess and King stuff going or the others would wonder what was going on.'

'The ordinary Morris dancers, you mean, the ones not involved in the – er – cult.'

Wilhelmina nodded again.

'So what happened then?' asked Fran after a short silence.

'Diggory wouldn't help me with any money,' said Wilhelmina, 'said he'd got a lot of other things on his plate. He was investing in his business, or something.' She shrugged. 'He always seemed to be out, if you ask me. Doing deliveries, he said.'

'Of his bread?' asked Libby.

'Yeah. So I thought I'd go and see John.' She looked down at her mug again. 'And he was – I don't know – strange. Different.'

'You said angry?' said Libby.

'Yeah. He kept striding about the place and

291

saying things.'

'Saying what?'

Wilhelmina's eyes slid sideways. 'Not really sure. Kept saying it was disgusting.'

'What was?' said Libby and Fran together.

'I don't know. Then he was talking about – you know – that night.'

'Beltane? He meant to go?'

'Well, he *did* go, didn't he? He was still a Morris dancer.' Wilhelmina's tone indicated that Morris dancing was on a par with drain cleaning.

'So what was disgusting?' pursued Libby.

'I've told you, I don't know.' She looked up at Libby and quickly away again. 'He mentioned Bill.'

'He said Bill was disgusting?' Libby was bewildered.

'I've *told* you! I don't know!' reiterated Wilhelmina, suddenly standing up. 'What I want to know is, do I tell the police?'

'Well, of course you should, even if it does seem insignificant to you,' said Libby. 'They'll want to know if he mentioned seeing anyone, or if he knew he would be doing something different that night. They'll also –' Libby stopped as a thought struck her.

'Also what?' asked Fran.

'Also be pleased to know that he was alive that afternoon,' said Libby slowly.

'Course he was,' said Wilhelmina. 'He was killed at night, wasn't he?'

'Yes.' Libby gave her a small smile. 'But they'll still be pleased to know.' She contemplated her hands for a moment. 'So why did you need my

292

advice about this, Willy? You knew what you should do. What is it you aren't telling us?'

'Nothing.' Wilhelmina sat down again. 'I just don't have experience with the police. I didn't know what to do.'

'Were you frightened?' asked Fran softly.

Wilhelmina looked up quickly.

'You are, aren't you?' said Libby. 'What of?'

'I'm not scared,' said Wilhelmina in a shaky voice. 'I just didn't know – didn't want – well, I didn't. I just didn't.'

'Were you scared of other people like Diggory finding out if you spilt the beans about the Goddess business?' asked Libby.

Wilhelmina's colour started changing again. She and Diggory were like human rainbows, thought Libby.

'That's what it is, isn't it?' said Fran. 'Well, I don't see why you should be scared, but you can rest assured we won't tell anyone.'

'Right.' Wilhelmina was looking down again. 'So what do I do?'

Libby looked at Fran. 'Would you like us to get in touch with the police for you?' she said. Fran sighed.

'Yeah.' Wilhelmina looked up. 'Will they come here?'

'I don't know. They might want you to go to the police station,' said Libby. Wilhelmina seemed to shrink. 'I expect they'll come here, though,' she continued hastily. 'They usually do. Haven't they been here to talk to you already?'

'Yeah. Last Saturday after I'd seen you, Diggory

was here with me.' Her eyes slid sideways again.

'Right,' said Libby. 'Well, I'll – we'll – get in touch with the police and they'll make an appointment to come and see you.' She stood up. 'Was there anything else?'

Wilhelmina shook her head.

'We'll be on our way, then,' said Fran, also standing up. 'Thank you for talking to us, Wilhelmina, and don't worry.'

Out on the pavement, Libby let out a long breath. 'Cor,' she said. 'That was a bit difficult, wasn't it?'

'She's hiding something, isn't she?' said Fran, beginning to walk back towards the seafront.

'Sure she is,' agreed Libby, 'but hadn't we better phone Ian before she changes her mind about speaking to the police? I almost wanted to camp out there until they turned up.'

Fran nodded. 'For a variety of reasons.'

'Really?'

'Just let me call Ian,' said Fran, pulling out her mobile.

Libby waited impatiently while Fran left a message on Ian's personal mobile and another at his office. 'What then?' she said as Fran put the phone away. 'What other reasons?'

'Do you want that ice cream?' asked Fran as they reached the promenade.

'No! I want you to tell me what you mean,' said Libby, leading the way to a bench overlooking the beach.

'She was scared. We both agreed that.' Fran brushed the worst of the damp from the bench with a tissue before sitting down. 'She's scared that someone will find out she's been talking.'

'Who, though? Diggory? What they're doing isn't illegal is it? I mean, I know I told them last week the Black Mass was illegal, but it doesn't sound as though they're doing that. In fact, apart from the Cornish goings-on, it doesn't sound as though they're doing much at all. Why should anyone worry if the police found out about a bit of extra-marital shenanigans?'

'I'm not sure it's just that,' said Fran. 'She's scared of something else. I think Lethbridge said more to her that day than she's telling us.'

Libby frowned. 'Even if he did, nobody knows. Why is she scared?'

'Because of what he said. If he told her something was going on and she was – oh, I don't know – in the firing line?'

'In that case the best thing she could do would be to tell the police. Then they can go and arrest whoever it is,' said Libby.

'I don't think it's as simple as that,' said Fran. 'And unless she tells the truth, which she probably won't, I would think she's in danger.'

Chapter Thirty-one

'WHAT DID YOU MEAN,' said Fran, as they parted at Libby's car, 'when you said the police would be glad to know he was alive in the afternoon?'

'It suddenly occurred to me that he could easily have been killed earlier in the day. It didn't have to be during the Beltane thing.'

'But he was in full black-faced regalia,' said Fran. 'And it felt dark when I first – well, saw him.'

'It threw her, though,' said Libby. 'Do you think she was doing something she shouldn't?'

'I think she spends a good deal of her time doing things she shouldn't,' said Fran. 'I just want to know what Lethbridge was talking about.'

'If she was telling the truth,' said Libby.

'Oh, I think she was,' said Fran. 'About him being angry, anyway. And about calling Frensham disgusting.' She wrinkled her brow. 'It doesn't make sense.'

'A bit pot and kettle if you ask me.' Libby unlocked Romeo's door. 'I must get going. I said I'd meet Ben at the Manor at one o'clock. Let me know when you hear from Ian.'

It wasn't until Libby and Ben had stopped off at Peter and Harry's cottage on the way home from the Manor that Libby's mobile rang.

'I thought you'd be home by now,' said Fran. 'I've just left a message on the landline.'

'No, we often stop off at Pete and Harry's,' said Libby. 'What's up? Did you hear from Ian?' She struggled out of her sagging armchair and making "excuse me" signs in the air wandered into Harry's kitchen.

'I did. He was quite nice about it.'

'Has he followed it up, though?'

'He said he would. Said it was "interesting". He asked if we had any ideas about Frensham being disgusting, too.'

'Perhaps he should ask Monica,' said Libby, 'although I can't see her answering. And she said Lethbridge was kind, didn't she? Perhaps he meant the way Frensham treated his wife was disgusting?'

'But hadn't that affair stopped? Lethbridge and Monica, I mean?'

'Do we know that?' Libby frowned. 'Or did we assume it?'

'Oh, heaven knows,' said Fran wearily. 'Let's leave it to Ian. Nothing we can do about it now.'

Libby switched off her phone and stood staring at Harry's colourful shelves.

'Whassup, petal?' He came in and picked up various bottles from the dresser. 'Still figuring out whodunnit?'

'More or less.' She grinned at him. 'But Fran and I have dumped everything in Ian's lap and now it's up to him.'

'That'll be the day,' said Harry. 'Come on, now, drinkie-poos time. Wine or whisky?'

It was Monday morning before Libby heard from Fran again. Twice she'd dialled her number, but both times it was engaged. Knowing her friend's habit of forgetting her mobile entirely, she didn't bother trying to ring that. Instead, after a little desultory dusting, she went into the conservatory and stared at paintings for a while. When the phone rang, she jumped.

'Oh, it's you!' she said.

'Were you expecting someone else?' said Fran.

'No, it's just I've been trying to get hold of you this morning and you were engaged.'

'Sorry, I'm sure,' said Fran, laughing. 'I expect I was talking to Ian.'

'What did he say?' Libby went into the kitchen and moved the kettle onto the hotplate.

'He interviewed Wilhelmina last night.'

Libby let her breath out in a whoosh. 'That's a relief,' she said. 'I was dreading him finding her dead body instead.'

'I know. But apparently after I spoke to him he called her and she was still there, so he arranged to go round in the evening. Told her not to go out. But apparently she said she wasn't moving from the flat anyway.'

'She was scared. So what did she say?'

'As far as I can make out, exactly what she told us. It hasn't taken him much further, he says, except he's now wondering what it was about Bill Frensham that was disgusting, too. I told him you said he should ask Monica, and he said he intended to.'

'I'd like to be a fly on the wall in that interview,' said Libby. 'Anything else?'

'Well, there was one thing that he wasn't sure about. Apparently, Wilhelmina said that Lethbridge had said something like "positively Wagnerian".

She didn't say that to us, did she?'

'No,' said Libby, slowly. 'Was she referring to Frensham, or what?'

'Lethbridge said it while he was ranting and muttering, she said. She didn't get "Wagnerian" right, but Ian eventually translated it.'

'Perhaps he was referring to her,' suggested Libby doubtfully. 'You know, her name. Wilhelmina sounds Wagnerian, doesn't it?'

'Maybe, but I don't think Ian thought so. Any ideas?'

'Not right now,' said Libby. 'If you refer to something as "positively Wagnerian", what would you mean? Very heavy and long?'

'That sounds like a crowbar,' said Fran. 'What did he write?'

'Um, the Maestersingers? Was that him?'

'Oh, yes, of Nuremburg. Wasn't it? And the Ring Cycle.'

'Oh, of course. Brunnhilde, the one with the plaits and the breastplate.' Libby giggled. 'That's what you'd call Wagnerian. The voice.'

'Hmmm. Well, perhaps if Wilhelmina was going on at him and her voice got out of control that's what he meant?'

'Willy's voice just gets brash and hard. Sort of high,' said Libby, 'not what you'd call Wagnerian.'

Fran sighed. 'I don't know, then. He said would we think about it. Seemed to think it meant something.'

'Perhaps he was fond of opera. Could we ask Monica, do you think?'

'I expect Ian already has. I'll call him and tell

him what thoughts we've had so far and then ask him.'

'OK,' said Libby. 'Call me as soon as you know.'

She switched off the phone and stood staring at the kettle, now emitting irritated puffs of steam. She moved it back off the hotplate and turned to the window. Now she didn't know what to do.

'Women,' she muttered to herself, turning back to the sitting room. 'That's what Fran thought. Something to do with a woman. Which woman? Monica? Wilhelmina? Or Elizabeth Martin?'

She stood stock still. Of course! Elizabeth Martin! With her statuesque looks and fiery red hair. Wagnerian.

So how could she get to Elizabeth Martin? Both she and Ben were persona non grata at Frensham Holdings, even with the pleasant Barry Phillips, she suspected. Perhaps she could talk to Trisha?

The phone rang again.

'Libby, it's Ian.'

'Blimey,' said Libby, not bothering to hide her surprise. 'What do you want?'

'That's a fine way to greet an old friend,' said Ian, sounding amused.

'You're not an old friend,' said Libby. 'I've only known you a couple of years.'

'Don't quibble. Now listen. I know I said I didn't want you anywhere near this case, but, as usual, you and Fran have proved yourselves useful. So I want you to do something else for me. Completely off the record, of course.'

'What? I don't have my handcuffs with me,

'currently.'

'I want you to talk to Monica Frensham.'

Libby felt a frisson of apprehension. 'Why? What about?'

'Because she'll probably know what Lethbridge meant about being Wagnerian. Did he actually know his opera or was it just a phrase – a cliché.'

'I was just thinking about that,' said Libby. 'I wondered if he was referring to Elizabeth Martin. She's a fiery redhead. Could that be Wagnerian?'

'The avenging warrior queen. Yes, I suppose so.'

'But I don't see what he had to do with her. Or whether he was just talking about Frensham having had an affair with her.'

'No – unless there was some reason he shouldn't have.'

'Of course there was,' scoffed Libby. 'He was married.'

'But Lethbridge had an affair with Frensham's wife. He was in no position to disapprove.'

'I see what you mean,' said Libby. 'You mean another criminal reason?'

'I don't know either, but yes,' said Ian. 'But meanwhile, I want you to ask Monica if she knows what Lethbridge meant. Will you do that?'

'Just me?' squeaked Libby. 'Without Fran?'

'Fran's got cold feet, I think,' said Ian. 'She sounded very distant just now.'

'Perhaps she was being tactful because Guy was there.'

'I didn't think he minded her getting involved in your Miss Marple outings?' said Ian, in some surprise.

'He doesn't, but I think he's still a bit jealous of you,' said Libby. 'I hope you don't mind me saying.'

Ian chuckled. 'Not at all.'

'So again, pardon me for asking, but why aren't you going to talk to Monica?'

'Because it's a very small question within a very big case, and I'm snowed under. We've also got this drugs distribution ring we're trying to track down at the moment, which, of course, I didn't tell you about.'

'No.' Libby nodded to herself sagely. 'Of course not.'

'So, will you do it?'

'Yes.' Libby took a deep breath. 'As soon as possible, I suppose?'

When Ian had rung off, she frowned at the phone wondering if she should call Fran. How would she feel if Ian asked Fran to do something without her? Which of course, he had done, earlier in their association. But Fran had always apprised her of whatever the situation was. She punched in the number.

'He said you sounded distant,' said Libby, when she'd finished telling Fran what Ian had asked her to do.

'Nothing to do with him,' said Fran. 'Chrissie's here.'

'Omigod.'

'Quite. Can you cope on your own? I've got something you might want to hear, so I'll call you as soon as I'm able.'

'You don't want moral support?'

'I don't think she'd appreciate that,' said Fran, with a sigh. 'She's just sent Guy off with a flea in his ear.'

'Bloody cheek!'

'I know, but the quicker I listen the quicker – I'll have to go.'

'OK. Speak to you later.' Libby switched off the phone and frowned at it again. Whatever did Chrissie want? She sighed and went back to the kitchen. Time to formulate a plan.

The trouble was, Libby wasn't good at formulating plans. She needed Fran there to bounce ideas back and forth. The first thing, she supposed, was whether to ring Monica first or not. She could always ask her the question over the phone, although she rather thought Ian would want her to do it face to face. Anyway, it was a start.

'Will you be in this afternoon?' asked Libby, after introducing herself.

'Yes, up till about three,' said Monica. 'Why?'

'Inspector Connell has asked me to ask you a couple of questions,' said Libby.

'Did he not want to ask them himself?' Monica's voice had turned frosty.

'He's so busy – working on your husband's death, of course – and as this is a tiny little query he deputised me.'

'Oh.' Monica went quiet. 'Nothing very serious, then?'

'It could be,' said Libby. 'Can I pop over, then? I won't keep you long.'

'Oh, all right,' said Monica grudgingly, 'but make it before two thirty. I'm supposed to be at

Anderson Place just after three.'

'Oh, really? Are you going to see Sir Jonathan? He told me he had quite a soft spot for you.'

'Did he?' Monica audibly softened. 'You know him, then?'

'Oh, yes, quite well. Give him my love. I actually saw him on Saturday, but not for long enough.'

'I tell you what,' said Monica, obviously thinking as she spoke, 'why don't you come over here and ask your questions, then we could both go and have tea with Sir Jonathan.'

'That would be lovely,' said Libby, 'but I wouldn't want to intrude.'

'Oh, you wouldn't be,' said Monica blithely. 'He'd be delighted, you know he would.'

'All right then,' said Libby. 'I'll be at yours around a quarter to three. OK?'

How surprising, she thought, as she went into the kitchen to find herself some lunch.

The journey took slightly longer this time than last, partly because Libby was distracted by some particularly lovely views, which she had to stop and look at. This was the part of Kent the tourists didn't see, the tiny lanes that would give Devon a run for its money. The real country, with real country people, real farmers and real villagers, not incomers (she felt a pang of guilt at this) who bought up and prettified the cottages and priced the locals out of the market. Or built houses like this, she thought, as she turned once more onto Monica Frensham's gravelled drive.

Monica, in pale green to match her furniture,

opened the front door, a sparkling smile on her face.

'So nice to see you again!' she said. 'Do come in for a moment. I won't offer tea, as we'll have some at Anderson Place.'

'Thank you,' said Libby, sitting in the same place as before. 'It was very nice of you to agree to see me.'

Monica shrugged. 'To tell you the truth, I've hardly seen anybody. At first I couldn't bear to talk to anyone, except the children, but now I wouldn't mind some company, most people seem afraid to talk to me. That was why I was so grateful to receive Sir Jonathan's invitation.'

'He's an old sweetie, isn't he?' said Libby, and found herself telling Monica about her previous adventure involving him and Anderson Place. 'And he's already offered to help with this investigation,' she finished.

'Really? You've talked to him about it?' Monica's tone became fractionally colder.

'Oh, no, not really. You see Fran and I were at a hen party there and one of the other guests worked for your husband's company.' Libby hoped this rather incomplete version of events would satisfy Monica. It did.

'Oh, I see!' she said. 'Who was it? Might I know them?'

'A girl called Trisha,' said Libby. 'I think she works for Barry Phillips?'

Monica was frowning. 'Trisha? Is she blonde?'

'Ye-es. Rather a nice girl. A bit – um – ditsy, I suppose you might call it. She used to work with the girl who was getting married.'

305

'Ah, yes!' Monica's face cleared. 'Not that I know her well, of course, but I did meet her. Now, what was it you wanted to ask me?'

'Well, it's a bit delicate,' said Libby, clearing her throat. 'We need to ask you something about John Lethbridge.' She stopped as she saw Monica's face change. 'No, please, it's just that you knew him better than anyone else we've talked to.'

'Except Wilhelmina,' said Monica.

'That's just it. We and the police have talked to Wilhelmina, and we rather think you knew him better than she did.'

A faint expression of gratification passed over Monica's face. 'In some ways,' she said.

'He made a comment, in Wilhelmina's hearing, about something being positively Wagnerian. Now,' said Libby, leaning forward, 'this probably sounds pathetic and petty, but she had no idea what he meant, didn't even know what Wagnerian was. In view of the comment, the police would like to know if John really knew Wagner, or if it was just a – a – oh, you know, a well-known phrase or saying.'

Monica frowned. 'You're right, it does sound pathetic and petty, but I'll take your word for it. John loved opera. It was one taste we shared, although I prefer the ballet. So if he described something as Wagnerian, that's what he meant. In the true sense of the word.'

'And what would that be? In your opinion, of course.'

'Wagnerian? Oh, large, grand. In fact Grand Guignol, almost. Perhaps without the horror.'

'We thought of Brunnhilde,' said Libby. 'She'd

306

be the female personification of Wagnerian, wouldn't she?'

'She would!' Monica clapped her hands, delighted. 'You know your Wagner, too, then.'

'The Ring Cycle, yes,' said Libby modestly, not admitting that her knowledge was based on the extremely funny Anna Russell explanation she had on a CD at home.

'Have you ever seen it?'

'No,' said Libby, 'and I can't say I'd want to sit through all twenty hours at once, either.'

'You have to do it on consecutive days,' said Monica. 'We did it – John and I – about a year ago.' She bowed her head. 'When we were getting to know each other.'

'Oh.' Libby made a face. 'I'm so sorry. I didn't mean –'

'It's all right.' Monica looked up. 'He wasn't mine, was he. I shouldn't be mourning him. I have my husband to mourn.'

Oh, goodness, thought Libby.

'Anyway,' Monica went on, sitting up straight and smoothing her brown hair, 'that's what John would have meant.' She paused, looking thoughtful.

'Have you thought of something?' asked Libby, after a moment.

'No.' Monica's eyes refocused. 'Sorry. I was just remembering. Shall we go?'

You weren't just remembering, thought Libby, as she stood up. You just thought of something. I wonder what it was?

Chapter Thirty-two

THEY TOOK BOTH CARS, although Monica offered to
drive Libby, but Libby wanted the means to make a
quick getaway. As Monica had predicted, Sir
Jonathan was delighted to see Libby, and took them
upstairs to his room on the first floor, where tea
things had already been laid out.

'I'll just boil the kettle,' he said disappearing into
a cubbyhole at the other end of the room.

'It's lovely here, isn't it,' said Monica, gazing
round.

'He's got an apartment right at the top of the
building, too,' said Libby. 'I think he's been very
clever turning what could have been an albatross
into such a thriving business.'

'I didn't do it all on my own, you know.' Sir
Jonathan came up behind them, beaming at Libby.
He put the silver teapot down on the tray.

'So, my dear, thank you for coming to see me.'
He handed Monica a cup. 'I was so sorry when I
heard of Bill's death. He was a good customer who
became a friend. A good supplier, too, of course.'

'Was he?' Monica looked puzzled.

'He set up their website,' said Libby. 'And did
the marketing.'

'And office supplies, of course,' said Sir
Jonathan. 'Always came personally to see me, even
though I don't really have anything to do with the
business. Our Melanie came via Frensham
Holdings, as well.'

A light went on inside Libby's head. Why hadn't she thought of asking Mel?

'I'm afraid I didn't realise,' Monica was saying. 'I only ever came here to functions. Bill never discussed the business with me. That's why –' she stopped.

Sir Jonathan quirked an eyebrow at Libby, who made a face.

'Why you want to find out what's going on there?' she suggested.

'Exactly.' Monica turned to her in relief. 'I told you, didn't I? That Elizabeth Martin is making it very difficult.'

'Forgive me, my dear,' said Sir Jonathan, 'but surely you're now the majority shareholder?'

'That doesn't mean to say they can tell me what's going on,' said Monica. 'I think Barry – Mr Phillips – would, but Mrs Martin, well, she just wants to keep me out of everything.' She shrugged. 'I don't know what she doesn't want me to find.'

Sir Jonathan frowned. 'I wish I could help,' he said, shooting another interrogative glance at Libby. 'I don't know the lady well enough.'

'You've met her, though?' Monica looked up.

'Oh, yes, at functions here, like yourself. I got the impression that she was taking over the supplies part of the business.'

'From whom?' Monica's voice went right up the scale.

'Well – your husband –'

'I meant who did you hear it from?'

'Ah – I'm afraid I don't know.' He was looking uncomfortable now. 'Someone in the office, I assume.'

'That's all right, Monica, we can find out,' soothed Libby. 'Don't worry about it now.' She smiled brightly at Sir Jonathan. 'Lovely cake,' she said, taking a slice.

'I'm sorry,' said Monica, shaking her head. 'I don't know what gets into me.'

Libby patted her hand. 'Your husband was murdered, that's what's got into you. It's enough to cope with by itself, without any added business complications. Now, cheer up and have some of this lovely cake.'

The tea party then resolved itself into more conventional terms. Sir Jonathan was the perfect host and treated Monica like precious china, so much so that by the time Libby deemed it suitable to take her leave, she was quite happy to stay when Sir Jonathan pressed her to a fresh pot of tea. Libby said goodbye and was accompanied to the door by Sir Jonathan.

'Thank you for smoothing over the awkward moment,' he said quietly. 'I wasn't sure what to do.'

'She's desperate to find out what's going on in the company,' whispered Libby, 'and to find out what happened to the man who they thought was Bill's killer.'

'And wasn't he?'

'No, it turns out he was already dead,' said Libby.

'Oh, dear.' Sir Jonathan pulled at his white moustache. 'I'll do what I can to keep her mind off it. But I really think they ought to let her into the business.'

'So do I,' said Libby, 'but they aren't keen on anyone getting inside, customers or shareholders.'

'Oh?' Sir Jonathan raised his eyebrows. 'We'll have to see about that, or I'll be changing my suppliers.'

'Is it all right if I pop in to see Mel?' asked Libby.

'Of course.' Sir Jonathan kissed her cheek. 'Take care, my dear.'

All that old world charm, thought Libby, as she walked down the staircase. If only I were older.

Melanie was found in her office at the end of the main corridor on the ground floor, looking far more like the Mel Libby had first met with Harry. Obviously not on front of house duties today, she was dressed in torn jeans, a studded leather collar and a T-shirt.

'I just wanted to ask you a couple of questions about Frensham Holdings, actually, if you don't mind,' said Libby, after the niceties were out of the way.

Mel put her booted feet on the desk and raised her eyebrows. 'Oh? Mrs Sarjeant Investigates?'

'Oh, you've heard.'

'We could hardly avoid it, could we? So what do you want to know?'

'I'm not really sure,' said Libby. 'Anything you remember from your days working for them.'

Mel put her feet down and leant her elbows on the desk. 'I didn't work for them,' she said. 'I worked for another of their clients. And I find this job far more congenial. More freedom. As far as I could see they didn't ever seem to let anybody know

311

what was going on.'

'Mmm.' Libby nodded. 'That's what Mrs Frensham's finding now.'

'Mrs Frensham?' Mel looked surprised. 'In the business?'

'Well, no,' said Libby. 'They won't let her get near it, even though she's the majority shareholder.'

'She was never interested before. At least that's what we were told. And Elizabeth Martin would never let anyone near old Bill, anyway.'

'Were they having an affair back then?'

'We all thought so, but there was another woman as well. We saw her a couple of times.'

'Blonde? A bit tarty?'

'That's her.'

'Wilhelmina Lethbridge,' said Libby, and told Mel all about it.

'We've had a couple of deliveries of office supplies since Bill died,' said Mel when she'd finished, 'but they've been using a third party delivery service. They used to come with someone in a car. Often it was Bill himself. Keeping in with old Jonathan, I think.'

'Yes, Sir Jonathan said he made personal visits. You don't sound as though you were over-smitten, though.'

'No.' Mel shook her head. 'Always felt there was something funny about the company. I mean, Barry Phillips was good at his job, and they had some good people working there, but, I don't know, the Supplies division always seemed a bit run down, if you know what I mean. I don't know if that was the first part of the company Bill set up, and then got

312

into marketing and media and lost interest. That's a bit what it felt like.'

'Well, somehow or other Monica's got to get in and find out. She may want to sell. I think I would, if it was me.'

'If the business is in good shape,' said Mel. 'They've been in trouble recently.'

'Really? My partner said he had a bad time getting money out of them. Perhaps that's it. Perhaps they don't want Monica to see the balance sheets.'

Libby was thoughtful as she walked out to the car. Had Ian looked into that? Had they put in a forensic accountant, or whatever they were? Was it fraud? She sighed, unlocked the car door and got in. And stopped. Just ahead of her was a white van with a logo she'd seen before. Diggory's. And sitting in the passenger seat was a woman she'd seen before. Elizabeth Martin.

The van drove off before she could even think about what to do, or what it meant. All she wanted to do was talk to Fran. And Ian, but preferably Fran. She shut the door, put on the seat belt and started the engine. Would Diggory have recognised her car? No, of course he wouldn't. And Martin had only seen it in the car park of Frensham Barn, and was unlikely to have taken any notice of it.

She drove carefully home, slightly shaken by what she'd seen and what she'd heard. Sidney welcomed her from the stairs, and, despite the two cups of Earl Grey she'd drunk at Anderson Place, she went straight to the kitchen and switched on the electric kettle. No time now to wait for the cast-iron one, a cup of strong builder's tea was what was needed.

When she had the mug in her hands, she called Fran.

'Are you free to talk?'

'Yes. Chrissie's upstairs in the spare room.' Fran sounded gloomy. 'With Cassandra.'

'Cassandra? The cat? Why? What's happened?'

'She's walked out on Brucie baby, that's what happened.'

'No! Omigod, Fran, that's terrible. She doesn't mean to move in with you, surely?'

Fran sighed. 'I think that's what she intended when she turned up on the doorstep this morning.'

'But she couldn't! There isn't room, and what about Balzac? He'd hate having Cassandra around. Remember when I had him here with Sidney?'

'As far as I could tell,' said Fran, 'she rather expected me to get rid of both Guy and Balzac.'

Libby exploded into laughter. 'You're not serious.'

'Oh, but I am. I told you she sent Guy off because she needed to, as she put it, "talk to her mother without non-family members butting in". Then she said "Put that thing out. I need to let Cassandra out of her basket."'

'So what did you do?'

'I said it was Balzac's home, and as far as I was concerned, Cassandra could stay in her basket until – and this was a master stroke – she went home.'

'And?'

'And then she broke down and said she wasn't going home. I made her tea and calmed her down a bit. That was when you rang. Then I had to listen to her for hours. Finally I told her to go and have a lie down before she drove herself home. She still wouldn't believe I wasn't going to let her stay.'

'I suppose you could, Fran. Just for a day or two.'

Fran sighed again. 'I know. She is my daughter, after all, but she's hardly been good to me, has she? And now I've heard the whole story, I think they'd be better sitting down and talking it through.'

'So what's been the problem, then?'

'She's suddenly decided she wants children. Or rather – A Baby.'

'Ah! And Brucie baby doesn't.'

'Well, quite rightly, he's confused. Cassandra was their baby – and how she'll take an addition to the family I dread to think – and they'd discussed it before and after they got married.'

'But you can't gainsay the old biological clock,' said Libby.

'No. And living here isn't going to make it go away, either. So tell me, what happened at Monica's?'

So Libby told her.

'Elizabeth Martin and Richard Diggory? But they come from different sides of the story,' said Fran.

'In a way, but they're both linked to Bill Frensham,' said Libby.

'It doesn't make any sense,' said Fran. 'Elizabeth Martin and Diggory. I don't get it.'

'Neither do I,' said Libby, 'but it can't have anything to do with my other thought, could it?'

'About fraud? I doubt it. You think Martin's trying to keep Monica away because they've been cooking the books?'

'Well, that would bring Diggory in, wouldn't it?' giggled Libby.

'Libby! It's a possibility and makes more sense than anything else. Have you rung Ian yet?'

'No. I'll do that after you. What do you think he'll say?'

'Thank you and goodnight, probably,' said Fran.

But Ian didn't. When he finally returned Libby's call, he listened attentively.

'Well done, Libby,' he said. Libby pretended to faint for her own amusement. 'I'll be round in about an hour. Have the kettle on.'

Chapter Thirty-three

IAN TURNED UP JUST as Ben and Libby were sitting down to supper.

'Honestly, Ian,' said Libby as she ushered him into the sitting room. 'Your timing's awful. I haven't got enough to offer you supper, and I refuse to let it get cold. So you'll have to sit here on your own until we're finished.'

'Can I watch television?' asked Ian with a grin. 'I never get the chance.'

Libby handed him the remote. 'Do you want tea? Coffee?'

'I'll have a coffee when you're ready,' said Ian, settling back on the sofa, 'but don't rush.'

'He's got a nerve,' muttered Ben, as Libby returned to the table.

'Not really,' said Libby peaceably. 'We're always trying to muscle in on his cases, and if he's nice enough to let us help the least I can do is let him watch our television.'

'*Our* television?' Ben gave her a crooked smile. 'That's a turn-up.'

Libby coloured. 'Well, of course it is,' she said. 'Now, eat up.'

When she took coffee into the sitting room, she had to shake Ian awake.

'Sorry,' he said. 'Haven't had much sleep recently.'

Ben carried the remainder of the wine in and put it and their glasses on the table in the window. 'Like a glass?' he asked, not too grudgingly.

'No, thanks. I'm driving. But thanks for the coffee, Libby.'

'That's OK.' Libby sat on the other end of the sofa. 'What do you want to know?'

'Tell me again what happened this afternoon.'

Libby told him again of her afternoon's meetings with Monica, Sir Jonathan and Melanie, followed by her sighting of Diggory and Elizabeth Martin and her subsequent conversation with Fran.

'And that's all?'

'What else? What were you expecting?'

Ian frowned. 'I was hoping Monica might understand the Wagnerian reference.'

'She said he knew his opera. Oh, and they went to see the Ring Cycle together when they were first – well, you know.'

'I expect they went to a lot of things at that time. Kept them out of the way of people they knew.'

'For a long time,' said Libby.

'Eh?'

'The Ring Cycle takes between fifteen and twenty hours to perform,' said Libby, watching Ben's and Ian's faces in amusement.

'What? You have to sit in a theatre for nearly a whole day?' said Ben in disbelief.

'No – it's four operas. Sometimes they're performed on consecutive days, sometimes independently.'

'Did Monica think the reference had anything to do with this Ring Cycle?'

'She didn't say so. You merely asked me to find out what he meant by "positively Wagnerian", not which specific piece.'

'Yes, sorry,' said Ian.

'What about Frensham Holdings?' asked Ben. 'I wasn't altogether happy with them as a customer.'

'You were a customer?'

'No they were clients of mine,' said Ben. 'I designed the conversion of Frensham Barn for them, then they adapted it and didn't want to pay me.'

'Ah.' Ian nodded. 'We've uncovered quite a bit about Frensham Holdings actually, and none of it good.'

'Really?' said Libby. 'You didn't tell me!'

'You're not on the force, Libby. I don't have to tell you things.' Ian smiled at her.

'No.' Libby looked down, embarrassed. 'But we've been trying to find out about the place – I even went there, didn't I? I thought you might have told me.'

'There is definitely something going on at Frensham Supplies,' said Ian. 'We're getting a warrant. We need a forensic audit.'

'I said that to Fran!' Libby said in triumph. 'That's why they want to keep Monica out of the business, isn't it?'

Ian frowned. 'It's possible, but I'm not sure it's necessarily false accounting. Well, not in the ordinary way.'

'So what is it?' Libby peered at him, eyes narrowed. 'Oh, I see. You can't tell me.' She looked across at Ben and grinned. 'How about if I make a guess?'

'I can't stop you,' said Ian, putting his mug down.

'You're investigating a local drugs ring, aren't you?'

Ian became very still.

'You told me that yourself,' said Libby. 'That was why you were so busy. Now I know you're often on more than one serious crime, but it struck me that this could easily have something to do with Frensham Holdings, couldn't it?'

'That's a bit of a leap of faith, Lib,' said Ben. 'How on earth did you come up with that?'

'I can't remember now,' said Libby, wrinkling her forehead, 'but it's sort of been in the background for ages. Oh – and I've just remembered!'

'What?' said Ian and Ben together.

'Harry told me. How could I have forgotten? He said Richard Diggory had started taking orders for Frensham Supplies. He told me days ago. That must be why I saw him and Elizabeth Martin at Anderson Place. Mel said they had courier deliveries now Bill Frensham no longer came to see them himself.'

'He delivered himself?' said Ian.

'Probably only to Anderson Place. He liked to keep in with Sir Jonathan, apparently.'

'Well, I'm not surprised,' said Ian grimly. 'I doubt very much if they needed a fleet of vehicles, or even salesmen.'

'Oh?' Libby looked puzzled.

'The little we have managed to see indicates that there *were* virtually no supplies. They must have bought in just enough to keep people like Sir Jonathan happy.'

'You mean they had no customers?' Ben was frowning.

'Not Frensham Supplies, no. Or rather, only a few. From before the new divisions started.'

'Media and Marketing,' said Libby. 'Yes, that's what Mel thought. She said Supplies seemed rundown. So why keep it going?'

'Come on, Miss Marple,' said Ben with a grin. 'Simple isn't it? As a cover.'

'Oh!' Libby looked annoyed. 'Bugger. Of course. So was he supplying drugs? Bill, I mean?'

'We've got our suspicions,' said Ian. 'He went out on deliveries but only made a few, rare genuine ones. So where else did he go?'

'How do you know he went out?' said Libby.

'That came out in our first round of questioning,' said Ian.

'So someone knew what was going on – and killed him for it?'

'In that case, John Lethbridge's murder is unconnected, which seems unlikely.'

'Round and round the mulberry bush,' said Ben, sounding a trifle impatient.

Libby scowled at him and Ian grinned. 'Absolutely right,' he said, and stood up. 'For what it's worth, I think Lethbridge was blackmailing someone. That's why he was talking about something being disgusting.'

'That doesn't make sense, either,' said Libby. 'If he was going round muttering when Wilhelmina got there it sounds as though he'd only just found out about whatever it was, so how could he have already been blackmailing someone?'

'He'd let someone know, then,' said Ian. 'And it was something important enough to be killed for.

Meanwhile, I have to find out more about both victims, so anything you can think of, let me know.'

'But haven't you already investigated Bill Frensham thoroughly?'

'Of course. But that was with the possibility of Lethbridge being the murderer.'

'So you were concentrating on Lethbridge and Monica?'

'Not solely.' Ian stood up. 'As I said, we now need to go a little deeper into both their lives. Find a connection.'

'Which has to be Monica,' said Libby. 'She was married to Bill and had an affair with Ian.'

'Which was over, as far as we can find out.'

'Have you looked at the gardeners' shed?' said Libby as she held the front door open.

Ian looked confused. 'Gardeners' shed?'

'At Frensham Barn. It was mentioned to me by Barry Phillips. They had a burglary there, but Bill Frensham wouldn't make anything of it. Didn't even report it to the police.'

'What? Why haven't I been told about this?' Ian's dark eyes almost flashed.

'Why should you have been? If it wasn't reported to the police, and there was no reason for you to investigate Frensham Barn.'

'I'll get on to it,' said Ian and began to walk to his car. 'Oh,' he said, turning back, 'and thanks, Libby.'

Libby returned to the sitting room and sat down on the sofa. 'I still don't get it,' she said.

Ben came and joined her. 'You don't need to. You've helped Ian, both of you. Now just let him get on with finding the culprit.'

'I can't get over the fact that the police don't seem to have done enough research into Frensham's life before this. That's the most important part of the investigation, isn't it? Finding out the victim's secrets, who they met, what they did. All that. Ian didn't even seem to know about the Goddess Cult and all those unsavoury practices.' She looked thoughtfully at the empty fireplace. 'Or perhaps he did and just hasn't told us. But he didn't mention it when I told him about my trip to Cornwall.'

'As he said, Lib, you aren't on the force and he doesn't have to tell you everything. Now come on, forget it. Let's see what's on the box. Take your mind off it.'

But Libby couldn't forget it. After Ben had gone to the Manor the following morning, she left a message on Gemma's mobile. Gemma would be teaching this morning, she knew, but maybe she would ring back at lunchtime. Then she called Barry Phillips, but only succeeded in reaching Trisha.

'They've been here again,' she whispered. 'The police. Did you tell them what I said?'

'Unofficially, yes,' said Libby, 'but don't worry. Your name wasn't linked to anything.' She crossed her fingers. 'It's just that now another body has been found they have to make even more enquiries.'

'Oh, no!' Trisha's voice wobbled. 'Is that why they've been into Supplies this morning?'

'I don't know,' said Libby. 'What did they want?'

'I don't know. Mrs Martin dealt with it.'

'Oh, yes. She would.'

'Yes. Look, I'm sorry to rush you, but I've got to get on. Can I take a message for Mr Phillips?'

'No, it's fine,' said Libby, not wanting to mention the gardeners' shed to anyone else. 'I'll try him again later.'

Fran wasn't answering either her landline or her mobile, and when Libby called Guy's shop, she learnt that she had volunteered to go back to Chrissie's house and try to mediate between the warring factions.

'With Cassandra commenting all the while, I suppose,' said Libby.

'That bloody cat. Kept me awake all night. God knows what it'll be like if Chrissie does have a baby.'

'Perhaps they'll have to give it away. It won't like the competition.'

'The baby or the cat?' growled Guy.

Libby put the phone down and wandered round the sitting room. Something was niggling at the edges of her mind, and she couldn't pin it down. Something that Ian had said last night, possibly? She leaned against the table in the window and stared out at the lane. Something she herself had said? She sighed and looked at her watch. Nowhere near lunchtime yet, so Gemma wouldn't be ringing back. What could she do until then? The obvious thing was to do what she had been going to ask Barry Phillips permission for, visit the gardeners' shed.

But just as she had locked the back door and found the car keys, the phone rang.

'Libby? It's Gemma.' She sounded breathless

and flustered. 'What's the matter?'

'Nothing's the matter, Gem. I didn't expect you to call me until at least lunchtime.'

'I thought – well, I thought something had happened,' said Gemma. 'Diggory's been ringing me.'

'Oh, dear. Renewing his suit?'

'In a way. Oh, Libby, you were right. He's quite horrible. He's been calling you names behind your back, too.'

'I'm not surprised,' said Libby. 'I've managed to uncover the nasty little group he and Bill were running under cover of Cranston Morris and more. At least, I think so.'

'We've been hearing about that,' said Gemma, sounding shaky. 'Is it to do with those sacrifices?'

'No, I think they were just to put people off the scent. They were doing sort of Black Mass things. Very nasty.'

'Oh, my God. Thank you for finding that out Libby. I don't know how we shall be able to carry on, now.' She took a breath. 'And was that why Bill was killed? He said he'd had a letter that morning.'

Libby froze. 'What?' she said eventually. 'What did you say?'

'What did I say? Which bit?'

'About a letter.'

'Oh, that. When we arrived for the start of the May Day parade Bill was cross. He was talking to Diggory and didn't seem his usual self. Dan asked him what was the matter and he said it didn't matter, he'd had a letter that morning, and he'd deal with it later.'

'Didn't you tell the police?' Libby almost shrieked. 'For God's sake, Gemma, don't you see how important that was?'

Gemma sounded even shakier now. 'No, why? What could a letter matter?'

'Because it was probably the reason he was killed, you idiot! Because the police could have been looking for that letter from the moment he was found.'

'Oh, God.' Now she sounded close to tears. 'I just didn't think. I'd forgotten all about it until now.'

'Never mind,' said Libby, 'I'll tell the police. Did they ask you about Lethbridge?'

'Yes. All I could tell them was John must have been late. There was a gap in the formation before we started, but when I looked back everyone was there.'

'Only it wasn't John, was it, because he was already dead.'

This time Gemma really did break down and Libby had to spend a good deal of time calming her down.

'Look, shouldn't you be in class now?' she asked eventually.

'No. Free period. That's why I rang you.'

'Well, don't you think you should ask to go home? I mean you're obviously not well. I'm sure they'd understand, under the circumstances.'

'I can't let the children down,' wailed Gemma.

'Oh, right.' Libby frowned. 'Well, ring Dan at lunchtime and see what he says. Tell him all about it.'

Next Libby called Ian's mobile number.

'Yes?' He sounded exasperated. Libby adopted a cowed and anxious tone and explained about Gemma and the letter. Ian exploded.

'Fucking hell! Bloody woman! Why didn't she tell us in the first place. My Christ, we could have had an arrest within a couple of hours. Good God, I'll give her hell.'

'Yes, Ian,' said Libby meekly.

'Sorry. God, Libby, I'm sorry. Thank you for that. Where is she?'

'At her school. In a state. I don't think she'll want you turning up there.'

'I don't care if she doesn't like it. God, this is unbelievable.'

Libby listened while Ian continued to rant until he finally ran out of swear-words and rang off, promising to update her later that day. Then she picked up her basket and her keys and left the house.

As she drove towards Frensham Barn through a brilliantly sunny late morning, she wondered exactly what she was trying to achieve. Last night she'd told Ian about the gardeners' shed. Surely that was enough? But she'd had the feeling then that it wasn't at the top of his list of priorities, and after their recent conversation it would have fallen even further. She wasn't sure of the significance of the shed, either. She could be barking up entirely the wrong tree, but she had to know.

Arriving on the forecourt of the barn, it was obvious that there was no one there. Taking out her mobile, she rang Trisha again.

'He's not back yet,' she said. 'Are you sure you don't want to leave a message?'

'Well – OK, then. When I met him before, he mentioned the burglary at the gardeners' shed at Frensham Barn. It's something,' she crossed her fingers, 'the police want to look into, so I thought I ought to come on a recce. I was hoping he'd meet me there, but obviously not.'

'No,' said Trisha. 'Could anyone else help?'

'Oh, no, don't trouble anyone,' said Libby hastily. 'I'll wait until I hear from Barry.'

Frustrated, she put the phone away. It was sweltering in the car, so she opened the door and climbed out. The air had that hot, silent shimmery feel that so rarely happens in England and she stretched, feeling her damp shirt pulling away from her back. Around the barn, the woods stood unmoving. Libby decided it would be cooler in there, and, anyway, she might as well reconnoitre as she was here, as she'd told Trisha. Taking her mobile out of her basket and sliding it into her jeans pocket with her keys, she set off for the woods.

As she reached the edge, she had the presence of mind to send a text message to both Ian and Ben, realising that her signal would probably disappear, and if she found anything she might need someone to know where she was. That, she thought, as she went into the woods, was where the heroines of fiction went wrong. They never let anyone know where they were.

She plunged onwards.

Chapter Thirty-four

THE WOODS WEREN'T AS thick as she first thought. After five minutes she came out to a patch of lawn surrounded by ornamental shrubs and roses. A path appeared to run from the other side behind a hedge of what looked like yew, so she set off across the grass towards it. Somewhere in the distance she could hear the faint sounds of a lawnmower, and it occurred to her to wonder what she would do, or say, if confronted by one of Frensham Barn's shadowy gardeners. So far, she'd given the existence of these creatures no thought at all. Barry Phillips had said they existed, so they did, but if so, how could Bill Frensham possibly have used the shed as a facility for anything?

As the reality of this thought hit her, her steps slowed. She'd been stupid. Just because Frensham hadn't contacted the police after the burglary, it didn't mean there was anything suspicious about the place. After all, Phillips had told her that he'd told their estates department. It could all be proved, and was presumably above board, so there wouldn't be anything to find and Ian would be furious with her if she'd sent him on a wild goose chase.

But, suddenly, there it was, in front of her. A white-painted, brick-built building with two doors, one at each end. The one long window between the doors appeared to be covered from the inside, but that was nothing so unusual. Libby went slowly forward.

The ground around the building was trampled, particularly round the door nearest to Libby. When she approached, she realised that the padlock was hanging loose, and when she tried the door, very gingerly, it swung obediently open. Her heart gave a huge thump and she stepped back hurriedly.

But all that met her eyes was a range of clean, but obviously used, tools hung neatly on the walls, hoses, flowerpots and strimmers ranged on the floor, and a large space in the middle, presumably where the lawnmower she'd heard earlier normally sat. Disappointed but relieved at the same time, she stepped back and pushed the door closed. And then realised that the gardeners' store only took up about a third of the building.

The other door was padlocked. Libby stood on tiptoe and tried to see in the window, but it was too well covered. Frustrated, she walked round to the back of the building. Here there was another covered window, but nothing else. She stood looking at it, listening to the sound of the lawnmower, which sounded nearer now. Which meant it was time to get out of the way fairly quickly. In fact, she thought, as she heard voices approaching, even quicker.

But she was trapped. The voices were coming from the other side of the building, so they were approaching from the same way as Libby herself had. How embarrassing. She stood against the wall of the building and tried to think.

'She's got to be here somewhere,' said the first voice, and Libby nearly fainted with fright. 'Are you sure that was her car?'

'Yes, certain. You don't see many of them around these days. There couldn't be two like it.' Diggory's voice was harsh. 'Nosy fucking cow. I knew she was trouble.'

'She doesn't know anything. She can't know anything.'

'But she's sicked the bloody cops onto us. You heard that Trisha girl telling Phillips.'

'Then they won't find anything. Come on, get that door open.'

Libby heard the sounds of a door being opened.

'They've already been turning over your bleeding offices. They know all right.' Diggory's voice faded as he went inside the building.

'Knowing and proving are two different things. I can manage to unload it all on Bill Frensham. Thank God he's dead.' And Elizabeth Martin's voice faded inside after Diggory's.

Libby's heart was beating so hard she thought she might faint. Could she get back round the building and back to her car without being seen? She would have to try, she thought, and began to make her way as silently as possible back to the front of the building on the far side to where she guessed Martin and Diggory had gone in. Very slowly, resisting the temptation to run straight across the lawn, she edged round, clinging to the shrubs. They knew she was here somewhere, although not exactly where, but at any minute they might come looking for her. At the moment, though, they were too busy clearing whatever was incriminating in the gardeners' shed.

As she came out into the car park she punched in

Ian's number again.

'Now what?' he said. Libby told him.

'Stay there,' he said. 'Five minutes.'

'They'll run if they hear a car,' said Libby, 'and I'm right beside their car now – or rather Diggory's van. And they know I'm here. They've seen my car.'

'Hide, then, for fuck's sake,' said Ian. 'Just stay there.'

Sweating and shaking, Libby looked round for somewhere to hide. There wasn't anywhere, unless she went round to the back of the barn, which meant traversing the wide open space of the car park. She began to pray that the gardeners would turn up. Perhaps they would save her. But then it struck her, as she slid to the ground beside Romeo and rested her head on her knees, the gardeners must know all about the contents of the other side of the shed. Unless they did, Frensham, Martin and Diggory, and presumably at one time, Lethbridge and Wilhelmina too, would never have been able to use the place. So who were the gardeners?

She was about to find out.

A shadow fell across her. She squinted up against the sun, and saw a large figure dressed in shorts and a T-shirt.

'Are you all right?' it said.

Libby cleared a dry throat and began to struggle to her feet. 'Yes, thank you,' she managed.

'I know you,' said the person when she finally stood upright. 'You're that woman.'

Libby looked at him. His round face was open, the narrow eyes friendly. Very little taller than she was herself, he held a pair of shears in one hand and a pair of gardening gloves in the other.

'That woman,' he continued. 'You know Mrs Gemma.'

'Yes,' said Libby, relief flooding through her. 'Have we met?'

Gemma taught in the special needs department of a local school, where she herself had visited.

'You came and showed us painting,' said the young man. 'Long time ago.'

'That's right,' said Libby, overcome with affection for this unlikely ally. She tucked her arm in his. 'And you work here now?'

He nodded vigorously. 'Not as good as painting,' he said.

'But very good. Have you been cutting the grass?'

He nodded again. 'Over there.' He pointed away from the woods.

'Do you work on your own?'

'Sometimes Mr Best comes to help.' He smiled at her. 'Mr Best's very good.'

Libby heard an engine and turned towards the drive as the first of two police cars drove up. The young man stiffened beside her.

'It's all right,' she said to him, patting his arm. 'They're friends of mine. They've come to catch some bad people.' She paused. 'What's your name?'

'Samuel,' he said. 'I live with Mr Best.'

Ian was approaching them.

'This is Samuel, Ian. Samuel, this is my friend Ian. He's going to catch some bad people.' She turned to Ian. 'Through those woods and out the other side, over the lawn and behind the hedge. But you'll be seen.'

'No we won't.' Ian grinned at her. 'Well done, Libby, even if you were a bit stupid to come out here on your own.'

'I didn't know this was going to happen,' said Libby indignantly, and watched as Ian and his team disappeared silently into the woods.

'I'm going to tell Mr Best,' said Samuel suddenly. 'It's his garden.'

'All right, Samuel,' said Libby. 'Where is he? Can I give you a lift?'

Samuel shook his head, looking worried. 'I must walk. Down there.' He pointed.

'All right, then.' Libby smiled at him. 'I hope I see you again.'

He nodded, gave her a brief hug and set off across the drive and vanished into a shrubbery. Libby leant against Romeo staring after him. Gemma taught many young people like Samuel, and strangely, his straightforward and obvious desire to be friends with her had wiped away the fear she had felt earlier. If there were nice, kind people like Samuel in the world, it couldn't all be bad, could it?

And then, for no particular reason that she could see, she thought of Monica and her children. Had there been a trace of something in the faces of those children in the photograph? Something – her mind made the connection – a little like Samuel? She frowned down at the ground, thinking furiously. But if both children were a little bit like Samuel, what did it matter?

She supposed she ought to wait for Ian to come

back with his prize, but she had no intention of facing either Elizabeth Martin or Richard Diggory, and if Ian found out enough to charge them with Frensham's murder, all well and good, although she didn't think he would. She wondered if he had talked to Monica about the letter yet, and suddenly decided to go and find out. She had to know who sent that letter. That would be the killer.

She got into the car and turned on the engine. Of course, maybe it was Martin who'd sent it. Not Diggory – Frensham had been talking to him on May Day morning, and there was still the mystery of the fake Lethbridge. She set off down the drive and turned towards Steeple Cross.

Elizabeth Martin. Still carrying a torch for Bill Frensham, and now apparently involved in whatever Frensham and Diggory had going on under the cover of Frensham Supplies. Drugs, presumably, although didn't Harry say Diggory had hinted at porn?

Who else could have sent the letter? Anyone, she supposed. Barry Phillips, Wilhelmina, even Monica. Or someone neither she nor the police were aware of. It could be anyone in the whole world. She screwed up her face. Address book – that would be a good starting point. Unless Ian had already stolen a march on her.

And what was it about? Hadn't she thought about blackmail already? But that was thinking that Lethbridge was blackmailing Frensham – wasn't it? By this time her head was throbbing and once more her shirt was sticking to her back. Her mobile trilled. Guessing it was Ian, she virtuously refused to answer it as she was driving.

She began to go through the ramifications of relationships. First of all, Monica and Bill Frensham. Then Monica and John Lethbridge. At some point in the past, it could have been Diggory and Monica. Then there was Bill Frensham, who had an affair with Elizabeth Martin, who still loved him, apparently, and Wilhelmina, who had also had an affair with Diggory. Bloody hell, thought Libby. Finally, there was poor old Barry Phillips, who sat on the sidelines and wasn't involved with anything, except that he was in love with Elizabeth Martin, which did give him a sort of motive.

She turned off the A2 and began to drive across country towards Steeple Cross. Had she missed anyone out? Of course, there was the Mannan Night crowd, and the Goat's Head Morris, all of whom could have the means to blackmail anyone involved with their unsavoury goings-on, but Bill Frensham's death had occurred two months before this year's Mannan Night, and, if there had been a reason to blackmail him, surely it would have been just after last year's festivities.

Her phone went again, and once again, she ignored it. She was now plunging deep into the narrow lanes that led between some of the few hop gardens that remained in this part of Kent. Praying that she wouldn't meet another vehicle coming the other way, she slowed right down and wondered what she was going to say to Monica Frensham. "The police have just caught your rival in love?" No, because she wasn't really a rival, was she? Perhaps "Did you know your husband received a letter the morning he was killed and do you know what was in it?" She sighed. Too bald, and anyway, Ian had probably already asked the same question.

Thankfully, she turned into the road leading down to Steeple Cross and the Frensham House. She was going to have to play it by ear.

Chapter Thirty-five

'DON'T WORRY, I ALREADY know,' were Monica's first words as she opened the door. Libby gaped.

'About Elizabeth Martin and Richard Diggory,' she continued. 'Your Inspector called me. He'd an appointment to see me, but he had to cancel, and as the barn is technically my property now, he told me why.' She shook her head and stood back for Libby to enter. 'I knew there was some reason that woman didn't want me looking into the business.'

'It certainly seems that way,' said Libby, following into the sitting room.

'It was kind of you to come and tell me, though,' said Monica. Libby was grateful she didn't ask any questions. 'You look very hot, though. Can I get you a cold drink? Or tea?'

'Could I have a glass of water?' asked Libby. 'And perhaps tea after that? I've had a bit of a morning.'

Monica smiled. 'Of course. Why don't you come through to the kitchen?'

The kitchen was much as Libby would have expected, very sleek, very modern, very clean. Monica took a filter jug from the huge American-style fridge and poured a glass of water. Libby perched on a stool by a breakfast bar to drink it.

'Did Inspector Connell tell you what he found in the shed?'

'Oh, was it a shed? He just said they'd arrested the two of them in possession of something at

Frensham Barn.'

'Yes, it was the gardeners' shed in the grounds. But didn't he say what he found?'

Monica shrugged, but Libby thought she saw something flicker in her eyes. 'No.'

'Did he actually say "in possession of something"?'

Monica looked confused. 'Perhaps he didn't,' she said. 'I thought he did.' She turned away as the kettle boiled. If he didn't, thought Libby, that means you knew they'd find something there. Interesting. 'Actually,' she said out loud, 'I wanted to ask you a question. The same question that Inspector Connell was going to ask you.'

'Oh?' Monica turned round. 'What was that?'

'Well, you know the police have to investigate the backgrounds of both your husband and John Lethbridge more thoroughly now?'

'Really?' Monica took milk from the fridge. 'Milk?'

'Yes, please. No sugar,' said Libby, noticing that this time there were no dainty cups, simply floral mugs. 'Anyway, since John Lethbridge's body was found –' she saw Monica wince '– they have to look further afield for your husband's murderer.'

'I didn't think they thought John was the murderer in the first place,' said Monica, handing over a mug.

'I'm not sure they did, either, but it was one of their theories. When he was found, then it was no longer a single, but a multiple murderer. And something must have linked the two men.'

'That's simple. Me.'

'Yes, I know, but in that case who would want to kill them? Someone who was jealous of them both? Did you have another – um – admirer?'

'Another lover, you mean?' Monica looked amused. 'Not recently, no. And as far as I know, no one wanted to be.'

'Right.' Libby looked down into her mug.

'So was that the question?'

'No.' Libby looked up. 'The day he died, your husband received a letter. Do you know who it was from?'

Monica's eyes widened. 'A letter?'

'Yes.'

'How do you know he did?'

'That doesn't matter,' said Libby. 'Did he?'

Monica shook her head. 'Not as far as I know. Where did he get it?'

'Here, I thought.'

Monica shook her head again. 'Not that I saw. We had breakfast together, then he went off. Perhaps he was given it when he met the other Morris Men?'

'Maybe.' Libby wasn't sure this was going the way she wanted it. 'We thought maybe it was blackmail.'

'In that case,' said Monica, almost scornfully, 'John wouldn't be linked with it, would he? He was already dead.'

I don't know where to go with this, thought Libby. I should have left it to the police.

'So where is this letter?' Monica picked up her own mug and gestured for Libby to go through to the sitting room.

'No one knows,' said Libby, now worrying that she would give away vital information and Ian would kill *her*.

'It doesn't seem as though there's any hard evidence of it existing at all.' Monica went to her leather chair. 'Why do you think it did?'

'The police were told about it.'

'Oh, for goodness sake! Who by?'

'Your husband was overheard talking to someone on the morning of his death.'

'And he said he'd had a letter? Sounds unlikely to me. If it was a blackmailing letter, surely he wouldn't have talked about it?'

'That's true.' Libby frowned. 'You're absolutely right.' She looked up and smiled at Monica. 'I wonder if Inspector Connell has thought of it? It does seem unlikely, doesn't it?'

Monica smiled back. 'Logic, that's all. Who would he have told about a blackmail letter? It's not something you would tell *anyone*, is it?'

'Oh, but he did.'

Libby and Monica both swung round.

'And you know who he told, don't you?' Wilhelmina's tone was vicious. She stood in the conservatory doorway, dishevelled yet menacing. The black leather and lace were back, and the mask-like make-up, but everything was slightly off kilter. Libby could see her chest rising and falling quickly.

'Go on, then, guess.' Wilhelmina strode across the eau-de-nile carpet to where Monica shrank back in her chair, and slapped her hard across the face. Tea went everywhere.

'You, then. You're so clever.' She turned to

Libby. 'You didn't get any of it, did you?'

'Of what?' said Libby, through dry lips.

'You didn't get what John was on about, did you? What he'd found out?'

'No.'

'And now your fucking Inspector has arrested Diggory.'

'What's that got to do with anything? And how do you know?' Libby could barely speak, but nothing Wilhelmina was saying was making any sense.

'They caught that cow Martin. He was – I don't know – out of sight, and he sent me a text. Knew they'd find him. Said it was your fault. And hers. They'll come for me next.'

'Are you saying Diggory killed Bill?' Monica's voice was bordering on hysteria.

'Diggory?' Wilhelmina laughed. 'He wouldn't have the guts.' She stumbled over Monica's feet and picked up the photographs from the mantelpiece. 'This is what it's really about!' She waved them at Libby, her voice cracking. 'That's why he wrote the letter.'

'Eh? Who?' Libby looked across at Monica in bewilderment. Monica just sat curled in her chair, a frozen bundle of fear.

'Who do you bloody think?' snarled Wilhelmina, and threw the pictures at Libby. One of them caught the side of her head and smashed, showering glass over her face. Monica screamed.

'You stupid cow!' Wilhelmina screamed back. 'John, of course! John wrote the letter.'

Libby shakily moved a hand to wipe the blood

342

trickling down the side of her face. John? Lethbridge? He wrote the letter? She looked down at the photograph on the floor, four faces smiling out of a frame. So alike.

She never knew why the synapses connected quite as they did, but suddenly it all made sense. At least, some of it did.

'Had Bill told him, Willy?' she asked as gently as she could.

'Course he bloody didn't.' She was shaking now, too, and had to hold on to the mantel shelf. Monica was moaning quietly in her chair.

'So what happened?'

Wilhelmina's legs suddenly gave way and she crumpled to the floor. 'John said –' she looked over at Monica '– that she should stop chasing him.'

'Monica was chasing John?'

Wilhelmina nodded. 'They'd had a thing going but it was over. John wanted me back.'

'Did he?' Libby was surprised and didn't altogether believe this. 'So what happened?'

'John went to see – her. She told him. Told him everything. He told me.'

'Monica told John the truth? So why did John write Bill a letter?'

'Oh, don't be a fucking idiot,' said Wilhelmina wearily.

'It *was* blackmail, then?'

'Bill didn't know. John wrote and told him.'

Libby's eyebrows rose to her hairline and she looked across at Monica who was still whimpering.

'Monica knew? And she hadn't said anything?'

Wilhelmina shrugged.

343

'But it wasn't Bill who killed John?'

'He was dead by then, wasn't he?' Wilhelmina stuck her legs out in front of her and leaned her head back against the wall. 'I loved him, you know.'

'I'm sure,' said Libby quietly. 'So do you know the truth, too? Why didn't you tell the police before?'

Wilhelmina shrugged again.

'Right.' Libby looked thoughtfully at Monica. 'And the police will be coming here. Monica!'

Monica looked up, her eyes unfocussed.

'You almost told me, didn't you?'

'Told you what?' Her voice was slurred.

'You told me about the Gods and Goddesses. And then you realised what John meant when he was talking about something being Wagnerian.'

Monica sat up a little. 'Did I?'

'Oh, yes. And I nearly got there by mentioning Brunnhilde, didn't I?'

Monica said nothing. Wilhelmina was looking puzzled. Libby eased herself towards the edge of her seat and brushed a little more glass from her shirt. She felt quite calm now.

'It's an opera,' she told Wilhelmina. 'And Brunnhilde falls in love with her nephew Siegfried, not knowing he's her nephew. And Siegfried himself is the son of Siegmund and Sieglinde, neither of whom knows that they are brother and sister.' She looked at Monica, who was sitting with her mouth open. 'That's right, isn't it, Monica? Brother and sister. Just like you and Bill.'

Chapter Thirty-six

'SO WHO KILLED JOHN and Bill?' said Libby.

'She did, of course,' came a quiet voice from behind Libby.

Ian Connell walked over to Monica and crouched down beside her. 'It was you, Monica, wasn't it? Did you join in on Beltane Night?'

Libby and Wilhelmina, their mouths open, sat motionless. Monica focussed on Ian and nodded slightly. A female police officer came quietly up on her other side and Libby was aware of further bodies behind her.

'What did you do?' Ian's voice was still quiet, comforting almost.

'John said he would tell Bill.' Her voice was rusty. 'I got out our son's old Cranston Morris costume and went and hid in the woods. Then I just joined in. And when we got to the edge of – when we got to the edge,' Ian nodded, 'I whispered to him, and he was so surprised. And I made him go down the hill a bit and then I hit him.'

'What with?' asked Ian.

'A hammer. Bill's hammer. He fell down to the bottom and I went on so I could join in the dances. No one noticed.'

'What about the clothes? And your black face?'

'I hid the clothes and got my make-up off before Bill got home. Then in the morning he found the letter. It must have been there the night before, although I missed it, because it was by hand. No post on Bank Holidays.'

'And you killed Bill?'

'I put the clothes on again. Danced with them. I used to watch them, you see, even if they didn't know I did. Then I stabbed him with his own paperknife. It was an old awl.' She was looking wistfully into the past.

'Why did you kill him?'

'Because he was going to end the marriage, of course.' She sat up straight, her face clearing a little. 'I couldn't have that. I've kept the secret ever since I found out.'

'When was that?' asked Ian.

'Before we were married. No one would ever find out. But then I told John.'

'Why did you tell John?'

'Because he wouldn't come back to me, he said I was married to Bill, so I told him that I couldn't be, not really. And he was – angry.'

'And he said he'd tell Bill?'

'So I killed him before he could. But he'd put the letter in the letter box. I couldn't have Bill ruining our lives.' She shook her head. 'So silly.'

Ian stood up and repeated the usual warning to Monica Frensham, who hardly seemed to take it in, and the police officer helped her to her feet. Libby stood up, though her legs threatened to give way, and stepped forward.

'If there's anything you need, Monica,' she said. Monica stared at her.

'Come on, Libby,' Ian put an arm round her shoulders. 'We're going to get you home.'

'What about –' Libby gestured to Wilhelmina

sitting on the floor.

'Unless you want to press charges of assault? I take it she threw the picture?'

Libby nodded. 'If she hadn't I might not have realised.' She shuddered. 'Brother and sister. How awful. How do you suppose she found out?

'I don't suppose we'll ever know, although she seems willing enough to talk at the moment.'

'She's not right, is she?' Libby went to get into the Renault, but Ian stopped her.

'Leave it here, Lib. You're in no state to drive, and your Ben will be fit to be tied when he hears what's been happening. We'll get you home.'

'I want to know what's happened, though, Ian. At the barn and everything. I did lead you there.'

'I know, I know. Once the paperwork is done, I promise I'll come and fill you in.'

'Tonight? Can the others be there?'

'Strictly off the record, but yes, OK.' He gave her a quick kiss on the cheek and saw her into a police car. 'Go on. I'll ring you and tell you when I can there.'

It was past ten o'clock when Ian arrived at Number 17 Allhallow's Lane. Fran and Guy had driven over, bringing bottles of sparkling wine, Ben, after reading the riot act, had persuaded Harry to send Adam round with a take-away, and Peter had arrived with a bottle of whisky. Harry and Adam promised to come round as soon as the Pink Geranium's customers had all gone home.

Ben gave Ian a large whisky and a plate of Harry's best vegetarian pate and bread.

'I hope it isn't Diggory's,' said Libby, eyeing it thoughtfully.

'I don't care if it is,' said Ian. 'I haven't eaten since this morning.'

Fran patted him on the arm. 'It was very good of you to come,' she said. 'You really should have gone home to bed.'

Libby sent her a fulminating glare, but Ian laughed.

'I owe it to Libby,' he said. 'She was the catalyst.' Libby looked smug.

'What happened, then?' asked Peter. 'Libby's told us more or less everything, but we don't know any of the whys and wherefores.'

'As long as you don't have your journalist's notebook out,' said Ian, and Peter looked down his patrician nose. 'OK,' he said, and took a swallow of whisky. 'When Libby called us to say she was at the barn and Elizabeth Martin and Richard Diggory were there, we'd already found a couple of clues in the offices of Frensham Supplies. It appears they were a distribution centre only, so we still haven't got anywhere near the major players, but Frensham and Diggory had a nice little business going. And you were right, they did a lot of business down in Cornwall. Malahyde is a distributor, too.'

'What about Bernie Lee?' asked Libby.

'His name hasn't come up,' said Ian, 'but it looks as though the – er – undercover arm of the morris dancers were a cover for drugs. Diggory will be done for supplying, as will Martin. They were keeping the business going after Frensham's death, though both of them suspected each other of murdering him.'

'What about Barry Phillips? Why did Martin say she wanted to kill him?' asked Libby.

'Best guess? He was as straight as a dye, and when he suspected something was going on and tried to interfere she wasn't having any. I feel sorry for the bugger. He's going to be left with the whole mess.'

They all looked solemn for a moment.

'Then of course, Monica. She told you most of it this afternoon. She'll be unfit to plead, I suspect.'

'Those poor kids,' said Fran. 'What on earth will happen to them?'

'They're both over eighteen,' said Ian, 'so they won't go into care.'

Fran shuddered. 'It doesn't bear thinking about.'

'When you went to see her after Frensham's body had been discovered,' said Libby, 'there must have been traces of blacking in the house. Didn't you search the house? And what about the hammer?'

'She was clever. We saw traces of the blacking in the cloakroom sink, and she said it was from her husband last night. She hadn't time to clear it up yet. And the clothes she simply said were his other outfit. She hadn't had time to do anything with them. The hammer she just replaced in the garage. No one suspected her of course, so no tests were made.' He made a face. 'It would have saved us a lot of trouble if they had been.'

'What about Lethbridge's car?' asked Fran.

'In the woods near the Tyne Chapel. She must have driven it there after she killed him. She told us that, too.'

'And no one really questioned her much after Frensham's murder?' said Ben.

'She really did collapse,' said Ian. 'Obviously because of what she'd done, but at the time she appeared prostrated with grief. All the doctors agreed she'd had a sort of breakdown. Which she had, and when she heard about Libby and Fran investigating, it began to send her over the edge again.'

'But she didn't look as though she intended to murder me,' said Libby.

'No. I don't think she would. Wilhelmina, on the other hand –' Ian grinned at her.

'Yes,' said Libby, putting a hand up to the bump on her head.

'What will happen to Wilhelmina?' asked Fran.

'She definitely knew about the drugs, and took part in the parties, but other than that she's guilty of nothing but bad judgement.' He grinned. 'And throwing a picture at Libby.'

'How did you know where I was though?' said Libby. 'You turned up like the god from the machine in the nick of time.'

'Diggory started talking. Not about Monica being the murderer, but saying she knew all about the drugs. We decided we'd better round her up as well. When we arrived and saw your car, and what we now know is Wilhelmina's – almost as bad as yours, Libby – we changed tactics and crept in. In time for me to hear quite a bit of your rather one-sided conversation.'

'And did she know about the drugs?' asked Fran.

'We think so. There wasn't actually much she didn't know about the business, she just pretended not to. We think she could keep tabs on her husband that way.'

'But she asked me to help.' Libby frowned. 'Wouldn't she have been better keeping quiet?'

'As far as we can tell, she wanted to point the investigation in a different direction, and she couldn't do that with us – the police – so she picked on you. Like a good many people in the area, she'd heard about your adventures.'

'Interference,' corrected Ben.

'Humph.' Libby scowled at him and turned her attention back to Ian. 'But why did she go ahead and marry Bill if she knew that they were brother and sister?'

'She's an obsessive personality, isn't she? I expect by that time she'd set her heart on him and wasn't going to give him up. They were both adopted and she didn't think anyone would find out. That's what she said to us.'

'I still don't understand why she had to snoop round Frensham Holdings if she already knew about the drugs,' said Fran.

'She wanted proof. Then she could have held it over Martin and Diggory and either cut herself in or exposed them.' Ian shrugged. 'She wasn't making much sense when we got to that point.'

'Well,' said Ben getting up to fetch another bottle of fizz. 'I suppose all's well that ends well, and I'm glad I wasn't wrong about Bill Frensham and his company.'

'Are we still going to have a retirement party?'

asked Libby. 'I think I need something like that.'

There was a sharp rap on the front door and a scuffle in the hallway.

'Hello?' Harry put his head round the door. 'Have we missed Poirot's explanation? And did I hear something about a party?'

About The Author

Born in Guildford, Surrey, Lesley spent her early life in south London, before marrying and moving all over the south-east of England. Lesley fell into feature writing by accident, then went on to reviewing for both magazines and radio. She writes for the stage, she has written short fiction for women's weekly magazines and is a former editor of *The Call Boy*, the British Music Hall Society journal. Her first Libby Sarjeant novel, *Murder In Steeple Martin,* was published to much acclaim in 2006, followed in 2007 by *Murder At The Laurels* and *Murder In Midwinter*. In 2008, Lesley's ever-increasing number of fans welcomed the publication of *Murder By The Sea*. 2009 saw the publication of *Murder In Bloom*. In addition to *Murder In The Green, Murder Imperfect* will also be published in 2010.

Her passion for the theatre is reflected in her first non-fiction work, *How To Write A Pantomime,* also published by Accent Press.

www.lesleycookman.co.uk

The Libby Sarjeant Series
by Lesley Cookman

9781905170159

9781905170845

9781906125028

9781906373306

9781906373771

9781907016080

9781907016462

Also available from Accent Press

The HEARTBEAT Series
by Nicholas Rhea
now a much-loved TV series

"...an account of the hilarious happenings to the county's rural policemen" **Yorkshire Post**

"Rhea's strengths are his sharp portraits of people and absorbing detail of a country copper practising his craft." **Northern Echo**

9781906373375   9781906373405   9781906373399   9781906373429

9781906373382   9781906373412   9781906373368   9781906373351

Accent Press Ltd

Write a review and win a prize!

Please visit our website
www.accentpress.co.uk
for our latest title information,
to write reviews and
leave feedback.

We'd love to hear from you!